Virtue & Vice

by

Steven C. McCullough

The Wild Rose Press, Inc.
PO Box 708
Adams Basin, NY 14410-0708
Visit us at www.thewildrosepress.com

Publishing History
First Edition, 2024
Trade Paperback ISBN 978-1-5092-5697-6
Digital ISBN 978-1-5092-5698-3

Published in the United States of America

"We have all become like one who is unclean,
and all our righteous deeds are like a polluted
garment.
We all fade like a leaf,
and our iniquities, like the wind, take us away.
There is no one who calls upon Your name,
who rouses himself to take hold of You;
for You have hidden Your face from us,
and have made us melt in the hand of our
iniquities."
Isaiah 64: 6-7 (The Holy Bible, ESV)

Chapter 1

By definition, a Virtue is a veritable manifestation of one of the twelve base elements that constitute our waking world. They are not 'alive,' in the sense that most would perceive the word—they have not intrinsic physical anatomies, nor do they require external sustenance as would any other creature—but rather they exist in conjunction with all other living beings.

Some specimens have even gone to such lengths of adaptation to our physical realm as to develop personalities and traits that set them apart from other Virtues of the same type. This is for reasons we have yet to understand. Just as one Wind Virtue may manifest on this plane as a kind of eagle or some such bird of prey, another Virtue of the same element may choose to manifest as a small, inauspicious insect. It is unknown why the Virtues choose to adopt differing forms even within the same ecosystem or why they so often choose to mirror species of natural origin therein, though some speculate that their individual levels of potency—the totality of their substance and ability to manipulate the element of their existence—has much to do with it. It is also unknown to what degree their consciousness and control of free-will can be measured. Virtues are, even still today, an enigma of which we have only just scratched the surface.

The twelve elements as labeled by the Institute of

Virtue Studies (Case Study of the Elemental Manifestations, IVS, 2385), and by deduction types of Virtues, are as follows:

Fire
Water
Wind
Mineral
Electric
Evolutic
Entropic
Gravitic
Darkness
Radiance
Force
Void

Each of the Virtue Branches cohabitate with creatures of the realm as if they were themselves the very same, though they do not or cannot exist and operate in a similar manner. Without diet, lifespan, reproductive capabilities, or any other component of what constitutes a physical and living being's existence on this plane, we would naturally assume that Virtues have a limited interaction with the environment around them. But studies have shown a significant variation on test environments that directly correlates with the types of Virtues found therein. Higher Evolutic Virtue count in a region tends to correlate to increased reproduction rates with all fauna nearby, while the inverse population of said Virtues appears to tie with a decrease of those rates from national averages. Likewise, a larger percentage of Entropic Virtues regulates flora and fauna lifespans in a region to less than national average. Therefore, one can surmise that even though Virtues are not often physically involved in the realm in which they manifest, their manifested numbers directly correspond with that environment. Some scholars believe that the population of Virtues is but a representation of the existing level of that element in the environment while others conclude that said population of the Virtues is the direct cause of such radical differences in elemental levels.

Whatever the case, further studies are assisting research teams with more definitive answers than we have seen since the first recorded manifestations of—

(Basic Aspects of Virtues, Chapter One, Pages 1-2a, Bernald, 2392)

"And what about you, Jameson?"

The words rang out in the stone-cold classroom, hollow and meaningless. With no reply, much to her expectation, Madam Traeger tried again.

"Jameson. *Jameson Innis!*"

Jay felt his head twist upward from the textbook. It was a kneejerk reaction to those forlorn syllables: *Innis*.

Gaze now unglued from the tattered pages, he focused on a highly displeased woman draped with both sharp, black attire and the many evidences of age. Madam Traeger was gaining rapid ground on his desk, eager to hear a verbal response or cast out a round from her limitless bag of punishments.

"Oh, um…sorry, Madam Traeger. I didn't hear the question." As soon as the words stumbled from his lips, he could hear the telltale snickering of Wade and others from behind.

"I was *saying*," the teacher began irritably, "That tomorrow is quite possibly the most important day of your life, and you have ample ability to *fail* should you be caught daydreaming rather than paying attention to *my lecture.*"

Jay only sank farther into his seat as she continued her derisive assault.

"Now, if you would be so kind as to answer my question: *what type of virtue are you pursuing to bind during tomorrow's exam and why, Jameson Innis?*"

She stooped low then, speaking in a whisper that only he could hear, "You may be an adult by society's standards, Jameson, but you are still a child and a student while you are in this classroom." Swift as a breeze, she turned away from him and resumed her position at the head of the class, awaiting his answer.

Jay considered for a moment, making certain that Madam Traeger could see his thoughtful expression.

"I uh–I really don't have a preference," he said blandly. "I'm gonna bind them all at some point, so I guess I'll just snag whichever I find first."

His answer—confident and common in this scenario—drew a mix of mocking laughter and scoffs from the rest of the class. He had learned to ignore them.

Madam Traeger wiped at her overbearing brow, shaking her head from side to side. The ample skin beneath her chin trailed in negative motion as if in agreeance with them all. "I honestly don't know what to do with you sometimes, Jameson…"

Jay slid farther into his seat in sync with her sigh and averted his gaze.

Angling her attention toward the student in front of him—whether by mercy or a desire to get on with the class—Madam Traeger continued her questioning, receiving various answers as she progressed across the room. Every other student named a precise element, some even going as far as detailing the specific attributes they sought in the virtues of the wild near their hometown of Glendale. Wind, water, evolutic. Fire, mineral, electric. The list went on, and with their hopeful responses came the typical reasonings:

"I want to bind a chill, water virtue so I can get a job at the marina. You know, lay out by the lake all day. Who wouldn't want that?"

"I'm going to bind a strong mineral virtue so I can take up my family's stone-shaping business after my da."

"I'm after a radiance virtue so I can find work in the hospital of Highwater City. I hear they're always looking for fresh residents with experience in ultraviolet therapy."

Jay had heard them all before. The same ambitions that had been recycled through their small society for ages.

"If you want to work in a specific field, Jay, you'll be best served to pursue the virtue that supports it."

His snarky guidance counselor with far too many pimples for a middle-aged man had drilled it into him from day one at the Academy.

Virtues were like degrees of certification honored by all employers across the Pangaea continent, attesting to the abilities of the applicant without a single interview. They weren't necessarily *required* to find work—many people didn't have a virtue bound at all—but they certainly increased the value of a citizen in the long term.

With an elemental companion basically handcuffed to his will, Jay would be able to manipulate its type with practice and determination, offering skills that companies respected and compensated. Pandering for employment aside, *that* was what Jay was after.

5

A bound virtue enabled its binder to have a manner of governance over the element in question. It was nothing so fancy as summoning windstorms and earthquakes in the beginning, but with a lifetime of dedication to the arts, such incredible feats *actually could* be accomplished. What more could a guy ask for than the ability to summon fire from his fingertips?

For Jay and all his unimagining classmates, though, Mr. Pimply Parker's advice boiled down to only a singular course of action: *get a job, you bums*.

So if anyone wanted to work the power plant on the east side of Glendale, he or she would probably need to bind an *electric* virtue during the exam, seeing as the work would involve electricity on a daily basis. Though electric-binders couldn't exactly become human conduits, a measure of control over such an element had its benefits—namely, not dying a violent death after crossing two incompatible wires.

If anyone wanted to work the fields for crops or study new ways of farming, he or she should chase after an evolutic type, the virtue over the elements of growth and life. Work the forges over in Red Pillars, then fire. Work the quarry outside of Highwater, then mineral. Every virtue type had its own unique advantages, but somehow, Jay had always known he would never be satisfied with just *one*.

He had bigger dreams than the others of his class and even all of Glendale it seemed. They often looked at him like he was mentally stunted for believing that he could bind all twelve or even a solid pair at that rate. Turns out, very few people have bound more than one virtue, and even fewer had the desire to do so for some reason. It was a complicated and expensive process, yeah, *but there was just something about it* that made the price worth it. Something that tempted Jay to spend whatever it would cost, do whatever it took.

But clearly these people never had the drive. It had been burning in Jay's veins from the moment he signed four years of his life away to this grueling school, and it burned hotter now than ever.

"All right, class. Remember: we won't be meeting here at the Academy tomorrow. You will all gather at the East Gate at first bell. Be sure to come prepared with the items I instructed. Dismissed…"

Jay perked up again as the roar of moving bodies filled the room. *He had to stop zoning like that.*

"Yo, Jay," a voice echoed out through the crowd.

Jay turned to find Wade standing a few desks back, working his way closer. His dark skin seemed to meld seamlessly with the black Academy uniform. Another thing Jay loathed about the system… Uniform codes were just another play in the tyranny handbook.

"Hey, Wade."

"Dude, you gotta learn to at least *fake* being normal sometimes," Wade chastised, a contorted expression on his face.

"Uh, yeah. Wait, what do you mean?"

"Susie—you know, two rows back Susie, hot as a flaring phoenix—has had a thing for you for like the last six weeks. Don't know why. I told her you were dumber than a rock, and you look like someone keeps you locked in a basement. Seriously, side note: you need some sun, man." He quirked an eyebrow, though Jay could see the grin hiding there. "But as soon as you started swinging around your wild fantasies, I'd wager she cut that crush short."

Jay pinned him with a glare. "Well, Susie can keep her clothes on. I'm not interested in dating right now." He paused before adding, "And they're not *wild fantasies*, Wade. I take this seriously. Thought you backed me on this…"

Wade held up placating hands. "Listen, I'm one-hundred percent behind you on your dreams, bro. Do I think you'll actually accomplish them? *No*. But I'll stand by you…even as you're ridiculed and possibly mauled to death by a feral horde of virtues. That said, *I like women*. Especially gorgeous women like Susie. And you announcing your insanity to the world vicariously cramps my style."

Jay grinned and slapped a hand on his shoulder. "Well, that might actually matter if you *had* any style."

Wade frowned, offering Jay a hand up. "Come on. Let's go get suited up for tomorrow. I have a couple things on the list that I need to pick up at Jenson's."

Jay took his arm and stood. "Yeah, so, *what list* was that again?" He grimaced, trying to retrace the last half hour.

"Dude, *seriously*? Do you *ever* listen in class?"

****

"Okay," Wade started, scanning over a crinkled notebook outlined with doodles. "Looks like we both need a binder's sleeve. We should be able to pick those up free of charge at the Academy Warehouse. And *then*… I'll need a map of the Eastern Glens. What about you? Got one?"

Jay shrugged into his jeans and slipped a light tee shirt over his head. They decided to change into more comfortable clothes before the shopping spree.

"Um, yeah; I should have one of those around here

somewhere."

He pulled open a series of drawers, rifling through wads of paper, soiled clothes, and other undefined paraphernalia. One drawer, stuck from years of disuse, groaned under his weight as he pried at it. With a final sigh of protest, it released its age-old grip and vomited its contents all over the floor. Something akin to a rotten fruit peel fused with a tattered sock soared past Wade's head, grazing his ear. He gagged hard enough to summon his noonday meal.

"You have got to be the most unorganized person I've ever met." Wade leaned back against a desk near to toppling from the mounds of books and unfinished projects cluttering its surface.

"Try living in a big house all by yourself for three years and see how it is." Jay spun away, pulling open a closet that promptly spewed more clutter onto the already untraversable floor.

Wade nearly shot a retort, but the nature of that conversation was a fragile one. His forced silence, though, turned out to be worse. Jay turned back and ran a hand through his dirty-blond hair.

"I didn't mean—"

"Relax," Jay cut in with a smile. "I'm just messing with you. Three years has been time enough to deal with their deaths. Emotionally, that is. Mom and Dad left me more *junk* than I could deal with in decades."

Wade appeared relieved, but he still steered away from that direction. "So let me revise the question. What on this list do you have that is *easily accessible*?"

Jay shrank into the bed, sending a wave of laundry into the growing pile on the carpet. "Let me get my money. We can just start fresh…"

****

Glendale wasn't very large in comparison to the other nine cities of Tier One, but it offered everything that an average citizen would need. It was surrounded by sparse forest on all sides, sectioned off by cardinal direction. The Eastern Glens were, of course, to the east side of the town, and they bordered the Valley of Pyres, the second of six regions that spanned the Pangaea continent. The Northern Glens spilled out upon the edge of Cityscape, which gave way to a brilliant blue ocean and a fair fishing trade. The Western Glens was a lightly forested area with a wide and well-kept highway bridging Glendale to the larger Highwater City, where most commerce originated in the Tier. And finally, the Southern Glens snaked through the countryside toward the higher Tiers of Cityscape, lands which few of the common-folk of Glendale had the privilege of crossing into.

Jay and Wade studied the recently procured map, one of a higher quality and detail than the elusive copy hiding somewhere in Jay's residence. They had rarely spent any time poring over such geographical details as they were seeing now. Though the lack of any sincere education dedicated to the topic had made Jay curious on occasion, he had never given it much thought. The Academy's only boast toward world geography was a fuzzy holographic image of the globe in its main lobby, but it was likely more to showcase their growth in technology than their interest in the arrangement of the Earth's crust and mankind's pioneering. Now, though, he held an intricately defined map in his hands, and a spark seemed to ignite in his chest.

"Check this out," he said, drawing Wade's attention

to a raised point on one side of the dense plate.

He clenched the knob between forefinger and thumb and watched as the lines on the map began to shift. What appeared only moments before to be ink now revealed itself to be some sort of glowing goop embedded between the two glossy layers of what Jay assumed to be tempered glass.

"*No way*," Wade said mystically. "This map shows more than just the Glens?"

"Jensen said it's a full-scale *world* map," Jay answered giddily. "Problem is, you can't fold it up." He lightly tapped the hard surface to illustrate. "It'll barely fit in my bag."

"Still, that must've cost a fortune," Wade prodded, looking dismally at his own small map, printed in black-and-white on a piece of folded parchment.

Jay smiled openly at his sulky state. "Don't worry. You can use it anytime."

"Respect, man."

Wade took a few steps away from the eave of the shop and stared out across the sprawling city. He pulled the list from his bag and marked off the few items they had gotten from Jensen's General Store.

"So how much money did your parents leave you anyway?"

Jay reluctantly peeled his eyes away from his new treasure and calculated.

"Well, I started off with a little over thirty thousand, but I had to pay off the house first thing. Mom and Dad had it down to half of the original mortgage, so it only cost me about twelve thousand for a full settlement. After that—and paying my next three years at the Academy—I was left with a little under ten. Haven't spent much since then."

Wade's eyes nearly bulged from their sockets. "You're kidding."

Jay shook his head, snatching the list from Wade's hands. "Nope. I guess I never mentioned that my parents were pretty wealthy when we first moved to Glendale. Dad was an engineer with the power authority up at Highwater, and Mom was a researcher with one of those weird-named tech labs. When Dad was offered a position out here, he took it. Said he was tired of the big city life, and they had plenty of funds to keep Mom from having to work too."

Wade whistled. "If you don't get stupid, you're set for a while, man. Got a house all paid for, got more spending money than most people make in five or six years. You're gonna be all right here."

"Yeah," Jay said distantly. Before Wade could pick up on his sudden shift in mood, Jay pointed back to the page. "Let's make a trip over to The Traveler. I can grab a few things from the list there and pick up some other stuff while I'm at it."

Wade shrugged and led the way to an adjacent district of the town. There weren't many major trade stores in Glendale, but what Jensen's lacked, The Traveler made up for by far. It was a continental brand, which meant that merchandise could come in from the far sides of the mainland and not cost a fortune as if they had purchased it from a roaming merchant. Long-range travel was difficult and costly, driven mostly by the more potent—not to mention *rare*—wind virtues. But The Traveler stores had monthly deliveries from their own enigmatic sources, beckoning folks over for their more exotic needs while keeping the retail margins reasonable.

Jay was finally letting himself feel the excitement of capturing his first virtue; he had been diligent in taming his fervor over the last few years. Ever since leaving base-school at seventeen, he had set his course with the Academy, dedicating the next four years of his life to the premiere institute of virtue studies in the region. It was a rite-of-passage for anyone interested in capturing one of the anomalies of nature.

Binding the elusive buggers wasn't as easy as heading out on a lax fishing trip and waiting for something to take the bait. It took years of study on both practical knowledge of seizing, maintaining, and controlling the virtue as well as where the particular types could be found. This was all without mentioning the carefully regulated sale of binder's materials needed to forge the bond in the first place. Some called it a racket, but Jay only saw it as the path he had to take. The Academy was the only source in Glendale where the tools could be found, and they were only available to graduates. So graduate the Academy he would.

He had never quite understood the restrictions on binding, given the abundance of virtues that seemed to outnumber humans ten-to-one. There was just an unspoken agreement across cities that not everyone should be allowed the privilege, hence schools like the Academy of Glendale and Highwater Institute reserved it specifically for *certified* binders.

One of which I will soon be.

Finally, all his hard work, all his dreaming and planning was coming to a head. Tomorrow, the trial would complete this stage of his life…and then would come graduation. In a way, purchasing all these supplies was like the first step to the rest of his life…

"Hey, Wade."

"Yeah?" Wade replied, looking over his shoulder to find Jay lagging behind.

"What are you gonna do after this?" Jay's feet slid to a stop on the gravel path.

"Probably go home and have a sandwich."

"No, like, after graduation. Are you going to hang around?"

Wade half-shrugged but then stopped to consider it seriously. "I don't know, man. I guess I'll stay here and help the family over at the orchard until another opportunity comes along. Joanna practically *bleeds* apple juice. She'll never go anywhere else. And Peter essentially runs the place next to Pop. They really don't need me, but what else?"

"And if another opportunity never comes?" Jay asked, propping up against the side of an old stone building.

"You're getting at something," Wade guessed, donning a perplexed smirk.

Jay held his gaze for a long moment before twitching away. Wade had been his only real friend since his family moved to Glendale. He was reluctant to speak the next words, as if they would suddenly fracture any ties they had forged during the past five years.

"I'm leaving, Wade."

Wade cocked his head, now even more confused. "What do you mean *you're leaving*? Leaving Glendale?"

Jay nodded solemnly, chewing on his lower lip. "I've thought this through... Once we graduate, I'm gonna travel. Maybe head toward the higher Tiers of Cityscape where I have a chance of binding better virtues. Or head east across the Valley. I don't know, I just…I just wanna see the world, you know?" He trailed off, looking out over the city as if taking it in for the last time.

Wade was silent for a moment, kicking at the ground with the toe of his dirt-stained sneaker. "Guess I saw that coming. You got no reason to stay."

"Wade, that's not it and you know it. You're family to me. Your mom and pop are like my own. But I have to be realistic; I have *no chance* of binding all the virtues if I stay here. Some of them aren't even *in* Tier One. I'll have to go to Waterwall or even farther to find types like force and darkness…"

Wade didn't respond, so Jay tried, "You could come with me, you know?"

Wade shook his head dejectedly. "Nah, man. You know I can't do that."

Jay started to protest, but he heard his name called out by a voice he had long ago learned to loathe.

"*Jameson Innis!*"

Both Jay and Wade spun to find Carlisle DeMoro, the fattest, richest, most pompous dunce in existence. He had made Jay's life a little darker on the day they first met and insisted on belittling his dream ever since he had learned of it.

"What do you want, Carl?" Jay asked flatly.

"Oh, I was just happening by when I spotted you two. Curious how many virtues you've bound by now? Better get started if you want to snag them all, you know." His double-chin bounced with subdued mirth.

The jibe was worn-out, though. It didn't take.

"Funny seeing you here, Carl," Wade retorted. "They just popped out a fresh batch of cookies over at the bakery. Figured you'd be first on the scene."

Carl's eyes drew down into two slits nearly submerged beneath his imperious brows. "Oh, ha ha. The fat jokes just get better by the day."

He turned his attention back to Jay. "As much as I enjoy having fun at your expense, my father sees something in you that I cannot. He wishes for you to dine with us tomorrow evening after the trial. Seven o' clock on the dot. Do not be late."

With that, Carl turned and wobbled off in the opposite direction.

Wade nudged Jay's arm and nodded that way. "Ten pips says he turns left toward the bakery."

Jay only smiled and shook his head as Carl stopped for a split second before taking a hard left past the laundromat. Wade grinned from ear to ear, but it faded as he considered what was said.

"What do you think Mayor DeMoro wants with you?"

Jay shrugged. "No idea. But I think I like that man even less than Carl. At least with chubs, you get what you see. His father seems more like a snake in the grass."

Wade nodded soberly. "Apple actually fell pretty far from the tree there. Carl looks and acts nothing like his old man. Anyway, come on. Let's wrap this up. I'm starting to get hungry."

Wade stepped ahead on the path, but Jay lingered. His gaze continued tracing Carl's lumpy form hobbling off into the distance. Eventually, he let his suspicions drop and followed Wade. They still had a lot to gather in order to be ready for tomorrow's trial, and something about Carl's words made Jay want to work that much harder to prove the lout wrong.

Chapter 2

Jay felt like a man readying for a world-rounding excursion. With the incessant prodding of his shopaholic friend, he had ended up purchasing a new travel pack, a few trinkets and tools that he could use on the road, and an assortment of freeze-dried rations that rivaled what he kept in his pantry at home.

Though Wade had originally pouted at the idea of Jay's vacation from Glendale, a quick glance at the wares of The Traveler made him forget his woes. He scoured the shelves like a child while Jay had to temper his spendthrift nature from the side.

Although a vast warehouse of odds-and-ends, in contrast to its namesake, the many needs of long-term travel weren't top priority at the corporate storefront. The meager and frankly *strange* collection was dust-covered and stuffed in a back corner of the shop where few patrons frequented and the floors rarely saw a mop. Apparently, the market for a wayward man's needs wasn't priority.

Jay hadn't been exposed to many different cultures in his twenty-two years on this Earth, so he was hesitant to draw stereotypes. But one thing he knew for certain was that folks around Glendale scarcely moved from city to city. Most were quick to turn noses at the mere *idea* of a nomadic lifestyle. What he didn't understand was *why*. To him, seeing the world seemed too mystical an idea to forsake, especially as a young and single man with no ties to bind him. During his many years in the rural walls of this stuffy town, his imagination had spun such wild and fanciful webs of the "out there" that he was now captured in their tacky grasp. He *could not* stay. It was no longer an option. The world outside called to him with promises of virtues and adventure and *purpose*.

He sidled into his bedroom and plopped the purchased bundle onto his bed, shifting it in amongst the piles of *other* lingering there. He found a vacant chair— a rare breed amongst the mess that was his house—and slumped into it. Tomorrow couldn't come soon enough. His heart raced at the thought of all the many virtues he might face and subsequently bind.

Sadly, the equipment he now held would only be good for a single catch. Despite his lengthy protests to garner more, he was turned away and refused like a begging urchin. He lifted his left arm, studying the elongated black sleeve that stretched tight from fingertips to neck. Two plates adorned the mostly elastic fabric, one on the back of the hand and one on the crest of his shoulder. Each of the silvery slabs held a single socket where a binding stone could be placed. Jay sighed, disappointed. Only one of the hollows was currently filled.

Why even give me the second plate if I can't have a stone for it too?

He fingered the small, foggy gem inlaid against his hand. One side of it faced outward, while the other side protruded through the plate to rest against his skin. In order to successfully enact a binding, he would have to make physical contact with the virtue using the exposed portion of the stone. It acted as a sort of transmitter, relaying what he had been taught to think of as *soul codes*. Just as any piece of the recently emerging brands of technology operated based on a series of coding computed through some mechanical brain, Jay had learned to think of binding in a similar manner. The stone now jutting from his sleeve was the interface through which the coding that made up *him* traveled to the virtue he intended to bind, and vice-versa. Once both codes merged, the two would be inextricably linked for life.

That was another thing. He couldn't be frivolous with his choice. Even though he intended to bind them all, once he was connected with a certain type of virtue, he could never bind another of that type no matter how hard he tried. It was as if his soul had twelve individual slots of its own, and filling one was a permanent decision. Bind a weak virtue now, and he would never get the chance to replace it with one stronger.

Jay leaned back, hearing the chair groan beneath his weight. The decision would be critical. The *whole day* would be.

I should get some sleep. He yawned. Seeing the effort it would take to clear out a space on his bed, he sighed. *Chair it is, then.*

****

At first, there was only light, *bright, scorching light.* It burned his eyes through opalescent lids. Dark veins and red hues and fluttering streaks of white…

Jay moved to brush away the morning sun, block it from its harassing position over him, but his swipes failed to create any relief.

Then heat. It came so furiously, so suddenly, that Jay startled. It was almost enough to rouse him. *Almost.* But still, he held firm to that sweet abyss.

It was the *screams* that finally brought him awake.
****

Sober vision found him as quickly as his lashes spread. There was no grogginess now, no slowness to wake. The scene that met his eyes was enough to shatter sleep and return him to consciousness like a sheet of icy rain.

Everything was red.

Expecting to find his house ablaze, he was surprised when only an *open field* sprawled out in his sight, torched and buried in ankle-deep ash. His mind spun.

How had he gotten here?

There were *people* running in the shadows around him, some crying for help, others stampeding toward a perceived safety. He couldn't see anything at all save an ever-reaching fire, like an unholy barrier across the sky, a meteor that refused to fall its final feet. It hovered like doom manifest on the horizon. He couldn't take his eyes from it.

It pulled on him.

It tugged at his essence like two halves meant to meet, to reforge, *to become one again.*

Someone suddenly teetered past Jay on his right, clothes burning like the community bonfire they held every spring in the town square. The smoke rose off of him in constant skyward rapture, a pillar of sacrifice to the deity that lingered out there.

Jay felt his stomach churn at the sight, the sounds and the stench of the dying man, but before he could heave his meal away into the crimson night, another vision caught his eyes. He looked up and ahead to find the culmination of every childhood nightmare, something birthed from the very pits of hell clambering down from the fiery skies and across the plains. Its steps singed the world.

And somehow, he knew. *It was coming for him.*

****

The sun pierced the veil of his bedroom curtains, searing Jay's pale skin like a heated cattle-prod. He leaped from the floor, gaze darting around the room and refusing to believe.

What happened to the field? The people? The burning man—

He hauled his mind away from that last image even as it still stood in his memory like a figurine cast in stone.

A dream.

Confused but relieved, he shoved away the bulk of laundry blocking a mirror on the back of his bedroom door and examined himself. He was soaked from matted hair to the soles of his feet. Sweat dribbled down the crook of his nose. His eyes were dilated, his skin flushed, but there was no evidence of the burnt flesh he expected. He swept a hand through his tangled locks and sat back hard against the mattress, drawing deep breaths.

Just a dream.

It took him a few minutes to gain confidence in that, but he managed to convince himself of the stress. He had a big day ahead of him. That was it. Just a little stress.

What little sleep he found outside of the nightmare on the plain had been elusive, quick to leave him only shortly after ensnared. He rubbed at his swollen eyes, scanning the room as if it was something foreign now. His pack was laying on its side at his feet, toppled like an overstuffed giant. He touched the sleeve still on his arm, ensuring that the precious stone within hadn't vanished in the night.

****

"*Jay!*"

A voice came through the walls like thunder. He chirped and stumbled into a mock mannequin, once a lamp.

"Jay! Come on, man! We're gonna be late!"

Jay shook his head and shuffled drearily toward the front door, dodging more masses of untidiness along the way. Fumbling with the latch, he finally popped it open in time to catch Wade rearing back for another knock.

"I'm coming, I'm coming. *Geez.*"

Wade grabbed his sleeve, tugging him out the door. "Dude, we have ten minutes to be at the gates! Let's go!"

Jay stood a little straighter. "*Ten minutes?* Are you serious?" He peered up at the sun as if he was adept enough to read its precise position.

"Where's your bag? Get your stuff and let's go!"

Jay spun around, dashing back to his room, heedless of the ripples he sent out across the sea of litter. He peeled his bag away from the carpet and slung it over one shoulder. Shoving his feet into his boots, he didn't bother to tie them as he sprinted out after Wade.

"Didn't get much sleep, huh?" Wade asked as they ran side by side down the main thoroughfare.

People were already out and about, eagerly tending to chores, languidly sipping their coffee, or dressed down in preparation for the day's work.

"Less than an hour of anything good." Jay fastened the pack a little tighter as he spoke. He shot a brief glance at the crystal-clear sky and felt another surge of relief gain foothold.

"Yeah, same here. Too stoked for this."

Wade took their last turn at a gallop before sliding

to a stop, planting them squarely before the massive steel gates that led to the Eastern Glens. The connecting walls were imposing, forty feet high with tines of jagged metal threaded down every linear inch. Though there were ample signs of age across its surface—rust, weathered pockmarks, and vines as thick as Jay's ankle—it held as fast as the day it was built. No virtue or wild animal had ever crossed it high or low save for those with wings, and the city guard was always quick to run such intruders away.

In truth, Jay wasn't exactly sure why Glendale, Highwater City, or any other large settlement for that matter insisted on building such formidable defenses against nothing more than nature and its "virtuous" counterparts. He had heard of the rare instances where large and dangerous virtues had weaseled into city limits and wreaked a fair amount of havoc, but even in those cases, their entry was never due to a weak perimeter. It usually happened when hapless sentries left their posts unmanned or the gates unlatched after rounds on the exterior. Jay thought that, even at half their size, the walls and gates of Glendale could still repel any creature interested in touring the town.

"What do you think you'll spot first out there?" Wade asked, drawing his attention back to the upcoming task.

Jay tried to shrug, but the puffy pack pressed against his shoulders like stone. "Don't know, but if it's as infested as they say, I don't think we'll have to look long."

"I've lived here my whole life and haven't been through the Eastern Gates *once*," Wade lamented. "Pop always said it's twice as dangerous as any other direction. All the nasty stuff stays close to the edges of the Valley, I guess."

"Guess that's where I'm headed then," Jay said with a smirk.

"Your funeral," Wade countered with a laugh, scratching at the stubble on his chin. "Professors aren't gonna pull us out of this one like they do during training. We're flying solo."

Jay slowed, falling in line behind the milling crowd of about thirty students. Three of the head professors from the Academy stood before the group, seeming to take attendance.

"Let me begin by declaring the rules and the goal of this trial."

Madam Traeger stepped up to the center of the group and stood atop a small pedestal ostensibly designed for her more ample girth.

"You will each have until sundown—approximately eight hours from now—to locate and bind the virtue of your choice. Bear in mind that in order to graduate, you *must* bind the virtue within this allotted period. If you fail to do so, you will have the opportunity to retake this semester and attempt the trial at a future date. Your binder's sleeve, and thus your binding stone—filled or not—will be forfeit back to the Academy, however, barring you from attempting any exercise outside of Academy supervision. If you bind a virtue outside of the time slot, you will be reprimanded and refused a certification of graduation from the Academy. *Pay close attention to the time.* Am I understood?"

"Yes, Madam Traeger," the dull response followed.

"Good. As for the other rules, there are only three. Do not, under any circumstances, interfere either positively or negatively with any other student during this exam. Do not travel beyond the Glens; there will be markers erected along the boundaries to prevent you from blindly wandering beyond. And lastly: *do not pester any virtues that you do not expressly intend to bind.*"

She eyed a ragtag group of rowdies at the head of the class who promptly snickered to one another.

"You will each be given a data-feed module which will visually record your progress and behavior and send it back to one of us for review. Tampering with this device will automatically fail you in this trial. Losing this device will incur a substantial financial charge to your student account. These are precious computational devices, the likes of which are very rare and very hard to procure. Am I understood?"

"*Yes, Madam Traeger.*"

Wade nudged Jay and nodded toward a tall man waving over the crowd. With his gesture came a sudden gust of wind, rising playfully around them and bearing aloft the aforementioned monitoring devices. They floated about lazily until a single unit hovered directly over each student. Gasps of awe echoed from the group, some even declaring they would seek out wind virtues solely because of the showmanship.

Jay plucked his out of the air and clipped it onto the strap of his pack, pointing the little lens toward the enviable Professor Farsk.

"*Show-off,*" he puffed.

"At least he has it to show," Wade whispered. "I'm a little jealous."

Madam Traeger lifted her hands to regain their attention. "Remember your training. Remember what we have taught you. Be diligent and swift, and above all…" She paused, locking eyes with nearly every student before stopping to pin Jay with a hard stare. "*Choose wisely*. This decision is *permanent*."

Jay returned it, unflinching. He had never come to words with the woman, but he had always known deep down that she mocked him for his grand intentions. Though it was common enough amongst his peers, something about a teacher's belittlement—an instructor of the renowned Academy no less—dug at the thin reins holding his temper.

Wade shuffled past him, trailing behind a trio of women that Jay recognized as Susie and her two friends, Haley and Freya. Wade melded into their group, no doubt layering their conversation with charm, leaving Jay to his lonesome. Jay meandered behind the crowd, opting to let them pass through registration first. There was no sense in bum-rushing the place. They would all have plenty of time to complete the trial.

As he spotted the first vacant station, his gaze found Professor Farsk standing over it, waving him forward. Jay obliged, moving idly closer.

"You may want to do something about those boots," Farsk stated flatly.

Jay looked down to find his laces still loose and sliding through the dust to each side of his shoes. He knelt and cinched them up as quickly as he could.

"Jay, *look at me*."

Jay lifted his head in time to catch the man's beefy hand coming to rest on his shoulder. His gaze inclined further to land on the chiseled jawline and gleaming green eyes that had earned more than a fair share of feminine attention.

Almost conspiratorially, Professor Farsk leaned in and whispered, "You can do whatever you set your mind to. *Anything…*"

Jay stared at him as if he had sprouted horns. Farsk had never been rude or demeaning in all the years that Jay had lived in Glendale, but he had never been particularly kind either. Something about the man's abounding success at wielding his virtue's abilities—not to mention his overwhelming popularity and general magnetism—always seemed to grate. But in those few simple words, every predisposition Jay had built up about him seemed to melt away.

"I uh—thanks?"

Farsk smiled. "*Fire.*"

"Excuse me?" Jay asked, unsure what he meant.

"If you are going to try to catch multiple virtues, *fire* would best suit as a starting point. It's amongst the strongest in raw potential and can easily overwhelm other types if it comes down to a fight. *Choose fire.*"

Jay's mouth hung wide, unable to form a response. A flash of the dream he had the night before flickered across his mind, but before he could respond, Professor Farsk simply pressed him through the station and waved the next student forward.

Semi-dazed from the exchange, he stepped through the Eastern Gate where Wade caught him.

"Yo, you ready for this?" He emerged from a group of women grinning like the proverbial school-boy he was.

"Yeah. I guess I am," he answered with his mild shock still evident.

"What's gotten into you?" Wade asked, quirking a brow.

Jay shook the stupor. "Nothing. Let's do this." He clapped Wade on the back. "Good luck, man. I'll see you at the end."

Wade grinned. "Just don't get yourself killed."

Jay returned the smile, spun, and sprinted off down the grassy, cobbled roadway that led toward the far reaches of the Eastern Glens.

****

He passed by several students already delving into the thickets and dense patches of forest for their prey. They would likely find something perched within despite their nearness to the gates, but Jay didn't care for the ease of such a pursuit. The likelihood of weaker virtues aside, Jay had never been the type to take the easy paths. He liked the challenge, which may well be a large factor in his ultimate goal of binding all twelve virtue types. And he knew the challenge awaited him farther out. So he streaked past them all, knowing that his trial would take at least a few hours more than the rest.

The edge of the Valley of Pyres was nearly a two-hour walk from the gates according to his map, meaning that he could cut the time in half if he hurried. That should give him a solid six hours to hunt before he would need to turn back.

As he progressed down the primary road, he kept an eye out for any suspicious movement. Just because he liked the challenge didn't mean he would let an opportunity escape him. Mostly, he saw only small critters, natural wildlife scurrying away from his storm toward the border, but as he passed a small stream-crossing, he slowed. When the flicker in the trees came again, he hunkered low behind the nearest hedge.

It was of a radiant blue—cerulean to be precise. The

color and visible aura often gave away the virtue, he had been taught. It could be one of two types: water or evolutic. Water virtues, on one hand, tended to be a lighter shade of blue with some level of translucence to mimic their affinity for their titular substance. But evolutic virtues could be any number of brighter colors, designating their vibrance and origins in the natural order of progress and growth.

Jay watched silently as the creature dove down from the treetops once more, splashing through a deeper portion of the stream. It rested just atop the shimmering surface, seeming to blend into the refractions of the sunlit ripples.

Water it is, then.

He watched for a time and wondered at the oddity of its form: a winged manifestation, though unlike any bird that he had ever seen. Sky-blue feathers fluttered at its side, shaking the gleaming droplets from its coat. Its head bore sharp features, a coned beak and crystalline eyes. It was beautiful, entrancing him with poise and a clearly keen perception.

Suddenly, its twisting neck stopped, its gaze falling on his skulking position. With a single, swift motion, the virtue was airborne again, the water beneath it roiling and rising to shield it from view. Jay leaped up and started after it, but as the water splashed back into the pool, the winged virtue was simply *gone*.

"*Shoot*," he exclaimed, kicking at the undulating waves. "Ah, well. Not sure I really wanted that one anyways."

It was going to be difficult, he realized, to bind anything that could move so quickly. He had to make physical contact, after all. Undeterred, though, he shrugged his pack a little higher and restarted his journey to the edge.

****

After nearly thirty more minutes of jogging, he came to a crossroad. The crisp, green forest wall loomed before him, cutting off his easterly trek. The pine-fragrant air danced across his skin, cooling him from his hard press as he surveyed the lot. There were no signs or markers that foretold of the end-results of either of the new roads, so he pulled his pack down and unsheathed the large digital map he had recently purchased. After a few clicks and pokes to bring the contraption to life, he narrowed in on his presumed location, quickly finding the junction illustrated there. According to the screen, heading right would carry him southward toward the second tier of Cityscape. Taking a left would carry him northeast, eventually dropping him off at the border to the Valley of Pyres, the area he had originally planned on scouting.

"Looks like a left from here..." he muttered, still resolved.

He slipped the map back into the bag, resituating it on his shoulders. Just as he was snapping the restraints together, he heard the rustling of something moving through the woods ahead. Instinct kicked in. Squatting low, he eased closer, planting himself behind the largest of the trees outlining the copious beyond. His gaze roved, half-expecting the disturbance to be nothing more than a merry band of squirrels. Long seconds passed, and just as he was readying to call off the search, a sharp snap sounded *behind* him. He spun, heart leaping into his throat, just in time to catch a red blur streak across his vision.

"*What the!*" he cried out.

He had never seen anything move so quickly; he couldn't even pin a figure in the blur of motion. His mind reverted almost instantly to Wade's insinuation of danger this far out. Virtues weren't averse to killing unwary travelers.

Jay pressed his back against the towering oak, scanning the road and surrounding forests for any sign of the red blur again. He reached for his only form of defense, the single item that The Traveler carried suitable for repelling all types of wild virtues. It was an orb, no larger than his palm, designed to emit high frequencies and blinding lights when cracked. Something about the pitched stimulants reacted painfully with the virtues' anatomies, forcing them to flee.

Jay held the orb in front of him, readying to whip it into the moss-draped stones at his feet. The area was silent and still though, not even a breeze to disturb the languid leaves overhead. After brief deliberation, Jay decided to retreat slowly toward the Valley. He wanted a strong virtue, but he wasn't willing to die for the chance.

Turning away from his protective trunk, he took two steps toward the road again and froze.

The air warped in front of him.

A line of fire trailed in its wake, scorching the stones and casting a wave of heat across his body. He cried out again, stumbling back over himself and landing hard in the dirt. The orb flew high into the air, coming down beside him with a loud *crack*. A small explosion followed, sending an ear-piercing alarm through the serene glen and blinding Jay with a shockwave of light.

He rolled away, growling with pain from the sudden

sensory overload. But he couldn't stay there. *He had to move*. Blinking away a flood of tears, he managed to make out bare outlines around him. He scrambled to his feet, sprinting as hard as he could down whichever stretch of highway he found first. The red lines of a hazy shape shot across the road twice more, canceling any remaining grip he held to logic. He shouted maniacally, swatting the air with empty hands. He could feel the phantom fingers of a nightmare swiping at him as he ran.

He wasn't going to make it. It was too fast.

He slid into a sharp bend in the road, vision beginning to return like blurred pixels. There was a hollow in the woods ahead, a large stone hovering over an opening in the damp soil. It called to him like shelter in a storm. *If he could just get—*

His step faltered. The red stripe suddenly raced *toward* him from that narrow distance. Hitting the ground a second time, he curled up into a fetal position, body locking down on him in terror.

This was it. This was how he died.

He was going to be ripped to pieces by this monster, left there in the road as a mangled testament to his failure.

What a way to end. He would be the laughingstock logged in all history books to come: the man who thought he could claim them all *killed* before he could even bind his first.

As the myriad of thoughts crossed Jay's mind, he realized the time it had taken to process them all…*and the fact that he was still alive to do it.* He unfurled like drying bark and sat up slowly, afraid that the motion would be his last. When the road came into clear view again, he saw a red figure dancing across the cobbles, and suddenly, the howling of pain entered his ears.

Jay was still for a long moment, watching with disbelief. The creature that had been, just moments ago, the bane of his existence now stumbled about, subdued and on full display.

It was small. Shockingly small. It stood nearly knee-high on him, crimson and black fur covering most of its body. From Jay's vantage, it appeared uncannily like a dog, canine from its four legs to its tail and even the whiskers on its snout. The differences could be summed in glowing ruby eyes and sharp spines of obsidian erected from its back in a long, linear design. It continued to blunder drunkenly around the road, whimpering and howling at what Jay realized was the continued assault of frequencies on its ears.

Like a thunderclap, he bellowed out the most absurd laugh he ever had. It was unstoppable, something dredged up from beneath the receding panic and fear. The noise boomed through the trees, derisive and unbelieving.

"You have got to be kidding me!" he called out at the doggish virtue. "*You*? *Look at you*! I'm losing it! How did *you* do all of *that*?"

The virtue slowed as the frequencies began to die out in the distance, the bauble clearly exhausting whatever energies supplied its rant. The dog's ears perked at Jay's shaming taunts in tandem.

"You looked so much *bigger* before." He held a hand to his head, chastising himself, "*Aw man*, I just wasted my only repellent sphere on you."

The virtue opened its fiery red eyes wide, pinning Jay with a glare. It seemed to understand what he was saying, even donning an offended stance to prove it. Jay only shook his head, sighing.

"Wasting my time." He checked his watch as the canine figure continued inspecting him with affronted eyes. "I have less than six hours now. Thanks a lot."

He spun and began walking back to the crossroad, ensuring that he took the right direction. As he turned his back on the virtue, though, he heard a distinct growl echo down the corridor after him. He looked over his shoulder to see the canine hunkered low, aggression returning.

"Just chill. I'm leaving, see? No need to get your whiskers in a bunch."

He snickered, continuing on and leaving both the virtue and his shame on the road behind him. As cool as those tricks were, it was obvious how weak the dog was by size and stature. Jay needed something with a little more flare, something imposing and impressive to drive his capability home to the naysayers. He needed something in between this puny predator and a virtue capable of mauling him to death.

Dismally, he realized that the professors would have seen everything that just transpired, as he was wearing the small recording device still. There was no telling how difficult it would make his life if the footage was to get out. Something told him that one of the professors—likely Madam Traeger—would 'accidentally misplace' the film of his downfall to a weak virtue. It would inevitably be for open viewing within the week.

Back at the crossroad again, he took the correct route this time and resumed his hunt. The next hour was slow, little more than insects and the occasional bird flying high overhead to give him company. Several false leads carried him deeper into the woods only to reveal natural wildlife or worse: *nothing at all.*

On his way back out from one of the latter excursions, he spotted the culmination of his hopes. A formless figure of energy hovered aimlessly through the air several yards ahead. It was a deep violet, shifting with glimmers of blue and white across its surface every few seconds. It floated languidly amongst the trees, occasionally brushing against something that would immediately begin to float alongside it until losing the levitating energies and plopping back to the forest floor below.

He watched in silent awe, celebrating his luck. For one thing, it was a *gravitic* virtue, as rare as they came in these parts. On top of that, it was documented that some of the more powerful virtues refused to take a consistent form, instead opting to remain as the amorphous essence of energy that truly constituted their existence. By binding this, he might possibly have one of the strongest virtues in all of Glendale.

Jay crept closer, unsure how to keep from being noticed. The thing didn't have eyes or ears or any standard form of perception-oriented anatomy that he could avoid triggering. He decided to move in as non-threateningly as he could, standing straight and making slow progress.

The virtue hummed with power, and Jay could feel his steps growing lighter as he closed the distance between them. His heart thrummed hard in his chest, excitement threatening to overwhelm him. He felt like a spacewalker bounding across the surface of the moon. With a gravitic virtue as his first, there was no telling what all he could accomplish...

"*Just a little closer,*" he whispered, trying to speak soothingly.

Every fiber of his being was buzzing with eagerness, urging him to leap the last few yards and seal the deal. He could feel the smile splitting his face. All he had to do was touch the blob with the back of his hand and—

Suddenly, a blur caught the corner of his vision, drawing his attention away. Before he could even register it, the beast lunged into him, carrying his near-weightless form into the air and far away from his prize. Once outside of the influence of the gravitic virtue, his body regained affected mass and plummeted back to the ground. He felt branches break beneath him, cracking like the bones he half-expected to join them.

Eyes now wide, they settled on the form of a red-and-black canine virtue, clawing into him with puny paws. He shouted angrily, kicking and punching at the miniature wolf until it relented. Regaining his personal space, Jay took a few steps back and held his wounded chest. There were shallow scratches at most, another testament to this pest's lack of power. He bellowed his defiance at the creature but quickly reeled it in as the gravitic virtue fled into the thickening brambles.

"No! Wait!"

He dashed for it, but the persistent hound cut him off, snarling.

"What's your problem!" he screamed, grabbing a stone and hurling it at the beast.

The fire virtue only sidestepped and increased its rumbling volume, as if they had engaged in a shouting match.

"I don't have time for you!"

He snatched one of the larger branches that composed his earlier cushion and swiped furiously. It backed away, quickly regaining an aggressive stance, but it soon realized that Jay was not going give up easily. He continued rushing the virtue, slashing through the air with the branch like a madman. Eventually, it took the hint and bolted, but not before casting a swift, disdainful look over its shoulder.

"Ugh!" Jay roared in frustration.

He had been *so* close. It was a *gravitic virtue* for crying out loud. He traced the path that it had taken but soon found that its formless nature left almost no evidence behind.

"*Stupid-fire virtue ruining everything-flippin' dog,*" he mumbled beneath his breath in chorus as he took to the road once more.

"*Okay,*" he coached himself, "Just get it together and keep looking. There's bound to be more out here. And who knows what I could find?"

****

With only two hours left to the trial, Jay was at his wit's end. He had actually found three more virtues worth the risk, but each attempt at binding them ended up in a similar state as the gravitic.

The first was a wind type nesting serenely in the lower reaches of a tree. His climb was interrupted as a branch gave way, planting him yet again on the hard dirt and sending the virtue flitting into the fading sky. The following attempt at an evolutic type got the best of his already-boiling temper, as every time he neared to touch the snaking ethereal vine, it whipped away playfully. Half an hour of that was nearly enough to break his resolve. He left the infuriating evolutic and found its counterpart, an entropic virtue, not too far away. The swarm of what appeared to be festering gnats was equally maddening as he couldn't seem to connect with anything solid enough to bind it. He looked like an idiot—adding to his embarrassing footage—swiping and punching the unmoving mass until he was out of both breath and patience.

Now, he was back on the road and nearing the end of his searchable area. In visible distance, he could see the tall, blinking markers signaling the end of the Glens and Cityscape, and the beginning of the Valley of Pyres.

He exhausted his breath and anger toward the falling sun. He looked like he had been beat up, dragged through the woods by his ankle, and emotionally abused at every turn.

He sat on a stump in a small clearing, trying to rebuild the dedication that he had recently lost to the annoying trio of virtues. The Valley sprawled out before him, a sight he had only ever seen in textbooks. It was barren and uncovered by the dense foliage that constituted the Glens. It seemed to stretch into an endless distance. *Breathtaking.* He tried to enjoy the moment despite his shortcomings in the trial.

Pillars of liquid fire sprang forth from the Valley floor en masse as far as his eyes could see. They stood and stooped in tandem, hundreds of them dancing toward the sky in asynchronous and violent fashion. One day, he was going to go there, spend weeks, months, maybe even *years* camping out near the molten sprays until he had bound the best virtues that the land had to offer.

He shook his head at the thought, though.

"I'll *never* do that. I can't even catch the virtues here," he lamented. He plopped his head into his hands, staring out into the mesmerizing skyline.

After a time of sulking and brooding, something strange caught his eye nearby. In the clearing around him were three odd stones, black as night and rather lumpy to be extrusions of something like obsidian or coal. It was as if the sky dropped three large meteorites, foreign to this land, flat onto the dell. Their dusty surfaces had scratches and gouges all about them, some joints between the lumps even appearing purposeful.

"Huh," he mused, standing and approaching the nearest. A few feet out, he saw the telltale signs of shuddering movements in those joints and beamed. "*Gotcha!*"

The solemn word seemed to bring the behemoths to life, stones grating on stones in a world-churning motion that continued until all three giants were standing tall and menacing over him. The one nearest was twice his size, body made up of the boulders that once littered the ground, each conjoined at mystical intervals like magnetized materials.

Jay shook with sudden excitement again. It wasn't a gravitic, but a mineral virtue this size *had* to be powerful. That familiar notion of deadly fear crossed his mind, but he waved it away for the impeccable timing. His trial was nearing its end, and these beauties had been practically handed to him on a silver platter. With their type and size, they would move like molasses in winter, which should give him plenty of time to bind one and get away before he was pummeled to death.

He pulled his arm across his chest, readying to make contact, and sprinted forward. All he needed was a quick tap to the closest stone and—

A familiar red streak flashed between him and the first golem.

"Oh, no you don't! Not this time!" he barked, rushing the stone giant before the crazy canine could stop him.

But even at a full dash, the little fiery pest was faster. It caught his leg head on, tripping him face first into the dust. They both stumbled forward in a heap. Before Jay could stand again, he spotted the golem's gargantuan limb coming down faster than he anticipated. He rolled several times to the left, barely escaping the impact. The vibrations rattled his teeth and bucked his body away from the baked soil.

He managed to clamber back to his feet in time to see the second and third golems gaining slow ground. There was still a window, though. It was small, but if he timed it right, he could get within reach of the first giant and make contact before escaping the others' collective wrath.

He angled forward again to run, but the infuriating dog was back, cutting into his trajectory with impressive resolve. If the whelp wasn't actively attempting to foil his plans and future, he would've given it props for persistence. He was beginning to regret his insensitive words. The virtue had obviously taken the taunts to heart.

It barked and growled as menacingly as it could, but the sight of the golem in the background put the little guy into minor perspective. It held its position, though, daring Jay to make a move, all while the mass of living stones behind it prepared another assault. This time, the leader was no longer targeting *Jay*.

Jay faltered. Against every instinct and every logical node in his mind, he felt a wave of empathy crash into him. He wasn't sure if virtues could die, but if he didn't do something, he was going to find out expressly.

"Listen! Whatever I did to spite you, let's call it even! Just leave me alone!"

He stepped to the side, but the fiery virtue mimicked. The golem's fist was at its zenith, preparing to reverse directions even as the other two took up positions to follow suit.

"*Just move!*" he screamed. "You're gonna get yourself killed!"

The canine barked back, as if demanding he make it.

Then the first boulder dropped. Something in Jay stretched taut enough to snap. *He couldn't let it happen.*

Screaming and running and calling the dog a dozen different demeaning names, he leaped at the last moment before the first fist fell. The fool virtue never even saw it coming. Jay clenched his eyes shut, feeling every muscle in his body seize. He collided with something, and then his world blacked out.

Chapter 3

Jay saw fire. *Again.*

Billows of flame and smoke and rings of angry red surrounded him in every direction. It was his nightmare all over, but this time *he felt it.*

His skin *burned*; his hair, his eyes, *everything*. He tried to scream, but no sound came. There was nothing but the song of the blaze. The crackle, the pressure, *the pain*.

Suddenly, he was back to reality. It all happened in a flash. His numb body tumbled end over end, no longer feeling anything but the ground moving like jagged wind beneath him. When he finally stopped his forward momentum, he curled into a ball and groaned.

Everything hurt.

His bones felt like applesauce in leather tubes. Raw agony lingered across every inch of his skin. He wore it like a tight-fitting suit, felt it embrace him more with every beat of his heart.

Pulse-pulse-pulse.

It was like he had been hit by a hammer—

He surged upward into a crouch, mind returning to the present. His throbbing gaze landed on the three golems now regaining their stony feet as well, as if their own attacks had thrown them completely off balance.

'*But we were right beneath them*,' he thought, confused.

And then the 'we' in that thought took hold. He stood shakily, scanning all around for the idiot dog that nearly cost him his life. But there was nothing; only the three uneasy golems and he remained in the clearing. Just as he thought the beast must have fled, ungrateful as it obviously was, he cringed. The dots were beginning to connect, nodes snapping together with treacherous lines of truth. Bringing his wrist to bear, he saw what he had so desperately wished he wouldn't.

"*No*." He palmed his forehead. "No! No way! *No*!" he shouted. You have *got* to be kidding me! I get one chance, and I bound *you*?"

He thought back to the moment he collided with the obstinate mutt. His gem must have made physical contact, sealing the fire element to his soul and forever filling that portion with a virtue that he loathed.

He plopped back onto the ground, soberly considering it all for a time longer, moping at his luck turned sour, but eventually he was forced to move or be beaten to a pulp by the sloth giants. He resituated his gear, checked his watch, and made a slow and somber return to the Gates.

****

A few times, he attempted to feel the power that the virtue had supplied, even going as far as trying to start a flame from ambient energy as the textbooks suggested was possible, but in each instance he stopped. He just couldn't find the will for it. After all that he had been through, nearly catching rare and potent virtues, nearly *dying*, he had ended up with a petty fire-type that, quite frankly, he now *hated*. He dreaded telling the group that he had captured such a weak variant at the start. He could imagine the rest now, laughing at him as they recited their tales of monstrous and powerful virtues captured at every turn all while he ended up with the shortest straw of the lot.

When the Gates came into view, he hung his head, afraid to make eye contact lest someone ask him about it. He found a seat just outside the closed portal where they had been staged for all returning students until the time was up. He could hear chatter between fellow trial-takers, some excited, others exhausted, but all seemingly proud of their accomplishments. And there he was... Stuck with his mistake for life...

"Jay?" a sweet voice called his name, shaking him from his brooding.

He looked up to find Susie sliding down a few seats to sit next to him.

"Hey," he answered, unable to hide the disappointment in his tone.

Susie's sympathetic gaze lingered on him. "What's wrong? Did you bind anything?"

He held his wrist up to display the glowing red gem as response.

"Oh!" she replied excitedly, but her eyes held confusion. "So what's the matter? You seem upset?"

Jay shrugged, stifling a sigh. He didn't want to be the party-pooper, but he couldn't pretend either.

"I almost had a gravitic virtue," he said, trying to sound animated. "And these massive mineral golems too. *Huge*." He extended his hands to illustrate their height.

"Yeah?" Susie sounded, perking up. "That's incredible! What happened?"

Jay's gaze dropped again. "Then *this* happened." He tapped his wrist. "Stupid fire virtue wouldn't leave me alone. Kept interfering. I accidentally touched it."

"*Oh*," Susie said again with new inflection, realizing his predicament. "Oh wow. I'm really sorry, Jay."

Jay waved her compassion aside. "What about you?" he asked, intent to take the attention off of him. "What did you get?"

Susie displayed her blue gem proudly. "Water! It's what I always wanted. Kind of a weird form, but it seemed like a strong one, so I nabbed it."

"Yeah? What did it look like?"

"Here! I'll show you."

She held her hand out and closed her eyes. Slowly, blue lines of essence began to leak away from her palm, floating toward a single point where they coalesced. When the last lines escaped her skin, the blue orb reshaped into a familiar winged figure, complete with crystal eyes and all.

Jay grinned with a touch of awe. "Hey, I actually saw that one. Pretty neat how it made that curtain of water and vanished."

"You saw him too?" Susie asked, giggling as it now waddled toward them with childlike interest. "He did that same thing to me! I chased him for hours! Eventually, I caught up when there was no water around. He couldn't perform his mystical vanishing act then."

Jay nodded appreciatively. "Say, how'd you do that? Summon him back out? I've never seen that before."

"Oh yeah, I read a book by Gareth Filimore about it. Not many people know how; most cities across Tier One frown on virtues being allowed to roam. Once you release them like this, you can call them back pretty easily, but you can't manipulate the essence until they're fully recalled."

She scooted closer, taking his hand in hers. "Here, it goes like this. Hold out your palm and envision the way it looked before you bound it."

He watched her, studied her crisp blue eyes, her golden hair. She smiled at him with ruby red lips, nudging her hip against his.

"Close your eyes, silly. It helps."

He obeyed, although reluctantly. She really was a stunning girl. Maybe Wade was onto something.

Clearing his mind, he envisioned the stubborn pup.

"Now, *push* the virtue out of you. Will it to reform physically exactly as it was before you bound it."

Jay watched in his mind's eye as the canine took shape, red eyes piercing the darkness there. Even in his head it seemed hellbent on defying him. He continued, though, keeping his lids closed and focusing as long as Susie held his hand upright. When she let it go, he peeled them open with a start.

"Ah! He's so cute!"

Susie leaped from her seat and knelt down to the summoned creature. The exclamation drew the attention of several other bleeding-heart women who joined her to dote. Jay only narrowed his eyes.

"Wish I could just let *you* have him."

Susie peered back up. "Oh, don't be like that. He's sweet!"

She reached forward to pet the virtue as if it was any other household dog. It growled and snapped at her, turning circles to bark at the others closing in.

Jay just grinned as Susie's shocked expression turned on him. "Not as sweet as you thought, huh?"

She looked back to the fire virtue and scooped up her own, inching away.

"He's a little menace, is what," Jay went on scathingly.

The canine turned its fiery eyes on him, black and red tail whipping out behind it in slow, methodical sweeps.

"*Okay*," Susie started, "Guess I can see why you were upset."

"So how do I recall the demon dog?" he asked, leaning down to square up with it. "That's right," he taunted, "You're *mine* now."

"Same as before," Susie replied, holding her virtue tight as if its fire-branded cousin would lash out at any moment. "Just will it to reform as essence and connect with you again." She demonstrated with the water virtue, setting it down and recalling it in mere seconds.

Jay's virtue sat like chiseled stone, gaze still pinned on him in sinister insolence. Something about that posture was a little *too* smug. He closed his eyes and began the process. He tried to envision the ball of energy, the strands of essence extruding from his hand and connecting with his new companion. But something was wrong. Even as he saw it happening in his mind, he would only open his eyes to find the dog still there, scornful expression unchanged.

"What's wrong? You're doing it like I told you, right?" Susie asked with mounting trepidation.

"Yeah!" Jay said, frustration bleeding through.

A hushed murmur suddenly buzzed around them. They had drawn a crowd it seemed, which only added to his rising temper.

"What am I doing wrong?!" He looked up in a mild panic to find Susie, pale-faced and eyes wide this time.

"*Oh no.* Jay, I didn't think this would happen, I

swear."

"Wait, what? That what would happen?"

Susie took a step back as if her words would bring physical retaliation. "I'm so sorry. I don't think you *can* recall it."

Jay froze, letting his arm fall like a weighted shaft of ice. He spoke as calmly he could under the sudden anxiety, "*Susie. Why* can't I recall it?"

"It-it almost never happens," she stuttered. "But some virtues can block the connection once they're resummoned. They have to be really strong-willed to do it, at least have a stronger will than the host. I mean, it's still bound to you, and it can't wander far, but—"

"But I can't put it back," Jay finished flatly.

Susie shook her golden-draped head side-to-side.

"And now I just lost my ability to manipulate its essence."

She nodded this time, bright eyes foggy with tears.

"Great. *Just great.*"

He turned back to the self-satisfied mutt and could swear that it was grinning at him. He wanted to kick the thing square in the face, but the crowd would likely disapprove. Instead, he fell back into his seat, refusing eye contact with it. Susie sat a few seats away, silently consoling and apologetic.

"You could try and befriend him?" she suggested after a long, tense silence. "Him, right?" She tilted her head, earning an approving grunt from the pup.

Jay laughed bitterly, but he stopped when he realized how harsh that must sound to her. She was only trying to help.

"Not sure that's gonna take, Suz."

"Well, you could at least give him a name. Pets tend

to respond better to their masters when they have frequently-used names."

Her suggestion brought both Jay's and the dog's eyes up in sync.

Jay grinned, seeing his chance for payback. "Well, he's not really a pet, but I *am* his master." He shot his own scathing look at the virtue. "How about Fleabag? Or Dunce-hat."

"*Jay*, be nice. What about Cinder?"

Both Jay and the dog looked away.

"Or maybe Sparky?"

Jay chuckled as the virtue half-whined, half-growled at her. "How about 'Jerk that shouldn't have interfered and we would both be happy right now?'" He sneered at the crabby creature.

"No, be serious! I think it could really help. How about *Blaze*?"

At that, the dog perked up. It stood and approached Susie in a manner of agreement. Jay was beginning to wonder just how intelligent this thing was…

Susie slid away hesitantly, but the virtue only drew closer. He bowed his head to her, causing Jay's eyebrows to twitch upward.

She giggled, reaching gently forward to pet it again. "I think he likes it. Don't you, Blaze?"

He actually nuzzled against her hand this time.

"See? I told you." "All I see is that he likes *you*, not me."

The dog looked back at Jay with its radiant red eyes, seeming to agree wholeheartedly.

"Well, maybe you should take what I am saying seriously! He seems friendly enough. Maybe it's *you* who has the problem." She winked and returned to petting the newly-named Blaze.

"Jay's got more than one problem," a new voice entered the conversation.

Wade approached from the road and stopped as soon as he saw the free-roaming virtue squatting at their feet.

"Um, what did I miss?"

Susie smiled. "This is Jay's new companion, Blaze!"

"She means that it's the new plague on my life who stole my freaking fire virtue slot!" Jay shouted at the dog, leaning over to swat at it.

"Woah, man. *Chill*. That thing could rip you a new face-hole." Wade took a seat between Jay and Susie. "So how's it, you know, *out*?"

"You can summon your virtues to their physical form by envisioning—"

"I wouldn't recommend it," Jay cut in. "Blaze here doesn't wanna go back into his cage."

"Yeah. Not sure I wanna risk mine either," Wade said with a wan expression.

"What did you get?" Jay asked, finding a measure of hope in his best friend's success.

"Well," Wade started a little uncertainly, "It's a wind virtue." He held his wrist up to display the light greenish gem glowing there. "And it definitely seemed like a strong one when I was chasing it, but…"

"But what?" Susie asked as he trailed off.

Wade grimaced. "I think it may be a little *challenged*."

Jay snorted. "Like how? Start at the beginning."

"Right," Wade nodded, standing to illuminate his storytelling. "So I'm deep in the woods between here and the Valley, see? Been there for maybe two hours when I first spot it. It's squawking and chirping—it took the form of a bird by the way—so I move in to see what's going down. That's when I spot it and this other virtue duking it out—I think it was an entropic type or something; it looked like the weirdest snake you've ever seen. And this wind virtue starts smacking the snake around, divebombing and pecking the hell out of it. Casting up whirlwinds and fighting like there's no tomorrow. Straight savage. So I'm thinking this is my boy, right? I rush in to catch it off guard, but it spots me and gets away. But I'm on the chase now. Finally catch up to the bugger, and, well…it's acting a little funny this time. Like, it keeps running into this tree, headfirst and *hard*. I check to see if it's attacking something else, but as I get a little closer, I realize there's nothing there. It's just a tree and the dude's going nuts on it."

Jay jumped in at a lull in the tale. "So why'd you bind it then? If it was a cracked-up bird, you could've walked away and found another."

Wade shook his head dismally. "I had less than two hours till the trial was over. And besides, this thing was a scrappy fighter, you know? I figured that if I bound it, it's not like I would adopt its crazy."

"I'm not sure, man. You're acting a little more erratic than usual," Jay prodded with a grin.

Wade sat back down and slapped his shoulder. "At least mine is still stuffed inside its cage."

Jay leered back, and Blaze began to growl.

"All right; we're cool!" he assured the dog and turned wide eyes on Jay.

"Trust me; I know," Jay replied dryly.

****

Once every student was accounted for, Jay was

ushered through a documenting station where they registered his virtue type in the Academy database. Blaze meandered alongside him with languorous interest, never straying far as if psychically leashed like Susie described. He gained several odd looks from students and teachers alike before Madam Traeger finally approached to settle the issue.

"Jameson, you need to recall your virtue at once. It is not appropriate to have the creatures, especially one as newly-tamed as yours, wandering around in physical form."

"Yeah, I wish that was possible, believe me, but it won't listen." Jay shrugged nonchalantly. Though he was certainly more upset about the matter, he knew it would get under her skin.

She huffed, straightening her already pristine attire. "What do you mean, it *won't listen*? Simply recall it the same as when you summoned it. Which, by the way, you should have *never* attempted without Academy supervision."

Jay continued through the line, signing the necessary forms as he spoke, "I *mean* just that. I tried to recall it, and the stupid thing won't come back."

"*Jameson Innis*, I will not be toyed with! Recall your virtue at once, or I will—"

"Ruthenia, I believe Master Innis is telling the truth."

Jay and Madam Traeger turned simultaneously to find the Academy Dean and founder-descendant, Walter von Quake, approaching. His tall and imposing form was slightly bent with age, but he nonetheless exuded authority as the ranks parted around him.

Jay had always thought the old man an enigma, but

he was likely the most polite and supportive official in all their ranks. The Dean had personally attended and spoke at Jay's parents' funeral despite barely knowing them, a kindness that endeared him since Jay was still an outsider at that point.

"Walter," Madam Traeger scrambled, "I'm sorry that you have to see this. Jameson is refusing to recall his virtue, and it is upsetting the other students."

The Dean looked from Jay to his teacher to the rebellious—albeit momentarily docile—virtue at their feet. Slowly, he scanned the milling crowd. "I see no disruptions that would warrant a recall, Ruthenia, do you?"

She stammered, but he only continued over her.

"And, as I stated, I believe that Master Innis is being forthright about the nature of this predicament."

The elderly man knelt to the ground, a great and exhausting task from the sight of it. He studied the dog with his bottomless brown eyes, searching for something. Then he spoke in a softly mystical tone, "This virtue defies you, Jameson. A rocky start to your relationship, I would venture to guess?"

Jay nodded somberly.

Walter's crinkled lips twitched into the worn groves of a smile. "It holds a fire against you that will not cease of its own accord. You would do well to extinguish it before it grows."

He turned his glimmering gaze upward and held a hand out to Jay, beckoning assistance. Jay took him by the arm and escorted him back to his feet.

"I-I'll do what I can," he stammered, trying to decipher the cryptic charge.

Walter chuckled with perceptive humor. "Oh, I'm

sure you will." Just before he turned to move away from Jay and the bewildered Madam Traeger, he smiled again and whispered, "Blaze is a fine name, indeed. It suits."

As he retreated back into the milling crowd of both students and now-flocking parents, Blaze puffed at him, standing and adopting an indignant pose.

Jay watched the exchange curiously, wondering just how the Dean had known the virtue's given name, but Madam Traeger's angry gaze drew him away from the thought.

"Figure it out and recall him," she snapped and stormed off.

Jay washed his hands of the entire scene and continued through the registration process. Blaze followed still, like a true dog who had been recently neutered and stripped of its reason to live. He toddled around, inspecting people and objects alike with unimpressed notice until his path crossed Jay's again, to which he simply snorted and flashed his tail as he hurried away.

Just on the other side of registration, Jay passed by Professor Farsk who drew him aside with a wave of the hand.

"*Fire*," he said appreciatively.

Jay shrugged and explained his predicament.

Farsk reached down to pick Blaze up, but the virtue barked and hopped away. He promptly wrapped the dog up in a curtain of condensed air, restricting him, and stooped to try again. Blaze wriggled and struggled against the trespass, but all to no avail. A few gouts of flame arose around the pair, but the man's aptitude with wind shown true as they all died with sudden whipping gusts.

"*He's feisty*...but that can prove valuable," Farsk said, inspecting Blaze carefully. "The fighters tend to be stronger manifestations. You know, most people keep their virtues caged in deference to popular opinion, but there are groups in this world that prefer to allow their virtues free roam, believe it or not. It's been documented that these can be refined and grown to a higher potential if left to experience your world in such a way. You may find that allowing it this freedom is a wise decision, despite the handicap to any skills of your own. Two can often be better than just one."

Jay cocked a brow, skeptical. "And where could one find *such people*?"

Farsk frowned. "Don't be snide, son. As a matter of fact, you can travel to the eastern ends of Waterwall this very moment and find many factions that have adopted the habits. Not to mention a few cities in the higher tiers of Cityscape. It's seen as a statement of beauty and power to showcase the elegance of virtues there."

He handed the dog over to Jay, who took him reluctantly. Blaze suddenly stopped struggling, falling limp and relaxed in his arms despite its canine sneer at both humans hovering over it. Jay felt a strange feeling of relief come over him in tandem.

"You know, you now have a bond with this virtue as true as any you've ever had. It is as much a part of you as you are yourself. Don't forget that."

"Hey, Jay!"

Jay turned again to find Wade emerging from the crowd.

"Check your watch, man! You're gonna be late!"

Jay's gaze connected with the circular timepiece on his wrist, and he blanched. He had less than a half-hour to get cleaned up and to the Mayor's manse for the mysterious dinner request delivered by Carl.

"Sorry, Professor Farsk. Gotta run."

He spun and took to a jog, pack and dog bouncing against his body in sync with his steps.

"I'll see you at graduation," Farsk replied, smiling and turning to the next student in line.

Jay waved back and let the dog plop to the ground beside him. Strangely, Blaze continued running in pace obediently without Jay so much as uttering a command. There truly was much to consider about this new relationship, as the professor had hinted, so much to test and refine. But he couldn't dwell on that right now. He had a meeting with Glendale royalty and the clock was ticking.

****

Shallow minutes later, Jay was in the best attire he could find—a wrinkled button-down and a pair of brown slacks—and stepping lithely up the endless stone stairway that prefaced the Mayor's oversized abode. Sweat beaded on his forehead, the walk from his house to Carl's a notable distance. Blaze meandered alongside him, shoulder cold to his new partner but seemingly compliant with the evening's plans.

Jay paused at the last step, eyeing the lightning rod before him. He shuddered with a wash of unbidden memories but quickly stuffed them away. Three stories of brick and stone dedicated to sheltering a family of four, if you included the ornery cat that had Carl beat for fat-to-body ratio.

He was still unsure why they had invited *him* over for a meal. He had never even been acknowledged by Mayor DeMoro in the few times they had crossed paths in public. And now, out of the blue, he had been summoned to dine with him, an occasion that wasn't regularly offered to people outside of political maneuverings.

Shrugging at the curiosity, he took the last few strides toward the front door and planted a series of hard knocks with the extruding brass handle. The sound was sharp against the dense wooden surface, quick to bring attention.

Jay backed away as the door cracked open, shedding a bright light onto the gloomy front porch. Carl stood as a sudden sentry there, backlit by dual chandeliers drooping from the foyer ceiling beyond.

"You're late, Innis."

"Fashionably," he replied. "Are you going to invite me in?"

Carl looked down, noting Blaze in the darkness behind Jay. "Not with your mutt trailing." He pointed at a small box several paces out into the yard. "You can leash him there."

"He's not a dog, Carl," Jay responded flatly. "I'm sure you and everyone else in a fifty-mile radius already know that."

Something akin to a smirk flickered across Carl's fat face, but the evening shadows swallowed the expression. "*Oh, yes.* I had heard about that little incident. Nasty situation. Might teach one to better consider his actions before blindly rushing into them."

"Blaze is coming in or we can cancel this little soiree," Jay said curtly. "You can tell your father that I sincerely appreciate the offer, but his son was too rude to allow my virtue's company."

"*Oh, you would like—*"

"Carl!" a deep and husky voice boomed from within the house, cutting off his snappy response.

Carl spun swiftly, ample rolls following in delayed suit and then jiggling with the jarring stop. A woman, larger even than her titanic son, stepped around a corner within Jay's vision and beckoned again.

"Carl...is that our guest standing idly outside while the meal awaits?" she posed dangerously.

"Yes, mother. I was just letting Jameson in."

There was a brief pause where Madam DeMoro held Carl with a violent green-eyed gaze, and then she turned, allowing her son the dignity to usher in the waiting Jay.

"Watch your tongue, Innis. This is my home, not a classroom suited for banter."

Jay relented, seeing the sudden need for prudence, though that didn't necessarily mean that he couldn't offer the occasional veiled jab at his copious cohort. He followed Carl inside, Blaze lingering only momentarily until he saw the door swinging shut. He leaped through the closing gap and scampered across the marbled tiles, tracking in dirt and bits of leaves with every step.

"Innis! If I have to so much as sweep up a *mite* after your mutt, I will make sure it costs you."

"Relax, Carl," Jay said, moving past him. "You have maids for things like that. Besides, it wouldn't hurt you to do a little physical labor every now and then."

Before Carl could respond, Jay was within earshot of the lady once more, cutting off any sass that might have been flung his way.

"Madam DeMoro, it's a pleasure. Thank you for having me over." He tried to emit his most cordial tone, though it probably sounded more like an actor spouting lines.

The woman merely grunted and waved for him and her son to follow to what Jay supposed was the dining area. They passed a sitting room, a study, and what appeared to be a bar equipped with every color between honey-yellow and dirt-brown liquor known to man. Of course, each room was outfitted with the best of the best—taxpayer's money going to good use—but the dining hall was a sight above the rest.

Jay stepped through double doors of aged iron and wood to find a table of over two dozen seats. Platters of food fit for feeding a tenth of the town littered its surface, shimmering silver beneath the single massive light fixture in the room. It hovered precariously close to their heads and held more candles than Jay could count. He found himself wondering just how long it would take someone to light each of those by hand.

A movement summoned his attention from the other end of the room, though, bringing his gaze back down to find Mayor Leon DeMoro seated at the head of the enormous oaken table.

"Please, sit," the man said, voice smooth and silky.

Jay looked first to Carl and then to his mother, who both only waited for his obedience. Feeling altogether awkward, Jay decided that he wanted to sit close to the host and moved down the length. With every chair he passed, he felt more and more like an idiot, but Blaze's sudden saunter past him sealed the ultimate embarrassment. The salty virtue waltzed right up to the Mayor and began to growl a serious, threatening rumble.

"*Blaze*!" he hissed, willing the beast to back away from the man but only watching him refuse. "Blaze!" he called louder, asserting his voice.

The dog spun, the strangest look in its glowing red

eyes, as if shocked at the rebuke.

"*Here*," Jay called warningly, pointing to the floor next to the seat he had slid away from the table.

The Mayor only grinned as if it had been some sort of joke to which he was the only audience that understood. Carl and Madam DeMoro broke away from their solemn stances at the opposite end of the room as Jay sat, but instead of finding a seat as well, they simply vanished back through the doorway. Jay's mouth moved to question their sudden absence, but he let it go, converting his breath to another series of syllables instead.

"I...apologize for that." He turned his attention to the Mayor once more. "I just bound him today, and—"

"I know," the host interrupted, sipping lightly on a glass of wine. A line of the blood-red liquid lingered at the corner of his lips before he dabbed it away with a linen napkin. Setting the now-stained cloth back down between them, he continued, "You summoned him and he refused the recall."

Jay nodded, and silence fell once again. He took the chance to make fresh note of the man. It had been some time since he last saw Mayor DeMoro. Pale skin, dark eyes to match his long, wavy locks. A pitch-black goatee framed his lips, tight and sinewy as they were. He was substantially thinner than the others of his household—Carl likely had him two-for-one on weight. He was barely grazing six feet in height and just turning down the back slope of middle-age. But there was something about Leon DeMoro that always hinted at ulterior motives despite what was shown on the surface, like a snake coiled and prepared to strike...

"Some virtues can be hassle," he spoke again,

breaking into Jay's quiet observation. "You will learn this lesson a most difficult way, I believe." He extended long fingers toward the multitude of platters splayed out before them. "Please, eat. We can speak at leisure."

Jay looked down at Blaze who had returned to his side, refusing to look any other direction than at their host. Although he was no longer growling, the virtue maintained a hard stance. Unsettled at the joint tension in the room, Jay simply eyed the food and began to fill his plate as suggested.

"You have grand days ahead of you, Jameson," the Mayor picked up, adding a solemn roll to his plate with the sharp tines of a fork. He jabbed the innocent chunk of bread like a fish attempting to escape his snare. "Graduation tomorrow, the world after that."

He wiped the fork with the stained linen napkin before setting it down to the right of his plate. His bony fingers drummed the table around it, but his gaze was fixed on Jay.

"I hear you have significant dreams, son. Tell me about them."

Jay hesitated just before his plate was overloaded and decided to restrain himself for the sake of manners. He let the tongs plop against the side of the nearest platter where they slipped languidly into the buttery glaze that lined its edges. He cursed himself immediately for the faux pas. But his attention was swept aside as he realized the question that lingered on Leon's lips.

"Well," Jay started, clearing his throat, "I intend to bind all twelve virtue elements. I know it sounds crazy, but I honestly believe that I can do it. No one else has ever done it, but someone has to be the first. Why not me?"

There was a stark silence as Leon continued staring at him, like his answer wasn't quite satisfactory or complete.

Jay tried again, "I guess I'll start in the lower tier of Cityscape here and try to move my way across the west side of the continent before I head east over the Valley of Pyres. Eventually, I figure I'll have the chance to see and bind them all if I travel from place to place."

The Mayor nodded his head curtly, moving to tuck a fresh napkin into his collar. Jay snatched his, realizing proper etiquette, and folded it across his lap.

"So you intend to travel quite a distance then?"

Jay inclined his head, waiting anxiously for his host to take the first bite of his measly helping so that he could dive into his. He was *starving*, especially now that the food was casting its alluring aromas at him within tantalizing proximity.

"That's the plan. I can't catch some of the rarer types in this region alone."

"Indeed."

The Mayor lifted the jagged fork and joined it with a knife, slowly sawing into his roll with precise motions. Jay took it as fair signal for him to start.

"I have a request of you, Jameson," Leon started, words slow and deliberate, "Or rather, I have an *opportunity*. I would that you hear me out."

Jay peered up over his fork, mouth still working its revolutions on a lump of exquisitely braised pork. "What's that?" he asked with the subtle grace of barely retaining all food particles behind his lips.

The Mayor seemed not to notice. "I have an…*acquaintance* in Tier Three that I would like for you to meet. As a matter of fact, he has requested your presence specifically. Now, I told him in the kindest manner that you were not to be burdened with such a long journey—I try to protect all citizens of Glendale from such frivolous and dangerous travel between the cities—but he quite insisted that you make the visit. And now that I can verify that you would be traveling of your own accord, I feel it prudent to pass the message along to you." Leon finished and stuffed the miniature bite of bread into his mouth before leaning back to await an answer.

Jay hesitated, taking the time to finish chewing before speaking again. Something about the way that the Mayor was 'offering' this information was strange, like a pot of golden coins presented, but they were all somehow tarnished and cursed. But it had his attention nonetheless. Jay could hear Blaze below him growl as he took the bait.

"Who is this acquaintance?" he asked, finding it as good a place to start as any.

"His name is Mr. V. To be honest, I'm not entirely sure what his full name is. He's only ever called Mr. V. in the circles I maintain. A rather elusive man. He minds his privacy well, but he has significant pull in the southern stretches of Cityscape. You would find him a good ally and asset in your pursuits, I am certain."

Jay furrowed his brows, considering the words. "What does a man like that want with *me*? How does he even know who I am?"

The Mayor allowed a thin smile at Jay's skepticism. "He knew your parents and apparently funded one of your mother's projects at her laboratory in Highwater. I don't believe he has ever met *you* before from what I gleaned of our conversations, but he must assume the intelligence of your family tree descends to you. When he learned of your desire to bind the full spectrum of virtues, he reached out to me. Your little dream has made ripples across certain media, Jameson."

Jay's lips turned down at the Mayor's use of adjectives, but the simple fact that someone all the way in *Tier Three* of Cityscape heard about his vow to bind all twelve virtues consumed.

"How did—" he started, but Leon cut him off.

"Mr. V is not the kind of man to turn away, Jameson. I trust you will take this request seriously."

Jay nodded slowly, eyes still twitching back and forth as if calculating some unseen equation.

The Mayor snapped his fingers smartly and a maid rushed in from an adjoining chamber. Jay looked up, surprised at the swiftness of the answer to the summons. She held a round, copper tray out before her, atop which sat a single piece of parchment. Leon snatched the paper off the tray and waved the maid away. He then extended his hand to Jay, paper offered up.

"What is it?" Jay asked, lightly plucking the piece from his grip.

"It is a writ of passage, one which you will need to cross the borders between Tiers. This will take you all the way to Godsreach, via Mr. V's authority."

Jay nearly choked. "*G-Godsreach? Are you joking?*"

The Mayor didn't so much as smile. His face stony, he answered, "No."

Jay stared at the writ, seeing the Mayor's own signature scrawled pristinely across the bottom of the page. Another signature joined it, a single letter in defined cursive script: *V*.

He knew there were barriers to cross in order to transition from one region to the next in Cityscape, but he had simply forfeit the considerations of admittance. *No one* crossed the borders into higher Tiers without express permission and a *very* good reason. But even had he gained the necessary permissions somehow to move into Tier Two or even Tier Three, never had he expected to get *anywhere close* to Godsreach. It was the capitol of all Cityscape and seat for the most powerful and wealthy patrons in the entire world. Rumors held that the rarest and most potent virtues were forming near those forlorn walls, as if they themselves were attracted to the high and mighty in society's standards.

"I…Mayor DeMoro—"

"Tell Mr. V that I send my best when you see him."

Jay looked up to catch a full smile now, predatory white teeth shining back from his host. Another wave of uncertainty coursed through him, but he pushed it all away. Regardless of whatever motivation the Mayor could have for giving him this writ, Jay could only celebrate his luck. This was a greater graduation gift than he could have ever hoped for, and he wasn't about to turn it away.

****

When Jay had finished his plate and spent a few more long minutes admiring the writ of passage now in his possession, Mayor DeMoro offered his polite, albeit eager, retirement for the evening. Jay was escorted out by the impetuously curious Carl, who had been restrained from eavesdropping on their meeting.

"Carl, *nothing happened*; I promise. Your dad was just explaining how he wished *I* was his son instead of you. He said something about putting me in his will or whatever, but—"

Carl pushed Jay out of the door with pudgy hands. "Oh, you *are* the world's greatest comedian. Have fun failing for the rest of your life, Jameson."

And then the door slammed promptly in his face. But Jay didn't care. He couldn't stop smiling. Blaze maintained a different demeanor, consistently looking over his shoulder to growl at the retreating residence. But even the odd behavior of his canine cohort couldn't bring him down. He had scored a writ of passage to *Godsreach*.

Just wait till Wade hears about this.

****

But Wade was nowhere to be found that evening. Jay stopped by the orchard, the Academy, and even strolled the streets for a time, but no one had seen him in hours. Thinking his friend had simply snuck away for some solo virtue training session, Jay opted to retire himself.

Blaze obediently trudged along as they veered toward the house, but as they stepped through the front door together, the virtue stretched and moseyed away like the place belonged to him. He quickly found a bundle of dirty laundry and dug a burrow into it. Bed created for the evening, he climbed inside and plopped down, facing away from Jay.

Jay only stared at the dog curiously, wondering how it knew this was home and why in the world it would want to make a bed. Virtues didn't require sleep. But now that he thought about it, just because they didn't *require* sleep didn't mean that they *couldn't*. Jay just shook his head and went to burrow into his own hole for the night.

In his room, he fell into his mess of a bed, holding aloft the writ of passage for one last longing look.

"*Soon,*" he whispered, almost reverently. "No more Glendale, no more Academy, no more cynics talking down at me, and best of all: *no more waiting.*" He rolled onto his side and set the paper gently next to his pillow.

As sleep crept up on him, he couldn't help but feel a tug against his heart at the concept. Leaving Wade behind was the hardest thing by far. He would be alone, *truly alone* after this… But the horizons were bright, and there was so much potential out there beyond these stuffy city walls. He had to remind himself of that.

He could always come back and visit.

He could always come back.

Couldn't he?

Chapter 4

Jay was in his assigned seat at the ceremony hall before anyone else stirred on the grounds. Blaze loafed just next to him on the floor, a growing theme, Jay noted. The lights were all off save for a few pilots that only offered a dim ambience to the inclined chamber. Just under forty chairs were arranged in neat rows facing an empty audience of over three hundred. Each and every one of those seats would be filled when the time came. It was a momentous day for students and parents alike, a day that signaled the transition from youth and education to adulthood and profession.

And Jay desperately wanted to skip it.

It wasn't like he *had* to be present in order to graduate. The ceremony was more of a formality, a chance for celebration under the spotlight for an hour or so. And after all the work they put in as students for the last four years, it was the least the Academy could do. He would still be officially disbanded from the drudgery of school and handed a diploma that would authorize him for a higher level of pay and responsibility from his employers if that's what he wanted out of life. But despite the air of excitement and evolution that the day would bring, Jay could only see the dismal absence of *his* parents in the mix. Times like these only seemed to highlight loss, giving way to a subdued celebration that just couldn't provide joy.

Jay's family had always been a small one: no living grandparents; any uncles, aunts, and cousins all residing in cities too far away to connect with; and no siblings either. When his parents died in the accident, it effectively left him an orphan, albeit a nineteen-year-old one. But still, the loneliness was tangible. Wade's family took him in for a year after the storm, treated him like one of their own, but it just wasn't the same.

How could it be?

Sitting in that quiet, empty room, his mind inevitably faded toward the deadly night of three years past. Much as he had come to terms with it over all this time, the sharp memory still left red lines when it passed by.

He could see his mother and his father standing in the doorway, calling for him. Their voices were pitched with panic, their clothes whipping and snapping in the violent wind that rushed just across the threshold. Jay joined them there, heart pounding in his chest as the entire house creaked with abnormal pressure. The night beyond was black as death, invasive fog and icy mist swirling together to blind and bind most other families to their homes. But Jay's father insisted that they had to move somewhere safer, that their house couldn't withstand such crossline gusts through the Glens. And so, they braved the dark.

The next thing Jay could remember in the chaos was the lightning. It was stark against the endless clouds above, striking faster than a brood of serpents, blue-white and angry. The violent lights served to guide them in frequent bursts, his father still leading them to what he assumed was safe shelter. But there was never any shelter waiting.

By the time they made it to the Mayor's manse, a place that was undoubtedly better fortified than the rest of the town collectively, it had already succumbed to its own dire fate. Several of the trees around the perimeter of the enormous building had fallen, crushing sections and lighting them ablaze like toppled candles felled by wind and electricity. Jay's father only stood in the streets, gaping at the sight, his hopes literally crushed. And his recourse came too late.

Jay could still hear the snap of severed wood, feel the ground shiver beneath his shoes as it did in that wicked moment. An ancient oak, likely only a sapling when Glendale was first founded centuries before, had made Jay its target. It toppled over like a drunken giant, intent on crushing him beneath its bulk, but his father...*he*—

Jay honestly couldn't recall what happened then. His father did something, shoved him, tackled him, transplanted himself where Jay had stood only seconds before. Whatever the case, the fallen tree claimed Paul rather than his son. In a flash, his father's life was gone, stolen away by a death that should have been his. And it still wasn't over; his mother was next. She was taken by a bolt of lightning as they tried to dig Paul out from beneath the shattered and splintered bark, a sight that still burned like a jagged blue tattoo on the back of Jay's eyes. It reached out like a ravenous tentacle, connecting with the skyward branches and coursing through the mammoth conductor until it ended in the explosion that sent Regina to her sprawling death. The outlines, the lights, the sounds—they were all seared there in Jay's mind, a final memory and testament to the horrors of that unprecedented act of nature.

The tempest took others and demolished half of Glendale in the end, but it spared Jay. He never was able to understand why or how he made it out alive when so many others did not. He hid somewhere and could barely recall anything after that nightmarish moment. It was as if the squall simply passed him by after that, content with the lives already taken, satiated for the time-being.

"*A freak storm,*" people still called it and would continue to do so for history to come. Glendale hadn't so much as felt a heavy wind since that night. It was as if the weather built up directly over the town, discharged, and returned the world to normal. But Jay's world was *far from normal* now.

His gaze fell to Blaze at his side, testament to his trajectory in life going forward. The snoozing pup stirred under his scrutiny as if it somehow felt his emotions churning behind those dark eyes. In consideration, he supposed his idea for leaving and binding virtues was in large part *an escape*. Staying in Glendale, just like sitting in this ceremonial chamber, was a vivid reminder of a past he would rather not relive. His parents were dead and his ties here, other than Wade and a select few others, were severed. His future was elsewhere, removed from the haunt of this dead-end town.

****

Just then, a grating creak resounded in the hall, causing Jay to jump in his chair. Blaze rose to all four, a snarl resounding in the back of his throat. Jay's eyes snapped up to find Professor Farsk entering down the right side, trajectory carrying him to the light panel. Jay tried to stand and sneak out, his opportunity to ditch the graduation rapidly shrinking.

"*Sit, Jameson.* You're not going anywhere," Farsk's

deep voice rang out.

Jay bit his tongue. *The man had eagle-eyes.*

Farsk flipped a row of breakers, closed the box, and moved to do the same on an adjacent panel. The arena screamed to life with buzzing light, causing Jay to recoil back into his seat.

"I had a feeling I would find you here," Farsk stated matter-of-factly as he strolled down the ramp toward Jay.

Blaze maintained a defensive stance, already on ill terms with the man. He was in his official attire for the ceremony, long, black robes spilling down his undoubtedly muscular figure. That was another reason for Jay to hold a measure of animosity against him. Not only did the man have the genetically strong features of the handsome elite, but he took care of his body in a way that Jay never had the discipline to do. Of course, he had never been amply-weighted like Carl DeMoro, but his thin frame, pale features, and lack of muscle mass spoke volumes for his careless lifestyle.

"Most people never admit to being a stalker," he responded dryly, tapping Blaze on the head so that the dog would lose feral focus.

Blaze blinked hard and looked up at him with narrowed eyes. Jay refused the contest. The last thing he needed was for his unruly virtue to assault a teacher and give credence to Madam Traeger's warnings.

Farsk stopped just before taking a seat next to him and shot over a calculating stare. "I can never tell when you're serious."

Blaze barked once in response before turning to find another perch.

"Feisty," Farsk dubbed the dog again before continuing, "I know why you're here, Jameson. Sitting in this room all alone, hours before the ceremony starts. And it's not because you're *eager* for it."

Jay held his tongue from a smart retort. The man had been kind to him thus far; he at least deserved a measure of respect. "I don't need a pep talk. You can save it for the others when you're behind the podium."

Farsk snorted a laugh. "I think there has never been a more blatant lie."

Jay's eyes snapped over, unable to conceal the glare.

"Touchy, I know. But you need to hear what I have to say."

Jay sighed, looking away. "I don't suppose I could stop you."

"Oh, I could certainly talk until the sun goes down, but you need to *hear*."

Jay remained silent, which Farsk took as permission to continue.

"I was twenty-four when I graduated the Academy, you know? Two years older than you are now, I presume. Two years later than most. Do you know *why* I graduated so late?"

Jay shook his head. "I have a feeling you're going to tell me, though."

A crooked smile formed in the corner of Farsk's lips. "I had a mental handicap when I was growing up, Jameson. A sub-cranial cyst formed at birth that was *just* big enough to apply pressure to my cerebrum." He tapped his skull lightly. "The malformed tissue was minor by most counts, not serious enough to operate on, but it affected my ability to learn."

Jay peered up from staring at the polished wooden stage. "I didn't know that," he said softly, feeling more than a little awkward at the revelation.

"Few do," Farsk answered, dismissing the guilt. "You see, I tried to hide it during adolescence, but it was obvious to my fellow students that something was amiss. Simple concepts such basic mathematics and spelling were to me like calculus and foreign language. I just couldn't grasp them like the others in my class. And so, I was held back twice, forced to dedicate year after year to the basics before I was allowed to move on to the next level."

Jay felt a shrug pulling at his shoulders, but he restrained it. "I'm sorry to hear that. But what does that have to do with me?"

"Nothing," Farsk admitted, "But the story doesn't end there. After my second attempt at the sixth level of education, my parents decided they'd had enough of me. They apparently couldn't handle the pressure of loving an idiot child, so they sent me away. Packed me a bag one evening and stuck me on a wind carriage going north. Sent me from our home in Tier Three to Glendale, where I had a cousin who just so happened to specialize in education. Ruthenia took me in like one of her own."

"Wait, Madam Traeger is your *cousin*?" Jay interjected, finding the genetic comparison nigh unbelievable.

Farsk nodded slowly. "She is."

"And you were from Tier Three?" Jay asked, perplexed. He shuffled in his chair, clearly gaining some interest now. "No one ever moves *down* the Tiers."

Farsk chuckled. "You have it right. It was not *my* choice, though. I was thirteen years old. My parents pushed me away, forced me to come here. Over the next seven years, Ruthenia taught me at my own pace, helped me understand, and showed me methods of retaining information that the previous school systems didn't employ. She treated me like an equal, like her own child even. And in all those years, I never saw my parents again. So I joined the Academy after I finally finished base school, worked odd jobs for the funds to pay tuition after classes. I was dead-set to show my parents that I was not the hopeless failure they thought I was, bound to shame the family in one way or another. And four years of exhaustion later, I found myself sitting exactly where you are now."

Farsk shuffled in his seat, turning to pin Jay with a serious gaze. "You know as well as I that this institution is not an easy diploma, Jameson. You have to *fight* for it, study hard, and remain diligent. And that's exactly what I did. I chased this degree through years of toil and sleepless nights. And when I sat in that chair," he prodded Jay's shoulder with a finger, "I knew I had *earned* the right to be there. This school, this world *owed* me a celebration. But like you, I slipped in an hour before the ceremony. Like you, I took my place and stared out over an empty room, wondering at the purpose of it all. And like you, I wanted to leave, wanted to ditch it, forsake what I deserved for one reason."

"Your parents didn't show," Jay said solemnly.

Farsk nodded, blue eyes glistening like gems. "*My parents didn't show.*"

Jay was quiet for a time, refusing to look back at him. He knew what was coming, what Farsk was trying to say, but it didn't match up.

"It's not the same," he finally whispered. "What happened to you and what happened to me... It's not the same."

Farsk stood, sliding the chair out away from him. He

stepped to the edge of the stage, knelt down to scruff a growling Blaze, and looked out over the empty audience.

"You're right. My parents *sent me* away, and yours were *taken* away. But, Jameson, don't miss the point: If you choose to escape this moment with your friends, with the faculty you've spent these last years with…well, you won't get it back. And you *will* regret it."

He took a step off the stage, leaving the fire virtue staring after him in a reluctant stance. "Stay, Jameson. And as soon as it's over, then you can leave. You can chase that grand and glorious dream of yours to your heart's content. Just, for now, *stay*."

Silence followed the word like a thick blanket cast across the stage between them. It muffled all but the footsteps that carried the man back toward the door. Jay watched him leave, considered his brisk posture, the finality in his charge.

Before he could make it to the exit, though, Jay called out, "Did you?"

The question stopped Farsk in his tracks. He looked back over one shoulder, his answer singular. "No."

Then he was gone.

****

Jay leaned back in his chair, blowing a breath through clenched teeth. Maybe he *should* stay. For Wade and his family at the least. Farsk made a point that he couldn't deny: if he left now, he would never get this chance again.

As if to press the idea home, Blaze strolled up and sat back on his haunches directly in front of Jay. There was no growl, no bark or bite—though Jay had grown to expect the trio—only a silent stare from the unnerving virtue. If the dumb dog was trying to make the same point as Farsk…it was doing a decent job.

"*All right, all right.* I guess we could stay for the main event. But as soon as it's over, we're gone. No hanging around to watch the others soak it up."

Blaze upped and strolled away, apparently satisfied with the answer. Jay lifted his bag, removing the black graduation gown from within. Smiling that he even packed it, he stood and sighed.

"Well, let's get suited up."

****

When the lights faded in the auditorium, Jay knew this was the beginning of the end for this phase of his life. A hush fell upon the crowd, larger even than he had guessed would show. There wasn't even standing room left once the masses rushed the doors. The place was packed tight, all save for the stage, which held thirty-eight graduates, a snoozing Blaze beneath Jay's seat, seven professors, and the headmaster of the Academy, Walter von Quake.

Jay turned to his right where, three chairs down, Wade sat wearing the widest grin. He wasn't alone. This was the most anticipated day of their lives as students. There were smiles and eager eyes to be seen on all the faces surrounding him.

Jay tried to get Wade's attention from across the gap, but he was focused on the headmaster now taking the podium. As it happened, Susie was one of the two in between them—sitting next to Jay—and caught the glance. She smiled and nudged him, insinuating that he, too, should pay attention. Jay complied, turning to face the front once again.

He had a conversation with Wade beforehand, but it was brief and shallow. Too many family members and starry-eyed ladies about to maintain his attention. He wanted to say goodbye, wanted to let Wade know he was leaving immediately after the service, but the opportunity never came. He only hoped that Wade would understand…

"Ladies and gentlemen, welcome to the class of '86! Could we have a round of applause for each of the diligent students presented before you today?"

Walter spun and waved his arms magnanimously toward the row of graduates behind him. The crowd erupted. Cheers, whoops, and whistles abounded as people from all walks of life stood like sprung instruments triggered by the words.

Blaze stirred beneath Jay's chair, obviously unsettled by all the noise. He attempted to wriggle out from the makeshift cage of feet but found only a hand waiting there to calm him. Jay kept his attention on the unpredictable mutt, primarily to stay a scene that it would undoubtedly make, but he was also unwilling to look out and find that there were no faces there cheering *him* on to this victory.

Just as Walter began to speak again, voice amplified to overcome the ruckus, Jay felt his cold hand being lifted up into the warmth of another. He peered up to find Susie's fingertips entwined with his, a wan smile framing her lips.

She knew.

She knew what he was feeling in that moment, and she didn't say a word. Instead, she turned back to hear the headmaster continue, hand still wrapped around his like a silent acknowledgment that he needed someone.

And he did.

Despite a rush of embarrassment amongst other

emotions, he squeezed her hand once to signal his thanks and let it be.

Walter von Quake, magnificent speaker that he was, continued to rile the crowd up before settling them down in a cycle that plucked heartstrings as deftly as a master musician. This portion of the ceremony was dedicated to the families and friends, the communities around the graduates, and all the support they gave over the last four years to see this day come to fruition. When Walter wrapped up his admonitions to continue in their undying support as the "children move on to new horizons," he passed the podium on to Professors Farsk, Rierdan, and Minelli.

"Now, ladies and gentlemen. Witness the potential that you have nurtured in these students and know that this Academy and their hard work both behind them and ahead can shatter *any* limits. Help me welcome three of our strongest graduates of years past, and enjoy the show."

Walter smiled and stepped away as another round of applause echoed throughout the room. To point, Jay was rather bored with the proceedings, but as the introduced trio took center stage, a new energy filled the air. And it wasn't from the crowd.

Jay sat up straighter, feeling the hair stand erect on his arms. Then, like miniature bolts of lightning, electricity began to crackle all around the chamber, and sparks ignited in midair. Professor Minelli maneuvered his hands back and forth like casting some fairytale magic, and the potency grew in waves. Professor Rierdan soon moved to stand next to Minelli, acting in synchronous motions and bringing forth roiling streams of fire to course around the popping bolts. Jay could feel the heat wash over him, beading sweat on his forehead testament to it.

Farsk wasn't far behind the dancing duo with his adept control of the air via wind virtue. A tangible current encircled the fire and electricity, settling beneath it all as a barrier to keep the energies from getting too close to the crowd. The heat dissipated noticeably at that point, and that's when the *real* show started.

Jay's mouth fell open as the pyro-electric verves pirouetted with one another, creating acts and visuals like he had never seen. One moment, an iconic version of a fiery dragon stalked the upper portions of the auditorium, and the next, a swarm of sparking and burning insects surged around the perimeter, battling each other like miniature armies in deadly combat. Jets and blasts of fire shot through electric ellipses like arrows, all while gusts of air brushed across the audience in time with the intense moments to draw cheers. *It was art in its rawest form.* Pure essences of the world manipulated by masters to paint something beautiful into existence.

Jay hardly drew a breath as the demonstration went on. The three controlled their respective elements with ease, coating the world around them with whatever came to their collective imagination. When the finale burst overhead—a searing spiral of all three virtue types coning down into a void—the room grew deathly silent.

Jay felt his heart thud in his chest, blood pumping with adrenaline behind his ears. *It was perfect.* It was exactly what he needed to refuel his desires and give him the boost to leave Glendale behind for good. *He wanted that kind of power*. That kind of *control* over the elements. He wanted that level of mastery, and not just over one, but *all* virtues.

Blaze, apparently feeding off his emotions, stood and pressed a way out from beneath the chair, searching around them as if the reason for his eager change was nearby. Jay reached down, despite his recent attitude toward the virtue, and patted the side of Blaze's neck. The dog's head snapped back, staring at Jay in dismay before awkwardly crawling back into his hole. Undeterred, Jay grinned. He had spent the better part of this day sulking and stuck in the past. *No more*. There was only a bright future ahead of him, and this was the send-off he needed.

Suddenly, he felt a tug on his right hand and Susie's fingers slipped away from his. He looked up to find the other thirty-seven students around him standing, he alone missing-in-action. He scrambled to his feet, seeing Walter von Quake back at the podium, now addressing the graduates. Jay had missed whatever was said, though he was sure it was just another encouragement to "do your best" and "reach for the stars." Applause died out after a few moments, and Walter lifted his hands to gather attention once more.

"Students—or should I say *graduates*—I have one final admonition for you, one last lesson to leave you with before you sail on to your dreams and your professions. Listen carefully, obey with passion, and your future will be great, your legacy undeniable: in all things, in all that you do and toil to do, *above all*, do it with your highest effort and give it your absolute best…and you will *excel*."

Walter stretched his aged hand, thin and willowy, to grasp the bill of his cap. With a single, fluid motion, he tossed the hat high into the air and let it drop to the wood of the stage. Like a ripple effect, hats began to fly all across the arena, graduates tossing them with glee, cries of celebration, and laughter joining the act.

Jay looked over in time to see Susie, tear-soaked cheeks and a smile that nearly split her face in two, hurl her cap into the distance like throwing a javelin in a competitive course. Wade's head was already bare—likely the first to be rid of it—and he was embracing those around him with enthusiasm. Jay made note that the hugs were largely shared with only women, some of which lasted a little longer than others.

Smiling from the contagion of it all, Jay reached up to take hold of his cap as well. Plucking the soft, black fabric from his head, he held it out, studying its thin lines with intensity. It was a last vestige, a symbol of a life he was soon to leave behind.

"Well?" a voice shattered his concentration.

He turned to find Susie anxiously awaiting the deed.

"Are you going to do it or not?"

"*Yeah,*" he replied softly. "Yeah, I think I am."

Spinning on his heel, Jay reared back and let the hat soar, watching as it disappeared into the distance, lost to sight and left behind for good.

Like his past.

Like Glendale.

****

The after-effect of the sudden hat-launching ceremony was a swift transition into food, drinks, music, and loud merriment. All formality was dropped as parents, family members, and friends alike stormed the stage to grab up their graduates and exclaim their pride. The party was in full swing within moments, a signal to Jay that his time to say goodbye had come at last.

He pressed through the growing throng, Blaze clawing and barking at every invader of space in an attempt to keep up. Jay paid his tantrum and their outrage little attention. He was on a tight schedule at this point. If he didn't make a line for the door, he was bound to be intercepted by people he didn't have the heart to dismiss. And he intended to keep his farewells to a minimum…

When his stash finally came into view, he hopped off the stage and made a run for it. Blaze stared him down sourly as he strapped the pack onto his back, cinching the ties tight.

"Oh, don't look at me like that. You were bound to have to wake up and *do something* eventually."

"*Jay?*"

Jay's head rocketed back toward the dog, bewilderment in his eyes until he realized that Blaze was not the source of the word. He turned farther, arm still at an awkward angle as he tried to settle into the pack just right, and found Susie standing at the edge of the stage steps. She was alone, the rest of the crowd several feet behind her and busy with their general commotion.

"Uh, Susie. Hey?"

She stepped gingerly closer, seeming to study the strange scene of Jay in the shadows, donning an obviously overstuffed backpack. If his night-long behavior had concealed any of his nervousness and anticipation for the coming flight, what she saw now could not be misunderstood.

Jay hovered in that teetering pose for a long, silent moment as his mind turned cartwheels. What was he supposed to do? *Deflect?* He couldn't lie to her—not now. Not after she had offered him comfort when he needed it. But he couldn't just tell her the truth either.

She would undoubtedly try to dissuade him, and if the words were right, he might not find the strength to argue. Even now, the echoes of her touch still buzzed on his fingertips.

This was one of the goodbyes he really didn't want to say.

Susie's bright blue eyes shimmered in the low light, and her lilted smile seemed to answer his silence. She closed the distance between them, bypassing a rumbling Blaze and stopping just before Jay. She leaned in close and let her soft lips touch his in a flash. It lasted only a second, *a fraction of a second*, but Jay felt his world grind to a hypersensitive halt. A thousand thoughts flooded into and through his head, too many uncomfortable, and that many more sending dreaded waves of doubt rolling over him. When his reality churned back into motion, though, Susie only stood quietly, scanning his reaction with utter care. Whatever she saw there both broke her heart and brought satisfaction to her watery smile.

"I hope you find what you're looking for, Jay. I really do."

And then she was gone, tracing her way back into the masses and lost to Jay's sight for what might be eternity.

Jay's heart suddenly hurt in a way that he hadn't quite anticipated. He knew this night would be the cause of so much pain, like ripping away a piece of himself and readying to bleed for years. But Susie, the realization of what he could very well have if he stayed. *That was unexpected.* And it was always the unseen blows that dealt the most damage. He couldn't prepare for them, couldn't build emotional walls to keep it all away.

A brush against his pant leg brought his attention whirling back to the moment. Blaze was standing there, staring at him, a strangely sympathetic expression on his canine face. If the dog actually could talk, Jay had a feeling he knew what Blaze would say: *it's time to go.*

Jay sighed, letting the heaviness wash out of him with the breath. He tugged the pack up a little higher and positioned himself for the door.

"Come on. Let's get outta here."

Every step he took felt weighted with lead. It could have been the pack, of course—he was likely carrying the equivalent of another human on his back—but he knew better.

Just as his toes broke the threshold leading to the crisp evening air, another voice caught him by the name.

"Jay! Wait up, bro!"

Jay sighed. He didn't have to look to know who it was.

"Wade, hey man. Sorry, I was just about to, you know, head out."

"Nah, man, you can't go." Wade pulled Jay back into the room, planting himself on the threshold. "You gotta wai—"

"Wade," Jay interrupted, frustration creeping into his voice, "We've talked about this. I'm sorry, but if I don't go now, I may never—"

"*Chill,*" Wade interrupted in turn, pressing a palm into Jay's chest. "I'm not saying *don't go*; I'm saying just wait a second. I haven't got my gear yet, and I need to give Mom and Pop this letter, see?" He waved a crumpled envelope in Jay's face.

Jay's wheels turned over and again until the meaning of those words finally clicked in his head.

Unbidden, a grin swept across his face. "Wade, are you serious? *Y-you're coming?*"

Wade adopted a similar grin and winked. "Man, you know I can't let you go alone. You'd bite the dust in a week. Besides, I got places to go, things to see…*like* exotic women from faraway lands." He twitched his eyebrows in emphasis.

Jay laughed, feeling a measure of the sadness shrink away. *This was big. Wade was actually going with him…*

"Wait, what about the orchard? Your family?" Jay stumbled to say more, but he knew his heart wasn't in the argument. He wanted Wade along likely more than Wade wanted in himself.

"Got that covered," Wade said, flashing the aforementioned letter. "And, Jay, I got to thinkin' about what you've been saying, you know? What you want outta life. And I don't think I'm the kinda guy who wants to be tied down to a *fruit orchard* for the rest of my days. I can always come back. Glendale isn't going anywhere. But if I let you walk out of those doors alone tonight. I won't see you or the chance to leave like this ever again."

Jay nodded soberly and clasped the side of Wade's neck. "Bro, you have *no idea* what this means."

Wade's grin grew three sizes. "It means either we're gonna die terrible, bloody, *horrible* deaths, or we're gonna make history together." He turned and scanned the crowd. "Three minutes. I already have a bag ready at your place. I'll meet you outside after I deliver this." He waved the white slip of paper again and dashed away.

Jay hovered in the doorway for a moment longer, stunned at the turn of events. Wade coming along was a boon that he honestly hadn't expected.

"*That makes two already*," he whispered to himself,

thinking of Susie's unforgettable kiss. He looked down at Blaze impatiently waiting on the other side of the door. "What else do we have to look forward to?"

Blaze only puffed a heated breath and continued trotting through the exit into the night. Jay followed, shaking his head at the grumpy virtue. Together, they found a small bench cornered by a trio of shrubs away from the door. It wasn't exactly hidden, but it provided enough cover to keep anyone leaving the party from noticing him and striking conversation.

****

Wade took several more minutes than the stated 'three,' but when he emerged from the revelry, Jay was glad he didn't rush the exchange.

"I take it that didn't go so well," Jay called out, drawing Wade's attention to his hiding place.

Wade shook his head vigorously. "Mom tore into the stupid thing as soon as I handed it to her!"

"She read it right there in front of you?" Jay asked with a wince.

"Oh, it's worse than that. She read it *out loud*. To Pop and everyone standing in earshot." Wade shambled over, falling onto the bench next to Jay.

"What did it say?"

"Ah, you know. The normal things a kid says to his parents when he's ditching duties and going on a dangerous cross-country trip. *Sorry, I love you, I'll come back some day, I'll be safe, don't worry*. Blah, blah, blah." Wade wiped at his face. "And then she burst into tears. Like grade-A weeping, man. Pop started yelling, going crazy on me right there in front of the whole auditorium. Caused a pretty big scene."

"I'm sorry. I didn't mean for that to happen," Jay

repented, now feeling a blend of guilt with his joy at Wade's joining.

"It's not your fault. I'm a grown man, and I made my own decision... Just so happens that decision caused my mom to pass out and my dad to nearly stroke." Wade sighed and stood again. "You ready to hit the dusty trail?"

Jay nodded. "My place first, right? Get your gear, and we're gone tonight—"

"Not so fast, gentlemen. I would have a word before you vanish into Glendale's memory."

Wade, Jay, and Blaze all turned in sync to find the Dean, Walter von Quake standing at the edge of the shrubbery, hands folded behind his back. Despite his age, Walter now held himself poised and proper with no signs of frailty for the years.

"Headmaster! We, uh—" Jay tried.

"I know what you're doing, son, and I know where you intend to go. I may be old, but I'm not senile, nor am I hard-at-hearing. I have caught wind of the Mayor's task to you, and I am here to offer a touch of wisdom before you go."

Wade looked to Jay, confused. "Mayor's task?"

"I'll explain later," Jay said, maintaining focus on the older man. "Wisdom? What do you mean?"

Walter unfurled his hands before him, revealing a small, cloudy crystal in each. Jay's eyes widened.

"Take these. You and I both know their rarity, yes, but I believe the Academy has enough to spare for aspiring young men such as yourselves."

Jay lunged at the offer. He scooped up the binding stone from Walter's right hand before reaching for the other. Walter's fingers clamped around the remaining stone like striking serpents, though.

"No, Jameson. This one is *his*." Walter nodded toward Wade.

Wade, obviously shocked as well, took a hesitant step toward the gem, glancing over at Jay as he did. He carefully plucked the small offering from Walter's waiting hand.

Walter suddenly twisted his palms and latched onto each of their arms before they could back away. His usually jovial demeanor became stone-cold serious.

"What you seek to do, Jameson—and you, Wade, by your association—is *not* unprecedented without warrant. Have you never stopped to consider why no one has before bound all twelve elements?"

Jay shook his head impishly, uncertain of the drastic change in the man's behavior. Of course, he *had* considered it, even found answers aplenty for the reasoning, but in the moment, he was unable to produce such a response. He had never heard Walter like this, timbre so grave...

"What you want is not only dangerous, Jameson, *it is forbidden*. By groups and beings and laws beyond your comprehension. You have *no idea* what you are getting into...though I fear you will find out soon enough. There are factors in this world that oppose Full Bindature with vehemence, and I cannot begin to tell you what would happen should you approach terminal vicinity of it."

He released their arms and spun to stare into the dead of night. The moonlight rippled off his black gown, giving him a sudden, eerie ambiance to match his words.

"Hear me and heed my words, boys. There is a reason why most of us restrict ourselves to a single binding—aside from the pressures of culture and the wisdom of our predecessors. Our very *souls* urge us to limit. They know better than the mind, *better than the body,* that we cannot handle what comes with that exponential addition of power. But *you*, Jameson, you are quite obviously different. Either you cannot hear that voice of reason, or you are producing your own reasoning by which to live in spite. Either way, you will find the same outcome: the closer you tread to your goal, the more difficult and dangerous it will be to you. With one binding, the body undergoes a strenuous transformation to allow room for that element and its control in your DNA."

Jay's mind flashed back to the intense pain he felt when he bound Blaze, the feeling of his body alight with those burning flames.

"With three," Walter went on, unaware, "your DNA changes again, expands to make more room still. With six, there is *no room* left in the average man, no boundaries to push. Therefore, something must be *removed* in order to free that space. And what is removed might be of more importance than what is gained."

Jay felt the tether to his dreams grow suddenly cold and brittle with the words. If what Walter was saying was true, then the more bindings Jay made, the more of *himself* he would lose. But he didn't understand. No one had ever told him that. *What did it even mean?*

Before he could work up the ability to ask, Wade beat him to the punch. "So what? Are-are you saying that Jay will lose his mind if he tries to bind more than six virtues?"

Walter shook his head morosely. "Not precisely, no. In honesty, I cannot predict what will happen to you, Jameson. I can only speak of what I know, what

I've...*experienced*. I had so hoped that you would abandon this foolishness long ago, given it up as childhood fancy. But I can see now that you are set in your ways."

"You've seen it happen?" Jay finally mustered, not missing the statement of experience.

"I have," Walter answered cryptically, "But that is not a tale I am inclined to share." He paused, silent for a long moment. "Jameson, this is a fair warning. *Know your limits*. What I spoke to the other graduates in that auditorium, to excel in all that they do, to shatter boundaries and aim for the stars. *I was not speaking to you*. What you seek has parameters that *must not* be broken. They exist for a purpose more profound than we can quantify. Find them and do not cross them, regardless of dream or goal."

"But, Walter—"

"*Enough*," he said sharply. "The South Gate has been opened for you. Should you leave within the hour, you will not be hindered or asked any questions. Keep these words to yourself and be swift."

Wade held up a hand, frustration evident in his eyes. "Wait a minute, you can't just—"

"Wade Wilkes!" Walter's voice rose an octave, warning in its wake. "*You* are his conscience now. Should Jameson fall to such temptations, know that his sins are on *your* head."

Wade appeared as if he had been slapped full in the face. Before either of them could retaliate, Walter was moving back into the auditorium, robes swishing out behind as his signaled goodbye.

"If you make it to the Arken Isles, find Pierre Kabolt and tell him I sent you. He will provide you with what he can."

And then Walter was gone.

Both Jay and Wade stared after the old man, mouths ajar and eyes wide. Jay had no idea what just happened. There were so many questions spinning through his head, so much revealed and yet so much still buried beneath.

"Uh, hey, let's—" Wade started before trailing off.

"Yeah, let's go," Jay finished, both confused and maudlin.

He lifted his pack onto one shoulder, the weight of it easy compared to the words Walter had pressed onto them. Slowly and silently, he led the way back out onto the deserted street, Blaze and Wade trailing behind in similar mood.

****

When they made it to Jay's house, Wade grabbed his bag and a pile of food from the pantry to top it off. There was little to nothing left after Jay's raid, but what he snatched would've been wasted and spoiled if left behind. And Wade wasn't a man to let a single morsel go to waste.

Jay moved about the empty house, double-checking that the electric breakers and water valves were all turned off for the indefinite vacation. He was leaving custody of the property with his neighbors, the determinately old and friendly Gilmores. They would keep tabs on the place to ensure there were no emergencies or the like. As Jay considered that, though, he wasn't sure what would come of such a situation anyway. If the place caught fire, it caught fire.He wasn't planning on coming back to tend to *anything* until he was finished.

Without words, they reconvened at the front patio,

where Jay locked the door for the final time in what could be the rest of his life. He glanced over its faded brick façade, considering all the memories that were stored behind those weathered shapes. Somberly, more due to their recent conversation with Walter than the idea of leaving, he reached up to lay a hand on the cool, coarse surface.

"Guess this is goodbye," he whispered.

Wade's hand struck Jay's shoulder softly. "That it is, man. Come on." He flicked his head back toward the South Gate looming high and beckoning in the dark distance.

Peeling away from it all, Jay led their silent charge out of Glendale.

****

They found the Gates just as Walter said they would be, unmanned and unlatched. The heavy, iron clasps hung loose, latches undone, and giant panels slightly ajar. No guard was stationed in the checkpoint booth. It was eerie, a sight that Jay had never seen in all his years in this clockwork town. Access in and out of the city was fairly restricted due to the saturation of dangerous virtues and wildlife in the area. For a station to be unmanned and a gate wide open was a severe breach of protocol.

"*What is Walter up to?*" Jay asked, still utterly confused.

Wade spun, hand already on the left gate and ready to press through. "What's that?"

"*This*," Jay pointed at the gate and the empty booth in succession. "This is all wrong. Why would he go to the trouble of doing this for *us*? I mean, I have a writ of passage from the mayor. The guard wouldn't have questioned us at all. So why leave the city vulnerable like this on our behalf?"

"I don't know, dude, but shouldn't we just move so we can close it behind us?"

"Yeah," Jay whispered before agreeing louder, "Yeah, go ahead."

They stepped through the gap together and shoved it shut just as Blaze ambled past. There was no latch on the back side, nothing to secure it with, but Wade waved away the concern.

"The guard will be back soon. He can fasten it up himself."

Jay only inclined his head, watching Wade as he started down the moonlit road. The bushy treetops scattered shadows all around them, but there was just enough light to walk by without the danger of tripping over their own feet. They needed to make it a few miles on the other side of the Southern Glens boundary marker before setting camp, meaning a heavy haul ahead of them before rest could come.

"That's gonna bother me," Jay admitted after only a few steps into the looming dark.

"What?" Wade called back over his shoulder. "The case of the missing guard?"

"Just think; how many times have you ever seen a post empty?"

"None."

"Exactly. So what's the deal?"

Wade stopped, kicking dust up beneath his faded sneakers. "Maybe it's like Walter said. We should keep the whole thing on the down-low. You know, binding all the virtue types."

"For one," Jay argued, "That secret's already outta the bag. Everyone here knows what I'm chasing. And even so, you really think there are people who would stop me?"

"I mean, I don't think Walter would lie to us, would he?"

"I guess, but," Jay kicked at a raised stone in the cobbled street. "*Full Bindature*."

Wade turned on him now, a funky expression on his face. "A full what?"

"Full Bindature. It's what Walter called binding all twelve like there was an official term for it or something. But I've never heard that in my life. You would think the Academy would've covered it."

"Jay, *brother*," Wade mewled, "All I know is that Glendale is behind us, and *the whole world* is ahead." He grinned mischievously. "Forget about what Walter said. Hell, forget about everything! We're explorers, baby!" He turned back to the road with sudden fervor. "Free to go wherever the wind takes us! The *whole stinkin' world*!"

Trying out his showmanship, Wade summoned a small gust of wind with his newly acquired abilities. A breeze, light but exhilarating, surged past them, whipping up dust and fluttering the loose portions of Jay's outfit.

"I'm ready to see it *all*! Of course, starting with all the hotties in, um…what's that city due south of here?" He wiggled his fingers next to his temple as if it would summon the word.

Jay chuckled, catching the mood. "Estelia Heights."

"That's it!" Wade snapped. "Estelia Heights, *here we come.*"

With that, he stormed the trail once more, pep in his step that was sure to fade over the next several miles. But

Jay felt better for the little speech, at least. They had a long trip ahead of them. It was better to face it with hope and enthusiasm than to sulk at the unknowable warnings of an old man. Besides, Jay wasn't the kind of guy to let potential dangers stop him. He wanted to be smart about it, yeah, but he couldn't afford to let fear slow him down. If problems arose, he would address them. But until then, he had eleven more virtue types to bind and a ticket to Godsreach to cash in.

Chapter 5

"Camping sucks."

Wade was resting against a smooth stone, tossing sun-dried sticks toward Blaze who was pointedly ignoring him.

"Yeah," Jay answered automatically. He was busily picking at the newly formed blisters on his feet.

"Dude, we've been out here *for five days*," Wade lamented. "We haven't seen a single virtue since we left, and I'm chafing something *fierce*." He dug his shorts away from his groin with a wince.

Jay chuckled. "Well, only about ten more weeks of this, and we're in Godsreach."

That earned a loud groan.

Jay had explained the details of the trip the first day out from Glendale, to which Wade's eyes nearly popped from his head. Ever since, he couldn't stop talking about how badly he wanted to *make it to Godsreach already.*

He couldn't exactly blame Wade for the eagerness, though, despite different motivations. *No one* from Tier One ever went to Tier Three, let alone Godsreach. Stepping into Tier Two was one thing—plenty of caravan merchants and political figures were allowed to cross that border—but even the most influential of the two lower Tiers would have difficulty making it across the Tier *Three* ley line. Jay was frankly astonished that Mayor DeMoro had the privilege himself. The authority to give it to another was an even greater mystery.

"How much longer till Estelia Heights?" Wade asked, clearly moping now.

"Map said it was another day's walk from here when I checked."

"*Finally!*" Wade exclaimed. "At least we're getting close to civilization again." He picked up another branch and hurled it out past Blaze.

"What good is a dog who doesn't fetch, huh?" he said, sneering at the lazy virtue.

"A better question is: *what good is he at all?*" Jay commented, grimacing. He took to stirring the small pot over the fire again, one he had been forced to start *without* the help of his fire-branded virtue. "I mean, he can't even start a campfire. Pretty useless."

Blaze's ears perked up at that, a distinct growl growing in the back of his throat.

"Oh, did I strike a nerve?" Jay prodded. "Well, if you're so capable, then you ought to prove it."

Wade laughed, tossing another stick, this time *at* Blaze instead of just over his head. "You act like the thing can understand you."

Blaze stood and shook his ruffled coat, apparently tired of the exchange. Without preamble, the virtue leaped at them with blinding speed, leaving a trail of inferno in his wake. The line of flames raced across Wade's pant legs and onto Jay's pack. Wade screamed and rolled to one side, beating at his clothes.

"*Blaze!*" Jay shouted angrily, lunging toward his bag to extinguish it before any of the contents could be damaged.

When they had the rogue flames under control, both he and Wade stared at Blaze with fury in their eyes. The unruly virtue, on the other hand, was pawing out a new spot to lay back into, freshly unconcerned with the world.

"*You*," Wade panted, "You need to get that thing under control!"

Jay hung his head, sighing. "If only." He returned to their stewing dinner and grabbed up the ladle. "Here, keep this stirred. I think it's about time Blaze and I had a little one-on-one."

"Ya think?" Wade snatched the ladle away. "Stupid thing almost killed me!"

"Oh, you're gonna be all right. Blaze, come on."

The dog twitched only slightly at the command.

"*Blaze.*"

Slowly, painstakingly, the virtue stood and eased toward him.

"We'll be back before dark."

"Yeah, yeah," Wade muttered, ringing the sides of the pot with the wooden spoon.

****

Jay led the way to an open field that they had passed on their way into the campsite. The road was a barren stretch of black stone, fractured and jutting sharp obtrusions out at every imaginable angle. The field, on the other hand, was level and smooth with only ankle-high weeds and ancient, rotting stumps left as a testament to a deforestation of the past. Blaze meandered up to one such pedestal and mounted it, observing Jay as if this entire endeavor would be a waste of his precious time.

Jay took a deep breath to quiet the rage inside. He still couldn't believe that he had been tethered to this infuriating hound. Of all the opportunities he was presented, one flailing mistake sealed his fate to *this*.

He approached the mutt, all too aware that he looked as if he was approaching a royal being on its throne. Blaze looked down on him with haughty eyes.

"Listen," he started darkly, "Let's get a few things straight, out in the open. I don't know how, but I know you can understand what I'm saying. At least enough to get the gist. So here it is: *I don't like you*." He enunciated each word with careful force. "And it's fairly obvious that *you don't like me*. Honestly, I think you ruined my life on purpose. I think you stole my chance at having an edge starting this journey. And I think I'm more of a babysitter to you than a partner, regardless of what Susie or anyone else says."

He locked eyes with Blaze, who was already glowering at him cagily. "But we're stuck together, all right? There's no getting away from you, and you're not getting far from me, either. So the way I see it, we have two choices. Either we learn to live together and help each other out, or I get mauled and eaten alive by some wild beast, *or worse,* and you…well, I'm not sure what happens to you when I'm gone, but I would wager it isn't pretty."

Blaze drew a sudden deep breath, nostrils flaring. He panted twice, dark gaze still fixed on Jay, but he never moved.

"Good," Jay chimed. "That's okay. You don't have to like it, but the facts are the facts. I can't protect myself out here without control over an element, and it just so happens that *you* won't return to me so I can have that advantage. Twice already, Wade has had to save my tail because *you* wouldn't help."

Blaze finally looked away, breaking eye contact with him. He wasn't sure, but Jay thought he could sense shame in the act. He took the chance to press the point.

"*Yeah*," he nodded intensely, "That's right. I almost bit it because my virtue is a lazy sack of potatoes and watched a *frickin' wolf* attack me! It almost ate my face! You could've at least done that little—" Jay waved his hands ambiguously, "Fire thing, where you moved super-fast and scared it away. *But no*! Thankfully, Wade was there with his *obedient* virtue to blast it off me!"

Blaze hopped from the stump and turned to trot away, clearly tired of being rebuked.

"Hey!" Jay shouted, running around to intercept him. "No way! We're doing this! We are having it out right here, and we are *going* to figure this out."

He stepped back and swiped a hand through his hair. "Okay, look. Let's just call a truce. I'll be nice to you so long as you pitch in and pull your weight."

Blaze stopped moving and looked back to Jay, something like a question in his canine eyes.

"Yeah, so all I'm asking is that you defend me when things get hairy. If we're attacked by something, or I need help subduing another virtue, you come to my aid. Deal?"

Blaze's gaze wandered for a moment as if he needed to consider the offer. Then he stepped purposefully forward within arm's reach. He stared at Jay with decisive willingness.

Jay sighed and knelt down to shake the dog's paw.

"Perfect. It's official." Standing again, Jay scanned the area, quickly finding what he was after. "There," he said, trotting over to scoop up a musty branch, ripe with fungus and rot. He paced out farther into the field and twisted the branch into the soil, leaving it standing and self-sustained.

"So I was thinking we could do it like this. We need a plan, a way to communicate in a bad situation. I'll give a command, and you—"

Jay trailed off as Blaze simply turned and waltzed back toward the road.

"Wait! Okay, all right... I'll give a *suggestion*—"

Blaze only hesitated, one paw still extended as if he would continue on if Jay didn't get this right.

"*You gotta be kidding*," he muttered under his breath. "A *request*, then. I'll ask you nicely to attack or do *something* to help. And you do your thing. All right?"

Blaze squatted on his haunches, awaiting the so-called *request* for a little practice.

"See that stick?" Jay pointed out the branch he'd recently planted. "That stick is the bad guy. It's the *enemy*. Now, would you *please* do whatever you can to subdue it?"

Blaze only stared at him like he was an idiot, something he was beginning to identify as the more he spoke to his virtue like a rational human being.

Jay moved back to the upright branch. "*This*," he tapped the tip of the wooden spire, "Is a *baaad guyyy*." He swung his arms in wide crosses as if performing the sign language to signify something undesirable. "*You*," he pointed directly at Blaze, "Don't like him. You should *attack*." He proceeded to fake punch the branch with horribly inept form. "The bad guy. See? Just like this."

Blaze stretched, yawned, and paced toward the choreographed fight scene between inanimate stick and his master. Jay stepped out of the way to see what his blazing virtue might come up with to topple the dubbed enemy. But instead of a spectacular show of fireworks and raw force, Blaze planted himself before the stick, looked back at Jay fixedly, and pressed one paw ever-so-gently against it. The wooden tower tilted forward gradually until it was parallel with the ground once more, Blaze's paw settled mockingly on its surface in triumph.

Jay shouted frustration at the dog who scattered before his tantrum. He picked up the branch and hurled it across the field, watching it shatter into a dozen rotten chunks.

"I hate you! I freakin' hate you! Why did I have to get stuck with *you*, huh? *Ugh*!"

Then he spun and stormed off, leaving Blaze behind.

****

His head was cooler by the time he made it back to camp, though now he just felt like an imbecile for the way he acted. Blaze trailed behind him, a smug countenance on the dog if Jay had ever seen one.

"How'd it go?" Wade asked, shoveling another spoonful of hearty soup into his maw.

"I don't wanna talk about it."

"That bad? You know, one of these days you're gonna piss off the wrong person, Blaze, and it's gonna come back to bite your scrawny tail."

Blaze ignored the admonishment and found his napping zone, settling in for another bout of pointless sleep.

Wade huffed. "What d'ya think? Should I kick some sense into him?"

"Nah, leave him be. Besides, I'm not sure it would do any good."

"Hmph," Wade mumbled, "When I acted a fool, Pop wouldn't hesitate to break out the belt. And after that, I didn't make the same mistakes twice, I'll tell ya that much."

"He's not my *kid*, Wade. You can talk sense into people. But he's a *virtue*. Not that he deserves such a title." Jay slopped a round of soup into a clean bowl and took a seat across the fire from Wade. "And that wasn't what I meant, anyways."

"What did you mean, then?" Wade asked, finishing his bowl and going for seconds, or likely thirds if Jay knew him at all.

"I'm not sure virtues can feel pain. Can *feel anything*, really."

Wade plopped back down into his seat of dust and stone. "Huh. That's a good point. Didn't we have a lesson about that not too long ago?"

"Yeah. They don't eat, they don't drink, and they don't *need* to sleep, despite how this one does nothing but—" Jay tossed a pebble at Blaze, earning an angry bark. "The same rules that apply to animals don't apply to them. They might manifest physically, but I don't think they *operate* physically."

"Operate?" Wade asked, slurping at the rim of his bowl.

"Well, you know. Virtues are supposed to be composed of raw energy, the pure essence of whatever type they are. And when they take a form on this plane, that shouldn't change. But somehow it does."

"So what are you thinkin'?" Wade asked cynically. "They *are* or they *aren't* the same as us?"

Jay shrugged. "I think they're still energy, just exposed in a different form. That's why they don't need sustenance. They *are* fuel, so why would they need more to burn? And they don't need to recover from any expenditure since they're kinda like little generators of their own."

"Well, what about the fur and the eyes and everything we see? That's not just some shared illusion. It doesn't feel like *energy* when you touch a virtue."

Jay considered that, adopting an innocent grin. "Yeah. Well, don't ask me. I'm not an expert."

Wade spat his soup, laughing. Thumbing to Blaze, he offered, "I say we cut him open and experiment a little. Who knows, we might be the first to find out what really makes them tick? Imagine the fame and glory from that."

Blaze appeared suddenly wary of their conversation.

"I'd rather keep my virtue, thanks. Dud or not, he at least shaves one type off the checklist." Jay stood and collected the bowls. "I'll go wash these off. It's getting late."

Just before he could make it out of the firelight, Wade spoke again, voice sobered now, "Hey, Jay. You still plan on going through with it? You know, after what Walter told us?"

Jay paused but never looked back. "Yeah. No stopping me now."

****

The night was restless, and the sun came back too soon. Jay felt like he had been beaten, bruised, and left out to marinate, of which the stony soil beneath his sleeping bag was the clear culprit. He woke with a crick in his neck that he knew he would come to curse. Wade was up already, mood similarly sour from the scarcity of sleep. Blaze, on the other hand, was snoozing in a way that Jay had not experienced since early childhood.

He stood, dusted off his clothes, and proceeded to kick the dog awake from spite. Blaze startled, leaping up and flaring with small combustive pops all along his bristling coat.

"Hmph. I guess he felt *that*," Jay pointed out, recalling their conversation from the night before.

Blaze gave a threatening snarl, but Jay turned away to ignore it.

"You awake enough to hit the road?" he asked Wade, "Give me a few minutes to pack and I will be."

Wade only nodded, refusing to release a word.

Jay gathered up his gear, stomped out the embers of the campfire, and suited up for another long and miserable walk. Whatever he envisioned this hunt for virtues to be, it was certainly less glorious in reality.

"Think we'll see one today?" Wade asked, the first words out of his mouth since before the starry night arrived.

"A virtue?"

"Yeah. Don't you think it's strange that we haven't spotted any since leaving Glendale?"

"Not really." Jay shrugged. "We were out of the Glens by morning that first day. This stretch is just a barren wasteland." He paused, reaching back into his memory to pluck a file there. "I read that virtue population tends to be higher around the cities and thinner out in the Midlands between them. Since we're getting close to Estelia Heights, maybe we'll actually start seeing some."

Wade fiddled with the empty binding stone on his sleeve. "Soon as you get a better sleeve, you're welcome to this one, by the way. I don't have any desire to bind more than Wisp. Figuring out how to control one is hard enough."

"*Wisp?*" Jay asked, not missing the name.

Wade grinned, though the expression was skewed

by the tired lines beneath his eyes. "You're not the only one who can name his virtue."

"You haven't even summoned him out yet. Let's see this *Wisp*," Jay insisted.

Wade shifted uneasily, looking out to the horizon. "Nah. We ought to get on the road, you know?"

"I figured," Jay grunted, amused.

"Look, I just want to make sure I'm in *total control* of this thing before I summon it. I don't want to end up—"

"Like me?" Jay finished, though he wore a smile still. "I get it, and trust me, you're right."

He stared down at Blaze with unveiled loathing. Blaze only appeared to soak it up like the rays of sunshine, feeding off his hatred.

Wade watched the exchange with hesitation. "Yeah, man. *That*," he pointed between the two of them, "Ain't healthy."

****

Estelia Heights turned out to be much smaller than Jay imagined. The party hobbled up to the gates after several more hours of walking, worn and weary. The pair of wooden walls were about half the size of Glendale's behemoth barriers and made from strapped rough-hewn beams, no steel brackets or braces in sight. Jay approached first and rapped on the wood, fist balled like a hammer.

"Anyone home?" he shouted at the weathered planks.

He could see movement in response through small cracks in the surface, but it was distant and unhurried. He settled in for the wait.

When they were within view of the city from afar,

Jay could vaguely see the ovular shape of the walls, stretching around a large hillside that continued to expand upward into the distance. Their last stint of the trek had been a real test of willpower and endurance. The elevation gain was exponential, and though he had seen the notes of warning on his digital map, he certainly wasn't mentally prepared for it. Wade was still puffing behind him, and Blaze seemed ready to drop with exhaustion—another note that Jay made on the physicality of virtues. Apparently, man, beast, and wild manifestations of the elements alike all hated cardio...

"Yuh. Give us a minute, then," finally came a muffled voice from the other side.

Jay tapped his toes anxiously, dying for something other than a bottle of water and a bowl of soup to fill his belly. He envisioned a grand inn just on the other side, golden banisters and crystalline signs inviting them forth as the first stop in their world-rounding adventure. Dining halls and lounges filled with exotic people and food and drink. A luxurious bed to mend the woes of his last few nights on the unforgiving ground. It would be a respite fit for wayward kings.

His mouth watered, and his muscles vibrated with eager anticipation. But as the worn and tattered gate to Estelia Heights creaked open, Jay saw no such thing awaiting them in the revealed stretch of city. Only a grossly rotund fellow set against a vantage of aged structures and dusty walkways.

"'Old it right there, gents," the apparent guard stated in his official tone as the trio came into view. "What brings you young lads to Estelia 'eights, and from the north no less? Odd direction. I bet I 'aven't opened this gate in three months or more." He added the last as almost a note-to-self, tone lowering as if he was only thinking aloud.

Jay studied the man gloomily, noting his faded britches, crooked guardsman patch, and messy mop of a head. This was not the glorious introduction to the outside world that he had hoped to find in their first city from Glendale.

"Just…passing through," Jay finally answered, fallen excitement clear in his tone. He looked back to Wade to find the same dejected countenance he knew that he now wore.

The guard couldn't help but smile, reading their postures like a hand-delivered letter. "Not what you were expecting, eh?"

Jay didn't bother hiding the fact. "No. We, uh, we were hoping to find a—" He stopped himself and recalibrated. "Sorry, we're from Glendale on our way to the southern border. We just wanted to stop in, restock supplies, and maybe find a place to sleep."

"Hmm," the guard murmured, thinking, "Well, that's going to be a fine challenge, I'd say. Estelia don't have no inns or 'ostels to speak of. Don't get many travelers coming through this way. If it's south, you're 'eaded. You'd normally bypass us—and the Cliffs of course—and go straight for Effervescence. Right fine city that is for the traveling type. Merchants and the lot stop there on their way to the other cities, sort of a 'ub 'fore they move on. But Estelia is just a 'umble town really."

Jay simply stared at the man as if he was speaking a foreign language.

"You're telling me you don't have a *single inn*?" Wade asked, belligerent.

The guard held up placating hands. "I'm not the city engineer, but it seems straightforward to me. Estelia don't get visitors so Estelia don't get an inn. Listen, you fellas come on in, and we'll figure somethin' out."

Jay followed the offer as the guard stepped aside, allowing them entry through the narrow gap. He hesitated, scrutinizing the way the man was keeping the gate near-closed rather than opening it wide.

"Afraid something will lunge in with us?" he asked, feeling as ornery as Wade was acting.

"You'd be surprised," the guard replied cryptically, shoving the door shut after Blaze. "I take it this is your virtue, by the way. Fire stone on your wrist and all, and 'is obvious affinity for 'ues of red." He reached down, attempting to pat Blaze on the head, but only earned an 'I dare you' growl that stayed his hand. "You'll need to recall 'im, of course."

Jay sighed, the sound raspy in his dry throat. "It's complicated, but in short, *I can't*. He won't obey."

The guard twisted his head to one side, peeking over his shoulder as if his commanding officer would be there. "Not sure what to do with an answer like that, chap, but it's the rules. If I let you walk past 'ere with a summoned virtue, we're both fried as soon as the captain catches wind of it."

"I promise, he won't be any trouble. It doesn't sound like we'll be staying long anyways."

The guard studied him carefully before submitting, "Okay, but try to recall 'im."

Jay's brow twitched upward. "I just said—"

"*Try*," the guard emphasized. "I'm not about to lose the only job I could land just because you *say* you can't do something. Try to do it so I can at least cover my 'ide if your little friend goes rogue."

Jay sighed again, looking to Wade, who only shrugged. He actually hadn't tried since the day of the trial, so he supposed it couldn't hurt. Perhaps his willpower over the stubborn virtue was up to par now.

He held a palm out over Blaze, who only sat and watched, motionless. Closing his eyes, Jay envisioned the essence of Blaze returning to him just as it had escaped on that dismal day. He concentrated for what felt like long minutes. When Wade cleared his throat, Jay's eyes popped open to find the virtue still there, staring him down with forced innocence as if he hadn't just fought tooth and nail to stay physical.

"*See*?" Jay moaned. "He won't listen."

The guard nodded suspiciously, eyeing them both. "All right. You got me there. At least now I can say I saw you try if somethin' 'appens."

"Can we go now?" Wade asked impatiently.

The guard stepped out of the way, but as soon as they were past, he caught them once more. "Just a minute."

Wade huffed, but the man waved it away.

"I remembered somethin' that might 'elp you fellas. Stop by the Broken Bone restaurant after you've stocked up for the road. Estelia isn't a very big city, so you shouldn't 'ave trouble finding it. East side, lower district, just past the retail quarter. Owner goes by the name of Nand Buetall. Funny fella, but I 'eard that 'e 'as an apartment available above that old restaurant. Could be that 'e lets you stay the night for a price."

Jay felt a sudden wave of relief wash through his blood at the words. He *did not* want to sleep on the ground again. A small reprieve was better than nothing at all.

****

Leaving there and topping a rise that seemed intentional from gate to main corridor, Wade tugged on Jay's sleeve and brought them both to a stop.

"We should probably get our bearings before we go wandering around. Just because it's smaller than Glendale doesn't mean it'll be easy to find what we're after." He peered out over the area ahead. "Looks like a lot of ground to cover, and I'm all walked out, bro."

Jay nodded and turned back to the city sprawling out before them. The cobbled, snakelike streets were much the same as in Glendale and Highwater—the only other cities he had seen in his life. But where Highwater boasted sky-scraping towers in shades of steel-gray, Glendale had been an eclectic mix of large and small structures, ranging from the Mayor's gargantuan property to the miniature housing district of the low-income and minimalist population. The buildings here, though, were altogether different from both predecessors. Squat, elongated shapes, none more than two stories if he had to guess. The theme was dirt brown in every direction, evidence of the stony landscape beyond dotting the city with crags and scalped earth. Glendale's greenery had faded and fallen away to showcase the bare bones of the planet beneath their feet. Jay looked to the towering peaks in the hazy distance, the infamous *Cliffs of Ascent* referenced earlier by the guard.

"Didn't he say the retail quarter was on the east side?"

Wade nodded.

"So let's head that direction. We can stop and visit this Nand guy while we're there. Who knows?"

"How much cash you got? Cause I'd be willing to pay him just about anything for a soft bed."

Jay chuckled and started toward their goal, feet clopping on the stone highway. "Me too. I brought everything I had. Here—"

He swung his pack around, digging into the main pocket. When his hand came free, it was adorned with a rolled wad of bills stamped in the center with the national emblem of Cityscape. Wade's eyes bulged.

"This is half. You keep it with you in case one of us loses a pack."

Wade reached out greedily, snatching the roll away. "Dude! This has to be...at least *four grand*!"

"Thirty-eight-hundred and some change. Should keep us alive for a while." Jay stopped, observing the drool leaking down the corner of Wade's mouth. "And *no*. You can't just spend it on whatever you want. *Especially* not on girls."

Wade glanced up. "What? You serious?"

Jay laughed, shaking his head. "No! We're going to need every pip! Unless you want to pick up odd jobs along the road, we won't have any income to replace this with. We need to make it last."

Disconsolate now, Wade shoved the roll into his bag and frowned. "Fine. But I'm at least going to buy some new kicks. These sneakers are giving me some nasty blisters."

"That's what you get for wearing *sneakers* in the first place."

****

They found the retail district with no hitches, refilled on food and other necessities such as quality boots for Wade's worn feet, and then went on to search for the elusive Broken Bone restaurant.

After nearly another hour of walking, asking for directions, and keeping Blaze from attacking bystanders who risked entering his personal space, Jay finally spotted the stained wooden sign that displayed their destination.

This portion of Estelia Heights wasn't quite slum quality, but it was certainly borderline. Sadly, such places seemed to come with every commune of people regardless of where, when, or how many. There would always be some who were wealthy, some who were poor, and some who would do anything to move from the latter to the former. Jay could feel those types of eyes on him even now, hungry for an opportunity to take another step toward wealth. They couldn't know how much money he actually carried with him, but he supposed it didn't matter. Sometimes, it only took the shine of a single button to spark greed in a person's eyes.

"Let's get inside," Jay whispered, gaze still pinned on a group of rowdy-looking teens across the street, leering at them.

"Yeah," Wade whispered in agreement. "I feel like if we stop moving, I'll catch something—a disease or a knife in the back one…"

Jay turned and pressed into the dilapidated doorway, hearing not-a-few things rattle in the threshold that likely shouldn't have.

Light surged into the darkened foyer, visible dust fluttering through the rays of foreign sunshine. Wade coughed twice, the sound followed closely by a sneeze that wasn't his. Jay looked down in time to catch Blaze sneeze again, casting a spatter of canine mucus across the scarred wooden floor. He paused to consider that, perplexed that a virtue could be subjected to respiratory reactions, but a voice deeper within the building caught his attention.

"*Find seat and give me moment.*" The voice was husky, masculine, and thick with an accent that Jay had never heard in his life.

Wade looked back to show his obvious fear for the scene, but Jay only pushed past him. Despite the dim interior, the near-*condemned* status of the building, and the sinister tone of their faceless host, Jay turned out from the foyer and into a wide area that could roughly be considered a dining hall. The dark stain on the wooden walls nearest them appeared purposeful until he spotted differing hues and shapes across the rest of the surface beyond. The same mysterious coating created splotch marks along the floor planks—a single row of which was simply missing, revealing dry ground a few feet beneath. Wade turned to make his exit at that point, but Jay caught him by the sleeve.

Three tables were erected in the center of the room, though only one appeared sturdy enough to hold anything heavier than a glass of water. Jay led both man and mutt to the table and stripped off his pack.

"*You can't be serious,*" Wade said, scanning the room disgustedly. "Even if he does have a bed available, I would sleep on a stump before we stayed here."

"*Relax,*" Jay calmed him, "Let's just talk to the guy and see what the situation is. Then we can make a decision."

Wade was clearly put-off, but he slid out a chair anyway. It groaned with ancient pain as he sat, a wince on his face as if he was soon to share it. But it held, as did Jay's, despite the slight and unnerving wobble. Blaze meandered away from them as if he had better things to do, and Jay frankly didn't care to correct him.

"So what if this guy is a serial killer or something?" Wade whispered across the worn-out table.

Jay only rolled his eyes.

"*Does this not look like the lair of a serial killer to you?*" he pressed.

"Then I guess we're about to die," Jay countered flatly.

"*What you want for drink? We have water and tea.*"

The rumbling voice came so suddenly from behind Wade that he nearly leaped out of his chair. Jay saw the silhouette of a hulking man across the room, frame wider than the doorway he stood behind.

"Um, water is fine. For both of us."

"Hmph," the host muttered as he turned back into what must be the kitchen.

Wade's eyes suddenly fixed on Jay with a plea. "*Let's go,*" he whined.

But before Jay could respond, their host stepped back through the dwarfed porthole carrying two foggy plastic cups of what he hoped was clean water.

"Have no menu," the man stated as he tromped across the rickety wooden floor toward their table. "Have soup and sandwich this time of day. Which you want?"

Jay stared back at Wade, hoping he would keep his cool in front of the stranger. As the cups slapped onto the table, though, Wade released a shallow whimper and winced.

"What kind of soup?" Jay answered quickly, taking in the behemoth's now unveiled features in the dim light.

Not only did he look like a world-class bodybuilder, he had more scars from his neck up than Jay had on his entire body. His head was shaved down to short stubble, matching the scruff on his craggy face. A seemingly perpetual frown sat in placid lines of a home position on his lips. But his eyes belied it all, a soft, sullen blue, weary with an age that Jay didn't think belonged to the man at perhaps forty or fifty years. His glassy gaze seemed to press past the two patrons at his establishment into a lonely place that Jay couldn't begin to understand.

"Is just soup. Plenty to fill you up."

Jay's gaze roamed awkwardly before landing back on Wade, who was of little help. "Two bowls of soup then, please."

The man simply turned and lumbered back into the kitchen without another word. Wade immediately relaxed, drawing a breath for the first time since the water touched the tabletop. Jay lifted one of the cups, inspecting the sanitation of the utensil.

"I definitely wouldn't drink that, man," Wade warned.

"Would you just chill?" Jay started, "We're in the middle of a city at a place *the guard* referred us to."

"They could be in this together!" Wade hissed. "The guard lures unwary travelers to the lair, and Nand butchers them up and serves them in his mystery soup!"

Jay chuckled. "Do you hear how ridiculous that sounds?"

Wade shrugged, glancing back over his shoulder. "Maybe, but I don't want to tempt fate. Let's cut our losses and dash before he comes back. I'd rather risk another night with your poor excuses for a meal than sample some of his homosapien stew."

"Two soup, ready for you."

Wade cringed visibly, slinking deeper into his seat.

He donned a hopeless expression, their opportunity clearly gone.

Their host set the bowls down gently this time, plopping a spoon into each before backing away. But instead of returning to the kitchen, he only stood and awaited their reactions, like a master chef ready to hear a review of his finest dish.

Jay hesitantly lifted the spoon, gaze fixed on the bubbling bowl of who-knew-what. Gingerly, he scooped out a minuscule bite. He blew on the serving slowly, more to delay the inevitable than to cool its contents. With Wade watching in horror, Jay shoved the spoonful back, swallowing without allowing it to touch his tongue. There was a brief moment of confusion in the air before Jay quickly spooned out another bite and let it settle onto his taste buds, actually *savoring* it this time.

"*Wow*," he stated after the second swallow, sounding genuinely surprised. "This is really good!" He turned to the watching cook, seeing a faint twitch of that frown rise at the words.

"Is specialty of my homeland. *Farruchey*. Chowder made with helial root and bison blood. Give strength to warrior, strong bones, and much protein."

Wade exchanged looks with everyone around him, including Blaze, before turning to stare at his own bowl. Warily, he tried his luck and found the same surprise that Jay had moments before.

"*No kidding*," he said, shocked, "Is this, uh,this how you got—" Wade waved his hand at the man, implying his broad figure.

Something that could have been either a laugh or a grunt of pain echoed from deep within the man's chest. "No, but is still good for body. Enjoy."

He turned to leave the room, but Jay caught him.

"You're Nand, right?"

The man turned slowly, nodding his head. "Is my name, yes."

Jay cleared his throat, still feeling the lingering spices there disrupting his coming words. "The guard at the gate told us to come see you. W-we were hoping you might be able to help us. We're not from Estelia Heights; we've come down from Glendale, headed toward the border to Tier Two. We need a place to stay tonight, but there are no inns or taverns around that offer accommodations—"

"And I have apartment upstairs," Nand finished dully for him. He pulled out a chair, easing his bulk down into it. The wood squealed in pitched protest. "Tell me. Why you go to next Tier?"

Jay squinted his eyes, curious at the question. "Well, we have some business there." He tried to keep the answer vague, unsure why Nand would want to know. "A meeting with someone who might be able to help us."

"You have long way to go." He nodded slowly, his giant head bobbing back and forth mechanically.

"Yo, Nand. Tell me more about this soup," Wade interrupted, clearly relieved of all ill suspicions toward the man. He was shoveling it back faster than he could swallow it, some spilling down his chin like a starved animal.

Jay frowned. *My cooking wasn't that bad.*

"Farruchey is nomad's cuisine. Suits you with such trip as you make. Easy to gather ingredient if you know where to look. In my homeland, ingredients abundant. Here, not so much."

"Where are you from?" Jay asked, intrigued.

Nand turned to him, eyes glossing again as if returning to that faraway, lonely place. "Starscythe Plains. Long way from here." His words were soft now, filled with forlorn emotion.

Jay shuffled in his seat, noting the reference to one of the six regions of the continent but feeling awry to continue his inquisition. Instead, he pivoted, lifting the flap on his pack and unzipping several pockets until he found the focus of his search. Turning, he placed his digitized map on the table, pecking at it until it lit up with a full-scale representation of the entire continent. Nand seemed suddenly interested, scooting closer to peer over the device.

"So *this* is Starscythe Plains?" Jay asked, pointing at a large portion of the map to the far east. He knew it was, but he figured asking would get Nand to open up a little. Perhaps if he could get the owner to a friendly state, his apartment might become suddenly available for the night…

"Yes. Is a wonder," he said mystically, gesturing to the fancy map.

Jay grinned. "It's pretty handy. So what area did you live in?"

Nand waved his finger over the whole swathe of land. "All of it. Starscythe a nomadic land. Tribes travel in rotation, spend season in one place then move on to let next tribe in."

"Nomadic, huh?" Wade chimed. "I don't think we ever actually studied the cultures of other regions, did we?" He aimed the question at Jay, who only shrugged.

If they had gone over it in any portion of their schooling, it had likely been brief and vague. Seeing as how they lived in Cityscape, it was assumed that the students would never venture elsewhere. The Valley of Pyres, Waterwall, Starscythe, Eternity, and the Reach—sometimes referred to as the Forgotten Reach—were all but mysteries to be discovered.

"It was simple life," Nand went on. "Only possess what need and only take from land what it gives. Not like here. Here, possess too much and take too much. Land is *stunted*. Covered by many cities of excess. Land not produce because Karaclasts are not honored."

"*Karaclast*?" Jay asked, not catching the reference.

Nand inclined his head in a nearly reverent manner. "You call them...*virtue* I think? In homeland, Karaclast their name. Sacred. Is tradition to honor Karaclasts. From their power comes life, fruit to fields and health to beasts that keep men alive."

Wade slid his empty bowl away, looking hungrily at Jay's as he nursed the steaming stew. "You worship virtues?" he asked impertinently, leaning in with his spoon to help himself to the unattended portion.

Jay swatted at him with his own, fending off the hungry scavenger.

"Worship? No. We *honor*. Karaclasts are spirit of life."

Wade gave him an exasperated glance, but he let it slide.

Jay had a thought. "So Nand... If your people honored the *Karaclasts*," he tried the word again, "Did you ever bind them? Like we do here?" He pointed to Blaze and then to his binder's sleeve.

Nand nodded at the sleeve, but he seemed to avert his eyes from Blaze. Jay made note of that, curious as always. Even as Blaze strolled up to the man and sat at his feet, Nand still refused to recognize the fiery dog.

"In Starscythe, it privilege of tribe leaders to mingle with Karaclasts. Common man not mingle. Considered dishonoring to Karaclasts."

"By mingle, you mean bind?" Jay prodded.

"Yes. You say *bind*, but our word for this translate to *mingle*. Or better: *intertwine*. When tribe anoint new leader, leader proves worth by trial. Trial is to mingle with Karaclasts until one deems worthy. Then new leader return to tribe with Karaclast companion and is sworn to headship."

Jay was so lost in the prospect that he never noticed Wade finishing off his bowl of soup with ravenous scoops. "Did your tribe have to use one of these?" he asked, pointing again to the sleeve stretching up his arm.

Nand shook his head vehemently. "Not the way we mingle. Stone *force* Karaclast to obey. This dishonors Karaclast. Tribe leader mingle with Karaclast by choice and Karaclast mingle by choice. In this, we honor."

Jay was floored. Never in all his life had he heard of an alternative to binding virtues by stone. *He had to know more.*

"How is that possible? What do they use if not a binder's stone? You mean the virtues just choose to follow someone and share their power?" He rattled off the questions like fireworks, eager to know more, but Nand seemed to adopt a morose expression.

"I not know how." He waved his beefy hand through the air dismissively. "Nothing to tell you. I was never worthy of leadership…"

"Say, Nand, why don't you tell us all about how you wound up here in Cityscape over a couple more bowls of this Farra…Farruch…"

"Farruchey," Nand corrected, sliding his chair away

to stand.

Jay stared daggers at Wade, just realizing that his bowl, too, was bone dry and stacked lopsided in its empty sibling.

"*For real?*" he asked, incredulous.

"I was hungry!" Wade defended, looking to Nand for support. "Besides, it's not like the man can't whip us up some more."

"I have fresh bowls brought out," Nand agreed, turning to amble back into the kitchen.

Once out of earshot, Wade leaned across the table, summoning a vibrating *pop* before removing his weight hastily. "Seriously, though, do you notice how his mood keeps shifting?"

Jay cocked an eyebrow in response.

"It's like he can't decide whether to be nostalgic about his past or depressed by it. Ten pips says he's a fugitive or something, running from the law over there and hiding out in this backwater city."

"And here I thought you were over the prejudice," Jay snarked.

"Just because he makes a killer stew doesn't mean he isn't a *killer*." Wade waggled his eyebrows suggestively. "Either way, here he comes. Tread lightly with your interrogation, bro. I saw the look in your eyes; you were ready to threaten him for information. And I don't want this to be my last meal, regardless of how good it is."

Jay started to make another snide retort, but he stopped as Nand stepped back into sight. Wade shot him a cautionary glance and prepared himself once more for the feast. When Nand set the bowls down, he eased himself back into the protesting chair again, gaze fixed on the floor. Wade pulled both bowls close to him, inspected them, then slid the one with a mite less soup to Jay. Jay paid it no mind, intent on learning more about Nand's culture and how they were able to commune with virtues in such a unique way.

"You boys interested in many things. Remind me of myself when I was lad."

Jay smiled. "We just graduated the Academy in Glendale. It's the first time we've ever been outside of the city walls really."

"Eager to learn. Let me give lesson of great importance. You both listen good, yes?"

At this, he stared fixedly at Wade, who stopped slurping at his bowl long enough to notice. Jay nodded, feeling a sudden weight settle in his chest. He was beginning to give new credence to Wade's suggestion of Nand as the mood grew grim.

"You boys want to know why I move here, to Cityscape. It long story but one I willing to tell if you willing to *listen*."

He said the word with strange intonation, impressing more than just open ears. Resituating in his chair, he ran his thick fingers through the scruff of his beard. Jay thought the sound like sandpaper on chiseled shafts of stone.

"I was young lad, younger than you when it began. My tribe was Yyatva, strong tribe, long generations. Proud warriors of Plains with wise counsel of woman leaders. My mother one of six leaders, father a man of honor at her side. Yyatva was renowned in region, honored above many lesser tribes. But one tribe, Jaskiav tribe, *loathe* Yyatva. Jaskiav make war, but Yyatva choose not to retaliate. Goes on many years like this, and many good people lose their lives, but still, Yyatva leaders not change their stance."

Nand paused, sighing a great and heavy breath of air into the dusty dining hall. "I not agree with inaction of leaders. I was young and angry, and so I gather other young and angry people and I lead attack on Jaskiav tribe."

Wade slowed in his eating long enough to breathe and form a sentence. "Sounds like they got what was coming to them."

Nand only shook his head, maudlin. "I was fool. We kill many, wound many more, and even capture tribe chief. Major victory in eyes of foolish people. But when we return to Yyatva camp with prisoner, my mother looks at me with disgust and punishes whole war party. Leaders shun us and refuse to speak. I made grave mistake…"

Jay straightened in his chair, eyes indignant. "Why would they do that? If this other tribe was attacking yours and killing your people, it sounds crazy to just ignore them. Something had to be done!"

Nand allowed a small smile to creep onto his stony lips. "You think like me, boy. I did not realize something *was* done. Leaders make ceasefire with Jaskiav and other tribes, creating peace treaty to last for ages. But our attack broke treaty before it even start."

"You couldn't have known that," Jay offered with a wince.

"No. But we should have trusted leaders. Yyatva convince Jaskiav that attack was unauthorized. Treaty eventually signed, but Jaskiav create anti-migration clause against Yyatva. Today even, clause in effect because what we did."

"What's an anti-migration clause?" Wade asked, finally satiated and scooting away from his bowl.

"This where story continue. Clause prevent people from one tribe moving to other tribe or even do trade. Breeding ground for more hatred. *No contact at all.* Yyatva must stay far away from Jaskiav. But one day, I stumble on Jaskiav camp. I was still angry boy, older but still foolish. I wanted to attack again, wanted to kill Jaskiav people for making fool of me, but-but I saw *her.* Despite clause, I saw her and could not look away."

"*Ooh*," Wade cooed, "Always a woman. Had to make your move then, right?"

Nand stared at Wade as if he couldn't quite translate the language. "I…was taken by her. Beautiful woman, skin like the endless sands of Valley, eyes like burning torches, build of graceful gazelle. *Woman of my dreams.*"

Jay finished the poet's thoughts as he trailed somewhere back into his memory, "But she was of the Jaskiav tribe."

Nand nodded somberly, cold, blue eyes flashing for a split second before fading again. "It could not be. But for second time in my life, I broke peace treaty between tribes and took what I should not have."

"I mean, if she's worth it, she's worth it," Wade interjected seriously.

"Not if tribes return to war," Nand stated sourly.

"You mean that the Yyatva and the Jaskiav started fighting again just because you were fraternizing with a woman from the other side?" Jay asked, perplexed.

"We tried to keep secret, but we had something special. She loved me like little child, and I loved her like bloodkin. I wanted to wed Ashelia, but with clause, we could not. So I approached tribe leaders with request."

"That couldn't have gone well," Wade commented.

Jay kicked him under the table, earning a yelp. Blaze scrambled away from the battling boots that followed, giving them both the stink-eye.

Nand went on, unaware, "It did not. When they learn of our secret, they were furious. I was imprisoned for breaking clause, but Ashelia was sentenced to death."

"That's insane!" Jay exclaimed. "Just for falling in love with someone?"

"It justice, boy. *Listen* to what I say." His voice rose an octave, and that was all it took to make Jay shut his mouth. "We broke law. Consequence is punishment and cannot be escaped. I wanted to serve time, but I could not let Ashelia die. I thought I could free her, and we could run."

"So you broke her out and came here?" Wade wrapped up, ushering the tale on.

"Yes, we fled tribes together. We thought Cityscape would be different, no tribes here, only towering cities with many people and no war. But...punishment followed us. Two years we lived in new region before Ashelia become sick. Deathly sickness, rare and incurable. No doctor to help. She passed, leaving me exiled in new land alone, prisoner on foreign soil as surely as prisoner in Yyatva camp."

Jay felt like he'd been punched in the gut. He wasn't exactly expecting a happy ending, but Nand's story left little room for anything other than grief. "Nand, I'm sor—"

"Lesson is this, boy," Nand spoke over him, "This world have rules and rules must be followed. Break a rule, and you will suffer consequence one way or another."

Jay stuttered but snapped his mouth shut. For some reason, his mind rocketed back to the words that Walter had spoken before they left Glendale.

What you want is not only dangerous, Jameson, it is forbidden.

"That's an oddly specific and grim lesson, Nand," Wade said, grimacing. "Not sure that I'm picking up what you're dropping, but you certainly taught me one thing today." His frown flipped. "Jay needs to be replaced as camp cook *asap.* You looking for a gig?"

Nand again only stared at Wade as if trying to interpret a barking animal. Turning back to Jay, who he now clearly noted was the brains of the pair, he said, "I can see in your eyes, boy. You seek something you should not, but you *want it.* And nothing will stop you getting what you want. Just be ready for consequence."

Nand stood, effort eternal as he reached his full height. Jay now saw the man in a different light, revelations of his past adding depth to the distant blue eyes and the slope to his shoulders and neck. *A man who had lost everything...*

"You could come with us," Jay found himself blurting Wade's previous suggestion. He had no idea why, but he felt like the concept of Nand being there could provide something that he simply didn't have.

Nand stared blankly at the two for a time, but he eventually turned, wordless, to return to his work.

"Oh, come on!" Wade called after him, "You said it yourself. You don't have anything keeping you here anymore. It might do you some good to get out of this dead-end town!"

Nand stopped. "You miss lesson, boy. *This is*

prison. And I haven't yet served time." He continued walking but spoke once more before exiting the room, "Meal is on house. When you ready for sleep, tell me. Apartment yours for night."

Wade turned to Jay with a grin, blocking his view of Nand's retreat. "Look, I know I said I would rather sleep on a stump, but now that we know Nand isn't a killer—well, a killer of innocent people outside of the Jaskiav tribe anyways—I suddenly feel a lot more susceptible to the idea."

Jay sank back into his chair, letting his tense muscles relax. "Yeah, I'm cool with that."

Wade quirked a brow. "Feeling overly empathetic?"

"Nah, that's not it."

Wade sobered. "You're thinking about what Walter said, then, aren't you?"

Jay shrugged. "How can I not? It seems like everyone is telling me to give it up. First, I have to listen to all the teachers and students scoff at me, and then the one man I thought supported my dreams tells me I'm chasing something forbidden and might *lose my mind* while I'm at it. Then some stranger we just met gives me a lesson about how my choices have consequences and—"

Wade slid away from the table noisily, interrupting his pitiful rant. Stepping around the loafing Blaze, he suddenly whopped Jay on the side of the head.

"What the hell!" Jay cried, glaring at Wade and scooting away.

"Needed to knock some sense back into you, so there it was," Wade said seriously. "Look, you're losing it man, and I'm not gonna let that happen. I didn't come out here into the *lost dregs* of society to watch you mope and give up on the only thing you've cared about for as long as I've known you. *No way.* Forget about what they're saying. It doesn't matter. It's like Walter said, anyways; you've got me as your voice of reason." He stood straighter, posing for Jay.

"And how can that ever go wrong?" Jay muttered, hand still planted against his throbbing head.

****

They killed a few more hours in the city, aimlessly wandering and checking out the local sights—most of which were women that Wade steered them toward. After consistently being turned away by the opposite sex, however, Wade confessed that he was off his game and decided they should turn in. On the way back to the Broken Bone, though, Jay's feet dragged to a slow stop, his gaze pinned on the western horizon.

"Hey, what's up?" Wade called, but his voice quickly faded as he, too, spotted the sight.

Hovering in the distant sky, like a floating orb of expelled lava, was the setting sun in all its splendor. It drew the eye with intense gravity, not of physics but of *sheer beauty*. Swathes of every hue between red and yellow painted the empty air around it, cloudless and endless and clear. The dull brown stones of the Cliffs lay stretched out beneath it all, coated in similar colors like a canvas under the spilling paint pails of the Heavens. Jay found his eyes locked there, drinking it in, unable to peel them away. It made him feel so suddenly and completely *small*. Like everything he was, everything he was aiming to do on this grand trip of theirs was just a speck in the midst of everything else, insignificant despite his intentions of trying to change the world.

"*Crazy*," Wade whispered reverently, all signs of his

130

witty and flippant personality lost in the moment.

Glendale had never been so captivating. At least from their point of view, it hadn't. Beautiful, yes, with greenery that stretched on for miles, the thousands of different types of trees and plants and critters forming its ecosystem. But the utter vastness of the cracked and jagged Cliffs beyond this tiny shelter of mankind known as Estelia Heights was something entirely *different*. Everything here was exotic and new and inciting.

"We're really doing this," Jay said softly as if this scene was the final nail in the door that sealed their past behind them.

"We're really doing this," Wade mimed, affirming.

It was a significant moment, Jay would soon come to realize, a final recognition that there would be no going back.

****

They eventually broke away from their trance, trudging back up the cobbled hillside toward Nand's rickety establishment. The climb up the ancient staircase to their nightly accommodations was the last exhausting chore of the day, and when they pressed the door wide, Jay felt his knees wobble with eagerness to relax.

He fell into the bed, not quite as dingy as he and Wade originally guessed but still in a state of long-term neglect. Blaze clambered up with him, giving him a grudging look, before nestling in at the foot under a wad of blankets. Wade crashed into a couch of similar condition, and together, they all met dreams within minutes.

****

Jay slept fitfully at first, waking every few hours with a strange feeling in his chest that something was *wrong*. But after seeing Wade and Blaze both still snoozing and the room void of any imminent danger, he only fell back to that blissful sleep each time.

The fourth time Jay woke, he checked his watch to find that dawn was nearing. Frustrated that he wasn't making the most of this reprieve with a soft mattress, he slid out of bed to search the apartment for a cup and a faucet. A quick drink to wet his parched lips and he would go back to sleep until noon if he had to for the maximum effect. But as he slunk past Wade's snoring figure on the sofa, another sound infiltrated his ears that originated far from their sleepy nook above the Broken Bone.

"*Wade!*" he hissed, shaking his friend awake from an obviously deep slumber. "*Wade, wake up!*"

"Huh, wha— It wasn't me, I swe—" Wade blinked blearily at Jay, confused as the day he was born.

"*Do you hear that?*" Jay asked, keeping his voice low but urgent.

"*Huh? Hear? Do I what?*"

"*Shh! Listen!*"

They both sat still as stones for a few long seconds. And then it came again, unmistakable.

Wade's eyes seemed to snap suddenly into focus. "Was that a scream?"

"It sure sounded like—"

The noise came again, this time closer, cutting off Jay's reply. He felt his heart jolt into action, thudding against his ribs with heavy beats. Before he could summon the courage to investigate, though, he heard the sound of weighty footsteps stomping up the narrow staircase from restaurant to apartment.

Jay looked to Wade who had his hands outstretched,

ready to do all he could to repel whatever ghoulish nightmare was soon to join them.

"Blaze!" Jay yelled, panic for his own defense summoning the mutt from beneath the blankets.

Blaze only stared at him with angry red eyes, indignant that his rest was interrupted.

Jay couldn't even reprimand the virtue. The door swung open with incredible force, nearly rupturing away from its rusty hinges. Jay fell back a step, gaze scanning the darkness even as his vision tunneled. An enormous form filled the shadows there, emerging into the small studio inch by inch, slowly rising like black smoke until the entire wall behind it was blocked from view. Wade whimpered, hands glowing with a faint green light that did little more than illuminate his huddled position on the couch. Jay could feel the air stir around them, dust and pieces of paper and fabric rustling about the scarred wooden floor, but no tornadic force of nature came to save them from the invader.

"*Boys. Wake now. Town is under attack.*"

Jay shot a hand over against Wade's, stilling his rising magic. That voice…

"*Nand?*"

"Yes. Come now. We must get out of building." Then the beefy shadow receded back into the floor where the stairs descended.

Jay moved to follow, but Wade grabbed his arm.

"*What are you doing!*" he cried.

"You heard him; we've gotta get out of here!"

Wade's head pivoted between Jay and the stairs. "What if he's…*you know*. What if it's a trap?"

Jay huffed and snatched his arm away. "If he was going to kill us, he could've just done it here."

Blaze hopped off the bed grumpily as Jay neared the stairs. He flipped the light switch, revealing a bewildered Wade and an ornery virtue by the single grimy bulb planted in the ceiling.

"Come on. Let's see what's happening."

****

By the time they made it outside to meet with Nand—who was unabashedly sporting a bathrobe over what appeared to be nothing more than a pair of boxers— Jay and Wade could hear the shouts and screams in full volume. The door swung wide to reveal a city in chaos. Jay could see small fires cropping up from their vantage all across the area; buildings collapsed inwards on themselves and many more were vibrating with intense warnings that they would soon follow suit. The ground seemed to shiver beneath their feet even as Jay watched. He had never experienced an earthquake before, but his guess was that he would soon check that off his list.

"What's happening?" Wade asked, jumping as the vibrations intensified.

"*Karaclasts*," Nand answered flatly, pointing to a firelit stretch of road where two scampering creatures bounded from house to house.

As Jay watched, the two grew to six, then ten. Before long, a small horde was crowding around a long building, pounding against it. The building shivered visibly before rattling apart at the seams.

"Those are virtues?!" Wade asked, fearful and confused.

"Karaclast, yes, but out of mind."

Jay looked up to Nand, noting the calm, cool demeanor the man still wore despite the clear chaos. "You've seen this before?"

"Two times," Nand replied with a sharp nod. "Karaclast lose mind. Attack people and tribes. Bad omen. They've been dishonored."

"What do we do?" Wade nearly shouted.

"Stay out of way."

Jay squinted at him. "We can't just let them do this! There won't be a city left when they're finished!"

Nand only shook his head. "Karaclasts are many. We are few. No stopping rampage without subduing all."

Jay turned to Wade and then Blaze. "Then that's what we have to do."

Wade groaned, shaking his head violently side to side, but Blaze held a different posture. There was something strange about the dog's manner. He stared ahead at the wreckage intently, serious and bristled for the first time since their evening at Mayor DeMoro's table.

"What do you think, Blaze? You willing to help?" Jay held the virtue's fiery gaze, seeing that same odd intensity staring back at him. "Can virtues be hurt, Nand? Can they be stopped? ...We've never had to *fight* one before."

Nand nodded again slowly. "Karaclast like man in many ways. Can be wounded, but not killed. Only *removed*."

"*Removed*?" Wade voiced, tone bordering hysterical now.

Jay could tell he wanted nothing to do with the idea, but they couldn't just sit back and watch as Estelia Heights battled for its life against these unlikely invaders. People were dashing past them, crying out for loved ones while escaping the havoc that seemed to be drawing closer.

"Yes, removed. Like," Nand paused, considering the next word, "*Unformed.* Karaclast form physical body when strong enough and in right place. Karaclast *lose* physical body if damaged severely or spend too long out of right environment."

Jay's face contorted. "You can make a virtue *de-manifest?*" he summarized, glancing at Wade with wide eyes.

Nand shook his head. "I cannot. Too weak. *He can.*" He pointed down at Blaze who was still glaring fixedly at the carnage in the distance. It was the first time that Jay had seen Nand look at the virtue, but even then, he seemed to want to look away as quickly as possible.

"So we have to fight virtue with virtue," Jay insisted. "Wade, do you think you can handle it?"

Wade reluctantly tilted his head forward.

"Good," Jay said. "Nand, we'll do what we can. Can you bring our things out of the apartment in case…well, you know, in case your restaurant—" He gestured to the nearest toppled building.

Nand drew a deep breath, considering them both as if he was debating whether to stop them from making such a foolish mistake. But with his exhale, he brushed past them toward his building.

"Attack is best when surprise. Stay hidden and strike from shadow. Karaclast cannot hit what cannot see."

****

The three-unit assault team shimmied down the main thoroughfare toward the nearest group of twisted virtues, slinking in the shadows and remaining out of sight.

Blaze was hunkered down, prowling and taking charge of their mission it seemed. Jay lent his companion a new confidence, but he still felt as if it was all a wild dream. He was jumbled by the myriad of things learned in such a short time, the fact that virtues could, as Nand put it, *lose their minds* paramount amongst it all. And how could they have gotten past the walls? Past the watch?

'*Sheer numbers*,' he supposed dismally.

But as he observed the terrorizing mineral virtues—as he could now tell they were all of a type—he had no doubt in his mind that there was something sickly and sinister about this raid. Their movements were measured and collected, synergy amongst the aggressive pods of virtues coordinated too well to be natural. They roamed from building to building, bystander to the next, teaming up to take down whatever stood in their way.

Jay had never before seen or even heard of virtues acting in such collective behavior. Attacking people and towns was one thing, but doing so in a harmonized effort was *unprecedented.*

One such virtue, a small goblin-like creature made of nothing but dark-colored gemstones, appeared to even be *enjoying itself* as it smashed into anything that it could find. If it ran up against a larger and more substantial foe, such as a solid wall or a marketeer's booth, it would thrash away at it until its abnormal powers disintegrated the standing form. Another band of smaller, but still just as devastating, virtues pounced on fleeing citizens, knocking them over and hurling pebbles and stones forged from the soil around them. Though none seemed interested in killing the pedestrians outright, they were actively terrorizing in ways that seemed *intentional.*

When Wade was close enough, he pelted the lot with a small tempest, tossing them high into the air and carrying them several feet away to land in a heap. Jay hesitated, applauding the skill. Though not as potent as some of Professor Farsk's showy abilities, Wade's control of the element was clearly improving. He felt a pang of jealousy again at *his* lack of control, but that notion quickly dissolved when Blaze finally made his move.

Jay watched in mute astonishment as the small and often infuriating mongrel completely redefined everything he had come to believe. Blaze rocketed into the midst of the toppled squadron of nasty virtues, spinning with lightning speed and coating them all in wide blankets of fire. Jay could hear yelps and cries of grating pain and flailing rocky bodies. But as Blaze leaped away and toward his next victim, the fires died to show a complete absence of enemies where there had once stood five. There wasn't even a pile of debris left behind to testify to their deaths.

It was working.

Somehow, when a virtue's physical form was damaged enough, it could cease to exist on this plane.

Jay, shocked to find Nand's statement true, turned just in time to see Blaze engage another, larger virtue with the build of a small golem, but his sight was cut off as the first rampaging goblin spotted them.

Jay yelped and fell back in perfect time to miss the gust of air Wade sent whirling at the creature. It fell off balance, bouncing back a few paces, but it quickly regained momentum. Its beady eyes watched them with glee, eager to make mincemeat.

"No, no, no!" Wade cried, trying to summon another mighty gust but falling short.

The goblin piled into them both, sending Wade

crashing back into a wall and Jay rolling end-over-end past him. He fumbled about, trying to stand, but the little fiend had apparently made him its prime target for dissolution. He took three stony blows to the face before Wade managed to knock it off again.

Standing and wiping the blood away from his chin, Jay sped past the scrambling goblin to find Blaze, his only source of personal protection. When he spotted the dog, though, his stomach lurched with fear. Blaze was lying on his side, panting furiously, while an enormous stone serpent hovered over him. Its mystically connected chunks of stone slithered against the ground, raking at the cobbles like a rattle shaking before the strike. The golems and all other enemy virtues seemed to have fled, but this new foe, ringed with cold, black, mountainous shards, was neither retreating nor showing signs of wear.

"Blaze!" Jay yelled, panic overcoming him. If *those* virtues could be killed, then so could he.

He surged forward, adrenaline fueling his stretching steps. The snake reared high, preparing to come down in a final blow to end its prey. Jay screamed, lunging to snatch Blaze up.

He was going to die.

Briefly, the thought struck him that this scene had played out twice now, this fool of a dog causing him to face off against mineral virtues twice his size. But as he rolled through the powdered dust, clutching Blaze tightly against his chest, he saw the slithering beast come back into view from a new angle, and he realized that they had been missed by slim inches this time. Fear overcame him. And then his mind emptied of all else, but one thought: *run.*

He leaped to his feet, sprinting as hard as he could

back toward Wade and the Broken Bone. He wanted to fight, wanted to help defend this city from whatever insanity was infecting the virtues here, but there was no way they could take on something that size, even if they had been better trained and more prepared. *Which they hadn't*. He was finding that the Academy certainly didn't cover all the bases for the life of an adventurous sort…

Wade spotted him coming and sent off a final deterring gust toward the feisty little goblin. It stumbled away, wrapped up in a cloak of air, as Wade sprinted to join him.

"Is he okay?" Wade panted, falling in step next to Jay.

Jay looked down at Blaze, unconscious in his arms. "I don't know," he answered dismally. *"Come on; stay with us!"*

Nand was on the sidewalk, ushering fleeing citizens past, when they came into view of the Broken Bone. The restaurant was gone. Nothing left but a ruddy pile of debris and two travel packs just outside of the fallout.

"Boys okay?" Nand called, waving them closer. *"Fool errand."*

"We're fine," Jay responded, looking warily at the limp virtue in his arms. "But Blaze—"

"Rampage worsen," Nand interrupted. "We need to leave, *now*."

He turned to lead the way, but Jay stopped him.

"Where are we going?"

"To outpost. Soldiers stationed there. They defend well."

"Are we abandoning the city?" Wade chimed in.

"Nothing here to do. Karaclasts continue coming. Something driving them to town."

"Something's *sending* them to Estelia?" Jay asked, but Nand waved the question away.

"Too many question. We go *now*."

They scooped up their packs, looking back to see the outline of the wicked stone snake in the distance, backlit by blazing fires. Buildings continued to fall, screams continued to fill the air, and Jay felt his blood freeze as the reality of what was happening finally set in.

This was no accident. It was no small band of rogue elements slipping in past city defenses to wreak a little havoc and go on their way. *This was a mass assault. A planned surge.*

Virtues were attacking people on purpose…

It was a nightmare.

The virtues were turning on them. And suddenly, Jay had never been so *afraid* in his life.

Chapter 6

When the sun returned to coat the land like a warm, radiant blanket, Jay felt less comfort than when shadows still ruled his sight. Now, he could see the billowing masses of smog and smoke streaking the horizon, a testament to the destruction that had come so swiftly in the night.

He turned to survey their final bastion, which had miraculously held against the alien onslaught of virtues. After only a brief recollection of the horrors of that previous night, Jay and Wade discussed the oddity that was the consistent type of each mad attacker: *mineral*. There were no fire, water, or wind types in the group, *only mineral*. Jay thought there was something important about that fact, but he couldn't quite put his finger on it.

Blaze still hadn't recovered from his bout with the stony snake. Unconscious and occasionally whimpering in his pseudo-sleep, the feisty virtue was being monitored by a local physician who was far from trained in the science.

"I don't know what to tell you," the man started, smock spattered with crimson lines borne from his recent influx of patients.

Jay cringed at the sight, knowing that there had been more than a few victims from the attack.

"If this was like any other animal, I would just say that it needs rest. Over-exertion and a measure of chronic hypertension by the looks of it. But this is a *virtue*, son. We don't exactly have histories of medical ailments and treatments for their kind. At this stage, I would treat it as if it is the very same as the canine form that it has taken. Ample rest and plenty of fluids—if it even *drinks*, that is."

"But what about—" Jay tried, but the man cut him off.

"Son, I have *real* patients to attend. Just take the advice and seek out someone who knows more than I do." He turned and moved hurriedly back into the makeshift clinic that had been erected for the survivors.

As the linen doorway sealed shut again, Jay huffed angrily. He looked down at Blaze lying limply in his arms with mixed emotions. He understood the severity of the situation with the amount of human lives at stake just inside that tent, but he couldn't let his only virtue fade from existence as he had shockingly witnessed was possible the night before.

"What should we do?" he asked, looking to Wade.

Wade swiped his head side to side. "I don't know, man. It's like the doc says; maybe just give him some time to recuperate." He hesitated, looking as if an idea suddenly struck. "You know, you could try to recall him now."

Jay's eyes widened comically. "Wait a minute."

He stared at Wade, unblinking, before turning his attention back to Blaze. Wade was right. *This was his chance*. He could finally be rid of the pestering mutt and regain his ability to manipulate fire… Perhaps if he resummoned the virtue, Blaze would even recover in the long run…

"Your call," Wade encouraged, clearly sounding in

favor of the concept.

Jay closed his eyes, focusing on the essence there, the feel of Blaze and his powers and his form. He pictured the energy withdrawing as it had first left him, returning to him and refilling that void in his DNA.

But he stopped.

A pang of guilt echoed through his chest, fighting the act. *Blaze had saved them*; he single-handedly defeated a number of dangerous virtues that held a threat to them and others around them. Jay wasn't sure that he could have done the same if Blaze's powers were his alone to wield, and on top of that, the fact that the virtue had cared enough to help—whatever the reasons—stayed his hand.

He let out a heavy sigh. "I can't."

"What do you mean *you can't*?" Wade asked skeptically.

"I just…"

He thought of telling Wade the truth, that he held a measure of sympathy for the dog now and that he feared that they might need Blaze in the near future, but he faltered. As his lips parted again, he found a lie spilling out to save face.

"I want him at peak strength when I take him back. I *will* beat him at this game. Doing it now just feels like cheating."

Wade nodded hesitantly. "I mean, I get it; I do. But don't you think stuffing him back in his cage now would save a lot of headaches in the future? *Winning* or not."

Jay simply smiled. "Gotta savor it. We'll be good." He looked around at the chaos still swirling about the outpost and found a chance to change the subject. "It looks like we're in the way more than anything. We should probably get a move on."

"Yeah, let's find Nand and see what he thinks about all this," Wade suggested.

As they circled the encampment, searching for their host, they discussed the possibilities that the attack brought to the remainder of their journey. It was a sobering and mysterious reminder that they were far from safe while wandering the wilds between cities. Travel through the Midlands was so sparse that they could find only a few sources of helpful information and none that could ensure they survived the deadly circumstances of a rogue virtue army.

"So what d'ya think happened?" Wade finally asked, getting to the heart of the matter.

"Beats me," Jay answered, mind still reeling. He shrugged Blaze up higher in his aching arms. "What I want to know is how we were never prepared for any of this. I mean, you would think the Academy, of all places, would cover all their bases."

He considered that for a moment. The Academy of Glendale was more than just a local school. It was a renowned institution for higher learning. Families from all across Tier One would uproot their lives just to immigrate to Glendale and give their children a fighting chance at being accepted. Even Jay had not been a shoo-in. He had to work hard, study diligently, and spend a small fortune just to earn his way. With some of the most intelligent educators and researchers in the Tier at its helm, Jay was wary of the sheer *ignorance* they were experiencing with their degrees.

"But after the Headmaster's creepy warning, watching Blaze interact with the world, and now this. I'm starting to think they left some lessons out on purpose. I mean, Nand knew *exactly* what was happening when the virtues attacked the city. How could he know and we not?" Jay shook his head. "Something's not right."

"I get the same feeling," Wade replied conspiratorially. "But maybe it's just not something they expect us to deal with, so it's like…*not important*?"

Jay shot him a deadpan stare.

"Yeah," Wade grinned wanly. "*Definitely* important. Who knows? Maybe Nand has the answers." He threw a thumb up toward a hulking fellow strolling nearer, toting a pair of cinderblocks in each of his beefy hands.

"Nand!" Jay called, rushing forward to cut into his path.

"Boys. How is Karaclast?" He leaned forward, dropping the four blocks onto the dusty soil. A small cloud puffed away from the ground, matching the one made when he smacked his hands together.

Jay looked down at Blaze once again, noting that the virtue was no longer moaning and whimpering in his sleep. "Better, I guess. He still hasn't woken, but the doctor seems to think letting him rest will help."

"Do not worry. Karaclast has strong spirit." Nand looked to Wade, who seemed to be examining the man with new interest. "What is it?"

Wade shook his head, gesturing at Nand. "Dude, you are *swoll*. How do you get like that?"

Now that they were out of the dingy restaurant and shadows of night, Nand was on full display, and Wade wasn't wrong; the man had muscles in places that Jay didn't realize muscles could grow. Wade was athletic, but he couldn't hold a candle to the giant standing before them. His friend was almost certainly thinking of ways he could bulk up like Nand for the benefit of the ladies.

"Eat well. Work hard. All you need." He turned back to Jay dismissively. "Are you preparing to leave?"

"We are," Jay answered, "But I had a few questions first: could you tell us more about what exactly happened to those virtues last night? We've never heard of or seen anything like that."

"Yes." Nand eased back, resting his haunches on the pile of blocks. "Tribe teach us that every so many year, group of Karaclast suddenly aggressive, attack people more than normal. Normally, attack only went provoked. Now, seek out people to hurt. Like lose mind, but not."

Jay scrunched his face at the last. "So it's *like* they go crazy, but they aren't? How's that?"

Nand waved an enormous hand at him as if he had it all wrong. "No. Not how; *why*."

Wade responded as a lull trailed his correction. "Nand, you're killing us, buddy. *Why*, then?"

"Don't know," he answered simply, as if that was sufficient to tell it all. Seeing that his audience was far from satisfied, though, he went on, "Tribe never find out. Some say leaders know but not tell. I do not believe this. Leaders would not lie to tribe. Either way, killing go for days, weeks perhaps. Then, all stop."

Jay quirked a brow. "It just...*stops*? The virtues go back to normal?"

Nand nodded firmly. "Like never happen."

Jay turned to Wade. "See, I'm telling you, man. There's something weird about all this. If it's happened in Starscythe, it's happened here more than just last night. Why haven't we heard of this?"

Wade shrugged. "Nand, why do you think our

Academy wouldn't teach us about virtues going crazy? Is Jay right? Does this happen here in Cityscape often?"

"Attacks happen everywhere. Perhaps too many years since last attack here. No one remember." Nand seemed immediately unsure of the answer.

"I don't buy it," Jay retorted quickly. As the next question came to mind, he fired it off, "One more thing: during the other two attacks you saw, were all of the virtues the same type?"

Nand's face glazed over with a strange look of consternation, as if he was attempting to translate what Jay had just asked. "*Type?*" he finally responded, testing the word.

"Right, like…" He pointed to Blaze. "Fire. Or water or wind or mineral." On the last, he waved his hand in the direction he thought the remnants of Estelia were.

Nand inclined his head, understanding. "Always same. We call Clast. Translate to *element*. Kara is *spirit*. Spirit of element. Karaclast." He hesitated, recalling the original question. His eyes held a new contemplation. "But yes. Always one Clast. Never two. Another strange thing…"

"I just don't get it," Jay said, thinking aloud.

Wade jumped in. "What d'ya say, big guy? Wanna join us now? I mean, your prison restaurant is kinda…well, *gone*."

Nand lowered his eyes. "No. I cannot."

"Oh, come on!" Wade protested.

"Must stay and help rebuild. Penance." He spoke the single word as if it said everything and more, but Wade only stared at him as if he was growing horns.

Jay nudged his friend before he could press the point. "We'll be heading to Effervescence, Nand. If you change your mind or anything, we'll be there for a few days, I'm sure. We really would love to have you tag along."

Watching Nand then, Jay had a distinct feeling that the man would actually love nothing more, but his so-called penance refused him the option.

"Boys take care of selves," was all he said before standing back up to tower over them. Cinderblocks once more in hand, Nand was off, stalking through the bustling crowd and continuing his labor.

Wade flipped a thumb over his shoulder, donning a perplexed expression. "That guy's odd, right?"

"I think he's made this place his self-imposed hell," Jay answered somberly.

"I mean, he did break some laws of that tribe, but this seems a little excessive."

Jay nodded. "I guess we should hit the road? You got everything you nee—" He trailed off as the furry bundle in his arms began to writhe. His gaze descended like dropped stones, landing on Blaze in time to see the virtue's lids peel open with notable effort. "Blaze!" he spoke excitedly.

The fiery dog blinked lazy eyes twice and twisted his head up to see Jay intruding personal space. With obvious angst, though, he could do nothing for it but stare helplessly at his captor.

"Nice," Wade encouraged but tapered as he noticed how weak the virtue still was. "Well, at least he's not dead."

"*Such words of comfort*," Jay snarked. Though trying to hide it, he was awash with serious concern, a level he honestly hadn't expected since their fateful first contact. "You sure did it this time. Bit off more than you could chew."

Blaze simply let his head fall back against Jay's arm, refusing to give him the win. And he didn't press it. Somehow, the gloating didn't really appeal.

Relenting, he amended, "*You did well*," nearly whispering the words as if they were something to be ashamed of.

"All right, all right. Let's cut this short before you get emotional on me," Wade barged in. "I'm ready when you are. Daylight's wasting, packs are full, and I'm ready for a less *depressing* scene." He surveyed the chaotic outpost pointedly.

Jay hoisted Blaze over his shoulder and sat the dog's rear in an opened portion of the pack he had preset for the purpose. Blaze, still having difficulty maintaining any balance or motor control, slumped forward, paws dangling over Jay's shoulders. Jay's arms would have sighed with audible relief if they could. With Blaze secured on his back, he looked to Wade and then to the road leading out.

"I'm not looking forward to this."

"Me either," Wade replied, punching his arm as he passed. "But the sooner we get it over with, the sooner we can see a new city and get away from whatever *insanity* broke loose here."

As Wade stepped ahead, Jay turned to look at Blaze. "Yeah, well let's just hope it doesn't follow us."

****

After setting the battered Estelia Heights to their backs, Jay and Wade trudged along the immense climb up the Cliffs of Ascent. Sweat-soaked and vacuuming deep, gasping breaths, Jay led the way with Blaze bouncing limply on his shoulders. The virtue had gained a measure of liveliness in the few hours since they departed, but to point, he still seemed too weak to carry his own weight. Jay grumbled more than once about how he should have recalled the chunky virtue when he had the chance, but Wade pointed out each time that he could always stop and try. Jay let the complaint fade in tandem, replacing it with a series of starving breaths.

The sun was no longer a comfort to cast away shadows and bring light and life to the land. Now, it was nothing more than an unforgiving *ball of fire*, hellbent on baking them alive as they traversed the stony soil that seemed to refract every blinding ray back into their eyes.

Wade tripped on an outcropping that he could've sworn blended right into the ground. Cursing and wiping at his now-caked body of sweat and dust, he stumbled onward while Jay noted that the rise was more than two feet high and impossible to miss. The climb was getting the better of them…

"I can't wait to get to Effervescence," Wade moaned, plopping down on a stone seat off the side of the road.

The endless lines of tan and brown streaking into the distance dizzied Jay as he looked up to respond.

"Are you gonna say that every time we leave a city? Can't wait to get to the next one?" He snickered, but the mirth died quickly under the assault of aches in his lower half.

"Dude, you can say what you want, but *this* is the reason people don't travel. Get a nice, cozy home in a city and *stay*."

Jay unwrapped Blaze from his perch and pouch and set him on the stone next to Wade. He wobbled away a few feet as if Wade had something catching and fell back to rest.

"You know, that raises a really good question," Jay posed. "We haven't seen a single person since leaving Estelia. No merchants, no explorers like us. I don't care how bad the trek is. That's kind of odd, don't you think?"

Wade shrugged, glazed eyes pinned on a tiny bug skittering across a dried-out and gnarled root at his feet. "After this climb, I'd be surprised if we see any signs of life for the next *hundred miles*."

Jay nodded absently, considering his own question. With the restriction on borders and the general absence of easy transportation—outside of slow pack animals and expensive wind carriages—Wade was right to think that they would find few folks on this stretch of road. But even so, that few was a pretty consistent factor: merchants, military and political envoys, research teams, and more, all duty-bound to cross the cityless expanse. It had to be rare to find a stretch of highway barren for so long, and Jay could only feel a piercing concern at the scarcity.

"I know this is a shortcut and all, but I'm starting to worry that there's a good reason no one takes it," he voiced.

Wade looked up into the distance, where the nearest plateau seemed to level out. "Yeah, but I would rather suffer the cardio for a short time than spend an extra *three nights* going the long way. Let's get up to the top there and take a look. Maybe we're nearing the peak?" His gaze bounced back to Jay with hope, a sallow grin carved into his dust-matted lips.

"Keep dreaming," Jay answered sourly, leaning forward with incredible effort. His legs wobbled beneath him, threatening to abandon their duty and plant him back on the ground.

Wade stood with similar groans and started back up the monstrous mountainside. When Jay stopped to scoop Blaze back up, the virtue only growled and meandered away from his reach.

He puffed with frustration. "Fine, have it your way. But you better keep up."

Blaze refused to acknowledge, slowly teetering up the incline. Jay watched with trepidation, though, hoping that the virtue wouldn't taper off and faint from the strain. He stepped in sync behind Blaze and silently encouraged him to keep going. His shoulders certainly enjoyed the reprieve.

****

When they all three finally mounted the plateau, Wade grumbled with renewed frustration. "What the hell is this?"

Jay approached and spotted the same impasse that had Wade fretting. Spanned out before them, connecting one sheer side of the mountain to the other, was the most death-defying and dilapidated rope bridge that he had ever seen. Even the makeshift creek-crossers they had forged as kids were like grand constructions in comparison. Frayed lines of cord tethered splintered boards to one another in succession, a tenth of which were simply missing from the assembly altogether.

Jay stepped closer to the deadly drop and stared out over the edge. A tiny stretch of slithering blue water over hundreds of feet below was the only color to break the dull monotony of brown.

"This can't be the only way across," he whispered.

"Think we've found your reason," Wade replied dourly, referencing his earlier ponderings of the empty road.

Jay backed away and let his pack slump to the ground. He dug around inside for only a moment before pulling away the digital map he had purchased in Glendale. With a few strokes of his thumb and forefinger, he expanded an image of the area, highlighting their recent revelation.

"No way!" he shouted defiantly. "How did I miss this?"

Wade scrambled over to see that this rickety bridge was, indeed, the sole means of continuing their journey into the Cliffs. He roared in similar disgust.

"I am *not* walking all the way back down there!" he cried, falling to the dusty stones and cradling his head.

Jay turned back to the bridge and tried to calculate their chances of safe passage. When the final, dismal odds presented themselves across the screen of his mind, he sighed.

"What do we do?"

Wade shook his head. "I don't know, man. Doublecheck the map. Maybe there's some kind of alternate route nearby. Even if we have to walk a distance to get to it, it beats going all the way back down and around."

Jay did just that, searching diligently for another option. After nearly ten minutes of flicking through the dusty screen, the sad reality was only reinforced.

"This is it. This is the *only* way."

He fell back onto the dirt, splayed out and sighing. Just as he did, he felt something vibrate beneath him. He twisted over to see if he had accidentally fallen on his map, but it was an arm's length away. As he laid his head back down, though, he felt it again.

"Do you feel that?" Wade asked, confirming that Jay wasn't going crazy. "Feels like—"

"An *earthquake*," Jay answered for him, though the rumble was so low and distant that he immediately reconsidered.

"*Great*," Wade stated sarcastically. "*Just great*. Not only do we have to cross a twenty-yard chasm on a shoestring, but wait! Let's make it *more* interesting by throwing in an *earthquake*!"

Blaze only watched them sulk as if it was a comedy bit. But as Jay studied the virtue a little more closely, he saw a strange note of tension in the dog's posture. But Jay steeled himself, refusing to let it deter their momentum.

"We're crossing it," he stated flatly.

Wade sat up like a sprung toy. "*Say what*?"

"We're gonna cross it! Come on."

"Hold up!" Wade countered, shambling to his feet. "I was just joking, dude. We're *clearly* going the long way around."

"*Nooo*," Jay drawled with a growing grin. "Let's do this. We can make it!"

"*Says who*?" Wade nearly choked. "Jay, look at that thing! It wouldn't hold Blaze, much less one of us!"

Jay decided to test that theory before responding, moving to put one foot out on the fickle walkway. The bridge immediately swayed with his touch, dried ropes crinkling beneath his fingertips. His foot met the first board with an audible creak.

"Seriously, man. Get away from that thing." Wade's voice was genuinely worried.

Jay pressed a little weight onto the foot, listening with a wince as the board popped. It echoed into the canyon like a gunshot. The whole structure shivered, but even as the sound faded, the vibrations continued. It took a moment for Jay to realize that it wasn't a result of his added pressure. The ground again rumbled beneath them as though a giant pranced in nearby fields.

"See!" Wade pressed. "It's a sign! The whole earth is telling us not to cross that bridge!"

Jay turned back to add a little more stress to his friend's panicked behavior, but he paused, seeing Blaze in that same strange manner as before. The virtue was looking around almost frantically now, as if searching for the source of the sudden tremors. Wade stepped between them before Jay could wonder.

"Look, let's just head back down to Estelia and take the other—"

Wade's words were cut off as the earth shook again, this time more violently. Jay felt his balance falter, the edge of the stone cliff suddenly as unsteady as the bridge beneath his left foot. He fell backward, stumbling twice across the rickety planks before finding himself fully off of stable ground. Wade's eyes tripled in size.

"*Jay*," he said calmly, as if an octave higher would bring the entire bridge crashing down. "*Slowly walk back to me…*"

Jay's body had seized though. He couldn't bring himself to lift a finger, much less a foot. He watched Wade bob back and forth in his tunneling vision. The entire world seemed to sway around him with the motion of the bridge.

"*Easy*," Wade breathed, posture hunkered over like he was the one out on the line.

Jay managed to crane his neck and catch a view of the bridge beyond. He felt a sudden, jarring rush of adrenaline and vertigo...*like a drug bidding him to defy*.

He looked back to Wade and Blaze, both standing at attention and watching his movements as though their own lives depended on what came next. He felt an abrupt pull in his chest, a tantalizing dare whispered by rushing wind. He smiled, knowing even as he did that the expression must look like the final moments of a madman. He lifted a foot, angling it at first toward Wade and safety before pivoting and planting it on the fourth plank out.

"*Jay!*" Wade hissed, his calm demeanor threatening to flee. "*What are you doing?*"

Jay turned his entire body into the next step, the other foot finding the sixth plank, as the one between was simply missing. Another surge of vertigo accompanied the move as the snaking river far below came into view through the absence. The bridge shook with his fearful tremors, muscles wobbling in every inch of his body. His smile never faded.

"*Oh, God!*" Wade mewled. "I'm gonna be sick. I can't watch this."

Jay took another step and then another. He paused as a sibling quake rattled the slats both ahead and behind, hiding the effects of his unsteady shaking. He held his breath. When the bridge settled again, he exhausted it into the vast gap of air between his feet and the beckoning ground.

Ten steps to go.

"*Okay*," Wade finally conceded, realizing his attempts to persuade were pointless. "You can do this. Just a little more..."

Jay dared to peer back over his shoulder, catching Wade turned in the opposite direction, refusing to risk seeing the abrupt end of his best friend's life. Blaze, on the other hand, was standing at the edge of the bridge now, staring out like a disapproving parent.

He turned back.

Five steps away.

They came to him like gut punches, each one potentially his last, but each one carrying him closer to the goal.

Four...three...two.

When he took his foot from the last weathered board and planted it on rocky soil, he felt a fusion of both joy and sorrow at the firm safety now beneath him.

He made it.

In the midst of silent celebration, he felt the adrenaline seep away and take with it that intense sensation. He had never felt *so alive, so bold* in his life. Caution in the wind. Walking on the absolute edge of primal fear. To succeed was to live; to fail was *death.*

It was exquisite.

It was raw and electric.

But like a snuffed candle, it was *gone.*

Still, he shouted triumph over the bridge as if it was an opponent lying in disgraced defeat.

"*Take that!*" he bellowed, rattling out a ragged laugh. "*Whoo! Get some! Yes!*"

Wade watched him punch the air and dance in disbelief. He wiped his eyes twice just in case he was suffering an illusion.

"No way," he mumbled with a wide grin. "No way! You're freakin' crazy, man!" he shouted across the gap, "Absolutely *crazy!*"

"So are you!" Jay shouted back, waving him forward. "Grab Blaze and just *do it!*"

Wade's pale expression returned. "Uh…yeah that's gonna be a hard *no* for me."

"Okay, I see how it is," Jay retorted slyly. "Blaze, show the wimp how it's done."

Blaze, as if enthralled to the command, bounded across the bridge with quick, light steps. His range of motion belied Jay's previous worries; he seemed to be recovering much more quickly now. He was on the other side, moving lazily past Jay in moments. Wade blanched even further.

"No choice now!"

"Oh, come on!" he complained. "Jay, seriously. I don't think I can."

"All right, we're going on without you I guess."

"No, wait! Just—just give me a second."

Wade paced back and forth, gaze never leaving the bridge. It seemed to stare back at him, taunting. He could see it already, the boards shattering, the ropes snapping in two and sending him down to his stony grave. It would be an awesome view for about five seconds, and then his world would end with a sudden, wet *thwack*.

He swallowed the growing lump in his throat. Stepping to the edge, he tapped the toe of his new boot against the cracked and weathered wood.

"Yeah!" Jay shouted, urging him on.

Wade only leaped back with the sound, afraid that his simple exploratory touch had already broken the thing.

"Hey, shut up!" he shouted back before self-coaching. "Okay, Wade, *you can do this*. Just one step. Gotta start somewhere."

He planted his foot onto the first plank, gripping the ropes to either side with lock-tight pincers. He half-expected them to snap like severed threads. When his weight was full on the board, he stopped. A crack like an explosion rang out, and the whole bridge shuddered violently. He thought he might have screamed, but he could hear nothing save the sound of that precursor to death.

"Displace your weight," Jay called. "Try to keep one foot on one plank, and the other on a second."

Wade wanted to reply, to tell Jay to go find a rock and suck on it, but he couldn't open his mouth. Teeth clenched as tight as his hands were on the rope, he took the advice and moved his right foot to the next board up. Slowly, *painstakingly*, he made his way across the hungry chasm.

At the halfway point, he couldn't go any farther. He had to stop. He needed to reset his nerve, recalibrate so that he had the courage to continue. But as he scrounged up the will, another loud snap echoed across the canyon. It wasn't the sound of a board, though, not the sound of rope breaking either. It was the dull pop of *stones* coming apart.

The telltale skitter of scree soon followed, avalanching down the side of the mountain. He looked up in time to see a boulder easing away from the wall where the bridge was attached, cascading with its many minions down into the depths of the chasm below. His eyes met Jay's for a split second before the quaking of the earth began anew, and the bridge careened to one side.

"*Jay!*" he screamed with all his might.

A rush of wind accompanied his words as if the crevasse below exhausted a breath of delight. He latched onto the left-side handhold, feet wedged in the crook between board and right-side rope. He could hear Jay shouting something, but the words made no sense; they were only jumbled syllables sandwiched together. Instead of a full lockdown, though, his body refusing to go any further, it seemed to take control of its own accord.

"*Come on!*" Jay yelled, the words finally forming in his ears. "*Just a little closer!*"

Wade sidled the upturned bridge like a professional rock climber. He shimmied with the best of them, foot to foot, hand over hand, clutching at any and every solid surface he could find. He could feel the wind urge him onward. It whispered to him, and something in him called back. He called to the power of the virtue inside him and begged it to help any way it could. And in sharp seconds, everything grew still as a void. Like a sealed tunnel, the breeze suddenly died. The bridge stopped swaying, the earth ceased to rumble, and like lightning, he was scrambling up the rock face beside Jay.

Jay heaved him backward onto safer ground, but Wade shoved him away, sprinting further away from the edge.

"Wade?" Jay called after him, watching as the crazed man just kept running.

He didn't slow until he was a full fifty yards away from the bridge, even then still moving deeper up the pass. Jay gathered his gear and nodded to Blaze, still wearing a confused expression.

When they finally caught up to Wade, Jay grabbed his arm to keep him from continuing. "Wade, you all right?"

Wade turned abruptly as if snatched out of a daze. He stared blankly back at Jay for a time before working up an answer.

"Am I okay? *Am I okay?*" He paused and furrowed his brow as if asking himself the question and awaiting an answer. Then it clicked. "I nearly *died,* thanks to you! I nearly…*I nearly*—"

He panted, heaving for breath as the panic finally took hold. Jay assisted him to the ground, measuring his breathing to ensure that Wade wasn't going to pass out. When his friend finally settled, he handed Wade a flask of water.

"You were *a boss,*" he said quietly with a goofy grin on his face.

Wade looked up, still panting. "Yeah?"

"The ladies would've swooned en masse," he agreed.

They sat there for a while longer, catching their breaths and stilling their hearts. When Wade finally returned to the land of the tempered and sane, they gathered their things and pressed onward.

Conversation centered on the daring triumph from that point till the moment they found an adequate campsite. Wade became more and more convinced as they spoke that *he* was the mastermind behind crossing the bridge, recalling multiple times that he *knew they could make it* and *insisted they give it a shot.* Jay let him have his delusions. The most important fact was simple: they were five days closer to their goal than if they had doubled back.

He wasn't exactly in a rush, but the thought of twiddling their thumbs on the road longer than necessary while *Godsreach* awaited was sickening. He was more excited now—with the daredevil in him breaking free— than he had been in a long time. He was ready to see what else this world had to throw at him, ready to challenge and overcome whatever they faced.

Exhausted and starving, they set to work on a meal and a tent to shelter them for the night. With Blaze still lax to share his powers, getting the fire going was a chore. The wind was fierce up on the bald plateau. It worked overtime against their efforts, scouring the dust and kindling into small whirlwinds and carrying them away into the night. Finally, Wade had to manipulate the currents around their site for a time until Jay could get the coals hot enough to stay alight.

"Told you that you should've withdrawn the mutt," Wade said, eyeing Blaze with blatant disdain. "Smug little—"

"Wade," Jay cut in, "Blaze obviously serves us better in a fight than if I had recalled him. I have zero experience with the element, and if we were suddenly attacked right now, I'm not sure I would be anything more than a soft target."

Wade sobered. "You think something will come after us up here?"

Jay stared out into the starlit deep. "Not sure."

The ground rumbled again, this time more intense than ever. Blaze sprang to his feet, a low growl emanating from the back of his throat.

"Settle down," Jay said sternly.

"What d'ya think that is?" Wade voiced. He looked as nervous as Blaze was acting.

"Earthquake? Has to be."

"Could be a volcano up here," Wade theorized. "I mean, we *are* in the mountains."

"Whatever it is, the sooner we get off the Cliffs and into Effervescence, the better."

Wade nodded fervently. "Yeah, I'm beat anyways. No sleuthing for tonight." He tossed his bowl to the fireside. "Catch you in the morning."

Jay tossed back a hand. He poked at the dying embers one more time, fretting the fireless night to come. But the wind only continued to whip the ashes upward into eddies that disappeared to darkness, killing any life left in the blackened stumps of wood.

He sat and watched Blaze for a time longer, curious as to why the usually unconcerned dog was now acting so spastic. Something about the quakes had him on edge. Honestly, though, Jay couldn't blame him on that front. The last thing they needed was for a rough shake to send rocks tumbling down on their heads, or worse, for the route to cave and trap them between a severed bridge and an impasse.

Eventually, Blaze's odd behavior tapered off, as did Jay's thoughts. Sleep soon caught him before he could even make it to the tent.

****

The night was cold. The wind screeched across the plateau, carrying away all warmth from Jay's skin. Several times, he found himself back awake, snugging the single blanket up closer to his chin. Finally, he decided the tent was necessary despite his reluctance to fully wake and move.

As he stood, he spotted the still lump of Blaze's crimson fur on the ground near the dead firepit. The small hound was shivering relentlessly, caught in the same chill breeze that pestered Jay to wakefulness. He turned his head toward the tent but stopped. Sighing, he stooped to lift Blaze up in his arms, earning a grunt of rebuke.

"Oh, shut it," he snapped. "You're as cold as I am."

Rubbing his eyes with his free hand, he continued to mumble, "No idea how; you're a stinkin' virtue for crying out loud."

Blaze wriggled once more out of spite and went still. Jay stumbled into the tent—stirring a restless Wade—and plopped down into the empty corner. He tossed Blaze next to him, pulling the blanket up over them both.

"Now, go to sleep," he said firmly, turning onto his side and trying to follow his own command.

Blaze watched him with dark eyes, unmoving from his designated place. There was a hint of curiosity there for the obedience, but it faded with consciousness as Jay nestled into a comfortable ball.

****

Jay woke again. This time, thin slivers of sunlight penetrated the fly over their shelter, tickling his eyes to open. But that wasn't what did the trick. The ground was shifting and shivering beneath him like quicksand. Wade's late-night assumption of a volcano readying to spew its contents all across the land seemed all too real in that moment.

He stood, stepping over the still-snoozing Wade, and made a line for the tent flap. The zipper buzzed with a swift crescent pull, releasing the thin fabric to whip away in the continuing winds. Before his foot touched the sandy earth, Blaze bounded past him, lapping the depleted fire pit once and coming to a sudden halt. Jay watched him cautiously, the air seeming to shiver around them both with sustained tremors.

"What's the matter?" he called out, catching the virtue's attention.

Blaze never budged, beady eyes still fixed on a

distant point down the slope back toward Estelia. Jay let his gaze trace that trajectory until they landed on two distinct figures nearly beyond his limit of sight.

'*Virtues?*' Jay thought with a growing fusion of trepidation and excitement. Perhaps the tremors were only some byproduct of a mineral virtue with more power than fairly due.

They had studied one such instance in detail during his first year at the Academy. A particularly potent and volatile electric virtue had set up residence near Highwater one summer several decades back. They had just recently upgraded the city's power grid to its current state of efficiency, and the act seemed to have either lured or spawned like virtues in the area. The culprit in question was so powerful, in fact, that it would occasionally discharge its excess energy into the environment as a sort of twin relief and warning to stay out of its territory. The expulsions would cause capacitor overloads as Highwater's nearby grid drank up the stray electrons, resulting in frequent blackouts until engineers could get on the scene and repair the damaged components. The series of unfortunate and frustrating grid failures eventually riled the city into action, but it wasn't until a woman ensnared the virtue and bound it that the issue was resolved.

The cogs behind Jay's bleary brown eyes were grinding out the seedling of a plan. If these quakes were caused by a powerful virtue with territory issues, binding that virtue would both give him abilities worth reckoning and pave a safer journey through the rest of the Cliffs. He glanced back out to the horizon, seeing the two figures slowly moving east. There was nothing for it but to check.

He took a few steps in that direction before Blaze suddenly broke away from his statue stance. The dog scuttled two paces in front of him and stopped, staring up at Jay with defiance.

"What are you doing? Get out of the way."

He sidestepped, but Blaze intercepted him again, growling.

"Blaze, I'm not kidding. What's your problem?"

He took a high lunge over the virtue, gaining a small distance, but Blaze barked twice, bringing his attention back around.

"Listen, I don't know what's been going on with you, but unless you figure out a way to write it in the sand, I can't help. I'm going to see what that is. You can come with me or you can stay here, but *don't* get in my way."

Blaze, nonplused, relented. His expression of sulky frustration faded into a don't-blame-me look as he meandered alongside Jay.

Jay ignored him, instead focusing his attention on the small lumps that slowly gained distinct detail as they neared.

The first was quickly revealed to be some kind of golem, not dissimilar to the ones he met during his trial. It was smaller, though, stature compact and colored near the same as the sandstone beneath his feet. It had the knobby form of a humanoid, one large boulder as its torso with many smaller stones to form two arms, two legs, and an assumed head. It moved with slow, grinding motions, feet clattering against the ground with scraping thumps. But despite its larger-than-human size, something told him that it was not the source of the still-thrumming earth.

Jay glanced to the second, its details still hazy from the expanse. He timed his forward momentum with theirs, pacing hunkered down as not to be seen. If he was going to spring on these two, he would need the element of surprise in his favor. His lack of any other skills to ward away dangerous attacks forebode an early demise if he wasn't cautious. And as he came within discerning distance of the second creature, his heart soared, demanding that he *definitely* spring on this opportunity.

It was tall and lanky, its sinewy arms nearly long enough to drag behind it as it continued down the slope. Though also in a bipedal form, this virtue seemed more like something out of a nightmare. It had stony wings draped against its back, charcoal gray and shedding an almost constant dust like two pieces of flint endlessly rubbed together. Its long legs were jointed twice, reaching out for great strides that ended with sharp talons piercing into the ground. Its head was a nearly featureless slab of black rock carved into a pyramid, point erect. Jay could only see faint lines crisscrossing its surface from where he crouched, hidden by a jutting wall of the canyon.

He watched breathlessly as the hideous being suddenly stopped and stared back toward the second of its kind. Without warning, it released the most bloodcurdling sound. Like a child screaming into the vast alleys of the canyon below, its voice was pitched and manic and evolving as it went on.

Chipping away the ice from his fear-frozen mind, Jay briefly wondered if this twisted visage of a creature could be a virtue at all, or if it was something else entirely, something more akin to *demons*. But the fact that it had befriended—or *commanded*—another obvious virtue sealed the question away.

Lesson one of the primary ways to determine a virtue from any other species was to gauge its surroundings. If it fraternized with other validated virtues, it was almost certainly a virtue itself. No virtue had ever been recorded to have a standing relationship with any other species in the wilds, their characteristically territorial nature proof of that. But in contrast, they often congregated with one another, sometimes to points that disrupted entire ecosystems, requiring outside intervention to break up the growing posse lest the area be warped to match the type inhabiting it. There was no doubt in Jay's mind: these two were both mineral virtues.

But now, he had to determine whether the sickeningly strange type before him could be the mastermind behind the tremors. If it was indeed the culprit, it could likely be more potent than he could handle. He would have to act fast, not let them see—

He hesitated then, all thoughts vanishing as the scene ahead changed. The two virtues on the cliffside became three, and then there were six. Before Jay blinked twice, there were over a dozen different kinds of virtues scrambling up the rock walls, soaring down from overlooks, and burrowing out from beneath the sandstone paths. With only a cursory glance, he could make a fair assumption that each and every one was *mineral*.

It was Estelia Heights all over again.

Suddenly, Blaze shifted against his leg. He peered down to catch an undoubtedly anxious glare. With only one more glance back toward the growing mass of virtues, he nodded at Blaze with new appreciation.

Somehow, the fiery dog could sense this volatile rally before it happened; he had known that they were gathering again, another crazed mob forming on the cliffsides around them. Had the earthquakes been some kind of warning? Some kind of alert...or a *summons* even?

With a start, Jay's gaze slid into the sight that answered him. He looked back up in time to see the mass of mineral virtues undulating on a single plateau no more than fifty yards away. In the distance beyond them, from the canyon that stooped down deep below the mesa and carved its way like a barrier to the lands of Estelia Heights, a new being arose, one unlike anything Jay had ever seen...or even *imagined.*

It was like the mountains themselves came to life like the Cliffs of Ascent had birthed some offspring from deep beneath the earth, gathering together and stretching up into the sky to tower over the many minions. Its stony form rose ever more, colors of gray, black, brown, copper, and white waving across it like royal garb. Jagged and craggy fissures rippled through its monstrous form in places. Seething darkness escaped those wounds like pressurized essence billowing out and over the dusty plains.

Jay studied it for long moments on end, thunderstruck with awe and fear. His eyes twitched. His heart stopped. And still he stared onward.

The only distinguishable appendage on the titan was a knoll atop its gargantuan figure, gaping hollows of scooped-out stone where eyes would presumably be. The voids seemed to churn with that unholy black mist, dark and sinister...*and appearing to stare right back at him.*

His legs finally moved of their own accord. He

scrambled out from behind his cover, heart suddenly alive again and pounding hard in his chest.

What is that?

His mind spiraled.

Blaze was already galloping up the hill, back toward camp ahead of him. He sprinted with all his might, daring only once to look back. He nearly fainted at the sight, seeing a veritable horde of mineral virtues screeching, crunching, grinding, and all storming after *him*. The monster in the distance only gazed down with dead, cavernous eyes, watching him flee for his life like an insect.

"*Wade!*" he screamed, his lungs burning as he expelled precious oxygen. "*Wade, get up! Get up now!*"

He continued shouting as he found the air until he spotted his oblivious friend stumble out of their tent, eyes squinting back down the hill toward him. When they registered what trailed ominously close behind, something in Wade's mind miraculously clicked in sync with Jay's. He began shoving everything he could into their packs. He barely had one shoe on when Jay rocketed past him, Blaze still in the lead. Jay snatched both bags, leaving tent, cookware, and much of their other stock behind. Wade fell into furious rhythm, one shoeless foot stomping the ground in careless stride.

"*What the hell is that?*" he cried, staring back over his shoulder at the goliath filling much of the early morning sky.

Jay shook his head vigorously. He couldn't speak. He was already giving out, his body shaking from adrenaline and exhaustion. Suddenly, all of Wade's attempts to make him exercise more had merit.

They ran.

They ran and ran until they could not run anymore. A winded eternity later, Jay had to stop. He couldn't go on, and Wade's foot was as raw as freshly ground meat. They slowed, clambering up into a tight crevice that they *hoped* was out of sight from anything that pursued. But as Jay pushed Wade into the carved crack, he hesitated. A brief glance behind them showed no sign of trailing, murderous virtues. The tan expanse was empty save for small clouds of dust kicked up by their stampede.

"*Wait*," Jay huffed, stepping back out into the open. "*They're…they're gone.*"

Wade slid back down, peering around the corner to find the same barren sight. He winced, falling against the stone and gingerly prodding at his foot.

"*Owww*," he moaned as if the pain had finally caught up to him.

Blaze pattered over, no sign of wear on his canine body save for the dust matted to his crimson fur. He eyed Wade's wounded stub with disinterest, brushing past to stand by Jay's side. Together, they surveyed the cliffs, baffled at the sudden cease of danger.

"What happened to them?" he croaked, voice hoarse.

"I don't know," Wade whimpered back, "But this is the worst nightmare I've ever had. Can I just wake up now."

Jay turned sympathetically. "I should have some bandages in the pack. We need to get that cleaned and wrapped pronto."

He tossed his bag to the ground and rifled through each pocket until his fingertips landed on the small medical emergency kit he had picked up from The Traveler. He sighed in relief at its presence, unlike the gear left behind in their rush. Snatching the plastic box open, he pulled out a roll of bandaging cloth, a small bottle of alcohol, and some antibiotic ointment. He was no doctor, but he at least knew that open cuts and scrapes would infect if not treated.

"Make it fast," Wade said through gritted teeth, eyeing the alcohol warily.

Jay nodded and dumped the entire container over Wade's dusty foot, the clear liquid cleaning away all of the filth to reveal jagged lines of split flesh and the occasional shard of stone jutting out of its embedded position. As if the dust was the only barrier clotting back the blood, Wade's foot turned crimson as the alcohol dripped to the ground. He hissed in pain, looking away from the sight.

Jay felt his muscles clench as the gore revealed itself. He quickly dabbed at the foot with a clean strip of the bandage, slathered it with ointment, and began wrapping it up as tightly as he could. In a few moments, it was covered and no longer oozing. He sighed and sat back, nudging Wade to slip a sock over it. While Wade worked to get the new bulk into a boot, Jay's mind unreeled back to the beginning of the morning, slowly working through each and every frame in an attempt to digest what they had seen.

To stack onto the mystery of the rogue virtues attacking a city and Nand's confession that it was not an isolated incident, they now had to add the morning's findings to the list. The strange and demonic virtue Jay saw with its golem compatriot; its sharp and eerie cry into the canyon; the sudden appearance of other mineral virtues in response; and then the enormous creature that rose like a mountain itself from the core of the planet. It was all connected to the attack and the quakes, Jay was certain.

He looked at Blaze then, curious at his ability to sense the impending doom. With a weak kick in the direction of the dog, he posed the question, "How'd you know that was coming? What was that thing?"

Blaze stared back with his typical superior expression, but Jay had to give it to him. He was right from the start and only tried to keep them safely out of harm's way. Still, it was another unknown to toss onto the already insurmountable pile.

"We need to get to Effervescence and warn someone," Wade croaked. He clambered back to his feet, scowling at the ache.

"I agree," Jay said shortly.

Without further discussion, they began a much slower pace down the barely discernable path. They had been lucky to stay its course during their flight, now having difficulty determining what was the main artery and what were side trails that would only get them lost.

****

The day tarried on with no more than a few *natural* critters scurrying along their route. No more virtues made their appearance, but Jay wasn't ready to give them up for gone just yet. He kept a wary eye open for anything out of the ordinary, startling more than once when stumbling across a nest of swallows and a small rattlesnake. They were dismissed and cast to the back of his worries. Jay thought that should they stumble across a mineral virtue though, it would not be such a simple encounter.

Chapter 7

Day became night, and night became day. Twice past, Jay woke up with an oddly-renewed spirit despite the bone-weary ache he felt in every inch of his body. The trip thus far had been aggressively miserable and bizarre beyond words, but it left them alive and nearer to their destination, and that was all that really mattered.

They had seen no more signs of the giant beast that either roamed these cliffs or was *a part of them*, but its sinister memory was enough to keep them on edge. They had, on the other hand, found themselves a few times in the vicinity of more of those tainted mineral virtues, but caution and stealth kept them from harm.

To Jay's mounting list of curiosities, he had seen no other virtue types at all, despite his careful hunt for them. If anything was to be found in the Cliffs, it was mineral alone, which was overtly strange. Even in places like the Valley of Pyres, where the land was covered in rivers of lava, geysers of gaseous flame, and an ever-present, stifling heat, there were more virtue types than just fire. Practically every kind could be found at some point across the region, but here, in the Cliffs of Ascent, there was only *one*. And that gnawed at him…

Wade had commented little during the journey, opting to safeguard his own opinions on the matter. Jay let him have the quiet, sure that he was just trying to stay sane. Blaze, on the other hand, was livelier than he had ever been in their company. Jay chalked it up to a smug attitude the dog had kept barely concealed, but he had to admit that he trusted the virtue's instincts now.

Blaze had not yet earned *much* respect, but at least he became prone to helping in small ways. The campfire was no longer started by match and lighter but by gouts of magical flame, and the warning signals to stay away from certain regions came as often as Jay requested them. Blaze had to be asked more than twice each time to pitch in, of course, but the fact that he cooperated at all was a sign of progress.

Still, the journey had been long, and they each wanted nothing more than to reach a city that could accommodate them for a long bout of relaxation.

When the final slope out of the monotonous mountains came, they stopped and nearly sobbed in relief. Stretching out in the distance below were the first traces of the color *green* they had seen in long days. Sallow shrubs and stunted lichens were the only fare behind them. And though wilted and dusty still, those signs of life were a more beautiful sight than they could have imagined.

"*Look*," Wade said, the first word out of his mouth in over fifteen hours.

His finger wriggled in the air, pointing out to a dainty sign nailed rather crookedly to a post.

Effervescence - 10 miles, Arken Isles - 106 miles, Halbert's Crossing - 182 miles.

Jay's mouth stretched into a wide, toothy grin at the words. Wade sucked in a deep breath and summoned the courage to lift his legs again. With fresh vigor, if only for a small time, they continued on.

Effervescence wasn't the sight they had hoped to

find, but it would be sufficient. The foothills of the Cliffs scooped down ever lower until they found their feet plodding across not dusty stone but slopping muck. Down still farther they went until the entire zone around them was nothing more than a waterlogged mire with underdeveloped cypress trees to cast it in shadow. The cool air, though sour with the smell of rot, was welcome in contrast to the unraveled section of road behind, sunscorched and shadeless. They never stopped across the ten-mile stretch from sign to gate, but Jay felt ready to fall out by the time they made it.

The walls stood tall and impressive, nothing like those of Estelia Heights. The slick stone perimeter canted out at an angle like the lip of a massive bowl. It proved its worthy design as Jay noted the countless number of grasping creepers trying to reach out from the swamp and climb its heights. At no more than a few feet up the sloping sides, though, each attempt had broken loose, gravity overcoming the rampant vegetation and sending it all hanging back toward the ground.

Though they never had a full view of the city from afar, Jay knew by the map he carried that it was nearly four times the size of Estelia. Population counts three years prior estimated just over seventy thousand citizens within the walls, a whopping fifty thousand more than either Estelia or Glendale boasted. Jay was eager to see such a metropolis in comparison despite having once lived in Highwater, whose population was substantially more.

Considering that, he realized that he remembered very little about his time in Highwater City. He was young when they moved away, though not so young that he should have no recollection of his time spent there.

Yet, no matter how he tried, there was simply nothing spectacular that stood out in his memories. His parents had worked through many hours of the day, often not making it home till past sundown. And his time with daycares and in elementary schools took up much the same. It was a boring routine, yes, but something nagged at him about the absence…

He drew his mind back to the present as Wade rapped on the man-sized portal affixed to a larger swinging gate. In seconds, the door opened to reveal a short, plump fellow wrapped from head to toe in metallic guardsmen attire and sporting a digital pad somewhat similar to Jay's map. He scanned them with dull eyes before pecking something into the screen.

"Trade, politics, or leisure?" he droned.

Wade peered over his shoulder and shrugged. "Say what?" he asked flatly.

The short man looked up with a sigh as if he was tired of having to explain himself. "Are you here for *trade*, *politics*, or *leisure*?" he said, each with belittling slowness.

Wade narrowed his eyes. "Leisure," he said with another deadpan tone.

The guard pecked something into the digital pad again and continued his interrogation, "Interesting. Not a common response. Where you from?"

Jay stepped up to answer this time, afraid that Wade would soon head down a path that could get them barred from entry. "We're from Glendale. Just passing through."

At this, the guard paused in his obviously stunted typing skills, pointer finger still rigidly hovering over the pad. He looked up, a curious arch to his brow. "Passing through *from Glendale*? You come over the Cliffs, then?"

Jay and Wade nodded in unison.

"*Stroke my whiskers*," the guard exclaimed despite his completely bald face, "You might just be the first lot to make it across those accursed stones in a decade. Why'd you go and do a thing like that?"

Jay, in no mood to explain their reasoning, simplified, "We're in a hurry to get to the border to Tier Two."

The guard bobbed his round head and seemed to size them up differently now. "Well, let's get you boys registered here and you can be off for a bath. Lord knows you need it."

He curled his nose upward, handing the pad over to Wade. Jay sidled closer to see and could make out a small grid of their alphabet checkered across the screen. As Jay watched his friend type, the name *Wade Wilkes* slowly appeared above the grid. Wade handed the pad back to the guard who pecked something once and handed it over to Jay. Jay followed suit, and when the pad was back in the guard's hands, he waved them through.

"All right then. I take it you've never been to Eff before?"

A simultaneous shake of their heads bade him on.

"This here's the North Gate Six, *N-6* for short. Now, Eff is a fair bit larger than Glendale, so it'll be easy to get turned 'round. If you're headed for the border, you'll need to cross through Arken Isles; that's gate *W-5*. Fastest route by far. The Isles are a nice place too. Took my wife there once on an anniversary. Rough trek of it even on carriage, though."

He paused as if something just occurred to him. "You have passage across the border, yeah?"

Jay nodded curtly.

"Good thing. There'll be no going through that gate unless you have proper passage. And don't even try to scale the border fence. Stretches all the way 'round the Tier, higher than you can climb, and it's built like a fortress. Some say it's even got ballistic turrets up on the battlements to ward off the unwanteds what get too close." He patted the small pistol at his hip in time with the words as if he would do the same to any unwanteds outside of Effervescence.

"What's the best way to get to the W-5 gate?" Jay asked.

"And what's the nearest place to eat and sleep?" Wade inserted, pausing before adding, "*Nice place.*"

Though Nand turned out to be a great guy and all, his establishment wasn't exactly the kind of quality that either was hoping to spend the next few nights in.

The guard gave his suggestions with fading interest, made note of the freed virtue and Jay's responsibility to keep it from making trouble, and the trio soon set out into the city, leaving him to his duties.

Jay took the lead, tired of walking and ready to make a straight line to the nearest of the aforementioned inns. Effervescence was certainly different from Estelia Heights in many ways, but there was nothing spectacular about its infrastructure that inspired him to explore. The roads either bordered lines of shops, housing, or the occasional sludge-covered waterhole that sent their noses up in protest. It was as practical and commonplace a road as any other he had tread in his twenty-two years. Everything was a solid greenish-gray, the weak rays of the sun doing little to liven the city around them.

According to his brief research, Effervescence had been largely built atop the only rise in the regional topography at first, but as it expanded, it had no choice but to dip into the recesses of lands less suited for living. Their current district was apparently one such poorly-planned development.

A gas bubble popped atop the surface of the filthy water to Wade's right, earning a loud groan.

"*That smells like genuine sewage*," Wade said loudly enough for a nearby merchant to hear. He wasn't pleased with the atmosphere and was clearly intent on letting the locals know.

"Who knows," Jay started with a grin, "It might be."

He made to shove Wade toward the pool but pulled him back at the last second. Wade didn't think it was too funny.

"If I go in," he said with a sour expression, "I'm going to make you *drink it*."

He stepped across the paved street toward a large brick building with a sign hanging limply against its face. It read: *Rambler's Reprieve.*

"Oh, *finally*. Maybe the air *inside* is actually breathable."

Jay cocked his head at the name, curious for only a moment until the guard's words in Estelia came back to him. Merchants often used Effervescence as a hub before moving on to other cities, meaning more travelers looking for a place to stay. He followed Wade inside, Blaze hugging his heels and staring around them skeptically.

The foyer was wide, a vaulted ceiling above their heads allowing them to see the bannisters for a second and third story. Decorations were sparse, but the walls and floors alike were covered with cherrywood panels, dark and reddish swirls worked into the stained planks to create a classy yet practical ambience.

A man stood at the far side of the room speaking in low tones with another. The sounds of lively chatter and music seemed to be coming from the doorway beyond.

Jay and his cohort stepped to the single stonework countertop in the area and waited for whichever of the two meant to run the desk to notice. Conversation interrupted, one of the whisperers pointed toward them and the other spun, appeared momentarily confused, and then bowed magnanimously before scurrying over.

"Welcome, welcome!" he said in an oily, though sophisticated voice. Sliding in behind the counter, he paused to consider them. "Sunkissed skin, dusty hair, grimy clothes. You boys have not only been traveling, but over the *Cliffs of Ascent* no less!"

He sounded as surprised as the guard had with the realization. Jay was beginning to wonder why the route was even listed on his map if it was so dangerously untraversed.

"How do you know that?" Wade asked flatly. "We could have just rolled around on the ground a bit before we walked in."

The man snorted, eyeing Wade as if he was a simpleton before reaching across the marbled surface and plucking at his curly hair. Wade jerked back, glowering.

"Hey!"

The man paid his cry no mind and simply thumbed the twin strands of dust-matted, crinkly tresses against his palm. "Because if you had come east through

Noterand, you would have dark, loamy filth all over you and you wouldn't be in my establishment in the first place."

He seemed to both smile and frown simultaneously, his thinly bearded face twisting into an unseemly shape. "The soil of the lowlands is dense and rich, nothing like the thin dust of the mountains. And the only people who frequent this business are locals and merchants with whom I have forged fine friendships over the years." He turned his gaze upward to study the floors hovering over them. "Haven't rented a room to any newbloods since the governor declared the Cliffs unfit for travel, the pompous lout."

"But you *do* have a room, right?" Jay insisted, already feeling his body argue against another long walk.

The man let his gaze fall back onto them, the frowning portion of his expression fading away. "Of course! Best rate you'll find in the northern districts, I assure you."

He hesitated, staring down between their legs toward Blaze who met his eyes defiantly. "And you'll be sure to keep your *pet* on a tight leash, yes? Damages to any property will be taken out against your tab at a double-retail rate of repair."

Jay nodded curtly, glad, at least, that they weren't refusing him entry and service due to his wandering virtue.

"*Wonderful.* Same room or separate?"

Wade shrugged and Jay opted to save the cash. "Same. *Two* beds," he added as if the point needed to be made.

"Second floor," Wade amended as well, "First if you have rooms down here. We've done enough climbing for a lifetime."

The host only smiled and thrusted a small digital pad across the counter similar to the one used by the guard. Jay was beginning to wonder about the technological state of Effervescence, and the other cities for that matter as they went on. Portable digital devices were only just now entering the market, and even so, the outlying cities were having a difficult time gaining access to the merchandise. The only districts that hosted the manufacturing facilities for higher grade tech like this were in Tier Two or beyond, leaving Tier One folks with the dregs. He was eager to see what kind of new and exciting trinkets were out and circulating this close to the border.

Wade flipped through the agreements without reading and signed at the bottom. Jay pulled a handful of money out of his pocket preset for just such an occasion and fingered the right amount onto the counter. It wasn't an absurd rate for a single night's stay, but it wasn't exactly *a deal* either. Regardless, he would've paid almost any price to climb into a hot shower and a clean bed.

"Splendid." The man took the pad back and tucked it beneath the desk, replacing it with a single key attached to a long, threaded lanyard. "You'll be in room 203 on the second floor. If you need anything at all, drop back by the front desk here and someone will be along to help."

He turned and gestured toward the doorway that continued to emanate the lively sounds of a crowd. "The bar is this way. Parlum is the finest chef this side of the Isles. You won't be disappointed with his menu. Be sure to leave a review with the barkeep. The man appreciates his feedback."

Jay nodded as he trailed off, spun, and ushered Blaze up the spiraling staircase. The room, only three doors down from the landing, was revealed to be quite the luxury. Jay reconsidered his earlier hesitance at the price as Wade sidled past him and leaped headlong into a sizeable bed swathed with pristine white linens. They quickly darkened a shade with Wade's filthy form rolling over twice to land face-up and nearly shaking with ecstasy.

"*Sooo niceee,*" he moaned, tugging the fresh blanket against his face and pulling in a deep breath of the laundered fabric.

Jay stepped inside, Blaze pattering past him, too, to hop up onto the other bed. He shrugged his pack onto the floor and took in the rest of the amenities they had bought into for the evening.

Standing lamps adorned every corner, and a large window on the far wall revealed a nice view of the city beyond. Billowing white curtains fluttered against its panes in the overhead air conditioning which brought a welcome chill to the room. There was a vanity opposite the two beds, equipped with a small sink and a fridge just beneath. He crossed over and popped the door open to find six separate bottles of purified water and two of orange juice. Slapping it shut again, he turned to see the bathroom door slightly ajar, beckoning him.

"I'm going to get a shower," he said, nearly running toward the door in case Wade had the same idea.

But Wade was apparently content to loaf in his bed unwashed for now.

Jay exited the shower feeling like a new man. He was clean for the first time in a week or more, and it showed in his mood. He sprang through the bathroom doorway, steam rolling out behind him in dramatic waves, and made a line for his pack. Before he ever touched the flap, though, his enthusiasm shrank. He might be clean now, but his clothes certainly *were not*.

He sighed heavily as he shrugged back into a pair of thrice-recycled jeans and a tee shirt that looked as if he had dunked it in a puddle of tie-dye liquid, if only the color scheme was more of an earthy sort.

The loathsome sound didn't stir Wade to sympathy, though, as his friend had already snorted a series of deep-sleep wheezes that sent vibrations throughout the room. Blaze was staring at Wade's prone form, one leg hanging limply off the bed, with a grim look of annoyance. Jay decided he didn't want to hang around and hear it either.

"I'm going down to the bar for something to eat. You can stay if you want—"

Blaze was already standing and stretching his squat legs before Jay finished the offer.

"Yeah, I didn't think so," he snickered.

They exited quietly and locked up before heading back down the stairs and across the entrance foyer toward the bar. Jay could already smell the sweet and succulent scents of fruity cocktails and mellow beers wafting out into the open air.

As he stepped inside, his senses opened to even more smells—some not altogether pleasant exuding from the patrons. But the sights of the ample entrees covering each and every table kept his appetite ready. His mouth watered, eyes suddenly locking on the bartender. Though she was a young and voluptuous brunette—more than easy on the eyes—she was not Jay's target obsession at the moment; he had his sights set on the platter of what appeared to be lamb chops, beef tenderloin, and a plethora of veggies ranging from black-eyed peas to brussels sprouts extending from her hand to a gentleman at the counter.

He eagerly slid into the first open seat he came to, Blaze hopping up on an adjacent pedestal as if he, too, would like to place an order for the scrumptious-looking plates.

The bartender turned in time with his arrival and appeared to study them both for a long moment before offering in a silky voice, "You're a new face. What can I get you, doll?"

"Everything on the menu," he said with a smile and paused to consider whether that was a joke or not. Deciding against being a *pig*, he amended, "Or we could just start with a menu."

The girl grinned and plucked one of the laminated folders from a nearby pile and held it toward him. Just as his fingertips brushed the edge, though, she pulled it away.

"Just so we're on the same page, you're not going to *eat* the menu, right? I mean, I've seen hungry, but that would be a first."

Jay's face adopted a look of confusion until he realized his choice of wording. "I meant to say that I can start by *looking* at a menu, then I'll decide what to *eat*, menu excluded." He grinned.

She handed it over and shared his smile. "I would say take your time, but I have a feeling you won't need it."

She pulled up a barstool on the opposite side of the counter and wiped away a pile of crinkled napkins from between them. Appearing ready to settle in for a long conversation, she propped her elbows up and calculated his appearance while he attempted to read the dishes listed bullet-point on the page. Eventually unsettled and unable to concentrate, he pointed to the first thing that sounded good and turned the menu toward her. She nodded sagely.

"One of the best-sellers. You can't go wrong."

"Then that's what I'll have," he said with resolution.

"And your little buddy?" Her round, blue eyes flicked to Blaze, smile never leaving her lips.

Blaze shifted on his stool grumpily, rumbling at her choice of adjective. She laughed and held up both hands as if to signify an apology. Blaze relented, though he turned his attention away to shun at least.

She was *pretty*, the kind that stood out all the more in a place like this: dim lights, jazzy music playing in the background, her auburn hair seeming to dance with the ample shadows. Her blue eyes, though, stood out like gemstones against the ambience. When they settled back on his, Jay nearly forgot to breathe.

"*Um*—" he cleared his throat, "Don't mind him. He's moody at the best of times." He could practically feel Blaze's indignance radiating with the synopsis, but he pressed on, "But Blaze isn't much of an eater. It'll just be me."

"*Blaze?*" she asked, testing the name. "I like it. Suits him." She turned back to study Jay again with those intense eyes. "*You* look like a *rambler*."

He tilted his head to the side, lifting a brow. "More like a *Jay*," he corrected with a smirk. "But I applaud the attempt. Judging by the name of this place, I'd guess you say that to every paying customer."

Though his tone was light, her shimmering smile

faded a shade. "Not every patron at the Rambler's Reprieve is a *rambler*," she said with a long pause to follow, "But I can see it in you. You're not the kind to let grass grow beneath your feet, are you?"

It was Jay's turn to study her now. Something changed in the blink of an eye; she seemed somehow sad, as if the assumption of his lifestyle had touched a nerve. But as quickly as it came, it was gone, her cheery and vibrant demeanor back in force.

"I'll get your order in pronto." And then she was gone, bounding through a set of swinging doors and leaving Jay and Blaze alone at the counter.

Jay turned to his furry companion. "That was odd, right?"

Blaze stared back at him noiselessly, but he could see the look of discomfort on the dog's face too. Before he could continue his one-way conversation, the woman was back, gliding into her readied seat.

"Talia," she said smoothly.

Jay arched an eyebrow.

"My name," she explained, "It's only fair. So where are you from, Jay?"

"Glendale," he answered quickly, keeping it curt.

This time, her brows arched with surprise. "That's quite a distance. What brought you to Eff?"

She reached below the counter and plucked out a clean glass, turning to fill it with what appeared to be house soda from a tap. The carbonation fizzled around the rim as she slid it across the counter toward him.

He took it and pulled a long draw, savoring the first sugary liquid he had tasted since leaving home. Something about her kind curiosity was putting him off guard now. It was as if she was working him with a magic that no virtue could supply. He felt like telling her his entire story, the dream that drove him here and beyond toward Godsreach.

Tempering himself, though, he answered, "Looking for rare virtues. Glendale isn't exactly a hotspot for the stronger types."

"Really?" she asked nonchalantly, stirring a finger through the condensation on the bar top. "Are you a collector or something?"

Her ruby red lips twitched into the kind of teasing smile that Jay was accustomed to receiving in these kinds of conversations. He was suddenly glad that he didn't spill his guts.

"I mean…I guess it's sort of like a hobby." He shrugged noncommittally. "So uh, what do you do, Talia?"

She glanced around pointedly before staring back at him with a growing grin. She knew she had him ruffled.

"Like for *fun*," he amended quickly.

"I like to make my cuter customers uncomfortable," she answered. With an overt wink, she fell quiet to do just that. Before Jay was compelled to speak something, *anything* into the silence, she went on, "I think that sounds like a nice hobby, chasing virtues. My father did something similar, though his was more for work than play. He was a lead researcher with Rylotek, stayed on the road for long periods of time, studying the different virtue types in different regions."

Her somber mood returned like a tidal wave then, washing over her features and somehow diminishing her. She reached a hand across the surface to pat Blaze as if instinctually looking for a creature comfort, and to Jay's surprise, he allowed it, though he seemed far from thrilled by the touch.

Jay shuffled straighter in his seat, not missing the cue. "You said '*was*.' What happened?"

She looked up, fighting to regain her previous air. "Went missing last month. He was supposed to be in Arken Isles, but no one has seen him since he left Precipice. It's not even that far between the two cities, but he just…vanished."

Jay suddenly understood her reactions. "Did he ever run into much trouble during his travels?" He hesitated before adding, "*Before*."

She nodded. "All the time. But he always had a team with him equipped to fend off even the most dangerous virtues. Or anything else for that matter."

"And the team?"

"Missing. All of them. I told him that he should've stayed, that moving back and forth through the Midlands like that was going to get him killed one of these days." She pulled her hand away from Blaze who seemed all-too-relieved. "Feel like I should tell you the same, *Jay the rambler*." She met his eyes again, but there was no humor in those deep, cobalt pools now.

Feeling the downward velocity of the conversation increasing, he changed directions. "So tell me about Effervescence. What's there to do around here for fun— *other than patronizing your patrons*." He smiled as brightly as he could, hoping it would bring hers back to life.

"Well," she started, pulling a deep breath and transitioning her finger to a small scar in the wood of the counter, "There are the festivals, though most of the cities in Tier One celebrate them, so it's not a particularly *Eff* tradition. The fishing is good, but you have to be pretty good not to lose your lures to the trees or the moss all around Green-Eye Lake. And, of course." She stopped and waved at the many customers tipping back glasses of beer, brandy, and wine. "There is always the booze."

Jay chuckled, turning to see the scene in full. But just as he was coming back around to comment, his gaze skidded against a pair of dark eyes watching him with grim intensity from a table in the corner of the pub. He connected with them for a moment, assuming the man to which they belonged would turn away.

He did not.

Jay spun back to Talia, feeling suddenly alarmed for a reason he couldn't explain.

"Talia, who is—" he started, but a sudden shout from beyond the swinging doors cut him off.

"Order up, Tal!"

Talia leaped off her stool and gave him a *be right back* glance. He watched her go but soon found his gaze gravitating back toward the corner table. As stealthy as he hoped to be with the furtive peek, the man there noticed and this time did not remain silent.

"Come 'ere, boy," he called, gravelly voice just one decibel above the din of the crowd. But Jay could have heard the words if they had been whispered at him, so intent he was on his apparent stalker.

He swiveled his creaky seat around slowly. Blaze seemed unbothered by the transaction taking place, his attention wavering between almost every person there as if they were *all* volatile threats. Jay took one more glance over his shoulder, hoping that Talia was back, but he was yet alone and without excuse to ignore the summons. He stood, the man still glaring at him, and stepped carefully over to the corner of the room.

"*Sit*," the man said as Jay neared.

Jay reluctantly slid out a seat and eased down into it. He could see the fellow better from this angle, the dim lights now revealing a long, jagged scar running from ear to nostril on his left side. His gray eyes were foggy, thin wisps of greasy hair following the color scheme and hanging languidly down his forehead. His clothes were dirty and matted with muck as if he had been traveling alongside Jay and crew during their last week.

"You're 'untin' virtues," he growled, the stunted words more an accusation than a question.

Jay worked his mouth soundlessly like a fish out of water until the syllables caught up, "I wouldn't exactly call it *hunting*."

The man grunted skeptically. "I know of a rare trophy in these parts. Nasty little virtue that's been causing all kinds of 'avoc. May interest you."

Jay let the surprise show on his face. "Really? What is it?"

"Tell me first: why do you chase these *monsters* if not to 'unt 'em?" His gray eyes seemed to penetrate Jay's thoughts, already knowing the answer before he asked the question.

Jay leaned in, careful not to let the entire pub hear his answer lest they laugh him out of the room. "I want to bind every type. I'm not in it to run them off or to...*kill them*." He said the last with a fickle tone, unsure that it was even the right way to describe what he witnessed in Estelia. "People say it can't be done; I want to prove them wrong."

The man barked an incredulous laugh that rattled the many empty glasses on the table between them. There was a hint of satisfaction there as if he had expected to hear such a wild response.

"Then I'll tell you everything, boy."

He plucked a pack of cigarettes from his coat pocket with two gnarled fingers, shoved one between his lips, and lit it. The harsh smoke wafted into Jay's face, sending him nearly tipping backward in a fit of coughs.

"There ain't many with such 'aughty ambition left in this world." He drew a deep lungful of the toxic vapor and let it trickle out with his words, "It's *void.*"

Jay felt his lids nearly shrink back into his head. "*Void?*" he asked with barely concealed excitement.

He hadn't expected to find something so rare this side of Starscythe Plains. According to his thirteenth-year class on Regional Composition of Elements, there hadn't been a single void-type virtue registered in Tier One for decades.

The man tilted his head back and forth. "And a strong one at that. Formless, like a floating mist 'overin' about the southern swamplands. Been chasing 'im myself for nearly three months, though I 'ave no intention of *binding* the foul thing."

"Why are you chasing it then?" Jay asked hesitantly.

"What else but to destroy it?" he answered plainly. Jay opened his mouth to speak, but the man continued over him, "I know what you'll say. Just like all the others, you wonder at me as if I don't 'ave my 'ead on straight, but *you've not seen what I've seen*…you don't know what I know."

He grimaced, leaning across the table to glare at Jay. "You think virtues are some kinda tools of the natural world to be 'arnessed and used. Bah! They're no more natural than aliens from a faraway planet come to conquer this sad little world. *But* at least you aim to bind as many as you can. I can work with that. Binding them removes 'em just as surely as banishing them completely. Most folk'll bind one or two 'round 'ere. *But if they only knew the truth about virtues and vices…ah*! I bet my left foot they wouldn't come within a mile of the nasties!"

Jay was looking at the man now exactly as he had presumed. A few screws loose would seem an understatement.

"What truth? And what's a *vice*?"

Strange as the man was, he had Jay's wheels spinning back to the myriad questions lying dormant and unanswered in his brain.

"*Is that like a really big virtue?*" he whispered conspiratorially.

The man sucked in another cancerous breath, puffing it out in a wide cloud. When he realized the seriousness on Jay's face, it seemed to flip a switch. His beady eyes widened to match, and he shoved out of his chair, moving to sit next to Jay now.

"*You've seen it,*" he said beneath a rancid breath. Pulling Jay's head closer to his, he hissed, "You've seen a vice? It's back? *Ohhh, I knew it…* It was only a matter of time before they—"

"Sylvester!" a sharp voice sounded from behind them, causing Jay to nearly leap away from table and chair.

They spun simultaneously to find Talia standing before the twin swaying doors, hot plate of food in hand.

"*Leave Jay alone.* He doesn't need you filling his head with those fantasies of yours."

She set the plate down with a clunk and swept out

from behind the counter, one hand rocketing toward the man's arm and hoisting him to his feet.

"Talia, listen! The boy's seen it! 'E can tell you!"

"Seen what?" she breathed, exasperated. "Jay, come on. Your food's ready."

She swapped her grip from Sylvester to him, tugging him back toward the counter. She guarded him until he managed to plant his rear back onto the stool next to a still-unconcerned Blaze.

Jay looked back to find Sylvester again in his original seat, mumbling angrily to himself. Talia's dark curls swept around Jay's periphery, though, and he returned his attention to her.

"What was that about?"

"Sylvie can be...*eccentric*," she said in an undertone. "Don't mind him, though. He's a nice enough guy, but he'll tell you the tallest tales you've ever heard and swear them on his mother's grave. You can't believe a word he says."

She slid his plate before him, the steaming entrée threatening to wash away all other thoughts save stuffing his face. But he stopped himself, thumb scratching the surface of his silvery fork anxiously.

"Talia, Sylvester said something just before you caught him, and—"

"*Nevermind him,*" she answered swiftly, shoving his plate a little closer. "Eat! I want to know what you think!"

She smiled at him again, her vivacious demeanor returned and affecting his thoughts further away. He took a bite and then another, nearly drooling all over himself with the flood of flavors. But all while he enjoyed the meal, that simple term haunted him.

Vice.

Somehow, he thought that Sylvester might be closer to the truth than Talia and the others realized.

****

He stayed and chatted with Talia for a time longer, eventually crashing from the full stomach and the culmination of his exhaustion. He promised to be back for lunch the following day and bid her goodnight, but as he stepped into the foyer, he took one last look at Sylvester, still brooding in the corner. The man met his glance knowingly and scraped away from his table. Talia intercepted him, though, just as Jay turned the corner out of sight. He waited in the foyer near the desk for five or six minutes, but he finally decided that the odd fellow had been detained for good.

Off to bed with Blaze close at his heels, Jay turned his question downward to at least verbalize it, "What is a *vice?*"

Blaze looked up at him with startling speed as if he had just hurled a particularly rude insult. He stopped on the last step and stared back at Jay with pinprick eyes.

"You know that word?"

Of course, Blaze didn't choose that moment to suddenly reveal his ability to speak, so no reply came other than the continued canine glare. It was silly to converse with the creature like this, but Jay needed something to rebound his thoughts.

"Do you think that thing we saw in the Cliffs was *a vice?*"

Blaze's singular huff was the only answer he got, but despite the dog's inability to share in his critical thinking process, he felt as though he was on the right track with that question.

If there were beings openly called virtues, it would stand to reason that their opposites, if they had any, might be called vices. But what exactly did that mean? The terms—who in the world dubbed them in the first place, he had no idea—simply didn't fit the bill. He had met and seen evidence of *virtues* that suggested a less-than-virtuous existence. Violent aggressors the lot of them were in more cases than not. But on that same line of thinking, would a vice be an even worse rendition of the virtues? Massive as the mountains and set on killing more than just those entering its territory…able even to rope their smaller cousins into their sinister biddings.

He wiped at his tired eyes, knowing that there was no amount of solitary deliberation that would help him arrive at an answer. And Blaze was already getting peeved at his lagging, standing at the locked door with an impatient stare. Jay sealed it all away in the recesses of his fading brain and shoved the key into the lock. He needed some sleep, and he intended to get all he could before setting one foot outside tomorrow.

Chapter 8

The sun was, *again*, a hateful thing.

Jay snatched the blankets up over his face, earning a smart bark of anger from the bundled Blaze at his feet. Even with the fabric snugly covering his eyes, the light seemed to penetrate both it and his lids with persistence.

He growled in tandem with Blaze, erupting from the bed to snatch at the fluttering curtains. Pinning them tightly together didn't offer a bit of help. It was as if the room had been positioned and equipped to eject guests at the earliest possible hour.

Wade, on the other hand, hadn't moved from his flaccid position since the evening before, filthy to the bone and still wrapped in his crusty traveling attire. Jay felt another stab of jealous anger at that.

With nothing left to do but wake and ready for whatever the day held in store, he petulantly scoured his pack for all clothing—opting even to gather Wade's despite his envy—and trudged to the bathroom to let them soak in the soapy tub.

When his mock laundry session was complete, he slipped back into his boots and moseyed mindlessly outside in search for something that could take his mind off the lack of sleep. Blaze chose to remain behind this time, whether for a little more loafing of his own or because he saw the dangerous volatility that was Jay's mood.

As the door clicked shut behind him, Jay blearily recognized the heavenly aromas of breakfast stirring in the foyer below. With a slight pep in attitude, he plodded down the steps and set his trajectory for the bar. To add to the cruelty of the morning, though, the attractive Talia was no longer manning her station; rather a gruff-looking fellow stood in her stead with none of the bubbly politeness of his colleague.

Jay slid easily into his seat from the night before, pulling a menu across the scarred surface to glance halfheartedly at its contents.

"What'll it be?" the man asked, gaze fixed on a glass of juice he was topping off.

Jay threw out the first choice that looked appetizing and waited in his sulky state until the food arrived. Wolfing it down in record time, he left his money, spun away from the bar, and found a pair of beady eyes watching him from the doorway.

"*Follow me*," Sylvester said in a low tone, turning to stalk back out into the sunlit foyer.

Intrigued, and with all the questions from the night before returning, Jay obeyed. He fell in behind the enigmatic man, no Talia or anyone else there to stop their coming conversation.

When Sylvester reached the dual windows near the exit, he stopped and turned back to Jay. "You ready?"

Jay squinted, unsure. "For what?"

Sylvester laughed. The coarse sound grated on Jay's ears. "*For what*, 'e says. To go and catch a blasted virtue, that's what!"

Jay's eyes went from slits to orbs. "You're serious? You'll take me?"

"Of course, I will," Sylvie answered soberly. "I need

'elp to manage that little fiend. It's too elusive for just one. We'll need a proper trap."

Jay felt his head bobbing forward so fast his neck threatened to give way. "Yeah! Yeah, lemme go get Wade; he's my friend, been traveling with me. And my stuff. I'll be right back down!"

Without waiting for a response, Jay sprinted back up the staircase, nearly blowing the door off its hinges. Blaze yelped, scrambling off the bed and into a fighting stance, while Wade only continued to puff out dreamy breaths of slumber.

"Wade!" he called, running to grab up his gear. "Wade, wake up! You've gotta hear this!"

Wade only continued to snooze.

Jay threw his pack onto the bed, shaking the comatose lout violently. Finally, Wade snorted twice, stirred long enough to open one eye, then writhed like a toddler brought out of a good dream.

"Wade, get up, man! There's a *void* virtue. This guy, Sylvester, is downstairs waiting on us. He's gonna take us to it! Just think, man: a *void*!"

If Wade found the prospect exciting, he didn't show it in the least. He swatted at the air between them, groaning.

"*Come on*!" Jay shouted, pulling on his filthy pantleg.

Wade kicked away and scrambled farther under the blankets out of Jay's reach.

"Suit yourself," Jay huffed. He turned to Blaze then, "*You're* coming though."

Without an option, Blaze hung his canine head and trundled his squat legs toward the door. The look he gave, though, told Jay that he would regret this forced jaunt.

Undeterred by the two killjoys, Jay sprinted back down the stairs to find Sylvie contentedly waiting.

"Ready now?" he asked.

Jay nodded. "Wade's not going to make it. This is Blaze, by the way. Ornery virtue that I accidentally let out of its cage. Long story."

Sylvester froze, staring the fiery pup down even as Blaze returned the look. There was a contest then, one to see who would back down first. Jay knew the outcome favored Blaze from the start, but he was both surprised and concerned to find his virtue turn away from Sylvester's dark glare after only short seconds.

"I don't like it," the old man finally said. "But I'll assume that you'll keep the mutt outta the way?"

Jay was only just getting the sense that Sylvester meant business about his dislike of virtues, but he nodded for the opportunity's sake.

"Good. Well, let's 'ave at it, then."

****

An hour later and several miles behind them, Jay, Blaze, and the untiring Sylvester spelunked through the swamplands that surrounded Effervescence. According to his compass, they were headed due east now, though they had been shifting directions every few minutes since they left the city gates. Lost and at the mercy of this near-stranger, Jay kept his wary eyes open for anything, most of all a void virtue.

"So where exactly did you last see it?" Jay asked, plucking his foot out of a miry hole that nearly stole his boot.

"*Shh*," Sylvie responded with a quiet hiss. "It can 'ear you, son. Don't wanna spook the pretty, now do we?"

Jay wanted to comment on how any virtue in a mile radius could hear their sloppy maneuverings, but he held his tongue.

"Not far now. It frequents a place just over that rise there." He pointed a crooked finger toward a small, overgrown hillock a little over fifty yards away. "Now, listen 'ere, Jay. These parts are dangerous for more reasons than one. Virtues thrive 'round 'ere, yes, but there are people too…*strange people* what call this muck their 'ome."

Jay slowed. "What do you mean by *strange*?"

Sylvie twisted his head side to side. "*Bizarre*. Won't come into town—no love for civilized folk. Attack the 'unters out in this region if they even wander near the camps. Rumors say they do wicked rituals on man and beast alike. Sacrifice 'em, imprison 'em…*eat 'em*."

"Wait, *what*?" Jay exclaimed.

"*Shh!*" Sylvie hissed again.

Jay tamed his tone. "*They eat people*?" he whispered back, nearly a hiss of his own.

What had he gotten himself into?

Blaze's head whipped back and forth between them and the woods as if he, too, found reason to fear these crazed and cannibalistic locals.

"Only rumors," Sylvie tempered, but his tone belied the point. "Still, best that we move forward with caution. Don't want either to come sneaking up on us unawares."

Jay felt his head grow suddenly light. It was one thing to be in the elements with virtues that could attack as suddenly as vipers, but it was another thing entirely to fear a group of people that might have him for *dinner*.

****

Their search continued with slow and paranoid progress. They managed to draw out a number of creatures both natural and not, but despite Sylvester's self-prescribed war against the virtues, he seemed to have eyes for only the strongest among them. He dismissed the majority as something beneath his notice, all-the-while mumbling manically about how he would soon best this bane of a void type. Jay got the feeling he had tasted defeat more times than one at the hand of their soon-to-be prey.

But Jay was not quite of the same mentality. He had to fight against his instincts to spring after each and every one they met. He wanted desperately to lay claim to an easy prize, especially the slimy and slow-moving entropics that littered the area. Like living piles of muck and sometimes masked as dead foliage or decaying mushroom fields, they were by far the most prominent entities in the swamp. He could bind one of those relatively easily, he thought, but he had to remind himself that his goal was not *them*. He had only one binding gem available. Why settle for less when *a void* was at his fingertips?

Blaze, on the other hand, was not opposed to lashing out at the least, sending gouts of roiling flame to spook even the most harmless of passersby. Sylvie was clearly not a fan of his antics as relayed by his constant shushing and evil glares, but Jay tried not to intervene in their duel of dominance. He was hypersensitive to the environment now, hawk-gaze roaming and readied to find the fabled virtue that would make this sickly soiree worth their time.

But as they delved ever deeper into the darkening bog, Jay began to spot things that brought back that demented notion of nearby cannibals. Twice, Sylvie saved him from falling into a pit covered over with brush and laden with spikes at the bottom. Once more, he stumbled into a net that, if not for Blaze's quick fireworks, would have snatched him by the ankle and hoisted him high over the trees.

"Just animal traps," Sylvester said as he untangled the ropes from Jay's legs. But judging by the size of the traps in question, Jay had reason to doubt that.

****

After an achingly long search, the trio finally stumbled into the gangly promenade that Sylvie assured was '*the right place*.'

"Now, listen," Sylvie explained, "We need to do this right. Voids are fast and feisty, and they've more tricks up their sleeves than I care to admit. So we'll split up. The goal is for *you* to bind it. Guess I shoulda asked before, but you gotta stone, don'tcha?"

Jay nodded, flashing his sleeve with one red gem while the other remained hazy and vacant.

"Good, good. Most times, the bugger'll react to light, so I'll get your little pal there to work me up a few torches. Makes 'em mad, see? They don't care much for the radiance, but it should keep it from bolting. If I can 'old its attention, you come in all quiet-like and *bam*. Done and done."

He reached into his coat for the tenth time, pulling out his pack of smokes. "Mind spottin' me," he asked, holding the cigarette toward a narrow-eyed Blaze.

Blaze puffed one superheated breath, catching both the tobacco alight as well as the sleeve of Sylvie's tattered jacket.

He patted out the embers, took a pull, and continued

205

as if nothing happened, "Biggest thing to watch out for is the vacuum. Pulls the oxygen right out of the air if you get too close, suck it from your lungs and leave you 'eaving for breath. You're gonna need to avoid that if you care to live." He took another lungful and let it trickle out between his lips. "Bugger won't mess around. And in order to avoid it, you'll need to stay unseen. Now, the kicker is, this fella don't 'ave no eyes."

"So how do I stay unseen?" Jay asked, recalling the exact same scenario played out with the formless gravitic virtue during his trial.

"Gonna need to act fast and follow my lead. You'll see me workin' my magic. If I wave you off, get outta there somethin' quick, you 'ear?"

Jay inclined his head, realizing that this would be a more complicated process than he originally suspected.

****

Sylvester and Blaze then collaborated on a set of burning wands with which the void virtue could be occupied while Jay peeled away on the hunt.

Cutting across the bog at an angle, he decided to start his canvassing from the highest point he could find. Just ahead, a small knoll rose up from the stagnant waters like a mossy mountain among various valleys. Planted in its center was something that Jay couldn't quite make out from where he stood. When he drew close enough, however, he thought twice of starting his search there.

****

Intruders beware-
Leave while you still can-

****

A violent chill raised gooseflesh across his arms. He considered again the people that likely scribed that ominous message. Shivering, he hurried away from the lopsided post, afraid of finding yet another trap lying in wait. The slope was treacherous though. He had to slow and plod carefully through the muck, eyes on the slippery slime beneath him. But suddenly, something called to his attention from another nearby rise. He paused, and his breath caught.

Twenty paces away, what appeared to be a cloud of low-lying mist hovered between a pair of cypress saplings. When it drew up into a bubbling orb of white haze, though, Jay knew it for what it was.

Scrambling backward, he spun to find Sylvie and Blaze in action, already having seen the void themselves. Blaze was hunkered atop a musty stump, growling his disapproval at the entire scene while Sylvie pranced ahead, shouting and waving his burning batons. The virtue reacted much as Sylvie said it would, warping and roiling with sudden aggression.

It was bizarre. Proximity to the strange virtue seemed to pull at the air in Jay's throat and wick the heat away from his skin. As if the element of *nothingness* had manifested before him, the void virtue appeared more like a warped segment of space that simply faded into emptiness. There was no color in the center of its agitated body, and yet Jay couldn't fathom how that was true. Everything had color to the human eye, but here, he only stared into oblivion.

But those existential notions could wait. He had to act fast. He had a narrow window. Even if the void kept its attention on the distractors, just the aura that it emitted was enough to siphon his oxygen in seconds. He would have to rush in and make contact all before he passed out.

"What're doing, boy!" Sylvie cried. "Get in there

Steven C. McCullough

and get the blasted thing!"

Jay moved without thinking. Pulling in a deep breath and sealing his lips, he scrambled after the blob. It was all or nothing now. If he didn't bind it, the virtue would be on Sylvie and Blaze in moments.

Fifty feet.

Blaze was barking. A flaming whirlwind rocketed forth from the dog, carving a path between it and the incoming void. It sizzled around the white haze, causing it to stutter in its rush. But Jay stayed on target despite the wave of heat that rippled his vision. He *needed* this virtue. It could change *everything*.

Forty feet.

Sylvie shouted something, but Jay couldn't make out the words for the rushing of the hot wind in his ears. *The vacuum had begun.* It pulled at the air like a black hole, hurricane of force swirling around it. Jay's eyes strained to stay open. Tears dribbled down his face only to fly away to the center of the vortex. It was excruciating, like stepping into the center of space.

Thirty feet.

He felt suddenly *cold*. His whole body seemed to slow, like he was sprinting through a blizzard gust. The heat of Blaze's attack was gone. Vaguely, Jay realized that his own virtue was huddled near Sylvester, succumbing to the effects of the void as surely as he. Reality seemed to fade around them, like a painting submerged in bleach. Jay steeled himself. He would bind this virtue or he would die trying.

Twenty feet.

The virtue was outpacing him now. He wouldn't make it in time. Sylvie and Blaze would be in the heart of the storm long before he could stop it. But Sylvester

208

was no longer there when Jay looked up. And neither was Blaze. Instead, there were three distinct shadows where the pair once stood, torches lying haphazardly on the sodden ground as the only testament to their previous existence.

Ten feet.

He couldn't breathe. He opened his lips, lungs burning for sustenance, but his pull was pointless. He choked on nothingness, chest constricted and screaming at him. He was suffocating. Black sparks flecked the edge of his vision and seemed to close in on the tunnels that remained.

Five.

It was only he and the empty cloud in an endless ocean of black. He reached for it.

Three.

He kicked away from the ground like a lead balloon. This was it. *Could he make it?*

And then time stood still. There was no darkness, no light, *nothing. Jay* was nothing. *The world was nothing. Existence…nothing.* An utter abyss. Emptiness.

Void.

Something had stolen the contents of the world and erased them so completely that even their memory was vanquished. And though it, too, did not truly exist, its *hate* for life echoed in this hollow like a long-intoned song.

Jay could sense it, feel its oppression exuding from an open wound in the dark. He had to escape. He needed to get back somehow. He reached for that tear and struggled to *be* again. But whatever *it* was, it refused him.

It craved his end.

****

Jay shuddered.

"*Come on, son.*"

Something pulled at him, rattled him back and forth until his lids finally fell open.

"*Ah, don't you be dead on me. Come on.*"

There was only an orange blur in his vision at first before it finally solidified into the wavering reeds of a distant fire. He moaned as his senses caught up and relayed the pain from every corner of his body.

"Thank the 'eavens," Sylvester whispered, helping Jay into a sitting position. "Thought you were gone for good, I did."

Jay cradled his throbbing head in both hands, watching as his heart pumped bright flashes through his vision.

"What happened," he mumbled.

"Was gonna ask you the same thing," Sylvie said, continuing to keep his voice low. "Right about the time you went charging in after that void, I was conked on the 'ead somethin' fierce. Woke up with these freaks standing over us."

Jay peered around them for the first time, truly taking in the scene. His panic mounted as he realized that he and Sylvester were sitting in a steel cage the size of a small room. Just on the other side of the rusted bars stood a pair of men dressed in long, patchy robes and holding torches aloft. The campfire beyond them that Jay noted as he woke was surrounded by a series of chatting lookalikes sporting the same drab attire. Though he couldn't understand what they were saying from the distance, the conversation seemed adamant and intense.

"*Where are we?*" Jay asked, suddenly frantic.

"Keep your cool," Sylvie warned, "Don't want more attention than we already got. Looks like those locals spotted us trampin' through their turf and decided they didn't like it so much. Guess this is their little village or what 'ave you."

Jay's eyes met the dark skyline then, finding another alarming fact. "How long was I out?"

Sylvester shrugged. "Dunno really. Several 'ours at the least."

"*We've gotta get outta here!*" he said, scrambling on all four toward the small hatch that was obviously locked. He rattled it anyways as if a miracle would reduce the padlock to ashes. Instead, the noise only drew the ire of the nearest guard who kicked at his fingers.

"Hey! Get back!" he shouted before turning to his companion with a sour grimace.

Jay skittered back to his original perch, unwilling to try his luck again. "*What do we do?*" he asked Sylvester quietly.

"Still tryin' to figure that one out," he answered in kind. "Say, did you ever manage to get the virtue?"

Panic pressed aside for a moment, Jay realized that he wasn't quite sure of that. He lifted his bracer to examine the gems. The red one shone brightly while the one just above it was crystal clear.

"I'm not sure," he started, studying the second of the two. "I mean, it was kinda hazy before, but now it's just like glass."

Sylvie nodded excitedly. "*That's the ticket,*" he said, satisfied look on his face. "Clear for void. You did it, you little devil. *You did it.*"

He patted Jay's shoulder once and turned to survey the camp again. "And don't you worry about your other friend."

He pointed discreetly toward a swathe of shadows wherein a patch of reddish fur could barely be seen. Blaze was hunkered down, watchful red eyes observing them intently.

"Been sitting there ever since I woke myself. Waiting for your word to strike, I'd suppose."

Jay felt sudden relief at the prospect that Blaze had not been caught with them, but his attention was rapidly gravitating to the fact that he had *bound the void*. He never remembered touching it. He could hardly remember anything at this point.

Conspiratorially, he changed directions. "Sylvie, what do you know about using magic? I've never had the chance to do it myself since I summoned Blaze."

"What're you asking me for?" he asked with a frown. "I don't mess with the little menaces. Never bound one myself."

Jay sighed. Though he thought he might be capable of breaking them out with his newfound powers, he had no idea how to call on them in the first place. Little good they would provide if he couldn't control them.

Before he could collaborate with Sylvie further on a plan of action, the voices that were once only unintelligible chatters now became distinct.

"*I'm telling you*, we have to handle this with *care*," the first of the three approaching villagers said to the others.

"You didn't see what we saw, Jerard," the second argued, a woman of middle years. "It was a *clear omen*. If we don't get answers quickly, rumors will spread and we will have a panic on our hands."

"Could you even imagine if two or more roamed the

world again at the same time?" asked the third, an older gentleman that walked with slumped shoulders. "It would be catastrophe on a level that we haven't seen in centuries."

The man named Jerard shook his head. "Just because you *thought* you saw Zero for a *split* second doesn't mean we raise the alarm. The boy simply bound a virtue. You could have witnessed spectral lights, the virtue take a strange shape, *anything*."

The woman tisked. "Would the virtue have grown to fifty times a human's height and bore an uncanny resemblance to Zero? *No.* Think before you speak, Jerard."

Jerard tried to counter again, but she snapped her hand at him in warning. Jay watched it all with a dreamlike sense of remoteness, as if he was seeing a drama production on display for only him. But when the trio stopped before the two guards and all five turned to stare at their prisoners, reality returned to him in force.

"Take them to the Reckoning," the woman ordered. "With the Elder gone, we will assemble the council to decide how to proceed. If there *is* some connection, we will derive it soon enough."

Jerard interrupted his female counterpart again. "This is *not* how Erik would handle this! We should wait for him before we rush to action! Julianne, you know better!"

"He's been gone for six months!" Julianne barked back. "If he was still alive, we would have heard from him! We *must* be proactive to stopping the threat."

She turned back to relay more instructions to the guards, but Jay was no longer focused on her. During their little spat, he spotted Blaze prowling closer from behind them, firelight flickering off his crimson fur.

Then it all happened in a flash. Blaze rocketed through the crowd, knocking three of the five off their feet and sending embers burning into their robes. The guard with the key fell closest to the bars, and Jay reached almost instinctively for the jingling wad of brass. Sylvester was on his feet then too, hand poking through the gap to grab onto the remaining guard's collar. With a forceful jerk, the man's head met the steel cage and he slumped to his fellow's side.

In the confusion, Jay managed to slip the lock and pummel his way through the flailing mass of arms and legs. Sylvie was right on his heel, swatting hard at anyone who stood in his way. Shouts trailed after them, then cries of pain as Blaze roared back through the squadron on fire.

Jay slid and stumbled through the soggy grounds, dodging tall stone monoliths, pools of muck, and the occasional unaware villager. As he passed more and more tents and assembly yards, he realized that the place looked too-much like a sanctimonious killing ground where victims such as he would be hauled into public witness before being sacrificed and subsequently eaten. He gained speed even as he considered that.

Blaze darted out beside him, seeming a small comfort for a time until he cut across Jay's path in order to dodge a lunging captor. Jay tripped over the careless mutt, tumbling end over end into one of the many ancient pillars that sprouted from the swampy grounds. As he stood again, cursing, to continue his race into the night, he hesitated long enough to note a strange and imaginative mural painted onto the side of the stone surface. A large monster represented as something decaying and rotten, skeletal frame showing beneath its sluffing skin, reached out over a group of people throwing spears into its fetid hide. There were other beings too, smaller but just as disgustingly decomposed as their larger cohort. It was a battle of some sort depicted in faded acrylic colors.

He was unable to consider it further as Sylvie caught up, snatched him by the collar, and dragged him back into motion. A mob of shouting men and women in grisly dark robes were close on their tails.

"Run, boy, *run!*"

Jay didn't need any more coercion. He high-stepped after his comrade, guards and villagers chasing and shouting and tossing lines of nets and ropes to trip them up. But their collective fear added too much speed for the throngs to pin down, and in short and breathless minutes, they were stumbling through the dark of the swamp alone. Torchlight faded, shouts died away, and all returned to a sickly silence.

Jay propped up against a moss-draped trunk, catching his breath and letting his eyes adjust to the night. Sylvie stopped just short of him, pulling first on the evening air and then on the butt of another cigarette.

Coughing twice, he spoke, "I…I think we lost 'em."

Jay, unsure where their fiery savior had gotten off to, searched the stagnant landscape for any sign of Blaze. The muck-covered mutt pranced up to them, displaying himself in heroic glory. If he was expecting a parade in his honor, though, the moment sorely disappointed. Jay swiped a hand across his head, ruffling his matted fur, while Sylvester only growled something that sounded like '*thanks.*' Receiving his meager dues, Blaze huffed and moseyed off.

"That was insane," Jay started, still reeling from the shock of it all. "What do you think they were going to do to us? And what were they talking about? *Zero*? What's that? *And that huge painting*."

Seemingly unfazed by the myriad questions, Sylvie sucked another smoggy breath in and answered, "Don't know, don't care to know. We best be on the move, though. Stick close to me and we'll get back to Eff double-time."

Jay only nodded, mind still churning over the pile of unfiltered information. As they trudged back toward town, he fell into a trance of contemplation. Trusting Sylvie to lead the way and call out any dangers, he allowed himself to process everything that had happened since leaving Effervescence what seemed like only hours ago.

He had bound another virtue. And not just any virtue—this one a *void*. It was unprecedented. No person in all of Glendale could boast such a find. And though that held some negative connotations—specifically that he had *no idea* how to call on void magic or what it even looked like—he was thrilled to be one step closer to his goal with one of the rarer types that was sure to have eluded him long-term.

Another interesting factor that he could not ignore was Blaze's actions during their brief captivity. Despite having shown little gratitude to the virtue, Jay realized that Blaze—frustrating as he had so often been during their past few weeks together—might actually be warming up to him. He didn't have to *request* the aid this time or anything. Of his own volition, Blaze mounted the rescue operation that quite likely saved their lives.

Looking down to the plodding lump of red and

brown in the scattered moonlight, Jay whispered, *"Thanks, buddy. You really saved our hides."*

If the confession swayed the virtue to a lighter mood, it didn't show, but Jay was happy at least to verbalize his appreciation before it had become a point of contention between them.

But his mind quickly returned to the conversation held by the arguing villagers and the thread of conspiracy that it seemed to tug free. They *saw something* when he bound the void. And the dream he had—it was slowly coming back to him in waves—the one of sheer emptiness, everything drained away from the world. It brought shivers across his skin.

What was this '*Zero*' they mentioned? Julianne, the feisty and seemingly-in-charge woman, said it was *fifty times a human's height*. Jay envisioned the mountains moving in the Cliffs of Ascent, the enormous being there coming to crash down upon them. Could that have been this *Zero* they were speaking of? And if so, why had they seen it when he bound the virtue?

Too many questions and not enough answers.

****

Sylvie emerged into a hollow of moonlit marsh just ahead of Jay, and together, they stopped for another breather. He plopped onto a swollen stump that collapsed slightly beneath his weight. Jay, opting for a sturdier seat along the way, dropped down and found the chance to gather an answer to at least one of the questions he had been mulling over.

"Sylv, what's a *vice*?"

The old man looked up, fingers once twiddling with a match coming to a rest.

"You mentioned it before, in the bar. I don't know

what that term means."

Sylvester drew a deep breath and blew it back into the night. The fog of it rolled through the chill air, framing his weathered face. "Can't give you an educated answer to that, son, but I can tell you a story."

Jay inclined his head, leaning forward. He was eager for *anything* that might shine a light on his recent discoveries.

"My pa told me this when I was a wee lad. Passed it on like a family 'eirloom. Told me never forget it."

He struck the match against the cuticle of his nail, waving the small flame across the cigarette perched on his lip. Blaze sidled up to him then as if the small fire was a beacon of familiarity in the dank darkness. Sylvie eyed the dog warily before continuing.

"Long time ago, the world didn't look like it does today. Instead of one great big mass of land, there were several smaller ones. See, we got what they call a Pangaea, a single continent where all the people of the world live. Broken up into countries, yeah, but you could walk one end to the other if you got the time. But before, the ocean was in between it all. 'ad to use big boats to get from one piece to the next. Anyways."

He drew another deep lungful of acidic fumes. "Said to me '*son, virtues weren't always around.*' Said they came from somewhere else, like an invasion of sorts."

"Like *aliens*?" Jay interrupted with a skeptical smirk.

"*Eh,*" Sylvie grumbled, waving at his flippancy. "Not from another planet or anything, just…not exactly from 'ere. When they came at first, it was just like this *strange phenomenon*, all of 'em formless like a buncha floating colors. Folks thought they were pretty and all but basically 'armless. Went on like that for years, it did, but after a time, the virtues started taking shape into the creatures of the wild and into strange renditions of other stuff. Every chunk of land, all over this big ol' ball, the little beasties started popping up, and eventually, the first one of their siblings came—"

"The first *vice*?" Jay inserted.

"Yup." The tip of his cigarette flared with orange light again before he went on, "Big ol' nasty fiend 'e was, bent on destroying the world. Like the size of a mountain 'e came down and started ransackin' 'ole cities, killin' folks left and right. And not just 'im, but all the little virtues came runnin' to 'is call. What folks thought to be peaceful little pretties ended up bein' their killers."

Jay felt his breath catch at the explanation, sure that what Sylvester was referencing was the very same thing that he and Wade had witnessed in the Cliffs. He leaned precariously close to the edge of his seat as the story continued.

"So powerful this vice was that 'e summoned all the 'elp of his little minions and *pulled* at the world. And *whoosh*!" Sylvie clapped his hands, causing Blaze and Jay both to jump. "What was once many lands came collidin' together to make one. It was the end of civilization. Those that survived couldn't fight back. They watched their cities fall as more and more of these little buggers infested and tore it all down."

He stared bitterly at Blaze then as if he was one of the many instigators of this fantastical history. But even as Jay tried to explain it all away, sure of Sylvester's cracked mind, he realized that he couldn't so easily dismiss the tale. In fact, he had never before heard of or studied any history of this world farther back than a few hundred years. That had never really bothered him, but now it was like a burning coal in his gut.

Could this man be telling the truth, however altered and twisted it might be for the years? Could beings called *vices* have ruined the world in eons past?

"So what happened then? How did the earth survive?" he asked, sure that he sounded like a toddler at the mercy of a tall tale.

"Well," Sylvie picked up, "Turns out the first titan wasn't the only one. More came after 'im. But the folks what survived found somethin' awful useful in the rubble brought up from the big land movement. Luck 'ad it that they stumbled on a goldmine of those little stones you got right there." He pointed his smoldering stub of tobacco toward Jay's sleeve.

"Binder's stones?"

"Yup. Somehow, they figured out they could capture the little minions by making contact with 'em and the rocks. Don't ask me 'ow they experimented on that, but I reckon a few brave souls were out there tryin' everything they could. Pa never did know the rest of the story word-for-word, but essentially, they found a way to fight back and best the vices. Course, they 'ad a lotta rebuildin' to do after that, which is why the world don't 'ave more cities than it does now, I reckon. But the lesson is that these fellas ain't our *friends* or our *pets*. They're our *enemies*. Quite nearly our executioners if the story is to be believed."

He stared at Blaze again, disgust evident on his shadowed face. Blaze didn't return the look, and Jay wondered at the sudden submissiveness that he had witnessed twice between the dog and Sylvie, almost as if a certain shame was hiding there.

"But at the bar," Jay redirected, "You made it sound like these vices could be back? Do you think...that they'll return or something?"

Sylvie wrung the cigarette butt against the moldy trunk and tossed it into the nearby marsh. "Dunno, really. Pa always said I should keep my guard up. Taught me to be ready for anything. Guess I just can't 'elp but worry that the fightin' ain't over."

He stood, stretched his limbs with groans of ache, and waved a wrinkled hand. "Enough chattin'. Let's get back to Eff. I'm ready for a beer and some sleep."

Jay stood and followed wordlessly. Blaze, still awry in his demeanor, trudged along, and more than anything, that seemed to drive the story home.

He considered afresh as they plodded through the muck back toward the low glow of city lights whether he should share his encounter with Sylvester or not. On one hand, the old man might be the only one who would believe him, but on the other, he was afraid of tying his wagon to the town outcast. If the people around Effervescence knew that he was in cahoots with Sylvester's worldview, he would likely find himself ostracized the same, and he couldn't let that happen.

He needed more information, and, most importantly, he needed to press on toward Godsreach. If something called a vice really did return to the world to wreak havoc again, it would be undeniable in itself. Striving to warn people of it ahead of time—even if they *would* listen—likely wouldn't make much of a difference in the destructive outcome.

But what about Estelia.

If they had been warned of the potential existence of some super-powerful being hanging around the Cliffs of

Ascent and its ability to summon countless mineral virtues to assault, would that have been enough to save even one life?

Jay ran a hand through his tangled hair, stomach roiling with fear and anxiety. He had no idea, but he wasn't sure that he was equipped to play hero or town-crier or anything for that matter.

'*Just focus on what's ahead*,' he coached himself.

And right now, the only thing ahead of him was a safezone from the creeps that almost ate him.

****

Wade was standing at the door to Rambler's Reprieve when Jay, Sylvester, and Blaze wandered up. They were covered in mud, slime, sweat, and a collective layer of exhaustion. It was a sorry sight, Jay knew, but Wade appeared to care only for their return.

"Where have you been?!" he practically shouted for the district to hear.

Talia, apparently hovering just inside the doorway, rushed out at the commotion. With glaring looks at all three, she skidded to a stop on Jay's apologetic smile. But even as the bartender's lip quivered toward a smile of her own, she planted a firm slap across his cheek, following it up with a kick at Sylvester's shin. Then she stormed back into the tavern leaving all four—Wade included—dumbstruck.

"What was that about?" Wade finally asked after a long silence.

Jay shook his head, mouth still agape and stinging.

"Talia's a sensitive lass," Sylvester offered, though the defense was lacking.

He moseyed past the two, angling after her, but Jay had a feeling it was not in an effort to console. The sour pitch of alcohol lingered in the air, calling the old man to partake.

Wade looked to Jay once more. "Okay, so what happened? I woke up alone, wandered around Eff pretty much all day looking for you, and suddenly you show up smelling like you went for a dip in the sewage pit."

Jay sighed, found a seat on a bench just outside the doorway, and spilled his guts. When the tale had been exchanged in full, all the bizarre details laid bare for Wade, there was only a stunned quiet left between them. Before Wade could work up some appropriate response, Jay stood again and waved Blaze inside.

"Going to get a shower. Could you spot the host for another night? I'll meet you for a bite to eat in twenty."

Wade, still agog, simply nodded and watched as the two muck-monsters clopped through the foyer, leaving trails of grime in their wake.

****

Shucked to his skivvies, Jay wrestled the filthy Blaze into submission beneath a wave of water in the tub. The dog barked and howled and spat fiery bolts at him, but Jay was relentless.

"*You…need to…get clean!*" he growled back at the obstinate virtue as they struggled. "*I'm not…paying for…your mess!*"

The clear liquid soon turned a milky brown, and by the time Jay was satisfied enough to let the dog out, the water was darker than a chunk of chocolate. Blaze shook the deluge from his coat, shot a scathing look at Jay, and bolted.

Clearing the tub, Jay took his turn, savoring the hot lines of cleansing moisture on his skin. When he could hardly find the shower curtain for the wall of steam

Steven C. McCullough

floating through the room, he cut the water off and decided to don some of his laundered and dried clothing.

Blaze, still infuriated at the mistreatment, avoided him as he emerged back into the bedroom.

"Come on, we need to go check on Talia."

Blaze's head peaked up above the bed, glowing red eyes fixed on him in protest.

"I know you don't *want to*, but you're coming anyway."

Blaze didn't move, so Jay did, coming in for another harassing grapple. As if conceding defeat, the virtue leaped across the bed and hovered by the door, refusing to look at him again.

"You're like a little kid." Jay huffed, returning to lead the way back out into the foyer.

****

Wade was just where he was told to be, sitting at the bar top, carrying a quiet conversation with Talia when Jay walked in. There was a quick flurry of words before he was close enough to hear, and then the pair fell silent.

"Talking about me?" Jay asked, pulling out a seat next to Wade.

Blaze pounced into it before he could plant his rear, finding at least a small way to win a victory over his master. Jay shook his head drolly and took another.

"Maybe," Wade answered with a smirk, but Talia only turned away.

"Wait—Talia," Jay stopped her.

He reached across the bar to touch her arm. She hesitated, looking down at his receding fingertips and then to him. There was an anger in those eyes that Jay honestly couldn't justify. He barely knew the girl, and yet she seemed to vehemently hold fault against his

224

daylong antics with Sylvester. But behind that anger was a sadness that couldn't be missed. And Jay started to suspect that he knew the reasons.

"Listen…I'm sorry if I worried you guys. Sylvie just offered to take me out and I had never seen this place before so I—"

"So you risked your life for *what*?" Talia interrupted. "A little stroll through the swamps? Do you even know what lives out there? How *dangerous* it is?"

Jay met her crystalline eyes, watching a mist grow in their corners. "I do. Sylvester warned me of it all, and we came back just fine. See?" He prodded his body as if showing that there were no signs of damage. And even though that strange, lingering pain from the void-dream flashed as he made a show of it all, he held a straight face.

Talia let her eyes fall. "I know. *I'm just—*"

"I know, too," Jay said, saving her the explanation. With a smile as bright as he could muster, he asked, "How about some of Parlum's famous food? I don't know about Wade here, but I'm starved."

Though it took a moment to catch, she eventually relented, grin growing on her face and now playful once more.

"I'll get right on it." She moved to the swinging kitchen door and stopped. "Glad you're okay…Jay the Rambler."

****

They spent the rest of the evening chatting amiably with Talia, Wade offering quips and jabs at Jay's expense while Blaze only seemed to egg it on with his punchline barks. Jay let them have it, though, happy for the time that things seemed to be looking up.

Despite the lingering pressure of the questions surrounding vices and Estelia's doom, Jay found his second of twelve virtues bound, another friend made, and laughter the theme amongst it all. Sylvester even joined them, reparations and apologies made to the beautiful barkeep, and Jay was happy to have another to add to the festivity.

When the evening wound down and most patrons scattered to their homes or rooms in the inn, Wade pulled Jay to the side.

"*Well*?" he asked vaguely.

"Well, what?" Jay whispered in kind.

"Oh, don't give me that," Wade smarted, "*Talia*. She's definitely into you!" He smacked Jay's chest. "Make a move!"

Jay snorted. "No way, she's just being nice. She's like this with all her customers."

Wade looked pointedly back to the bar as Talia stuck a finger in Sylvester's face and tore into him about something that they couldn't hear.

"Okay, so Sylvie's a different case, but so what? Even if there was a spark between us, what am I supposed to do? I'm not staying in Eff, Wade. You know that."

Wade sighed. "Bro, you are the most painfully dull person I've ever met. I would give my left leg for a chance with that woman! Look at her!"

He grabbed Jay by the base of the neck and spun his head back to the bar. Talia noticed and smiled, the image like something angelic despite the atmosphere. She waggled her fingers in a spirited wave before turning to swat Blaze away from the countertop he was stealthily crawling onto, basket of fries in his sight ready to be knocked askew.

Wade let him go. "You're going to give *that* up?"

Jay felt his heart flutter. "I...Wade, you know that I—"

"I know you wanna bind them all," Wade interrupted. With a mournful lament in his tone, he conceded, "But if you don't learn to stop and enjoy the things in front of you, you're going to miss the whole reason for this trip."

"That *is* the reason for this trip," Jay argued.

"No, it's not!" Wade countered. "Whether you want to admit it or not, this trip is about us becoming *men*. Traveling the world, experiencing everything it has to offer...and that *includes* capturing all twelve virtues. You gotta think bigger, man. What's gonna happen when you finally accomplish it but you've got no one left to celebrate with?"

Jay looked at Talia again, feeling that flutter in his chest return. Wade had a point. This was becoming something greater than just his self-prescribed goal, and yet he knew that he couldn't let himself catch an anchor just yet. Talia was brilliant and there was definitely something there, but was she the end to his journey? It wouldn't be fair to share an evening of romance with her if his intentions were to up and leave. Just like her father.

"I'm just not the ladies' man like you, I guess," he said flatly.

Wade could hear the defeat in his voice. "All right, all right. But I'm not poaching her from you, bro. Who knows where this *wild whirlwind* will take us?"

He attempted to show off by making a series of napkins float through the air. They scattered across the floor, earning a pick-them-up glare from behind the bar.

"Eff might bring us back around again, and you might get a second chance."

****

They cut up for a little while longer before Talia declared that she had to wrap it up. Sylvester stumbled out, waving his final goodbyes to Jay and Wade and wishing them luck on their travels. Jay wondered if he would ever see the old man again, and if he did, whether Sylvie would try to carry him on another crazy hunt for a virtue that was once, and perhaps even now, their *enemy*.

Wade, ever the romantic, grabbed up a snapping Blaze and declared that he was headed back to the room to crash. As he left the two alone, though, Jay knew better. He would likely be waiting just outside to catch the scoop on how well—or awful—Jay had made his parting.

Jay and Talia stared at one another for a time, grins still gleaming foolishly on their faces, before Jay broke in, "Kinda wish I could stay."

"Kinda wish you could too," she said softly. "You'll be safe?"

Jay bobbed his head. "I'll try my best." After a brief and awkward quiet, he cast his gambit, "I like you, Talia."

Her smile grew by a degree. "I like you too, *Jay the Rambler*."

"Maybe," Jay started, considering Wade's words from earlier, "Maybe I'll be back around some—"

He was cut off abruptly as Talia leaned across the counter and planted her lips on his.

Jay's world ignited.

There were colors and sounds and lights like he had

228

never seen before in his life. He thought he might have had a heart attack, but when Talia pulled away to watch him with a quirked brow, he found that there was still a thrum of life in his chest, however rapid it might be.

"Maybe you will," she said quietly. "And maybe *that* will give you one more reason to."

****

Jay stepped torpidly into the bedroom, head still spinning. Twice now, he had been kissed. Unprepared and unsuspecting both times. And the only other common factor was that he had been readying himself to leave both women in a place he knew he could not stay. His heart swam in his chest, though, desires mounting and convincing him otherwise.

He *could* stay here.

Get a small house, get a job. He could court Talia, make something of this romance.

"So?" Wade's voice rocketed into his ears.

Jay looked up to find him sitting on the edge of his bed, grin nearly splitting his face in two.

"Yeah," Jay answered.

"*Oh, man*," Wade exclaimed, "Give me the details. I can see it on your face!"

Jay, still flush with the aftereffects, took a seat across the aisle from his curious friend. "I mean, well…we kissed."

Blaze perked up from beneath a blanket then, gaining a curious stare of his own. Wade laughed.

"That's it? Oh, you gotta do better than that!"

"Well, *she* kinda kissed me. I just sat there."

"*Oof*," Wade breathed. "Okay, okay. That's not exactly a terrible thing. We can redeem this. Some girls find the flustered look cute and endearing. So then what?"

"Then we talked some more, and I left," Jay admitted dismally.

Wade wiped at his face, groaning. "Dude, you are the *literal worst*."

"We can't all be perfect like you," Jay retorted, wits finally coming back to him. "Besides, I don't see you out there killing it."

"*Oh ho*," Wade sounded. "Is someone challenging me? Man, I gave you the rope and walked away. If I had laid on the charm, me and Talia might be getting another room." He flicked his eyebrows.

"*Pshh*," Jay hissed with a smile. "So full of yourself." He fell back into the blankets, wrapping himself up and clicking out his lamp.

"Okay, so here's how this goes," Wade started, "Arken Isles. You and me. First one to make the kiss wins. Any girl, any way it happens; we just can't buy it."

"Buy it?" Jay asked.

"Yeah man, no money included. No fancy dinners, no begging to swap a buck for the win. Gotta *earn* the kiss."

"Sounds a little shallow," Jay chimed.

"Ah, no worse than you making Talia swoon then skipping town." Wade leaned over with that biting smirk to click his light.

"That's not fair, and you know it!"

Wade chuckled and then the room fell quiet for a time.

"*Void*, huh?" he eventually called out into the dark.

"Yeah," Jay answered with like wonder.

"What do you think it'll do?"

"Only one way to find out."

Chapter 9

The next six days were spent largely on a nonstop march from Effervescence to the fore of Arken Isles. Though this stretch was considerably more pleasant than their trek through the Cliffs of Ascent, the trio was already morose and miserable by the second evening. The pampered lifestyle of the Rambler's Reprieve reminded them of all that they had left behind when choosing to chase the wind like this.

With over one hundred miles to travel between cities, and little else to do but complain and succumb to the paranoia of unreal monsters, cannibalistic hunters, and every other imaginable threat to their lives, both Wade and Jay took ample time to practice their magical abilities in preparation for the worst.

Wade managed considerable progress by the fourth night. He could forge gusts strong enough to blow Jay off his feet or summon a plethora of dust-whipping whirlwinds in the blink of an eye. Jay applauded his developing acuity, knowing that the skills would provide protection to them both, but he couldn't help but sulk a little on his own behalf. His sessions proved much less effective.

He had been able to discern the general concept of void virtues and their inherent magics by delving through one of the books he bought on the subject before leaving Eff. But knowing and doing weren't exactly the same thing. There was a moment when he was able to pull on the air around him much as the wild virtue had when creating its defensive perimeter, but after experiencing the same sensation of suffocation as he had the first time, he opted to *never* do that again. If his goal was to protect himself and fend off any attackers, dying to his own defense wasn't a solid plan. Needless to say, the gained magic that was once so alluring quickly lost its appeal.

The text offered that popular practices were often tied with absorptive techniques such as what he attempted—dwindling forces and draining kinetic energies away—but Jay couldn't seem to create anything more than the self-destructive vacuum. He needed a teacher, someone who could guide him if only a little. With a solitary book as his mentor—one that didn't even cover the practical applications of void magic—Jay had simply gained a pretty binder's bauble and the second mark on his twelve-slot goal. Progress was progress, he supposed.

By the time the first signs of sunlit water glittered in the distance, he was ready to forget it all for a dip. Arken Isles, according to his digital map and its info pod, was an incorporation of four distinct islands that dotted the Ark Waterway—an enormous river that ran from the high hills of Tier One to the lowlands of western Tier Two before spilling into the sea.

Each island had its own *mini-culture*, so it said, but the namesake of Arken Isles was considered to include all four territories. Jay and Wade expected to find a conglomerate of lifestyles tossed into the melting-pot of the metropolis. Judging by the characters they had encountered so far in their journey, they weren't sure if that prospect was exciting or otherwise.

There were ferries that could carry them from one to the next, and Wade made it clear that they *were not* rushing this point of their trip. He wanted to tour and see each Isle before they ventured on, sure that he would find his winning kiss waiting on one of them.

"We should try to find that guy first, don't you think?" Wade said as the main bridge came into view.

A gargantuan gate hovered there, carved into the swathe of dappled stone like a giant's doorway hewn from a natural connection in the land. There was a dam stationed just beneath it, feeding off of the flow of the river. Massive turbines whirred in deceptively slow rotations. Jay could feel the buzz of generated electricity in the air.

"What guy?" he asked, sidling past a group of workers busy with what appeared standard maintenance of the bridge.

"*You know*," Wade rambled, "The guy the headmaster mentioned. What was his name?"

It came back to Jay in a flash. "Pierre Kabolt."

"That's the one," Wade said, holding up a finger.

Jay thought back on that odd conversation with Walter von Quake what seemed like months ago now. If he admitted, Jay would say that he had let it slip his mind in lieu of more pressing matters since, but now that he considered it again, it still chafed.

"Yeah, I kinda want some answers about all that," he confessed.

"What, about how Walter was being weird that night?"

"Exactly," Jay replied, "Let's see if we can hunt this guy down first thing. Then we take your grand tour."

They slowed to a stop behind a gaggle of teenagers

chirping on about some research project done in the day. Wade leaned against the weather-worn railing, waiting for the guards to swing wide the gates for the growing crowd. Jay joined him there and had to take a moment to catch his breath.

Leaning out over a two-story drop to the roiling waves, he thought that he had never seen a more beautiful sight in his life. Like a cerulean ribbon stretching from an eternity distant, the Ark Waterway snaked up toward the sundown horizon and into sight unseen. The second of the four Isles could be spotted just before the red radiance of the reflective flow stole the rest from view.

When Wade called his name, he hardly budged for it, but the creaking of the gate sliding open finally did the trick. He came away from his trance with wide eyes, staring into a new sight, less inspiring but something he would likely never forget. The streets beyond split from the edge of the island inward in a dozen different directions. They were each dotted with townhouses and shops and gazebos that all bared the brightest colors in the rainbow. Jay felt a wash of vertigo at the eye-twisting mix.

He fell in beside Wade, Blaze tarrying along with less eager stride. The virtue seemed to care little for their return to civilization, but to be frank, he had seemed to care little for just about everything since Jay bound him.

"Look at this place!" he exclaimed.

Wade wiped at his glassy gaze. "I've never seen so many colors in my *life*. It's kinda making my head spin."

Jay flicked his eyes from the yellow rooftop of one home to the brilliant blue bricks of another. The street itself was like a purple-pebbled roadway, resembling some kind of fanciful child's toy. But the colors didn't stop there. Even the people that wandered the city sidewalks were dressed down in flares of pinks and greens and golds. It was as if the aforementioned child decided to paint her toys and imagination into existence with an eclectic mix of whatever hues were on hand. Even the two guards ushering them in wore uniforms of the deepest mauve, broken only by badges of shining silver.

Wade stopped at the first of the pair. "Do you guys happen to know someone by the name Pierre...uhm...what was it again?"

"Kabolt," Jay cued.

"Right. Pierre Kabolt?"

The man bobbed his head once. "Master Kabolt lives on this Isle. You'll find his residence up the steps from the promenade and at the highest point overlooking the water. Can't miss it."

Wade gave their thanks and took the lead.

"*Master* Kabolt, huh?" Jay said, wondering what the prefix might mean.

"What if he's like a martial arts master and Walter sent us to him to get our tails kicked?" Wade groped at his backside as if he had just received one such kicking.

"Well, he didn't seem very happy with us, did he?" Jay answered.

About that time, Blaze chose to break away from them and accost a group of old men tossing their marketing lines into the crowd. One was shouting about having the best prices on fish in town, and apparently Blaze either thought he was lying or didn't like him raising such a ruckus for the matter. He barked in series and chased the old man until he ran, screaming curses, back into his shop. Satisfied, Blaze turned to give warning to the other shouters, watched them cower, and returned to Jay's side.

"*What are you doing!*" Jay seethed, kicking at Blaze's tail. "You're gonna get us thrown out!"

Blaze waggled his rear at Jay and scurried ahead, clearly content to know that he had struck a nerve. Jay groaned and watched him chase down another couple who were setting off fireworks into the air over the water.

"That dog is going to get us killed one of these days...*or worse.*" Wade whimpered.

"Worse?" Jay asked, curious what could be worse than *death*.

"Yeah, what if he runs off the girl of my dreams or gets in the way of my win." He flashed a grin.

"You have a *problem*," Jay replied flatly.

****

They strolled the boardwalk for the next twenty minutes, stopping occasionally to peek into merchant stalls and shops. They were continuously assailed by every imaginable color and sound. The people were as exuberant as their attire, eager to greet the trio despite Blaze's standoffish nature. But his summoned state didn't seem to bother them, and Jay caught himself wondering if one of their cultural norms included baring virtues back into the world.

Just as Jay took the first few steps into an enormous arena paved with orange and black river stones, a group of six misfits brushed by him, knocking him into Wade. Wade spun to sling snark, but he paused when he noticed the rowdy group on the other side. Blaze gave his best menacing snarl as the late teens pranced into the promenade, unaware or uncaring of their intrusion.

Jay noted that the large-and-in-charge guy, dressed down in dark leather with only silver chains to accent, looked *nothing* like the others on this island. He slid up next to a girl in the group, tossing an arm across her shoulder and saying something rather rude that drew laughs from all but her. The girl, same age and similarly clad, shrugged away from him and shook her raven hair. It swished out in languid lines, barely revealing a face that shared too many features with the comic to make her anything other than a sister. As if she realized that Jay's eyes were tracing her lithe curves from neck to foot, she cast a glance back over her shoulders to pin him where he stood.

Jay jerked his vision away, but the damage was done. Wade nudged him with an elbow.

"*She's hot*," he said blatantly, refusing to peel his own appreciative eyes off her.

When Jay snuck another peek, he caught the girl and two of her friends giggling before turning a corner out of their view.

"*Target in sight*," Wade cooed, rubbing his palms together hungrily.

Jay rolled his eyes. Despite Wade's proverbial tossing of the gauntlet, he had no intention of tangling himself up in another dead-end romance.

"Wipe that drool off your chin," he called to a lingering Wade, "There's the staircase."

Wade spun back to see Jay's point and joined him. "You're missing the sights, my man," he said with a dramatic sigh. "What did I say about rushing this?"

"I know, I know," Jay appeased. "But we need a base of operations if we plan on conquering the whole city before we split." He pointed up toward the top of the mountainous climb. "Let's see what *Master Kabolt* has to offer."

They trudged up the incline, breaths heaving by the time they mounted the final step.

"You'd think we'd be in better shape by now," Wade complained.

Jay opted to save his words since they would expend the precious little oxygen reaching his lungs. Blaze bounded past them both, though, unfazed and lively. Jay reached out to wordlessly reprimand the beast, but when his eyes fell on the structure Blaze was hurrying toward, he stopped.

As claimed, the building stood ever-watch over the Ark Waterway in sunlit splendor, a mansion of such grand proportions that Jay wondered if this Pierre Kabolt might be the mayor or the ruler of the whole city. Its whitewashed walls reached up high over every other peak in viewable distance. Large palm trees decorated the front lawn, casting slanted shade over the roadway and giving Jay a feeling of tropical wonder. White sand rimmed their trunks, but it was not natural by appearance, as its grainy reach only extended to a border of weathered wood that separated it from the loamy soil beyond. A lush green grass sprouted just on the other side, stretching around the building as another border of its own.

Jay stepped furtively closer to the apparent palace of Arken Isles, eyes jumping from beauty to beauty in its proximity. Wade sauntered past him toward the door, though, apparently not as perplexed by the grandeur as he was. He rapped twice on the ornate wood façade and waited.

Blaze sniffed at a particularly strange-looking flower as they waited for an answer that didn't come. Wade pecked at the portal again, tapping an impatient foot. Still nothing.

"Maybe he's out to—" Jay started, but Blaze interrupted with a growl that could match the roaring of thunder.

Jay turned to face whatever had the virtue stirred up and found an old man dressed down in white robes stained with grass and dirt. His hands were empty save for a pluck of root that he had apparently just snatched from the nearby ground. Jay looked beyond him to see a small garden stretching around the north side of the building.

"Who are you and what are you doing here?" the old man grumbled, casting a suspicious gaze between the trio before landing on the still-rumbling Blaze.

Wade scrunched his face. "You Pierre Kabolt?"

Jay sighed, opting to offer a mite more courtesy than his friend. "We were told to find Pierre Kabolt. We're just passing through Arken Isles."

The old man scrutinized them, tossing the root in his hands to the ground and folding his arms. "I'm Pierre. Who sent you?"

If Jay thought the experience would be easy or the man accommodating, he sorely misjudged the matter. "Look, we're not here for trouble," he started.

"Walter told us to find you if we came this way," Wade finished.

The man's eyes suddenly caught another level of suspicion, this time bordering outright hostility. "Walter? *Walter von Quake* sent you?"

Jay nodded, mentally willing the man to remain

calm. "We're from Glendale. The Academy. Walter was our headmaster."

Blaze's growl tapered off in perfect time, further reducing the tension. Jay looked back to find him, once again, preoccupied with sniffing things as if the entire exchange had never occurred.

"I'm Jay and this is Wade. We just graduated. Wanted to take a trip to get away from Glendale for a while, and the headmaster just mentioned that if we ever made it here to look you up."

Hoping that the simplification was enough, he looked to Wade and they together turned back to see Pierre's reaction. The old man appeared conflicted for a time, quietly deciding whether he should eject them from his premises or invite them in. Just when Jay was going to add more to his plea, Pierre spoke.

"How long?"

Wade was the first to respond this time. "How long *what*?"

"How long has it been since you left?" Pierre clarified with obvious disgust at having to explain the question.

"Um," Jay started, counting the days they had been on the road, "A little over two weeks? Eighteen days I think."

Pierre's expression softened, if only a little. He sighed, letting all the stiffness bleed out of his rigid posture. "Come on in."

And just like that, his curiosities were sated and his hospitality offered. He sidled past a bewildered Wade and pressed through the doorway, leaving it standing ajar. Though Jay and Wade both were still too perplexed by the encounter to accept the summons, Blaze leaped up the marbled steps and sprang right in. Wade finally shrugged and followed suit, leaving Jay as the single remaining guest still out on the lawn.

When he finally managed to clear the daze, he entered behind the rest to hear a new bark, this one not from his aggressive virtue.

"Get out of those clothes."

Jay turned to Wade, sure that the command had come from Pierre but not seeing him anywhere. Wade flashed a wary look, and Jay silently agreed that they must have both misheard.

Pierre came back around a corner. "Well?" he asked heatedly. "Drop the clothes! Now!"

Wade's hand instinctively moved to cover his delicate portions while Jay only backed away, fearful that they had entered the home of some sick stranger at their headmaster's behest.

Pierre growled and shook his head, apparently thinking them stunted. "You're not coming in this house looking like that!" He gestured to the filth and dust coating them both like a blanket. Extending an armful of robes, he tried again, "Leave those clothes at the door, and put these on."

Jay took the pile with fresh comprehension, and Pierre simply grumbled as he turned to stalk away. He looked to Wade.

"Not the greeting I expected, *but*."

Wade wiggled his head, exasperated. "I'm not cool with this, man. How bout we just go find an inn or something?"

"He's not gonna...*do anything* to us," Jay defended. "Besides, if Walter mentioned him, I think we should find out why."

Wade shivered visibly. "All right, but this guy goes in for anything funny, and I'm gonna drop him, you hear?" He took the proffered robe from Jay. "Old creep…ain't about to." he mumbled as he warily shucked his socks and shorts.

Once both of them had slipped into their robes and felt the luscious caress of its soft fabric, though, their collective mood lightened.

"*Soft as silk,*" Wade stated, suddenly aligned with the idea of staying a little while longer.

Jay grabbed Blaze as he tried to slip past, ran his hands rapidly through the dog's fur to free it of dust and debris at the doorstep, and let the ruffled virtue free again to his mischief.

"Come on," he beckoned to Wade. "I think he went this way."

They stepped into a long hallway with dim lighting, striding lightly on the cold stone tilework. To Jay's left was a row of pictures, most capturing unique landscapes and various virtues that he stopped to enjoy. He was once again reminded of the bizarre shapes and sizes that the spirits took in this world, oftentimes mimicking something natural only to morph and tweak the design to their liking. Blaze was a star example of that, canine in general form but in all other ways, nothing like the species.

His eyes caught another set of frames as he continued, and this time, both he and Wade stopped to study them for the familiar face within. Though much younger than the man they left behind in Glendale, Walter von Quake stood side-by-side with a group of four others, a younger Pierre among them. They all smiled up at the cameraman, spry and inexperienced.

Three men and two women, each of them lively in their youth.

From picture to picture, frame to frame, Jay witnessed the five in both serious stances and goofy moods. A woman not much older than he rode piggyback on Walter's shoulders in the next-to-last photo, grinning wildly as her mount sprinted through the image in a blur. It all seemed surreal to Jay, that the man he had so often thought of as mysterious and reserved had lived another life, obviously fun and free.

As they emerged on the other end of the hall, Jay spotted the old man seated in front of a vast row of windows that overlooked the rushing Waterway. The vaulted ceiling soared high above their heads, giving the entire room the feel of an observatory.

Wade sidled up next to the long sectional sofa, unwilling to move closer lest their host try something nefarious. Jay, not wanting Wade's circumspection to infect, plopped down on the outer seat. The soft fabric of the robe combined with the plush embrace of the sofa brought a sigh of relief. He was glad to be off his feet.

"Tea?" Pierre asked flatly.

Jay nodded gratefully and sat forward to pluck a cup off of the glass and steel cocktail table before them. Pierre, sitting to his left, eyes fixed on the goings-on of the world outside the house at that moment, waved a hand that signaled he should help himself. Jay doused his cup with the hot and fragrant liquid and sat back, letting away another sigh.

Wade, apparently unable to keep himself from the same comforts, finally joined them.

"So," he started, voice cautious, "What do you do, Master Kabolt?"

The old man's gaze finally snapped back into the room. "*Master?*"

Wade looked like a child who had just been caught at an insult. "It's what the guards at the gate called you."

Pierre rolled his neck then, removing his ire. "Idiot men won't stop spreading the notion." Before Jay or Wade could follow him down that trail, he spoke again. "So what did Walter say to you before you two left Glendale?"

Wade answered like a whip. He ventured to explain the situation in detail, even going as far as venting their frustration with the headmaster's warnings. While he spoke, Jay's attention wandered to another silvery frame adorning a nearby stand. In this one, the group from before stood in a line, hands clasped to each other in hugs or looped from arm to arm. But where there had once been five, this image only held four, the third and unknown man gone from their rank.

Overwhelmed by a strange need to know, Jay interrupted Wade just as he was moving on to describe their slip through the unoccupied Glendale gate.

"This picture," he said, pointing toward it, "Where is the other guy?"

Pierre looked up, visibly glad to have been offered a change of subject from Wade's complete debrief. "He died before that image was taken. They all have now, it seems. I am the only one left."

Though Jay could see the sorrow and reluctance to relive those memories, he couldn't help but point out the obvious. "No, you're not," he said plainly. "Walter's in that picture too."

Pierre, sadness still permeating his features, nodded slowly. "I didn't think you boys would have heard. News just reached me a few days ago and I have abundant sources."

"News of what?" Wade asked, eyes narrowing.

"Of Walter's death."

Jay felt the breath leave his lungs. "*Walter is dead*?"

"But we just saw him!" Wade exclaimed, sitting up straighter.

"Just shy of two weeks ago. Shortly after you left," Pierre explained darkly.

"What happened?" Jay asked, mind still reeling. He knew Walter had been an older man, but he seemed healthy when they last spoke.

Pierre sighed, the sound heavy and ragged in his throat. "Investigators don't quite know. They suspect foul play, though."

"*Walter was murdered*?!" Wade rushed to conclusion.

"Lightning struck him. Said it killed him on the spot."

Wade eased visibly; his skepticism returned. "Last I checked, Mother Nature doesn't exactly count as a suspect."

Pierre cast a warning glare his direction. "This was not *Mother Nature's* doing."

Seeing the coming debate, Jay rushed in, "But you said Walter was struck by lightning. How could that have happened?"

"How indeed?" Pierre posed. "He was found in his bed, in his home, and with no storm cloud in the sky for days. And yet witnesses say that they saw the bolt fall from the air, blow the tiles off the roof, and kill my friend dead. *How indeed*."

Jay was again at a loss for words, and to his relief,

so was Wade. They all sat there in silence, staring out the glass shield that kept them from the rushing wind rising away from the river. Eventually, when the pressure seemed too much, Jay broke.

"*Who would kill Walter?* He was so kind and gentle."

Pierre parted his lips as if to answer that, but he stopped himself. Instead, he redirected, "This *journey*. What is it that the two of you are after?"

Jay realized that Wade, likely in an attempt to spare him further humiliation, hadn't exposed the real reason why they left Glendale in the first place.

Instead of misleading, though, Jay laid it all bare. "I want Full Bindature."

Wade peered up with a concerned look, and Jay was unsure whether it was for the use of the foreign term or because he had so easily spilled their aims. Pierre, on the other hand, wore an expression of utter shock.

"Where did you hear that term?" he asked briskly, but before Jay could answer, he proposed the response himself, "I suppose Walter would have used it in his dissuasions." His dark eyes twitched to Wade. "This is what Walter harassed you over, isn't it?"

Wade nodded soberly.

"I see." Turning back to Jay, he went on, "So you have some grand vision of binding all twelve, eh?"

Jay nodded. "No one has ever done it. But I will."

Pierre snorted. "I can't tell if that's empty pride or sincere *stupidity*." He resituated himself on the sofa as Jay only scowled. "You have no idea what you're in for."

"So enlighten me!" Jay barked, finally letting free the response he wished he would have given to Walter, the response that Walter would now never hear. "If you think I'm so stupid for trying, why don't you share this infinite wisdom* of yours? Tell me plainly why I shouldn't."

If Pierre was flustered by the outburst, he didn't show it. He ran a wrinkled hand across his forehead and drew a deep breath before answering, "Because it will either kill *you* or those *closest to you.*"

Jay's frown deepened. "*Explain*," he said.

"You asked about the missing man in our photograph," Pierre began, earning a curt nod from his audience, "His name was Alden, and, like you, he thought Full Bindature something mystical and alluring. Walter took the four of us with him when he left his home of Highwater at twenty. We were young and energetic, the world our oyster. We had a certain...*task* that we needed to prepare for, and in order to do so, we needed to grow strong in our abilities with virtues. Most of us thought that this translated into excessive training with the virtues that we *had*, but Alden was different. He thought power came in numbers, not in ample experience with a single type. So as we traveled, Alden bound everything he could. At first, we assumed he would grow tired of the game, but his thirst only increased with every new virtue added to his arsenal. *And he was powerful*. He was right, you see. His potential for offensive might far overshadow the rest of us. But in response to his growth, something else began to change."

Unable to stay in the same position for long, Pierre hesitated, shifting his frail figure into a new arrangement before going on, "We saw it after the fourth binding. It was small, barely recognizable, but we knew our friend too well for it to go unnoticed. His mood became fragile, easily swayed to anger or depression or mania. We thought little of it for a time, knowing that life on the road was not easy for everyone. But when he bound his fifth, a darkness fell over him in a way that belied everything about his character. He was cheerful before, a contagious optimist that often kept us going through difficult seasons. But the Alden that emerged on the other side of that binding was brooding, secretive, *hateful*."

"What changed him?" Wade asked quietly, drawn into the tale as surely as Jay now was.

Pierre shook his head. "To this day, we still don't understand the science behind the metamorphosis. But as his body took on more virtue strength, it eroded other parts of his consciousness. The sixth was worse. And by the time he managed his seventh binding, we could no longer see the Alden we knew at all behind the one that took control of his body. His violence and unjustified envy made a decision for him one night, and it was either *our* lives or *his*. He attacked us; said we were plotting against him, that we had been looking for a way to rid him from our group, but his mind was cracked. The pressure of seven virtues vying for space in his head was too much. He nearly killed us all that night. *He was so strong*. But Kate caught him from behind, unaware. The branch broke his neck, and just like that, our oldest and dearest friend was dead."

"What if it wasn't the virtues?" Jay barged in, unwilling to let the sick and sad ending to Pierre's tale be the end to his. "What if he simply lost his mind for some other reason? You said it yourself, life on the road was hard. He could've cracked from that!"

"You don't understand," Pierre said warningly. "There is more to this picture than you know—"

"Then tell me!" he erupted again. "If there is more, then I want to know!"

"*You can't know!*" Pierre shouted back, finally at his wit's end. "It isn't for you to know or for me to share!"

Jay huffed, falling back into his seat. "Of course." he huffed sourly. "You're just like him. Walter wanted to give the warning too, but he didn't care to back it up."

"I count that a highest compliment," Pierre answered curtly, "To be like that man in any way."

Jay didn't respond. He brooded from that point on until Pierre finally stood to leave, catching their attention.

"You're welcome to stay here as long as you like. This is not an inn and I am not your maid, so if you need anything, get it yourself. *Do not* track mud into my home, *do not* bring guests here, and above all." He pinned them with a stare. "*Do not* leave the Isles without letting me know."

Wade caught the gesture and returned it with trepidation, but Jay kept up his offense.

"This isn't over," he said. "I want answers and I won't stop until I get them."

Pierre took an aching stride and paused. "*The same as Alden*," he lamented with a shake of his head. "For what it's worth, I hope you don't *end up* like him too."

He strolled up the tiled walkway until he was nearly out of sight. "There will be a parade tomorrow and a tournament. I suggest you check into the promenade before noon so as not to miss it." Then he was gone.

****

Jay loitered in the glass-walled room for over an hour after that, digging through the story that Pierre had given in search of any morsel of information that might shed a brighter light.

'How could binding virtues damage the mind?'

There was no science anywhere to back it up. Though, he had already found during his time away from Glendale that the Academy had been a poor excuse for a prep-school. There were many things that he had not learned there, so much information seemingly left out of his curriculum on purpose. He was beginning to think that there might be some grand conspiracy at work around him.

"It isn't for you to know or me to share."

They were the words Pierre had used to defend his secrecy. So somewhere, someone had already decided that there was a subject that Jameson Innis and his cohort Wade Wilkes were not allowed to know. And though Pierre Kabolt knew this information, he was barred from sharing it.

Jay growled in frustration, pounding a pillow with his fist.

What was it? What was this critical link between virtues, mankind, and a slow insanity that substantiated Walter and Pierre's claim against Full Bindature? Without knowing, Jay was determined to press on with his goal, but what if, by giving him the forbidden evidence, he could be spared from the same madness that took Alden?

'What could be so important about keeping such information secret?'

"Hey, man, you gotta see this!" Wade's voice barged into his thoughts.

Jay spun to find his friend with a bottle of soda in one hand and a snack cake in the other.

"This place is awesome! So it turns out Pierre is like

some kind of master craftsman or something. He has this room with trophies and plaques and all this weird stuff he's made."

"That's cool," Jay said, not entirely interested in the revelation.

"Nah, but that's not it," Wade said, "If you think *this* view is great, just wait till you see *the tower*." He swung a hand over his shoulder and turned to snatch up a lingering Blaze.

Blaze barked and wrestled with his captor, but Wade simply swatted at the dog until he resigned to lie limp and join them.

Jay followed the fuss, twisting and turning through the enormous mansion in tow with Wade. They wandered through parlors, kitchens—where Wade promptly grabbed another handful of snacks—more sitting rooms, and even an indoor pool, before arriving at a spiral stairwell that rocketed through the roof. Wade took the steps two at a time, Blaze bobbing grumpily in his arms. When they popped into the aforementioned tower, Jay understood the excitement that dripped from Wade's claim.

"*Wow*," Jay said, suddenly breathless, though not from the climb this time.

Together, they looked out the orbital dome to see the night sky lit with endless stars. Below, those same faraway sparks of luminescence reflected off the inky black water, mirroring the sight to make Jay feel as if they were standing inside a bubble drifting through the vastness of space. The moon gleamed its full white radiance over it all, adding to the sense of *smallness* that washed over them.

"Dope, isn't it?" Wade asked, voice nearly a

whisper.

Even Blaze seemed to take in the majesty for what it was, still and quiet in Wade's arms.

Jay drank in the view, eventually letting his eyes adjust to other sights visible from the height. He could see most of the island that they were now on, though it was large enough that details were scarce. The other three islands could be seen staggered from one another in the distance of the Ark Waterway. They were alive with lights and activity of their own, but when movement broke into the promenade below, he found his attention gravitating back there.

A group of six familiar shapes hovered in the massive square, and Jay felt a sudden desire to go see what the diverse drifters were up to.

He nudged Wade, bringing the man back from a daydream. "Wanna check out the promenade?" he asked, waiting for Wade to catch on.

Wade looked down to the same sight and grinned. "*The target has returned.*"

****

Dressed in fresh attire and back at the promenade steps, Wade and Jay looked out on the six stragglers raising a ruckus near a stand that read *Tournament Registrar.*

"All right, so here's the plan. I think I'm shifting directions. Hard dibs on the chick at the back."

Wade pointed to a girl standing next to the siblings, pink hair long and braided. She wore an overcoat that reminded Jay of a cross between a hitman and a fashion designer.

"You can go in for either of the other two. You know the stakes," he said, extending his fist.

Jay bumped it, shaking his head. "Yeah, yeah. How about we just see what they're doing before we go in on our knees with proposals?"

Wade grinned and rushed down the stairs like water, turning on his swagger switch to maximum capacity. Jay trickled down after him like the waves in his wake, primarily interested in seeing what this tournament was all about. But he couldn't lie. The girl from before certainly demanded his occasional glance.

"Lemme get in on this," Wade called, lunging into a circle of three kicking a small beanbag back and forth. He slid easily in next to his new "target" and began lithely showing his skills.

Just as Wade was nearing to his ultimate move, crowd gawking and girls giggling, Blaze sped into him, knocking him clear off his feet. He fell with a thud, scrambled back to standing, and let into the fleeing virtue with a tirade that threw him even further off his game. The crowd burst into laughter and the two guys in the huddle offered some timely jokes to add to the embarrassment.

Jay donned a smirk and made his line for the stand, opting to stay out of the scuffle, but he was almost immediately intercepted by the male sibling.

"Help you with anything?" he said, snide look on his face announcing that he was not actually interested in *helping* at all.

"Just checking out this tournament," Jay said, backing up.

"Yeah, see, this tourney's just for locals. *Sorry.*"

"Not looking to join," Jay lied. "Just seeing what it's all about." He tried to sidestep the fellow, but a hand wrapped in matte black bracelets and leather rings cut into his path.

"Sorry again, but no lookers allowed," he said with a fake grimace of sympathy.

Jay felt his fists tighten, nails digging into his palms. Just before he offered a less civil comment, though, another voice entered the mix.

"Raiza, let him by."

It was his sister, Jay saw as she approached the pair.

"*Oh, Raylin*, yeah I was just explaining that the tournament registration is closed."

"No, you said it was off limits to outsiders," Jay corrected with a hard expression.

"Get outta here, Raiza," Raylin demanded with a huff.

Raiza, still wearing the haughty smile that made Jay's hands clench ever tighter, conceded to walk away. He wrapped an arm around the remaining woman and loped down a side street.

Raylin, however, stayed exactly where she planted her feet, studying Jay with a smile that looked far less offensive than her brother's.

"What's your name?" she asked, voice smooth as glass.

"J-Jay," he said, stumbling over the word as surely as he stumbled into her amber gaze.

Those eyes, shining like the silhouetting moon, stood out against her raven hair and pale skin. When her smile grew, they seemed to brighten all-the-more.

"Well, J-Jay," she started, mimicking his stutter, "Are you looking to enter the tournament? I could always use more competitive fodder."

Jay broke free from the spell. "I might be," he answered, "*But I won't be fodder*. What exactly does it entail?"

"Four competitions, all based on your bond with your virtue. We do it every year. It's called the Manifestival." She glanced over at Blaze who was still running circles around a harried Wade and the three others who had been roped into the contest by 'accidents' of their own. "Looks like you've already got the summoning part down pat."

"How do you know he's mine?"

She stepped up to him, painfully close, and ran a lacquered nail across his forehead, pressing his dirty blond locks away from his eyes.

"*I can see the fire in you*," she whispered.

And as she backed away, Jay watched a ball of flame bloom from her palm before it slowly took shape into a four-winged avian of the element. She allowed it to flap around her for a moment, scattering embers to the ground between them, before withdrawing it back the way it came.

"We share an affinity," she said, waving him over to the booth. "I think you might do me some good if you join the fight."

Jay approached, again mesmerized. Before he had a chance to read the information layered there on the stand, she grabbed his hand and stuck a pen between his fingers. He wrote his name in the fifteenth square, and with a little more prodding from Raylin, he filled out the other slots of requested information as well.

"I don't even know how this works," he finally said, allowing himself a chance to protest.

"Where's the fun in knowing?" she replied, black-painted lips curved playfully upward. "I find the *mystery* so much more enticing."

Steven C. McCullough

She leaned in to plant a soft kiss on his cheek before pulling away and summoning her posse. At Jay's questioning gaze, she offered, "For the way my stupid twin brother was treating you, of course." Then she and the others capered down the same side street that Raiza had taken, leaving Jay utterly confounded.

Wade, having witnessed the affair, sprung up to his side. "Doesn't count," he nearly shouted. "On the cheek doesn't count. Gotta be full on the mouth for the win."

Despite not caring and having more curious concerns, Jay decided to give his friend a hard time for it. "That wasn't the rule before. Are you changing the guidelines in the middle of the game?"

"Nah, you can't play it like that Jamey-boy," he argued. "It's all or nothing. Just cuz you garner a sympathy peck doesn't mean you get the victory."

Jay held up placating hands. "All right, you got me."

Appeased, Wade finally moved on to other topics. "So she got you sign your life away, huh?" He hovered over the paper with a wince.

"Just a tournament," Jay defended.

Wade sucked a breath in through his teeth. "Always starts like that. Just some of *this*…a little of *that*. Before you know it, you're wrapped around her finger."

He sidled around the stand and pilfered through the brochures. Blaze, finally complete with his instigative rounds, returned to Jay and gave him a wan look.

"It'll do us some good," he said toward the virtue, knowing already that they were bound to fail the four competitions miserably if they were all based on *bond*.

Blaze sniffed the air snootily and sat back on his haunches as Wade spoke.

"Dude, you got *no* chance in the world." He held up

the first of four colored guides, pointing toward the scenes. "*A challenge designed to test reliance and cooperation*," he read aloud skeptically.

Jay looked to Blaze who apparently realized the fallibility of the decision as well, his beady eyes fixed in a disbelieving squint. "Like I said, *it'll do us some good*," he repeated.

Thumbing through the rest of the flyers, Wade whistled. "In over your head, bro, but I'm not stopping you. Not going to *join you*, but I won't stop you either."

"Come on," Jay said grumpily, his cheer dwindling with every pessimistic statement. "We should sleep if we're waking up that early." He gestured to the timestamp on the page that proclaimed the first gathering at eight in the morning.

"Gonna need more than *sleep*," Wade murmured as they took toward the stairs again.

Chapter 10

Despite the need for rest and the blissful opportunity on a feather mattress, Jay rose earlier than the sun. Stiff and sour, he decided to take a lap around the manse both inside and out, and by the time he made it back to his starting point, the sun had finally decided to stretch above the horizon.

He enjoyed the early-morning air with a cup of Pierre's tea from the evening before, helped himself to a breakfast of eggs and toast, and sat again by the wide bay windows overlooking the water. He half-expected the old man to emerge from a nearby room and join him in a shared silent sulkiness, but Jay only sat alone until the clock struck seven.

Decided that he should gear up for the morning's events, he returned to their bedroom to find Wade unsurprisingly snoring away while Blaze only shot him a suspicious glance before burying himself back beneath the blankets.

"I wanna get there early to scope things out," he pled. "Come on. Let's go."

When Blaze offered only silent rebuke, Jay scooped him out from under the covers. Instead of wrestling away as he had with Wade the night before, the virtue simply consigned himself to the fate. Though their bond was not the stuff of legends—unless the lack thereof could be considered—Jay thought they had at least made improvements over their time together. The pigheaded pup was a frustrating mess for the most part, but he was content, now, that they were not at each other's throats. They needed one another, and today, Jay needed Blaze to cooperate more than ever. He just wasn't sure how to make that happen.

****

In the promenade again, Jay strolled along with only Blaze as his company. The city seemed empty save for the few merchants preparing shops on nearby streets. He checked the registrar's stand once again and found that he had the time and place correct. At only fifteen minutes till the stated gathering, Jay was beginning to wonder if it was all some elaborate prank set up to humiliate him as an outsider.

Just as he was considering whether he should return to Pierre's estate, though, the sound of shuffling feet finally touched his ears. Then, like a march of madness, people of all shapes, sizes, and colors burst onto the cobbled streets en masse, stampeding in from different directions. There were sudden shouts of joy and ecstasy, fireworks popping in the air, and the hungry calls of merchants angling for a sale. It was as if they had all been waiting for a predetermined moment to hit the streets in celebration.

Abrupt as it was, it overwhelmed Jay in a flash, and both he and Blaze backed warily into the stand. Flyers scattered to the ground around them, but before he could stoop to pick them up, a storm of bodies flooded the courtyard, pressing in on all sides. Blaze began to bark in sincere panic, but his angry warnings were lost in the cacophony. Jay, on the other hand, snapped his eyes back and forth, searching for some telling reason why this riot of roiling people had come.

In answer to his unasked question, a single woman in a tie-dye hood, golden cords hanging from her neck and hands, stepped up to the topmost riser in the staircase ahead. With a wave of her rainbow hands, the crowd quieted. It was slow at first, but a hush soon fell over them all, including Blaze, who seemed at once curious and behaved.

Jay studied the flamboyant celebrant, watching carefully as she folded back her hood to reveal aqua-painted hair tied into a tight bun. A few free strands fell along her face, framing her long, curved lashes and high cheekbones. A tattoo of undiscernible design encased her neck, stretching up to paint the tips of her ears in the same inky color. When the crowd had fallen to such reverence that Jay could have heard a pin drop, she finally spoke.

"Would the competitors please make your ways to the central dais?"

The crowd parted like a machine then, feet shuffling and bodies scooting further toward the edge of the promenade. Though he hadn't recognized it before, Jay saw a large section of black and white cobbles in the center of the mostly orange arena that seemed to be there by some ritualistic design. One-by-one, fourteen other souls stepped into the oval confines of the dais. Jay recognized only two of them, twins in both blood and black attire.

Raylin spun on him with an unspoken summons, and with her strange magic that Jay could not describe, she drew him in. He stepped onto the dais with the rest, the fifteenth and final contestant.

Somehow knowing that he was the last of them, the

announcer spoke again. "This is a momentous occasion for each of you. Not only do you compete for the grand cup of the annual Manifestival, you do so on our two-hundredth anniversary!"

The crowd erupted in cheers and hoots. A chant even rose for the namesake of the city until the speaker quelled it.

"It is indeed a time to celebrate. But let us not forget the harrying challenges that await our competitors this day! We will cheer them all on toward victory, but only one will emerge the champion of the Manifestival."

In contrast to the crowd, Jay was feeling increasingly unsure. Raylin read his mind. Before he could back away to become another innocent bystander, she latched onto his wrist and pulled him between her and her brother. Raiza shot him a withering glance but quickly returned his attention to the speaker. Raylin, however, never took her unnerving eyes off him.

"We begin forthright," the woman atop the steps announced. "The first challenge awaits us here, on the Isle of Promise: The Trial of Bonds. Competitors, if you would follow me."

She descended the steps, carved a path into the crowd, and signaled the fifteen to follow. Raylin gave Jay another encouraging jerk, and he stumbled alongside her. They traced the speaker's path onto another street that ran against the flow of the river, the entire troop trailing behind them. Jay kept his lips sealed as they went, but Raylin apparently had it out for his nerves.

"No one's ever *died* during the challenges," she purred. "*At least not yet.*"

Jay frowned. "As much as I appreciate the info, you don't have to babysit me."

She bared her teeth in what could only be called a sinister smile. "Oh, I'm not babysitting anyone. *You're going to lose*. And it will be *epic*. I just want to watch you squirm as you realize it."

Jay's lips continued to slope in contrast to hers. "I'm beginning to think I like your brother better."

Raiza turned, apparently listening in. "Dude, you have no idea. *She's ruthless*." He gave Jay a harsh pat on the back.

"I'm just honest," she replied in an innocent tone. "The competition needs fifteen contestants to round it out. You happened to be my lucky number fifteen, but that doesn't mean I won't wipe the floor with you."

"Champion three years in a row," Raiza chimed.

"Soon to be *four*," she added, flourishing her raven hair.

"Or not," Jay said, feeling his confidence rise in the midst of their disparagement.

As always, when a '*you can't*' statement was launched his way, his blood began to burn with a desire to prove them wrong. The twins had just flipped the switch.

Blaze loped up beside him, apparently feeding off the tension that Jay emitted as he went on, "Maybe this is the year you finally meet your better."

"Oh ho!" Raiza sang. "Sis, looks like your boytoy here is calling you out! Do I smell *a rivalry* brewing?"

Raylin shoved him into another contestant who abruptly snarled. "We'll just have to see what J-Jay can do, won't we?" she asked, stuttering his name as he had the night before.

"Careful, sis. I think he can sense your *fear*." Raiza waggled his leather-banded fingers at her mystically.

Jay stepped in before it got dirty. "I'm just saying I won't be a pushover. Your win isn't guaranteed."

She spun back to him, amber eyes flashing first with anger but quickly fading to a playful curiosity. "We'll see about that," she said with a poised grin.

Suddenly, the crowd stopped moving, and the speaker fell still before a new arena. Jay looked around, drinking in the sight of filled stands arcing around a path of glistening water. Just as he was surveying the course that seemed to connect the end of this island to the fore of the next, busy hands ushered him and the other fourteen contestants into a nearby building. Jay tried to sneak a last peek, but the door slammed in his face, casting his eyes into readjustment for the dim lights within.

"Sit," the speaker said, gesturing to a row of benches along the wall.

Jay and the others did as told, lining up in a row. Though Raylin had been several paces away when the order came, she scrambled to take a seat next to him. He really couldn't understand this girl. Was she *into* him or was she still trying to mess with his head?

"As most of you know," the speaker began anew, "My name is Ansela Yune, and I am the broadcaster for this year's Manifestival. Some of you are new to the competition, so I will explain the process."

Jay settled into his seat, glad to finally have a name to attribute to the leader of this pack. Blaze hopped up into his lap, and for a moment, he wondered if the virtue might actually be taking this test seriously. But he quickly realized that it was only to get farther away from another summoned virtue in the shape of an ungainly rodent with fur molded like tufts of windblown grass.

Blaze growled down at the gangly creature as it passed to sit silently next to its owner, a middle-aged man with square-rimmed glasses and a hook nose.

"The Trial of Bonds is the first test each of you must undergo. There will be only five competitors at a time allowed, thus we will end up with three groups. Those who are not actively taking the Trial will remain here until your group is called."

She moved to separate each of the contestants into thirds according to how they were seated. Jay, sitting in the center five next to Raylin, realized why the girl had chosen to weasel her way closer to him before. She was in his group.

"This Trial is an obstacle course spanning from this Isle to the next, and it can only be properly traversed by relying on your virtue. In exchange, your virtue must trust and rely on you as well. For you must *both* reach the end of the course if you are to move on. The Trial is timed, allowing only four means of disqualification: failing to complete the course in the time allotted, falling out of the bounds of the course, recalling your summoned virtue, or interfering in any way with another competitor. Does everyone understand?"

Jay lifted a hesitant hand.

"Yes? You are?"

"Jameson Innis," he replied cordially. "So can we use any *other* virtues we've bound, or are we limited to the one summoned?" His question drew murmurs of confusion and awe.

"Do you have multiple virtues, Mr. Innis?" Ansela asked curiously.

Jay nodded, flashing his sleeve. "I have two."

Raylin looked at him with a new kind of respect this

time, though it bordered a fine line of bewilderment. Apparently, she, and the others, did not wholly approve.

"Well," Ansela started, caught slightly off balance, "It is not forbidden to use the aid of another virtue. However, even though it is not included in the rules, I am issuing a temporary restriction to *summoning* your second virtue during the remainder of the Manifestival. You may use whatever abilities it provides granted that you keep it withdrawn."

There was a groan of disapproval, but Jay quashed it. "It's void," he said flatly. "Doesn't do me any good. Just wanted to make sure *you all* didn't have an unfair advantage. I promise not to use any void magic for this trial."

Though he thought the confession would assist his credibility, the group only stared at him, dumbfounded.

Ansela explained, "No one here has a second virtue, Mr. Innis. Yours is a *very rare* condition, indeed." She said it as if it was a disease. "But we appreciate your candor and your restraint. You all heard him. He says he will honor the Manifestival by using only his summoned virtue for this first trial. Are we all in agreement that this is the proper course of action?"

A general consensus of nods followed, but Raylin wore a frown that attested to her cynicism.

"*I will*," he whispered. "When I beat you, it'll be fair and square."

He grinned as she narrowed her eyes, but Ansela drew their attention back before she could respond.

"We will start with your group, Mr. Innis, if you are so eager."

He looked up to see her waving them forward. The other four stood, and he joined them.

"Right this way," she called, stepping through another door opposite the one they entered.

They appeared on the other side of the squat building, emerging into the blaring sunlight once more. Jay winced, sliding to a stop with Blaze on his heels. When his eyes adjusted again, he could see the course rippling out across the waves before them.

There were ten tracks floating about the rushing currents of the Ark Waterway, spanning more than two miles from island to island. The tracks were identical in sets of two—one, Jay thought, for the contestant and the other for his or her virtue. Though he could see little more than vague details from where he stood, the missing links, high walls blocking paths, and general instability of the floating bridge bode ill.

He turned to Raylin. "We have to get across *that*?"

She found it her turn to boast. "Getting scared, J-Jay? Need to sit this one out?"

"You wish," he said, steeling himself.

Ansela planted her feet atop a large cylinder of metal that soon rose away from the ground with hydraulic pressure. At thirty or so feet, it ceased its skyward ascent, planting the broadcaster high above the heads of the cheering throngs. Jay again looked to see the thousands of people gathered nearby, the number seeming to swell even as the tournament neared its start. He felt the tremors of excitement and fear rush through him stronger than ever.

"Ladies and gentlemen!" Ansela boomed, a microphone now stretched across her scalp and positioned to amplify her voice. "Welcome to the bicentennial Manifestival!"

The crowd erupted with sounds that shook the

ground. Jay could feel the whole island shiver with delight as Ansela went on.

"We begin this magnificent fete with the Trial of Bonds! Fifteen competitors have gathered here today to showcase their skills, their determination, and above all, their virtues! But only one will become this year's champion. *Who will it be?*"

She swept a magnanimous hand across the stadium below to where Jay and the four other contestants stood, practically dancing with anticipation.

"Will it be our first entrant, none other than the reigning champion herself, the Prodigy of Flame, Raylin Hargrave?!"

Applause ruptured again as Raylin peeled away from the group and pounced up onto the lower stage. She waved all around, feigning modesty at their praise. But as soon as it faded, she summoned her flaming fowl to surge through the air above them, reigniting their awe.

Jay shook his head, smirking, but when *his* name echoed across the arena, he flinched.

"Or will it be our newest competitor, Jameson Innis?" With a pause, Ansela seemed to be considering a tagline to offer for the fresh addition to their Manifestival. "*The Dualist!*" she exclaimed in time with his foot touching the stage. "The first of our rank to command not only one virtue to bear, but *two!*"

The crowd *oo*'d and *ahh*'d at the note, but Jay simply waved and offered Raylin a shrug. Blaze, on the other hand, gave them all a show to remember, howling and snapping as if they had personally offended him with their admiration. Jay hissed at the dog, eventually earning the virtue's obedience, but not before the crowd noticed and offered a laugh for the antics. Thinking it at his expense, Blaze returned to his barking even as Ansela continued calling out names.

"Petri Devlin, the Little Devil!" she shouted, and another contestant took the stage.

Jay hadn't paid the others much mind until now, hearing the strange nicknames called out to the crowd for show. But as the *"Little Devil"* fell in next to him with what appeared to be a darkness virtue close at his heels, he thought the title stuck. The rather short man, perhaps slightly older than Jay, wore a mischievous expression that made Jay uncomfortable. His smog-like virtue continuously morphed from shape to shape until landing on a form that mimicked Blaze. And it seemed that Blaze didn't care for the flattery.

"Heather Gond, the Windrunner!" Ansela went on, overshadowing Blaze's sharp growl at the floating copycat.

Heather joined them, and Jay couldn't help but wonder at her nickname. She wasn't exactly the type to inspire notions of speed and running, as she was considerably overweight for a girl her age. No older than sixteen, Heather had round, youthful cheeks and a stature that wasn't much taller than the Little Devil to her right. But as her virtue, a wicked-looking beast of wind was summoned from her soul, Jay realized precisely why she had garnered it. Like a dire wolf of considerable size, the greenish and transparent virtue floated obediently to its master's side, casting Heather in its immense shadow.

"And finally, to round out the first of our three groups of competitors: Zane Daluth, or as you all better know him, Crazy Zane!"

Jay watched as Crazy Zane demonstrated his namesake, leaving little to the imagination. With a flourish, he snatched away clothes that had been lightly sewn together for just such theatrics. His shirt and pants, all one piece, fell into a puddle at his feet, revealing a tightly knit torso of muscle and only a skimpy pair of bright blue boxers to cover his shame.

He stomped around the arena at first, near-naked, like a chimpanzee, doing a commendable impression of the animal. Jay, thinking he was simply a lunatic, was surprised when the act had a point. With another flourish of his muscly arms, Zane summoned his virtue, a golden monkey that matched him for size. Zane impersonated his radiance virtue again, and Jay was surprised twice-over to see just how spot-on it was.

"What a way to kick this year's festival off!" Ansela cried, barely concealing her own laughter. "Well, folks, what do you say we get this show started?!"

The horde roared their approval again, and Jay found it a good chance to pull his attention back to the task. He stared out across the shimmering wake to where he would soon be racing the clock toward the other side.

"Competitors, are you ready?" Ansela called, to which they all nodded. "Take your positions."

As Jay suspected, the other four—all veterans by the looks of it—stepped up to their tracks while commanding their virtues to climb onto or hover above the track next to them. Jay suddenly realized the advantage that three of the virtues would have over his in this test: *flight*. The wispy smog, the insubstantial wolf, and Raylin's firebird were all capable of flying right over many of the visible obstacles. He was beginning to rethink his vow to play fair.

He took his place and gestured for Blaze to follow suit. When the virtue got a little frosty for the demand,

Jay had to kneel and make a promise he knew he would regret.

"Just do this *one thing* for me, *win this tournament*, and I'll do whatever you want. *Anything.*"

Though he thought the plea rather ridiculous and unlikely to sway the stubborn dog, Blaze actually appeared to consider it with his too-human expressions. Satisfied with the offer, he hopped up onto the track and watched Jay with a *this better be worth it* stare. Jay took the victory with a broad smile, disregarding what it would cost him later.

"On my mark, competitors, you will have thirty minutes to cross the Ark Waterway on your tracks. Should either you or your virtue touch water, you will be disqualified. You must work together in order to traverse this maze, and be warned that what you see is not all that awaits."

Ansela held up a hand bearing a small, silver flag. "May the Trial of Bonds...*begin!*" She let the flag fall, and with it, the game was on.

Jay watched as Crazy Zane, the Little Devil, and Raylin all sped down their ramps, virtues in similar tow. Heather, on the other hand, took her time, further belying her namesake. But something about her patience spoke of wisdom that Jay was not quick to dismiss.

He took a few slow steps, feeling out the shifting of the boards beneath his feet. They were no more than four feet wide from edge to edge, allowing little room for error. Blaze, on the other hand, took after the speedy crew, storming down the track until he was well out of earshot from Jay. Jay fumed. It would do him little good if Blaze reached the finish line while he was still stuck behind some obstacle the ornery dog was required to remove.

After acclimating to the unstable nature of the platform, though, Jay picked up the pace. He had half an hour to make it to the end, and though it certainly seemed like a solid couple of miles, he thought that he could make it, barring any major complications.

The first two hundred yards were riddled with relatively easy puzzles. A small gap here to jump, a rickety board there to circumvent, a fragile, breakaway tether that would send a section floating off down the river and ultimately out of bounds. They were all essentially trying to plunge the contestant into the icy waters below, but Jay was quick-witted and unwilling to let such simple traps catch him off guard.

When he made it to the first major obstacle, though, he was sure that the difficulty was increasing. An entire section of the track was missing, more than a measly hop could cross. At nearly eight feet to the other side, Jay had no way to reach it securely. He was no athlete, not confident at all in his ability to jump more than a few paces with a steady landing.

He stopped and took a frantic look around. Blaze was nowhere to be seen, but it was certainly hard to miss the bright red switch on the virtue's side that was sure to bring some floating filler up from below the cerulean waves. Jay called after the missing mutt, but his eyes eventually traced the outline of a harried Blaze much farther down the path, apparently having troubles of his own. He sighed and wiped his face.

"Okay, Jay, think." He spun back to the missing link. "How can you get across *without* him?"

He wracked his brain for options, and eventually, the breakaway section from before presented itself. He had been careful not to trigger that particular trap, and now, he celebrated his circumspection.

He sprinted back up the ramp, drawing distant sounds of confoundment and speculation from the watching crowds. Returning to the point of the track where he had seen the brittle binding, he snapped it with a sharp kick but held fast to the floating section lest it be swept away with the current. Hoisting it up onto the track with him, he proceeded to drag the segment back to the first major obstacle.

Though he had wasted a precious five minutes with the backtracking and return, he soon found that the trip was worth the cost. Sliding the section out into the vacant waters, Jay peeled his shirt off, ripped it down the seams, and used the fabric to tie the floating piece in place.

The sun scorched his pale skin, likely seeming a moving mirror to the onlookers both behind and before. Though his stint through the Cliffs had added a suntanned hue to his arms and face, his typically-covered portions were as pasty and reflective as the sand that awaited him on the second Isle.

Sweating and still catching his breath, he eased out onto the unstable addition, gentle in his movements. It dipped and shivered with his weight, threatening to allow some of the river water up onto the platform with him. He briefly wondered if he would be disqualified if it brushed the soles of his feet.

With half the original distance filled, Jay felt a mite more comfortable with the ensuing leap. He kicked away from the wobbly walkway with all his might and drew a sharp breath of fear when his foot nearly caught the edge of the next section. Jerking it back toward him like lightning, he examined his shoe and found no signs of wetness staining his body.

Letting the breath return to the air, he stood and examined the next portion. Blaze was yet in the same position as before, still pacing angrily at the face of a wall that rose well above his height. Apparently, there were no means for the dog to surmount the blockade, but in his stubborn stupidity, he was content to refuse coming back to check on his master.

Jay grumbled as he pressed on, again sidestepping traps. Tripwires, collapsing panels, and even more breakaway segments had been added to this stage, confirming his fears that it would only grow more difficult the farther he progressed. When he made what seemed the halfway point, the obstacle that barred Blaze's passage came into clearer view.

Blaze spun to give him a sickened look as if he had been wasting time.

"Oh, don't you start!" Jay shouted. "You left me behind back there! I had to figure it out myself!"

He groused even more as he stepped up to a large lever painted bright red and impossible to miss. Tugging on the steel shaft, he could hear gears working somewhere beneath the platforms, and the large wall on Blaze's track soon folded down to become a connecting bridge.

"*Don't!*" Jay warned as Blaze prepared to sprint ahead again. "*Don't you dare leave me.* We do this *together.*"

Blaze narrowed his eyes, but Jay didn't give him a chance to pout before he started at a jog. The virtue kept easy pace with him, and soon, they made it to their third major obstacle, this one on Jay's side again.

Jay examined the missing link, this time much

longer than the one before. On Blaze's track, however, there was no such gap; but rather, the platforms became considerably narrower. As he looked closer, he also noted that they were slightly raised from the one Blaze now stood on. Impatient and unruly as always, Blaze pranced across the first square in the line of differing pathways, and the section sank beneath his weight.

Barking in alarm, Blaze leaped away from the sinking segment, but Jay saw it, if only briefly. While Blaze stood atop the first square, the water at Jay's feet churned with activity. The puzzle formed itself in his head in a flash.

"No, Blaze, step back onto that square!"

The dog only stared at him like a madman.

"Just do it!" he shouted, fearful, now, for their time.

Hesitantly, Blaze pounced back onto the platform and waited.

It sank again, stirring him to move, but Jay held up a staying hand. When it stopped just shy of submersion, Blaze relaxed, and Jay celebrated. As suspected, the platform he needed rose up out of the water before him, giving him solid ground to stand on while Blaze moved to the next.

Instructions passed to his virtue, Jay made swift work of the obstacle. Blaze, whether by fear of falling in or of being left without his master, actually listened and obeyed. When they made the other side of the track, Jay offered his praise, which Blaze accepted in typical fashion—with annoying disregard.

Thinking the worst behind them, Jay sprinted onward, watching as all the other contestants, save for the Little Devil, gained ground ahead of him. He wasn't sure that this was an elimination round, but with the

Little Devil apparently lost in the rolling river—neither he nor his virtue was anywhere to be seen on their tracks—Jay thought that he might still have a chance. When his foot caught on one of the many tripwires planted along the path, though, he cursed his decision for haste.

Blaze slid to a stop as Jay faceplanted on the wooden bridge. When he peered up to wonder at the dog's worried expression, he realized it wasn't for his well-being.

Unblinking eyes of each snapped back to find both of their tracks fading into the waters below like dominoes. From the point of the previous obstacle to where Jay continued to lay in dumbstruck humility, the platforms sank one by one, closing in on him with ferocious speed.

He scrambled to his feet, a shout of panic pressing through his lips. Despite earlier directives, Blaze gave his master a farewell glance and bolted. Jay paid the remainder of the traps little mind now, moving too quickly for them to be of any effect. He plowed through still more tripwires, barely letting his feet touch a solid surface long enough to set anything else off.

He could see the last obstacle ahead, the writhing mass of the waiting crowd just on the other side where the white sands of the beach met the bridge. Still, it all collapsed behind him, chasing him down like a determined killer. Though in the back of his mind, he knew this was not life-or-death, the terror he felt in that moment belied it.

All that remained between him and safety was a single, paper-thin beam. On either side of the too-narrow walkway were a series of small pipes that thrust up out of the water like reaching hands. Though they didn't move, Jay somehow knew they were not as benign as they appeared.

Blaze mounted his beam first. So did Heather and her wind-walking virtue in tandem. In symphony, the pipes sang a song of such percussive might that Jay thought the plunging pursuit of his track had caught up with him. When rockets of water surged through the air toward their balancing quarries, though, Jay realized what the not-so-innocent fixtures really were.

Heather took one of the geysers to the chest, and it sent her headlong into the river. Her virtue, though visually transparent, was more substantial than Jay had first assumed. It escaped the wrath of the first three cannons, but halfway across the balance beam, it decided to forgo the act of walking in lieu of the air. Soaring upward into the sky, it met an invisible barrier that seemed to be a boundary for its bypassing intentions, and before it could correct its trajectory, a rocket caught it in the side, sending it flailing into the water next to its bobbing master.

Jay's eyes flicked down in alarm toward his own virtue, but to his surprise, Blaze was yet unscathed. With cowering swipes of his puny paws, the dog dragged himself across the beam in a slow and steady crawl that kept him just beneath the blasting cannons' reach. Apparently unable to angle downward any farther, they missed the creeping virtue entirely, sending their gushes of destabilizing water across to the other side.

Jay nearly forgot himself as he watched the ingenuity in action, a swell of pride filling him before he deflated back to *his* reality. Even if Blaze managed to make it across, how was *he* going to?

Just as his foot touched the beam, the collapse of his track ended, and the crowd seemed to hush.

He was the last in action.

The cannons to either side of his walkway primed, swiveling their mortar-like heads to lock him as their target. He cringed, knowing that there was no way he could make it without being struck.

He sucked in a breath, though, and committed. Head down and shoulders hunched, he bull-rushed. But before he could take two steps, he heard a new sound, a strange gasp from the audience. He skittered to a stop, bringing his gaze back up to find them all staring toward Blaze. Then the cause of their collective wheeze came again, and Jay saw it in full.

Blaze, eyes a burning red, sent jet after jet of sizzling flames into the cannons, aiming at Jay. One after another, they melted beneath the intense heat, coming spouts of water simply fizzling into steam and causing the entire system to buck from blockage. Jay, unsure if the tactic was legal to the game, decided not to pass up the assistance.

He rushed the ramp, balance his only worry as Blaze continued burning the blasters away and clearing his path. When the final enemy was down, Blaze let his fiery assault fade, and Jay leaped onto solid ground in time to slap the button that stopped his clock.

29:12

Jay first writhed like a popped balloon, unable to either comprehend or express his feelings. Finally, he screamed in guttural triumph, mentally, physically, and emotionally drained but *victorious*. The crowd screamed with him, and something about their cheer made the moment all the more real.

"*Innis, Innis, Innis*!"

The chant rose as surely as had Crazy Zane's, and for the first time in a long time, Jay felt what it was to be *praised*.

Blaze, unwilling to let him have all the glory, capered up to him and bathed in their reverence as well. Whereas he might have been opposed to their cheers before, he allowed his peasants and worshippers to pine over him now. Jay gave a wry laugh, but frankly, the dog deserved it. Even as a set of children, foreign and frantic, reached the virtue to lift him up in celebration, Blaze never flinched.

Suddenly, Jay felt soft, cold hands touch his bare torso and remembered that he had forfeited his shirt during the Trial. He looked down to see Raylin's black lacquered nails separating from his chest, and he traced them back to their source.

"Rough win, but a *win* nonetheless," she offered with a weak smile.

"Did you make it?" he asked, evading the taunt.

"First one through. Without a hitch," she boasted. "But you know, you were a close third."

Jay refused to let the goading sour his mood this time. "Tourney's not over," he stated with a wink before turning back to the crowd. "Just building momentum."

Crazy Zane sidled up to them then, eyes wild and ecstatic. Jay couldn't tell if that was normal for the guy or if the adrenaline of the moment still had him on edge.

"Wicked win, brother!" he shouted, slapping Jay's bare shoulder. "The way your dog just…vrew vrew vrew." He finger-gunned the image of Blaze shooting the jets of flame. "Burned 'em to a crisp! Never woulda thought of that! Hope they don't scold you for it. Looks like they're trying to patch it up now. Ha!"

Jay turned to see the target of Zane's gesture and found a series of mechanics in boats surrounding the melted pipes and charred beam, hands scratching their heads.

"*Oops*," he whispered.

"There will be no scolding," a new voice answered.

They all turned to find Ansela approaching, fiddling with her mic.

"Ladies and gentlemen, there you have it!" she boomed once the small device was in place, turning to address the hushing crowd. "Three of our five competitors will be progressing to the next round! And among them, the Dualist has set himself apart!"

She took Jay's wrist and pulled it high into the air. "Though his bond seemed weak at first—his virtue abandoning him in its eagerness—he proved that perseverance will earn respect and growth! His virtue."

She hesitated long enough to ascertain the name. Jay gave it.

"*Blaze* would not leave its binder to suffer loss! *No!* Without command or direction, it acted in the best interest of the team! And *that* is true loyalty!"

The crowd shrieked their approval of Blaze then, the virtue's congregation of parishioners swelling to an even larger size. Jay thought the acclaim a little off-color, since he knew the dog's true personality, but who knew? Ansela could be onto something about growth.

"Let's have a round of applause for all our competitors! And may the Trials continue!"

Jay met Raylin's tart inspection as Ansela finished her speech, and he noted that she didn't care much for a newcomer outshining her.

"Beginner's luck," she puffed, spinning away to recall her molten companion.

Before Jay could call her back, she vanished into the swarm of people.

"*Harsh*," Crazy Zane said, reminding Jay that he was still standing nearby.

"She's just competitive," Jay defended, though he had no idea why he felt the need.

"You got that right, brother," Zane answered, slipping back into a fresh pair of breakaway pants. "Gotta shirt if you need one."

Jay caught himself before refusing, realizing that he didn't really want to go all the way back to Pierre's just to grab a dirty top from his bag. "Thanks. Is this your first competition?"

Zane laughed, the sound pitched and manic. "Nah, brother. I'm a regular. Actually travel the Tiers to all sorts of competitions and festivals. Kind of a showman by trade."

"Wait, so you've been to the other Tiers?" Jay asked, sliding his arms into the overtly colorful shirt. He fastened the pearlescent buttons with mixed feelings about the style.

"Oh yeah, sure," Zane answered. "Tier Three is a buncha prudes, but they pay well. Don't go as often as I should, but hey, a man's gotta *enjoy* his job. Suck the life right outta me if I did every show I've been asked."

"How do you get back and forth?" Jay asked as they walked toward the stands. "It's really difficult to get passage."

"Gotta have a patron, buddy-boy. See, I'm originally from Tier Two. Born and raised in Lavish. Parents put me through a fancy school, but it just wasn't for me. Decided I liked performing for folks more than sticking my nose in books." Zane tapped the sharp tip of his nose and crossed his eyes. "Turns out the mayor of Lavish is somewhat of a performing arts fan. We partnered up; he paid the way for me to hop between Tiers and do shows like these, and I split the chum with him. Oh, and sometimes he wants private classes and showings, so he gets that in the deal too."

Jay took a step onto the first riser, quickly spotting a pair of dark-skinned arms waving frantically at him. He angled toward Wade, and Zane followed, apparently without a particular destination of his own.

"So you get paid for this?" Jay asked, making light conversation now.

"Sure do. Not a killer amount, but *this* festival is always a blast. I usually don't aim to win, by the way, so don't hold it against me. Just here to spark the crowd and put on a show."

"*Usually*?" Jay asked, catching the word.

Zane flashed a devilish grin. "You and the Molten Mistress there have a thing going. My money's on it spiraling down to the pair of you. Kinda wanna stick around and see how it plays out, you know, throw a little fuel on this fire."

Just then, Wade penetrated the wall of chattering people and caught Jay by the arm.

"Dude, I was looking for you all morning! Then I happen down to the beach, and I see you out tight-roping a beam in the river with fire flying at you!"

"I didn't wanna wake you," Jay lied. "You looked so cute all snuggled up on your bed. Who was I to take that away from the world?"

"Yeah, whatever," Wade ignored, "So where's

Blaze?"

Jay spun to look back, expecting that the dog would have been following him, but to his surprise, Blaze was nowhere to be seen. Before he could call after his missing virtue, though, Zane interrupted.

"Ah, he's just over there soaking up the spotlight." He flicked a finger toward a crowd of doting children from which Blaze's head soon emerged. Contrary to Zane's assumption, he appeared to be in full panic mode, struggling to get away.

"Guess I better rescue him," Jay sighed, parting ways with the pair even as Wade began questioning Crazy Zane on his recent stunts.

****

They waited out the final two groups of competitors, watching with avid interest from the second island as only four of the ten challengers made it safely across. Jay was impressed by even those that had not, with wily moves and adept control of their virtues, but the successful lot were certainly leagues above the rest.

Raiza, as seemed fitting, was the first of his fellowship to cross the track, both he and his electric virtue agile and practiced. Like Heather, the Windrunner of Jay's group, the next to finish was careful and concise, taking his time, whereas the others rushed it. There was a moment when he was near to taking a plunge, but his virtue, a gravitic, caught his fall from afar as he cried out for it. Though Jay thought the intervention of the virtue likely to raise protest, it seemed that they were as keen to allow it as they had been for him.

The next group yielded the same number of champions, an evolutic and a water virtue their companions, and the first trial was wrapped up. Jay,

Wade, Crazy Zane, and a still-hassled Blaze all stood to depart for the second round together. Their merry band of subscribers followed with excited chatter as to how well their adopted victors would fare in the next round. Jay's anxiety mounted the more they spoke, though, many of them reminiscing on past challenges and wondering what nefarious concoctions the Manifestival judges had decided to try this year.

"Any idea what we're in for?" Jay asked as Crazy Zane's wild gaze wandered his way.

"No such luck," he droned. "They keep the Trials fresh every year. Always follows a pattern though. The one we just finished is considered the Trial of Bonds. It's supposed to test binder-virtue compatibility and whatever. How well can you communicate, how quickly can you act together, synchronicity you know?"

"And the next one is the Trial of Strength," a familiar voice chimed in.

Jay turned to find Raylin merging with their ensemble. When her two female compatriots joined as well, Wade subtly slowed his pace to fall in stride with the one he had attempted to impress the evening before. She gave him a bashful smile as they took up a conversation of their own.

"What exactly are they going to be looking for?" Jay asked, choosing to stay on topic.

"That's the mystery," Raylin said with a smirk. "It changes from year to year, but like Zane says, it's always on theme. My guess is that they test how well we can fight."

"Like virtue combat?" Jay asked worriedly.

"Nah," Zane interrupted. "No way they'll do that this early. They can't eliminate so many in one round.

They'll likely save that for last."

"So wait. We *are* going to be fighting each other?" Jay asked again.

"Of course," Raylin answered with a perplexed stare before it returned to realization. "Forgot you wouldn't know. It's always part of the Manifestival. Competitors go one of the four rounds in elimination combat to see who can emerge the strongest."

"Or the smartest," Zane added with a wink.

Jay felt a prickle of worry in the pit of his stomach at the prospect. He stood no chance if it came down to *directing* Blaze in a fight. The dog simply wouldn't listen. Of course, if Blaze decided to hold up his end of the bargain and go for the win, they might be back in the race. He had absorbed all the adoration he could stand already, though, which left him with no incentive short of Jay's bumbling pleas.

When they broke away from the group to rejoin Ansela on the next stage—a new and larger courtyard in what seemed to center of the second Isle—Wade remained fastened to his consort of Raylin's friends, charm still laid on thick. Jay took his place next to the six other contestants and waited for Ansela to address the still-moving crowds.

Though he had been on the Isle for over an hour now, Jay suddenly realized that he hadn't yet taken in the sights and differences of it from the first. His mind had been wholly wrapped on the contest and his inner brooding. Standing there in the patient quiet, though, he had ample opportunity to gauge it all.

The color scheme was the first notable change, as this portion of the city was bathed in burgundies and whites, low and mellow purples cropping up here and there. Whereas the first Isle—the Isle of Promise as Ansela had called it—was a hodgepodge of spilled hues that rallied the brain, this soft and subtle theme set it at ease.

As Jay's inspection continued, what appeared a more feminine and flowery landscape at first glance soon showed signs of solid infrastructure and hard lines beneath. The roads leading into this central point of the island were plain and uncurving, straight from start to finish, and designed to let the eye escape into the distance. The buildings were squat and square, masses of what seemed to be hewn ivory cut into considerable size from floor to ceiling. Though the multitude of trees bloomed with cherry blossoms and dogwood petals, they were protected at the bases with stark pillars of iron and similar rings of warding lace between. The planter boxes that held the most brilliant bulbs of rose and tulip and lily were basic and bland, built for function rather than fashion, but they only seemed to enhance the beauty above.

"Ladies and gentlemen! *Wow*! *Just wow*!" Ansela boomed, bringing Jay's attention back around.

The masses seemed to share her single-word sentiment with a sudden hum followed by silence.

"What an exciting start to our day! Of our fifteen competitors, only seven remain. But not for long! The Trial of Strength awaits our brave challengers, and at the end, only *four* will proceed. Who will it be? The stakes are high, but the talent even higher!"

As she spoke, another pedestal rose from beneath her position in the central ring, carrying her into the sky to look over all the others. The crowd quivered with excitement, a rippling sea of faces that only blurred into flat colors when Jay turned to survey them all.

Waving a hand toward a semicircular amphitheater to her rear, separated by ropes and free of people, Ansela went on, "The Trial of Strength is an honored tradition in the Manifestival, hosted here on the Isle of Power for the past two hundred years. Over these vast generations, we have lived and learned of the ways of strength, of its many forms, and of the wisdom required to wield it well. Today, our challengers will be presented with a chance to prove their abilities to command such strength in conjunction with their virtues. By the generosity of our own Master Pierre Kabolt and his unfailing ingenuity, we have constructed the spheres you see before you."

Jay, gaze still roaming the referenced area, took note of the dozen spheres erected within the half-circle. With the stone wall as a high backdrop, the constructs appeared at first to be only decorative. But Ansela soon dismantled that presumption.

"Inside these well-built and sturdy designs lie switches that, similar to those of the previous Trial, will stop the clock for the competitor to whom it belongs. In order to reach the switch, each of our contestants will need to penetrate the reinforced hide of the sphere using only the strength of his or her virtue. Once the breach is made, the switch may be struck and the Trial completed. But it is not only a timed test! Competitors will be scored by our panel of judges on many more accounts! The number of actions taken to penetrate the sphere, the wisdom and guile used, and the presentation of power only to name a few. The four highest scores will earn the right to progress in the Manifestival!"

Jay could see the consternation on each of his opponents' faces. They were already considering how to best break into the vaulted domes, which tactics to employ for the swiftest access. He had no such need. Regardless of what plan of action he could cook up now, the truth was that Blaze would do whatever Blaze wanted.

He peered down at his virtue who, at the moment, seemed to care less for the tournament than he did for the rustling of a small bug in the grasses next to his paw. Jay groaned inwardly.

"Competitors, take your places!" Ansela demanded, to which everyone but Jay moved purposefully.

Not wanting to look like a *complete* idiot, he moseyed behind Raylin until he saw her step onto an area marked out for participants before one of the many steely orbs. He took his place next to her and waved Blaze forward to stand in the position marked out for virtues. In rapid fashion, six more virtues came to life around Jay, on his left and right, summoned from the souls of the others.

Raylin looked at him with a humored expression. "Why don't you ever recall your virtue?"

Jay cocked his head to the side. "He and I have an…*agreement*."

"Oh?" she prodded.

"I let him roam free, and he helps me with things like this." Jay gestured to the point of the Trial.

Raylin only nodded, lips pursed in amused lines.

Jay knelt down to face Blaze, who now watched Raylin with ominous interest. "It's all you, big guy. Just…do whatever you can to break into that bubble." He thumbed toward the sphere, and Blaze's gaze followed.

"*On my mark*," Ansela shouted again, voice echoing throughout the city. There was a brief pause before she screamed in unity with the crowd, "*Begin!*"

Jay withdrew from Blaze's panel. Fireworks, sparks, and loud crashes from Zane's gorilla filled the air. To Jay's right, the girl with the evolutic virtue—a stag with great, gnarly horns—was commanding it to take consecutive rushes to tackle her sphere. Slowly, the hide of the spherical shell, like dense but somewhat brittlely layered stone, splintered away beneath its onslaught.

Raylin, on the other hand, had her avian virtue drilling into the fore of the sphere with heated strikes of its long, needlelike beak. Rather than brute force, she was effectively using finesse to open a small wound in its side wide enough to fit her thin arm through.

"Having trouble?" she asked with a broad, triumphant grin as the bird cracked into a second layer of the sphere. Her amber eyes watched Blaze as he simply sat there, studying the others much as Jay was. "I'm beginning to think your virtue is a little stunted, J-Jay. Does it take after its owner?"

Jay turned to Blaze, afraid for Raylin now that the taunts had been extended to his virtue and not just him. He knew how to take a jab in stride. *Blaze did not.*

Blaze narrowed his piercing eyes at her, a growl rising in the back of his throat. The posturing did nothing to assuage Raylin's biting humor, though. Just before Jay intervened to keep his temperamental mutt from attacking a fellow contestant, Blaze moved. Like a flash of heat lightning, Blaze's body burned with red and white flames. The tempest of fire rose up around him, charring the surface of the stone walkway. Jay blinked with shock, and the virtue was simply gone. In the split second before he returned to sight, an explosion rocked the arena and shook the cobbles beneath the entire mob of onlookers.

Jay's head snapped to the source even as his feet left the ground. Blaze, in fiery glory, stood before the shattered shell of Jay's sphere, gaze still pinned on Raylin, whose rear had found the pavement several feet away from Jay's own landing point. The poor girl to Jay's right flew end over end into a row of shrubbery while her virtue stumbled away from its task to land into the next competitor's territory. The entire courtyard gasped in unison. A few of the judges even rushed away from their posts to assist the displaced contestants.

Raylin stood in tandem with Jay, and both stared absolutely *dumbstruck* at Blaze. The again unconcerned dog meandered back to the small square of his designated start and huffed proudly. Jay exchanged an equally bewildered look with Raylin before turning his attention back to the commentator. He could barely make out the words that Ansela was shouting, though they seemed surprisingly enthusiastic.

Jay waded through the rubble like a confused child. Strolling past the smug Blaze, who seemed to wink at him with one of his red-hot eyes, he stationed himself before the buzzer and slapped it numbly. It did not stop his clock, as the small and melted digital screen behind it showed no numbers at all. The large red button crumbled beneath the weight of his hand, adding more carnage to the mass of debris at his feet. He turned to face the judges' table with trepidation. The buzz of excitement there, however, thawed his frozen gut, and soon, the words Ansela was speaking came into focus.

"...has not let us down! Such a *magnificent* display of confidence and control by Blaze and the Dualist, folks! No hesitation, no concern for the competition! He has done only what it takes to win! Do we have our first of four?"

She held her words, and Jay held his breath. The judges, all of them now back at the table and hunkered in discussion, quickly agreed. A large card with the number ten painted onto it met the air.

Jay jerked his elbows back and nearly danced with euphoria. He ran to Blaze, scooping him up and holding the dog high above his head. Not caring for the show of comradery, Blaze wriggled free and fell onto his shoulder before skating down his back and away. But the crowd erupted with that familiar chant nonetheless.

"*Blaze, Blaze, Blaze!*" and "*Innis, Innis, Innis!*"

Jay turned to offer one more apologetic glance to both Raylin and the unknown girl before moving swiftly out of their vengeful reach. By the looks on their faces, neither was ready to forgive the trespass.

The competition progressed, and as Jay suspected, Raylin finished second. Then Crazy Zane followed by Raiza. Two of the remaining three finished with mixed results, but Jay's airborne neighbor decided to throw in the towel before her stag made it all the way through. Jay felt a guilty stain at that, knowing that Blaze's move had likely thrown her off her game, but there was nothing he could do for it.

When the numbers were called, the first four to complete the task became the victors to proceed to the next round. But Jay was not without his moment of embarrassment as the judges decided to give their reasoning to the crowd.

One of the judges, a squat man with a bold, black mustache and a thinning hairline, took the stage next to

Ansela and then her mic. "As for Jameson Innis and his virtue, Blaze, we admit that the tactic was brutish and unrefined, but the raw power displayed and the singular nature of the act that cracked his sphere was enough to demonstrate the heart of this Trial. Strength comes in many shapes and sizes, but the barest version of it, stripped down and returned to its roots, is often the most effective. Though Mr. Innis lacked what many of our other challengers portrayed in circumspection and precision, his virtue was the first and the most potent to complete the task."

The explanation met no resistance. Excitement still tangible, the crowds thinned again and readied themselves for another spectacular show. Most headed toward the ferry that would take them to the third Isle, but Jay lagged behind with Wade and Blaze. They plopped onto the first bleacher and eyed the dog warily.

"I think I have a new respect for you," Wade spoke reverently at the distracted dog. "That was *all-star*."

"Only problem is that you did it outta spite rather than for the win." Jay sighed.

Blaze nipped at a leaf swirling lazily on the wind next to his head. He seemed wholly indifferent to their considerations.

"At least he did it," Wade defended. "He could've been the usual lazy sack."

Jay turned his curious stare to his friend. "A few days ago, you were complaining that he was a *demon dog*. Now, you're his biggest fan?"

"That was before he became popular," Wade said with a grin. "Turns out the ladies dig my connection to the rising *Dualist*. You win this tournament and I'm as good as winning our bet." He mimed making out with an invisible girl.

"Well, we're only halfway through, so don't get your hopes up just yet." Jay reached down to swipe a hand through Blaze's hair. "You keep this up and I'll owe you big time."

Blaze puffed and scrambled away from his touch. Jay stood and signaled Wade along.

"Come on, let's see if we can catch the next boat."

They took the street that had, only minutes before, held the concentration of the masses. It pitched in perfect straightness toward the crystal blue river beyond, and above the heads of a few stragglers waiting for the next round, Jay could see the recently departed ferry toting its passengers into the distance.

The river wound away from this island like a snake, curving once, twice, and then a third time before it slunk off into unknown territory. Just before its escape, though, Jay could see the outline of the third Isle carved out against the horizon. It appeared considerably larger than the two that they had toured so far, but details were scarce at this range.

They waited in line, able just to make it onto the next boat before it reached capacity. It whined with electric engines and propellers as it carried them upstream toward their destination. Jay thought that, though the motors certainly seemed capable for this stint and back, they were unlikely to go much farther than Isle to Isle before needing a massive recharge. Nothing onboard seemed capable of generating the needed electricity to keep the beast moving aside from a few crewmates that likely controlled potent electric virtues.

But his attention didn't linger there. Instead, he found himself reviewing the Isle of Power as they departed. Even now, he could see the stark difference of two seemingly opposite mechanics strung together to make a sight most beautiful. The island was like a rose itself, soft colors and mortared petals rising high into the air, all suspended on a strong stem of bedrock and surrounded by protective iron girdles. There was something about it that struck a note deep inside him.

As he gazed back upon the Isle of Power and its meticulously opposing design that somehow harmonized so perfectly, he couldn't help but feel a well of foreign emotions and thoughts. The island was surely crafted by the hands of men and women with that strategy in mind, but the sight of it spurred him to consider a larger question.

Who made this world? He had never really considered it, and that felt...*wrong*. Who crafted the surface of this planet with its own intricate designs and its impossibly perfect harmony? Who caused this setting sun to rise and fall?

Or even nearer to his heart: *who made him*?

"Worried?" a voice broke into his musings.

Jay turned to see Wade propped against the rail of the boat, dark, crinkly hair catching the spray.

"About?" he asked in kind.

"What do you think?" Wade answered. "You worried about the next Trial?"

Jay shook his head. "Nah, at this point, I'm just having fun."

He nudged Blaze with the tip of his boot. Blaze gave it no mind, watching the water churn up in white froth beneath them as they went.

"What is it, then?" Wade pressed. "You got that look."

"*Look*?" Jay laughed. "What kind of look?"

"You know! That look you get when you're all serious about something."

"Oh, so, I have a look?" Jay mocked. "Tell me then, what does this *look* look like?"

Wade apparently didn't share the humor in full. "The same one you get when you talk about Full Bindature," he said, voice low and conspiratorial.

Jay sobered. "Just thinking about big stuff," he answered seriously this time.

"Like what?"

"Like…you ever think about who made all this?" He gestured around them.

"Some engineers, probably. A local company would be my guess. Who else needs ferries?"

"No," Jay sighed, "Like…*all* of this. *The world*, Wade."

Wade was quiet then, clearly unsure how to answer that. "Well. Guess I have thought about it a time or two. What's got you on it?"

Jay shrugged. "I don't really know. I guess growing up behind city walls left me sheltered. Now, we're out roaming this massive world and it just…begs some questions."

The boat bumped a series of rapids that jarred them back and forth. Blaze fell away from his viewing perch and steamed until they rode it out.

"It's no big deal," Jay inserted, "Just a random thought."

"Seems like a big deal to me," Wade countered wryly. "I mean, if I went and made a world, I'd kinda want people to say, '*hey, that's a big deal*!' "

Jay rolled his eyes but couldn't stop the smile from

splitting his lips.

"So I did a little investigation while you Blaze laid the smackdown earlier," Wade changed directions. "This next test is supposed to be the Trial of *Control*."

"You mean you talked about something other than yourself for a change? With a girl? I'm impressed."

Wade narrowed his eyes. "I see my assistance is unappreciated. Perhaps I'll offer it to Raylin instead next time." He waggled his eyebrows. "Nah, I play the long game anyways, remember? You win, I win. So this Trial typically measures how well you and your virtue can stay on track. Kylie said it's a lot of distractions, lot of illusions...stuff like that."

"*Kylie*?" Jay tasted the name. "Things must be getting serious."

Wade waved a dismissive hand at him.

"Okay, okay. So what did *Kylie* think this was gonna be?"

"She couldn't say," Wade answered. "But she suspects it'll be tough. They cut the four to only two after this. Last Trial is a championship match. Head-to-head. The Trial of Totality."

"Meaning the last two have to duke it out?" he surmised.

Wade could see the worry in his eyes. "Let's just win this next Trial before we have any meltdowns, yeah?"

They both eyed Blaze, who was paying them no attention at all.

****

Jay stepped off the ferry and felt exactly what he expected to feel when viewing this island from afar: *focused*. The landmass jutted away from the cool blue waters of the river, rising higher than the others, a spire to stand in stark contrast to its squatter siblings. *And it was gray. And that was it.* Jay could see nothing more of note from his vantage on the water aside from the theme of chalky gray granite in every surface both horizontal and otherwise.

The cliffsides reached up and around the large Isle, barely a brown or a green in sight to break the monotony. The buildings, similar to their foundations, were constructed of dark gray stones with occasional strikes of obsidian black running through them like webs of foreign invaders. The streets were simply chiseled out of the gargantuan mound, like a lump of boring clay cut away and pressed into something resembling a city.

As the trio struggled up the steep incline toward the center of the Isle, Jay felt the contrast in greater proportion. The newfound focus that had settled on him met its explanation: there was nothing here to steal away his attention. It was only he and Blaze, the tournament ahead of them the sole priority. Before, he found his mind wandering to the bright colors and the exquisite designs, but here, there was nothing but the task that awaited.

Ansela had already started the fanfare before Jay took his place in the grand quad. It was, as the Isle itself, larger than the last two, but the tedium kept Jay's gaze from wandering far from the announcer.

"Ladies and gentlemen, welcome to the third of our four Trials today! I can say with sound resolve that this has been the most thrilling and unexpected turn of events in all the years I have assisted with the Manifestival! Truly a competition worthy of our bicentennial celebration!"

Jay gave Zane a quick pat on the back and took his place beside Raylin. Raiza shot him a googly-eyed glance, but he honestly wasn't sure if it was friendly or not. Like his sister, Jay still didn't know what to make of him.

"Don't think you'll get away with those antics this time," Raylin whispered. "You're on *my* turf now."

Jay lifted his brows. "You live here?" he asked, catching the insinuation.

She smiled at him. "Yep. And everyone knows I'm the queen of this rock."

"...Isle of Prudence!" Ansela called out over their furtive exchange. "Here, we will host the trying Trial of Control! Can our contestants maintain their concentration and incentivize their virtues to do the same? Will they succeed in conquering the repulsing obstacles that await?"

She struck a pose, readying to wave a hand and reveal the course set out for the four participants to endure, but before she could say a word, the rotund judge from before hobbled up to her podium and waved her down.

Jay watched curiously as they held a quick and heated conversation. Ansela was obviously disgruntled at having been interrupted, but when the judge finished his spiel, she was smiling ear-to-ear. They separated, and the broadcaster reclaimed the stage while the judge stood idly by.

"Good people of the Arken Isles, do we have a treat for you! As recommended by our panel of judges today, this year's Trial of Control will take an unparalleled turn! A twist to keep our competitors on their feet, a little flare for the audience, and we will have a show we will not soon forget!"

Turning to the four wary challengers, Ansela explained, even as the obstacle course was revealed behind a series of thick, gray curtains, "During this Trial, you will be *paired*. Rather than take this test alone, you will support your partner through to the end. Two competitors, two virtues, and a hounding Trial!"

With a slash of her hand, she gestured between Raiza and Raylin, sealing Jay's fate yet again with his female nemesis. "Crazy Zane will be paired with Thunderstrike, while the blazing Dualist will work side-by-side with our very own Prodigy of Flame!"

Jay groaned aloud, suddenly wishing that he had chosen to stand next to Zane rather than her, but Raylin appeared somehow pleased with the verdict.

"The Trial is simple," Ansela went on, turning to pin their attentions on two separate stretches of track running lengthwise next to one another.

Jay could see barriers and pitfalls, pillars, and small gouges of water carved out into the stone. Unlike the first Trial's track, though, this one was no more than one hundred yards from start to finish.

"You and your partner must make it to the end of the course together. Your virtues are excluded this time from needing to reach that end in order to succeed. Only the binders are required to cross the finish line. Only two rules apply: do not step out of bounds and do not recall your virtue, whether by will or default."

Jay looked to Raylin with the last, unsure what Ansela meant by *default*.

Seeing that he was confused, the announcer explained off-mic, "If your virtue sustains too much physical stress during its summoning, it will automatically recoil into the safety of your soul, thereby recalling itself for protection and recovery. If this occurs, both you and your partner will be disqualified."

Jay reeled. His mind flashed back to that horrid night in Estelia when the town came under siege. The image of a beaten and broken Blaze filled his view, and he realized then that the dog, in his abysmal stubbornness, had resisted doing the very thing that could have protected him from further harm. He had never considered it possible, but it made perfect sense. If Blaze had simply allowed himself to be recalled that night, he wouldn't have risked whatever it was that happened to a virtue when it...*when it died.*

His anxiety spiked, worry flooding through him at whatever dangers this Trial might present, but he had no time to question anything further before the crowd demanded some action.

"Let's get this show started!" Ansela fed the flame. "Competitors, take your positions!"

Raiza and Zane trotted over to their track while Raylin practically had to pull Jay along by the wrist. Blaze followed unconcernedly, and Jay had to wonder what he would do if something went awry.

"Get your head in the game!" Raylin barked at him, flashing her hand to summon her fiery cohort. "I'm not about to lose this because you're worried about your little pal."

Blaze, now knowing he was the topic of her taunt, puffed at her warningly.

"And *you* keep your cool, you hear me?" she started, bending down to stare the dog in the eyes. "No more showing off. No more reckless charges. You *listen* to what we say, got it?"

Blaze stood his ground, unmoving. Jay intervened.

"Look, we can handle it. How about we just focus on getting *ourselves* across rather than worrying about what the other will do?"

She drew a deep breath and blew it out her nose. "*Don't lose.*"

"Same to you," Jay said smarmily.

Raylin turned her attention to the field before them, studying the lines carefully. Jay did the same, and even as he spun to survey, a handful of people stepped out from the crowds and into the arena of both their track and the other. Raylin wore the same expression as Jay, slightly askew, but both knew that it couldn't have been so easy. Stationing themselves like sentinels behind thick walls of glass and flashing their magical abilities in succession, Jay realized that the additions to the Trial would likely do whatever they could to stop the competitors from reaching the end.

"On my mark!" Ansela's familiar signal came. "*Begin!*"

Raylin was gone in a flash. Jay's mind churned through the pieces of the puzzle before him. Two sentinels stationed on either side of the course, left and right. There were small portions of cover scattered throughout, but none seemed to call to him with any measure of purpose. The ankle-high grass gave way to slabs of stone shortly past the jutting boulders and beyond, the finish line.

Raylin pressed toward the center, tucking behind a dividing pillar that split the track in two. Before she could make it to cover, though, the sentinel on the right began weaving an ethereal blue light between his palms. Specks of frost littered the ground around her feet and rapidly formed into full sheets of ice. Her steps planted in full sprint, she lost balance and slid headfirst into the stone column. The crowd groaned with her audible impact.

Jay, despite his earlier instruction to fend for themselves, lifted a boot in her direction, readying to join her. Even as he did, though, she righted herself, spat a few curt commands to her virtue, and watched as the bird swooped low to lay a run of fire down across the slick surface. The ice melted away but immediately began to reform as the caster continued working his magic.

Deciding to let her figure that conundrum out alone, Jay turned his attention to the sentinel guarding the left portion of the track. She was unmoving, simply studying him from behind her protective barrier. Jay couldn't initially tell if she commanded the same element as her cohort, but a quick glance at the other track suggested that she *did not*.

Zane and Raiza were in a similar bout of wills with their two defenders. Raiza was struggling to dodge what appeared to be a force caster as translucent bubbles of energy agitated the air before him. When one struck true, Raiza was blasted off his feet, his lithe, snakelike electric virtue caught in the propulsion as well. They both ended up dangerously close to the boundary before scrambling back to safety. Zane, on the other hand, seemed to be handling his darkness opponent rather efficiently. Clouds of tangible blackness seeped out from behind the woman's barrier, obscuring the way forward and hiding many pitfalls and traps that lay in her territory. Zane's radiant gorilla, though, flexed its magical muscles and expelled the darkness in a small beam that guided Zane's footsteps.

Jay realized he had no choice but to try. It was obvious that the guardian of his path wasn't going to present him with any information until he made his move first. Gesturing for Blaze to remain behind, he jogged into the mostly clear field. When he made it halfway to the barrier, he could see a bright red button mounted on a pedestal beside the sentinel.

To stop the resistance. So only one of us has to make it.

He made a line for it. Sprinting with all his might, he cringed when green tendrils of ether began to leak away from the woman's palms. He knew what was coming before it hit him. A tornadic force of wind smacked into him like a brick fist, sending him sprawling back several yards toward Blaze. The dog padded up to him, less from concern and more of a need to offer a shaming look.

Jay moaned as he stood, cradling what was sure to be a bruised rack of ribs. Without offering a word of protest to Blaze's vexing expression, he scooped the dog up and pinned him tight to his chest.

"*Be still,*" he said in a low tone as Blaze began fighting.

Like a snubbed candle, the dog's resistance winked out. Jay considered that curiously for a split second, mind returning to the moment when Professor Farsk handed him the virtue for the first time. Shaking the reminiscence, though, he refocused. He had a plan.

"We can do this, but I'm gonna need your help. See that little red button?" He turned the dog's head in that direction. "One of us needs to hit it. You're faster than me, Blaze. You can get to it if I can keep her distracted."

The wind-wall was still as active as when she first

cast it. Jay could see dust and pebbles swirling in small eddies about the ground ahead of them. Her hands were alive with green lights, her entire being raptured in focus to keep the spell going.

"We rush in toward the pillar," he continued, turning Blaze's head again to pinpoint the large stone wall that Raylin was moving out from behind in another attempt to skate the ice rink. "Once there, you charge up for a rush. I'll run out to catch her attention, then you make your move. Got it?"

Blaze didn't answer, of course, but Jay felt that he had explained it as best as he could for the hasty strategy that it was. Without wasting any more time, he tucked Blaze under an arm and shot toward the protective buffer. The wind coursed against him, but it wasn't quite as potent with his new trajectory. He had gotten the jump. He was able to press through and into cover before the caster redirected the gust across his altered path. Like a hurricane, though, the sound and pressure spiked in his vicinity, sending Jay hunkering down with Blaze falling in by his side.

"Get ready!" he shouted over the din.

Blaze, though clearly grumpy at being manhandled and forced into this predicament, powered up in preparation. Jay inhaled a lungful of air and leaped back into the fray. Before he made it three steps, though, he was swept off his feet again. This time he angled his body down to plant clawed fingers into the back side of a protruding stone lip. His body rode the breeze like a ragdoll as he struggled to hang on, grip weakening with every excruciating second. He shouted at the caster, heckling her for more. *And she answered*. The winds increased like a ranked-up hurricane, a smile widening on her face as she tried her best to blow him off the rock and out of bounds. But he had done his job.

Blaze erupted from behind his cover as the woman poured everything she had into a concentrated tunnel that hit Jay like a rocket. He let go and flew back to the start, barely catching himself before he, like Raiza, neared the boundary lines. When he looked back up, though, the wind had stopped, and the woman was backing away from a small red and black wad of fur. He celebrated as she surrendered the post, slapping the buzzer herself to show that she was giving in. Apparently, Blaze was taking her efforts personally.

Jay caught up as swiftly as he could, nodded a quick apology to the hassled woman, and pulled Blaze away before his threatening growls escalated to physical assault.

"Dude, it's just a competition," he assured.

But Blaze wasn't listening. His focus, like Jay's, seemed to gravitate to the next challenge. Raylin had already beaten them to the start. Instead of two separate paths, this center obstacle converged on a single point where an older man stood, triggering ground-shattering movements of the earth with every swipe of his hands. His mineral-based magic appeared to be leagues above the previous casters, as he was raising and lowering walls of rock to continuously block Raylin's attempts to pass.

"Don't just stand there!" Raylin shouted after him. "*Do something!*"

Jay broke away from his trance and sped to a trot. Like hers, though, his path split at a seam, and a ten-foot wall of stone separated him from one of the two points where he could sidle by the caster's barrier. There was a moat of deep water cutting across the course at this point, like the pillar before, forcing the contestants to deal with the obstacle before moving on.

Raylin's bird attempted to soar over the walls and chase the old man away, but he swiped at it lazily, sending a shower of dust and sand into the air to blind and distract. It flew awkwardly for a moment, knocking into a new stone structure forged by magic before toppling down to the ground. Raylin shouted for it to return, but it seemed confused, unable to tell her apart from the many monoliths around it.

"This guy's good!" Jay shouted.

"Yeah, you should join his fan club," Raylin spat. "Help me figure out a way past this!"

Jay started to move, but Blaze cut him off.

"What is it?" he asked, seeing the dog focusing on the top of the projected mountain before them.

Jay traced the climb and noted the somewhat smooth surface of the wall, the heady scent of lubricant on the air around them, and, ultimately, the seam that appeared too even to be cut by the edge of raw magic. He smiled down at Blaze, praising his perception.

"They're preset. So we just need to walk the maze."

Blaze, ahead of him on the idea, stepped around the massive barrier and met no immediate resistance. But after taking a series of canters toward the caster, a new wall sprang into existence about him in a 'U' shape. Raylin, still trying to surmount the wall blocking her path, gave a withering look at their calm demeanors.

"Well?" she shouted.

"It's a maze!" Jay answered. "The walls are predetermined. We need to find a way to navigate them."

Raylin sighed, planting the brunt of her palm on her forehead. *"Of course.* No wonder he can summon and maintain so many."

"Take it slow," Jay encouraged. "There's got to be a *right* way through this."

Raylin shot a piercing whistle through the air, calling her virtue back to her side. Finally overcoming the confusion that had stilled it, the bird flapped back over the wall and came to perch on its edge.

"Find the lines," she directed. "Fly high and see if you can locate a place where the walls *won't* be."

Jay and Blaze continued their ground search while Raylin awaited her virtue's return. Every few paces seemed to erupt with a new hindrance, but Jay took his time to mentally map them.

It was a frustrating challenge. They needed to best Zane and Raiza's time, but if they tried to rush this, it would only upset their attempts and cost them.

After a painfully long time, the pair made it closer to the center, from what Jay could tell, but they were still far from reaching the end. Raylin was lost to sight at this point, left behind in wait for her companion. Just as Jay was about to call out for her, though, the most recent wall barring his way shuddered. With a loud crash, the series of puzzling barricades plummeted back into their facets, revealing a wide, clear path to where Raylin stood, one hand planted on the red buzzer while the other rested on her hip.

"You coming or not?" she teased, spinning away to face the next trial.

Jay caught up with her, genuinely happy that she had succeeded, even if she planned on rubbing it in. When the walls fell, he could see that Zane and Raiza had already begun their final test, an evolutic caster by the looks of it. Ropelike tentacles of vines and limbs sprang forth from the ground and two nearby trees, encasing them by ankles and arms and continuously tossing them back to the start. He wished that he could swap courses with them in that moment, knowing that he and Raylin could simply burn the brambles away to make it to the end. But what he saw awaiting *them* made his heart sink.

"*Gravitic?*" Raylin asked, clearly thinking the matchup unfair as well.

She marched out away from the sitting mineral caster, who watched them with an amused expression. The purple veins of light in the air before the next and final caster were charged and awaiting them to make a move. Raylin did. But even as she proceeded into the exposed arena, her steps grew sluggish and strained. Eventually, her forward momentum came to a complete stop. She appeared as if the weight of the world was suddenly on her shoulders, unable to lift even the tip of her toes to take another step.

Jay closed his eyes, letting his mind wrap around the challenge. *What could they do?* It was an open field. The caster was likely capable of encasing all four of them in the gravitic magic. If they were all trapped, there would be no way to break free. *End game.*

He traced his thoughts back to everything he knew of gravitic magic—of magic in general. There had to be *something*. All those books he read, all the time spent researching.

Elemental Mastery and Casting Procedure: utilizing the bond with a virtue to open the door to their magic. Envisioning the desired effect and calling on the power of the dormant virtue to supply it. Summoning the effect into reality. The potency of the effect is equivalent to the potency of the bound virtue supplying it.

Nothing there. He kept digging through his memory. *Spell Maintenance and Limiting Variables: immense focus to retain the desired effect. Potency dwindles over prolonged casting. Overworked virtues tend to provide less power and capability. Casting new spells while maintaining priors expends at a higher rate.*

But Jay figured that this caster was well-stocked on power. Waiting out a failure on her part would certainly lose them the match. *So what else?* Jay felt like it was on the tip of his tongue, the precipice of his mind, just waiting for him to nudge it enough to fall away. *Another limit.* There was something he was missing, something—

Line of Sight.

There it was. He cast his gaze all around them then, finding Blaze in a similar stupor as Raylin and her virtue. But there was nothing here that he could use. He surveyed the other course then. *There.*

"Raylin, I have a plan. Do you trust me?"

His partner, still trapped in her sloth bubble, grunted through gritted teeth, "If it gets me out of this, then yes."

"All right. Get ready to run. When I say, don't look, don't think, just run as fast as you can to the finish line. Oh, and hold your breath too, okay?"

Her eyes twitched nervously, but she didn't argue. Jay looked down to Blaze, readying to place his bet.

"Can your fireballs reach over to their course?" He nodded toward where Zane and Raiza still fought their way through wilder fare.

Blaze cocked his head as if considering that.

"Just *try*," Jay coached. "But don't interfere with them directly. Try to burn the vines closest to this side of the boundary."

He pointed toward a wide swathe of where the

vegetation was out of control. Though it didn't whip and writhe like the rest, it still continued to grow under the influence of the caster's magic.

"Make it nice and hot. We're gonna need some *smoke*."

Blaze trotted a bit closer to the edge of their course, careful not to draw the scrutiny of the gravitic mage. He planted his paws firmly into the dirt. Body suddenly glowing with air-warping heat, Blaze barked out a series of burning bolts that caught the other arena on fire. It was far enough away from Zane and Raiza that Jay could argue against interference, but it soon generated the thick and billowing substance he needed.

Great waves of dark gray smog rose up over the second course, but Jay didn't let it linger there long. Sucking in a deep lungful of oxygen, he broke his vow to the other contestants and summoned his control of void. The air around him swallowed itself, vanishing into nothingness and tugging on everything it could influence. Jay strained to control it, but it felt like an unbridled animal refusing to heed his call. Slowly, though, the wild vortex funneled its draw on the environment.

The smoke began to move.

Lungs burning, Jay pulled the black cloud toward them, drawing gasps from the crowd that soon turned to chokes and coughs. When he neared vertigo from the lack of breath, he released his lungs but held fast to the magic.

Just a little more.

But he buckled to one knee and had to stop. He was *dying*, slowly suffocating from the empty atmosphere. When his control of void faded, tainted oxygen rushed back into his vicinity, and he drank it in rough and panicked gulps. To his astonishment, though, the cloud kept coming. The momentum was enough to bring it over them in sheets, and soon, he couldn't see his hand in front of his face. There was a blanket of darkness now, burning his eyes and throat with its acidic twang.

"Raylin, now!" he rasped. But he knew she had heard it just as he knew that the magic holding her to that fixed position was gone.

Even if the caster had not been surprised enough to let her focus wane, the smoke layering the arena was too dense to hold a firm image in the eye for long. *Line of sight*, one of the many limiting factors to using the magic that virtues imbued upon binding, had been broken. The caster could no longer summon an image of her target, therefore she couldn't properly envision the effect she needed the magic to enact. They were temporarily free of the gravitic hindrance that kept them from winning, but it had only been replaced by another.

Jay struggled to his feet again and floundered through the racing smoke. He had been angled in the general direction of the finish line before it overwhelmed him. He saw the red buzzer he was meant to touch on the other side just as the cloud buried it from sight. He ran as fast as he dared, trying to maintain that trajectory. To his blessed relief, he heard a blaring signal shake the stands to his right. *Raylin had made it.* Now he just needed—

Another signal blasted across the air, this time to his left. He could hear Raiza shouting triumphantly. *If Zane beat him there, it was all over.*

He lunged when he saw the white line beneath his feet. *The buzzer had to be close.* He crawled across the ground, swiping with frantic hands. The smoke was still too thick. He couldn't see anything. And there was *so much noise* now. The hype in the crowd had reached its crescendo. He shouted curses, scrambling to find anything that could help him regain sense. His hand touched something metal. He pulled himself up it, climbing it like a summit. And at the peak, *the prize*. He slapped it ferociously, hope swelling in his chest even as the bugle swelled across the arena.

"*Yeah!*" he croaked, coughing so hard on the acrid air that he nearly puked.

The crowd ricocheted his excitement. Chants once again rose over the stadium, and the wind mage from the start of their course worked the smoke away for Jay and the rest to see. When it finally cleared, Jay looked first to Raylin who was jumping up and down, thrusting her hands into the air in manic celebration. She shot him a look that suggested a further respect for his dangerous ingenuity. When he looked to his other side, he saw a dejected Raiza playing out the opposite of his sister, dragging his feet in sloth motions toward the course exit.

Farther along, Zane strode unhurriedly to his pedestal and laid a hand on its red surface. With a firm press, it shouted its successful song, and the masses gave their appreciative chant for his sportsmanship. But Jay saw the grinning interest on his face where the others could not.

He had to wonder if the strange traveling performer gave him the win or if he managed it fairly. The previous comment about seeing the show come down to him and Raylin hinted at the former, but that didn't necessarily mean that Zane had thrown the match. Either way, Jay had progressed to the final round, and he was going to celebrate it.

"What a climactic semifinal!" Ansela roared through her many speakers once more.

Jay looked up to find her rising on one of the many pillars controlled by the old mineral mage.

"Neck and neck, our two teams finished the courses within seconds of one another! *Incredible*! But the winners are clear, ladies and gents! The Dualist and the Prodigy will go on to face one another in the final, an explosive match to determine who will be this year's Manifestival champion!"

Raylin nudged Jay with her hip. He hadn't even seen her approach.

"You continue to impress, J-Jay," she said with a genuine smile. "But only one of us gets to take that trophy. Sorry to say that this is the end of our little soiree together."

Jay turned back to Ansela's continued instructions. "We can still be friends after I beat you," he said with a smug grin.

"I usually don't offer charity to *my* victims, but I might be willing to extend a little post-win mercy myself. Try to give me a good fight at least, won't you?"

She recalled her floating virtue once more while Blaze only jogged up to them, taking his place next to Jay's side with a 'you owe me' expression.

"You two have an odd relationship, you know that?" Raylin said.

Jay met Blaze's ruby-red eyes. "Yeah, we've got our own thing going."

"Well," she said, stretching and wiping her face, "We've got a little time before the final match. They'll kick it off right before sundown, just in time to finish up before the real festivities start. I think I'm gonna grab a shower. Smell like a campfire now." She turned up her nose.

"Guess I'll see you then?" Jay answered.

"Or," Raylin countered, "You could come with me? I could show you our place."

Jay twitched a brow. "Offering to consort with the enemy?"

"More like a little hospitality before I wipe the floor with you," she replied wryly. "Besides, poor Raiza will need some consolation to take his mind off the loss. You'll make a good distraction."

They both turned to watch the man in question kick sullenly at the base of a stone.

"Yeah, cuz a pity offering is just what he wants right now."

Raylin laughed, the sound like windchimes on a gentle breeze.

"All right, I'm in," he relented. "As long as you offer to let me clean up too. I'm not a fan of the soot myself."

"Oh, it won't be an offer. *I insist.*" She pinched her nose and walked away pointedly.

Jay shook his head and followed.

Chapter 11

Wade and Kylie caught up with the group as they meandered toward the Hargrave home, jabbering about the last Trial all the way. Raiza was none-too-pleased as they rehashed the details of Jay's and Raylin's win, but the duo seemed not to notice. By the time they made it to the leaden façade that Jay thought mirrored all the others on the island, Raiza was ready to part in a fury. He stormed up the steps two at a time, nearly knocking the door off its hinges as he entered.

"He'll cool off," Kylie noted at Wade's suddenly worried expression. "He's a bit of a sore loser. It doesn't last long, though."

Raylin only grinned at the summation, and Jay was beginning to think that she enjoyed disparagement in all its forms.

"Come on," she said, inviting them all into her home. "I'll put some tea on while we wait."

Jay and Blaze swiveled inside the door after her, pausing to gather bearing of the stark and dreary room. There were bare, bland furnishings lining the small chamber: a sofa that had seen better days, an end table lined with scars, and a set of dining chairs without their matching centerpiece. Jay opted for the comfort of the couch, falling into its frayed and worn embrace, while Kylie took what might have been her usual spot in the second of the freeform chairs. She tapped the one next to her, and Wade came to her side like a well-trained pup.

"I'll get it started," Raylin said, moving to a dark doorway and flipping on a light that revealed traces of a kitchen beyond. "Jay, you mind watching the kettle while I clean up?"

Jay shrugged and added a nod for good measure. He patted Blaze on the side as he hopped up to join.

"Thanks for the help back there," he muttered to the dog as he stood, sure that Wade and Kylie, still in their deep and *fascinating* conversation about the nature of tea leaves, wouldn't overhear.

Blaze puffed out a 'yeah, whatever' breath and snuggled into the silky fabric of the cushions. Jay grinned, letting him have his discounting ways, but he knew better. A few weeks before this, the virtue wouldn't have given him the time of day during the competition no matter how much he begged.

"Give it five, and it'll shout for you," Raylin said as she came back into the room. She swept her raven hair from her face and studied Jay curiously. "What's so funny?" she asked.

Jay wiped the stupid smirk from his lips and shrugged. "Nothing," he lied.

She squinted her tawny eyes, sure that she had caught him in a fib, but Jay met her gaze head-on and unfaltering. She was attractive. He quickly reminded himself by outlining the thin shape of her cheeks to her svelte figure. Despite her harassing ways, she could keep his attention. *And she knew it.* Her lips curved slowly upward as Jay continued to stare. With a sway of her hips, she left the room, Jay's eyes still locked on her retreat even as he fumbled to look away.

His hopes of Wade missing the overt display were

dashed as he came back around to see a giddy grin awaiting him.

"Not smart to fall for the competition," he mockingly instructed. "Better check yourself."

Jay threw a wad of fuzz relieved from the couch cushion at him. Wade hastily swiped it off, afraid of its origins, and turned back to Kylie.

"So do they live alone? Raylin and Raiza?" he asked.

Kylie bobbed her head, pink wisps of hair swaying with the movement. "Their mom died when they were born. Birth complications. I guess the risk grows with having twins. Their dad, though, well. He ran off a few years back. Met some lady from another city and decided he liked her better than his kids."

Wade's face drooped. "That's awful," he whispered.

"They learned to get on by themselves," Kylie rerouted. "Plus, they have us. Their friends, I mean. We're like one big family around here."

Jay kept an eye on the teapot from his position propped against the kitchen threshold. He wasn't willing to miss this conversation, a chance to get to know Raylin in a way that he doubted she would share with her new stranger-rival.

"Raiza works with the power company," Kylie went on. "He does pretty well for himself there. Seeing as they generate all the electricity for the area with virtue manipulation and the hydroelectric dam upriver, it keeps him busy and paid."

"What about Raylin?" Jay asked.

"She does odd jobs—nothing steady. Mostly hunting trips out toward the Deadlands."

"Deadlands?" Wade chimed.

Kylie giggled. "It's just what we call the region around the Tier-wall to the southwest. There's nothing out there, no settlements, no natural waterways, no forests. It's a buncha wasted, wide-open space. Good for hunting but not much else. They tell us not to leave the city, but what can I say? We're rebels at heart."

"Note to us:" Wade started, "*Don't* head that way."

Jay smirked. "Wasn't planning on it. We've seen what happens when we take detours."

Wade's face went white as he obviously recalled the giant monstrosity in the Cliffs that they had chosen to stuff into the dark recesses of memory.

"You know," Kylie began, unaware, "You still haven't told me what you two do."

Jay shared a look with Wade who decided to rush to an answer before his friend could spill his ridiculous dreams.

"Just traveling right now. Wanted to see a little of the world before we settle down, right Jay?" He gave a serious stare to carry the unspoken demand for agreeance.

"Yeah, that's right," Jay answered, letting his attention fade back to the whistling kettle. Truth was that he didn't care to reveal the details himself. What would Raylin think of him if he did?

He peeled away to let Wade have his private conversation again and began preparing the tea. The clatter of cups, saucers, and a steaming pot must have been a summoning bell for the lady of the house as Raylin came shuffling back into the kitchen, lustrous black hair still wet and pulled into a ponytail. Jay once again caught himself staring and unable to look away. Her sleeveless V-neck revealed a partial tattoo on her chest and shoulders that looked like a replica of her fiery virtue painted onto pale skin. When the light struck it right, Jay thought he could see it waving its wings in imaginary flight.

"Would you like me to pose for a picture?" she spoke into his stupor. "It would last you longer."

Jay broke away with a sharp blink and found her smiling openly at him. He cleared his throat and went back to pouring the tea.

"Sorry, just...admiring your ink."

"You got any?" she asked, stepping up beside him and commandeering the kettle back.

"Me? No, not a fan of needles."

She pulled away, cocked a hip, and studied him. "Hm...I wouldn't have thought that."

Jay mentally cringed as she busied herself again. Did he have to let the first real conversation with this girl start by ogling her only to fall into a revelation of his phobias? He regrouped.

"Kylie mentioned how you guys manage this all on your own. I'm impressed."

Her hands slowed in their work. "Yeah? Must not take much to impress you then."

"I wouldn't say that," Jay offered, leaning against the stone countertop and pulling an aged and wrinkly orange from a basket. "Living alone isn't easy."

"Not alone," she corrected, "I have Raiza."

"And Kylie and the others," he added for her. "But you know what I mean."

"I don't think I do," she said, tone gaining an edge. She turned on him with sudden ire. "What exactly *do* you mean, Jay?"

He took it in stride. "You've done really well

without your parents on the scene. I know that's not easy, and I just wanted to commend you for it."

"What do you know of it?" she snapped, turning back to her work.

"My parents died three years ago, right in the middle of my time at the Academy. Had to learn to cope just like you."

She sobered then. Her hand fell limp to her side, butter knife still pinched between her fingers. "I'm sorry."

Jay couldn't tell if that was for the aggressive behavior or consolation for the confession.

"Life goes on," he said somewhat drearily. "I learned to let the anger go and focus on what's ahead."

She glanced up at him. "And what is that?" she asked, a gleam back in her amber eyes.

"What's ahead?"

"Mmhm," she hummed.

Jay grinned. "Beating you at the final Trial first," he said, earning a reproachful smile in turn. "Then, who knows? See where the wind takes me."

She shoved a platter of buttered crumpets into his arms. "Yeah, well, let's see it take you back into the living room for now."

She grabbed the tray of tea and cups and moseyed out into the den. Jay followed and found Wade leaning in precariously close to a flushed Kylie, who held eyes closed and lips puckered. Wade backed clumsily away and shot Jay a scathing look before Kylie caught on and righted herself. Raylin seemed not to notice anything, but the couple kept their distance for the rest of the visit. Wade, sure that Jay had intervened on his winning move, watched sulkily as he provoked the shame with overt gestures to keep the awkward tension flowing.

Eventually, a steamed-out Raiza joined them, mood witty and upbeat just as Kylie had predicted. They sat and talked for a while, then Jay took a few minutes to freshen up before Raylin announced that it was time to go. Feeling livelier than he had all day, Jay pulled the door closed behind him and trailed the group toward the ferry that would carry them onward to the fourth and final Isle.

****

The sun was nearing the horizon as the boat rounded a bend in the river. Orange orb of fire to their backs, Jay set his gaze on the gleaming surfaces of a thousand metal, glass, and granite panes. He gawped as the fourth Isle came ever closer to them, revealing all its many wonders with every inch.

This island was three times the size of any of its predecessors. It was so large that the river, broad and powerful as it was, had to part into a multitude of smaller tributaries just to work around it. The largest portion of the flow was spotted with protruding stones and mini-islands itself, though there was enough channel to work a ferry through. Even with all its landmass, though, it still gave a cluttered texture as they neared.

If the first was eclectic in nature, the second cosmetic, and the third efficient, then this final Isle could best be summed as *energetic*. As Jay took the first step off the boat and onto dry land, his gaze scalped the top of the crowd to find electric lights buzzing in fervent fashion up and down the busy streets. Some displayed lettering and advertisements for local businesses and the upcoming festivities, while others simply shone white and yellow beams onto everything in sight. The buildings glistened all-the-more with the fading sun, glass windows of shops and cafes reflecting back the myriad rays to the crowd. The excitement seemed to swell here, like a bubble always ready to burst.

Jay found it contagious.

He couldn't hold his attention on one thing for longer than ten seconds before something else snatched it away. There was *so much* going on. Catcallers and impromptu theatrical troupes cast their sounds to the mounting audience. Searchlights on the three-story seam of buildings danced across the streets in spastic rave. Laughter, exhilaration, and hype covered every square inch of the endless populous. Jay felt his head constantly twisting in an attempt to absorb it all.

Flashes of memories that still seemed to elude him in full sprang up in his mind as he watched. Highwater City had been like this to an extent, busy and bustling with people and opportunity. But even as he tried to go back in time to that faraway home, he was dragged into the present again by Wade's exclamation.

"This place is *sick*!" he said, earning a fresh giggle from Kylie. "Jay, are you seeing this?" He waved an arm toward a venue to their left with an advertisement for wind carriage reservations—the only form of swift travel across the continent aside from beasts of burden.

"Walking right beside you, bro," Jay answered with a grin.

"Could you *imagine*? We could get to Godsreach in, like, *a day*!"

The group seemed to slow in unison at the statement.

"Godsreach?" Raylin asked. She held her gaze on Jay intently.

"Yeah, uh," he stammered, "We've got some business there, actually."

"*In Godsreach*?" Raiza pressed as if the fact simply didn't compute.

"I'll tell you about it later," Jay answered to get away from the topic.

Wade pulled the foot out of his mouth and assisted. "Guys, I need to see it all. *Everything*. This place is blowing my mind!"

"Tournament first," Raylin reminded them all.

Everyone could hear the unspoken threat against missing the match.

"Right," Wade amended. "*After* the tournament."

"Speaking of," she went on, "Here we are."

On cue, they stepped into a vast courtyard cut away from the clutter of the rest of the Isle. Already, Ansela and the judges hovered in the center while thousands of people lined the stands that appeared hastily erected across the grounds. The milling masses that had been walking with them from ferry to now parted like striking a wedge, moving to either the left or the right of the assembly.

Kylie tugged on Wade's hand, but he shot her a wink and broke away to speak to Jay in private. They sidestepped the others and put their heads together. Blaze tried to wriggle away, but Jay nabbed him before he could.

"Down to this, man. *You've got to win*," Wade encouraged.

"What d'ya think, Blaze?" Jay asked.

Blaze looked away, disinterested.

Wade nudged him with a toe. "You've been killing it out there! The ladies love you!"

As if the notion only scared the dog, he stood and reversed nearer to Jay.

"I think he's had enough love for one day," Jay snickered.

"Listen, whatever you do, go for the gold," Wade went on. "I know you've got a thing for Raylin—"

Jay started to protest, but Wade cut him off.

"You can't fool me. It's Talia all over again. She's cute, you like her, but you try to tuck it away and hide it cuz you can't let anything throw you off your game. Well, *this* is your game now. Forget about the binding thing for a few hours. Do you realize the street cred we can get from winning this? Kylie says that this tournament has given Raylin some serious connections in the past. Connections *we* need."

"I hear you," Jay appeased.

"Just saying, don't let her win this because you're feeling sappy."

"Look who you're talking to," Jay answered with mock outrage. "Unlike you, I don't exactly let romance dictate my life."

Wade stared off at the concrete. "Yeah, you know what, who am I to be having this conversation?" He turned his eyes after a waiting Kylie who stood paces away, batting her lashes at him. "Now, if you'll excuse me, I have some *romance* waiting for me."

"You ready or what?" Raylin's voice called after Jay as he pulled away from the huddle.

"As I'll ever be," he answered.

She grabbed his hand and waved Blaze along after them. "Let's give them a show," she said with a wink.

Strolling side-by-side to the stage, Raylin waved to the left while Jay followed suit to his side. Blaze hopped along, and Jay wondered if he was actually eager for the upcoming match. If the dog liked anything other than lazy loafing, he had yet to show it clearly, but perhaps they shared a common interest in proving naysayers wrong. They were clearly the underdogs in this match, which might be the spark to ignite Blaze's fire.

The sounds around them were thunderous, the vibration of voices and stamping feet shivering into Jay and making him dance with excitement. He reveled in it. He could hear his name called out by some, though many more were cheering on their hometown hero. But he didn't care. He let their cries soak into him like a song. *No wonder Zane did this for a living.*

Raylin planted her feet, and Jay slid in beside her. He drank her in one last time, savoring her beauty and the quickening of his pulse. Then he shut it all off. It was her against him now. Only *one* would win.

"Ladies and gentlemen, welcome back to the fourth and final round of this year's Manifestival!"

Ansela turned to face the two remaining challengers as the crowd's whoops died down. She sized them both up, surprised by one and apparently expecting the other. Her gaze lingered on Jay like an animal that she couldn't quite understand.

"What will this year bring?" she went on, tone calmer now as if asking a serious question. "Will our triumvirate champion make her mark a fourth time, or will this new and foreign challenger best her and break her streak?"

Raylin blew out an incredulous breath to which Jay only grinned.

Ansela spun in a slow circle to address the whole audience as she went on in her normal manner. "The Isle of Providence! The Trial of Champions! *Two* enter the arena, and only *one* emerges the victor. Will it be Jameson Innis, the Blazing Dualist?!"

There was a substantial resonance of applause. Jay almost thought he could hear Wade screaming out a lung.

"Or will it be Raylin Hargrave, the Prodigy of Flame?!"

The applause came again, this time earsplitting. Raylin peeked over to offer a belittling smirk.

"We shall see! Challengers, join me at the center."

Ansela stepped past familiar lines in the concrete that Jay knew would soon lift out of the ground. He, Raylin, and Blaze followed. As they took their places, Raylin summoned her virtue to complete the set.

"This Trial will be a test of will, of wiles, of endurance, and of power to combine each of the traits we have seen thus far in one bombastic duel. The rules carry from before. Your arena will consist of laser-measured boundaries. If your virtue goes out of those bounds, you will be disqualified. If your virtue is recalled for any reason, you will be disqualified. In this Trial, the binders must remain *outside* the boundaries while the virtues within battle it out. If you step into the boundaries, you will be disqualified. The last virtue standing wins!"

Jay and Raylin nodded in sync.

"You may forfeit at any time should you wish," she added.

Neither nodded this time. It was moot. *They would not.*

Ansela stepped outside of the marked arena. As soon as she was clear, the ground churned and rumbled beneath them. Slowly, it rose in a twenty-foot circle around the four. Two segments highlighted on the perimeter, signaling where the binders should stand. Jay led Raylin there, and he was surprised to find that they were made to stand *next* to one another during the bout. With a confident nod to Blaze, his virtue took its place in the center as well.

"The moment we've all been waiting for!" Ansela announced again as the cylinder reached its full height above the crowds. "The conclusion to our bicentennial Manifestival awaits! Competitors, are you ready?"

Jay nodded to Raylin, both wearing dangerous masks of determination.

"On my mark!" Ansela screamed.

Faint blue lines of light roped their way into a dome over the arena, cutting off Jay and Raylin from their virtues. Jay was slightly relieved to see that the boundary extended to the air as well, meaning that Raylin's avian virtue was not exempt from the rule.

"Be ready!" Ansela continued, building the anticipation.

Then, something else joined the mix. A series of pipes not unlike the cannons that attempted to take Jay off the balance beam in the first Trial rose from the ground around the webbed arena. Jay peered over to find that Raylin was just as surprised as he.

"Fight!" Ansela roared just before the rest joined her.

For long seconds, both Jay and Raylin stood there, still trying to decipher the additions to the match. Blaze and the flaming phoenix mirrored their masters' dumbstruck positions. But Raylin broke away first, and with a spastic command, the fight was on.

The bird dove toward Blaze, but the dog sidestepped like lightning. Corrected at the last minute, Raylin's virtue shot skyward again and surfed the inner wall of lights. It rounded the dome as if circling its prey. The crowds cheered it on to offense, but Blaze remained steadfast in his nonchalance. Twice more, the bird dove, and twice more, Blaze evaded the attack. Jay thought that his canine companion almost looked a little bored.

But just when he was falling out of high stress, the first of the steel contraptions—Jay didn't miss the material change—buzzed with life. True to his assumptions, the cannon fired a jet of high-pressure liquid that caught Blaze in the side, knocking him precariously close to the edge. The dog leaped back to his feet and barked a furious retort at the cheap shot. While distracted, Raylin shouted a new command to her virtue, and the flaming raptor flapped up a gust of ember-filled wind in Blaze's vicinity. Seeing the attempt at pressing him through the light wall, Blaze raced back to the center before it could make a difference. When he planted his feet in safe territory again, Jay could see that he was no longer interested in playing around.

The phoenix came close for a swipe of its infernal talons, but Blaze sprang into the air to catch it off balance. The two collided, and Blaze found the fowl in his clutches for a brief moment. He grabbed the bird by the back of its craning neck, teeth seeming to catch only ethereal flames instead of flesh, and wrenched it away from him. It soared uncontrollably into a new jet of water, meeting it with opposite force and flailing back toward the stage.

Raylin gasped, shouted, and stamped her feet as if doing so would kickstart her virtue back into action. Slowly, the phoenix rose, but Blaze offered no quarter. He pounced again, slapping the bird with a paw. It slid closer to the barrier, and Blaze bounced in for another strike, like tapping a ball inch by inch toward the winning hole. Raylin screeched, and Jay saw a series of waterjets vomit their contents onto the platform. He couldn't prove it, but he suspected that the judges controlled those cannons in order to prolong the fight for the crowd's enjoyment. Case and point, *all* seemed to be aimed at Blaze now.

The dog danced in and out of the liquid beams, but he wasn't quick enough to escape the full gambit. He took one to the face, earning a low groan across the audience, and then another to the rear. He slid back toward the center, righted himself, and found that the bird had once again taken flight.

Jay watched all of this like a spectator himself, studying Blaze's movements, Raylin's commands, and her virtue's unerring obedience. He offered no constructive advice himself; he simply stared and calculated. Raylin seemed to notice his inaction, too, as she frequently looked over to examine him as if he had succumbed to a stroke. But he was developing a plan that would make Blaze the victor of this match. He just needed the right opening.

The scorching bird now watched its quarry with hawk eyes. It circled again and again, searching for its chance. Blaze offered none. Tired of waiting, the judges fired up the cannons for a new round, and the water flew like bullets. Short, staccato bursts of fluid orbs darted across the stage, causing the two virtues to cease focus on one another and survive the barrage. Raylin continued barking out her commands while Blaze barked foreign words of his own.

The burning hound rolled end over end as a series of

water shots pricked him from different directions. Though their force wasn't comparable to the flatlined beams from before, Jay could hear the thumps of contact and thought that repeated exposure to their pummeling would leave bruises on human skin.

Finally sick of the aggression from beyond the dome, Blaze released a roar that sent chills down Jay's spine. It was angry and feral, a sight and sound that Jay had not seen from Blaze since their first encounter. This was getting personal. When the echo of his anger faded, Blaze began to pace in a small circle around where he stood. With every revolution, his speed increased. In seconds, the dog was moving so fast that Jay's eyes could not follow. When the wind whistled, and the air in Jay's lungs felt hot and stuffy, a tempest of such fiery force escaped the spinning blur that Jay felt the beading sweat on his skin wicked away as if with a dry cloth.

The blazing tornado stretched away from the stage, and shouts of fear and excitement rebounded across the stands. It caught the first three cannons nearest its scraping vicinity, and when it passed them by, only one appeared whole enough to continue operations. Steel or not, two of the pipes hunched forward like old and arthritic men. The ensuing shots leaked away from their barrels with no more force than a water faucet. The tempest made its rounds, clearly controlled by the unseen Blaze. Apparently up for a temporary truce, Raylin bade her virtue to follow suit and destroy the hindrances to a fair match.

Jay stole a quick glance at the judges and found that both they and Ansela were obviously displeased about the unruly response to their interventions, but the crowd, on the other hand, seemed to enjoy the spectacle. When the majority of the cannons were divested of function, Blaze and the phoenix squared off once more, truce ended and battle back in action.

They danced away from one another, strikes and fiery attacks either missing entirely or landing only grazing hits. Raylin continued to conduct her symphony of instruction while Jay only continued to watch. She was growing frustrated, he could tell. That her prized virtue had not bested its opponent yet was something both unprecedented and unacceptable. Her demands took an edge, and slowly, they devolved into contradicting tactics that only confused her partner.

When Raylin shouted a longshot drive to her virtue, a kamikaze strike that might turn the tide, Jay realized his opportunity had come.

"Blaze!" he shouted, gaining the attention of his virtue as signaled only by perked ears. "Seize the opportunity!"

It was the first command he had given all evening, and it would be the last. Raylin turned to stare at him with both surprise and intrigue. His call was vague. There was no visible advantage that she could see.

He had her attention.

"Raylin," he began, voice calm and controlled despite his racing heart.

He took her hands in his, turning her to face him. There was a split second where she turned back to the match, watching as her virtue dove recklessly toward Blaze, following her last command. But he pulled her attention back with the tightening of his fingers on hers.

"I need to ask you something. I've been waiting for this moment since we first met. There's just something about you…something I can't ignore."

His words came faster now, his voice rising to overcome the shouts and the battle. Her amber eyes watched him with *utter confusion*. He lowered his body to one knee, and all the chatter of the crowds seemed to stop.

"*You make my heart race*. I could see this moment from the beginning!" he practically shouted for all to hear. "I can't pretend that I don't have these feelings for you, for *this*. I need to know! I just need you to answer *one thing*."

Her eyes were as wide as the rising moon coming to take its place on the skyline. The sandstone orb in the distance seemed to shimmer in tandem with them. Jay felt her breath escape over him, exhumed from her chest by shock. There was a bark in the background to signal him onward with the question that would end it all.

"*Would you*," he began, licking his lips in sweet anticipation. "*Would you accept…*"

The world watched them with bated breath. They couldn't believe it. Their silence, like hers, was like a gavel waiting to drop, waiting for the question that they expected to come.

Jay savored the moment. When the word rolled forth, he felt such heart-bending glory that he was fearful of fainting.

"*Defeat?*"

He snatched his eyes away from hers and gestured to where Blaze stood alone in the arena, strutting back toward them from where he had bested the fiery phoenix of the three-time champ. The embers of the climactic clash slowly flitted to the ground as the avian competitor dissolved into ethereal mist. Raylin hadn't even realized its need to be recalled. But the crowd did. And they let the city know that the match was over in one explosive return to sound.

Jay stood, exultant in the chant that named him the Manifestival Champion, grin plastered across his face in contrast to the pale and slowly-understanding slate of Raylin's.

Ansela was speaking again, trying to overcome the hullabaloo that shook the stadium, but her words were simply swept away in the incessant tide. The judges leaped from their seats, exchanging wild words between themselves and, even a few, money obviously cast in a gamble.

Jay, on the other hand, was growing increasingly worried as Raylin's demeanor never changed from that shocked quiet. He was afraid she might hit him, might throw him off the platform to a swift and painful death for having been tricked.

He had gathered in his ample observations that she relied too much on vocally leading her virtue rather than allowing it to act on its own. Though he and Blaze didn't have a model relationship, the involuntary independence that they had forged worked in their favor this time. Blaze was his own being. He could make decisions and act based on his own personality and experience. And that had ultimately won them the tournament. When Raylin gave the order for an all-out attack, Jay knew that should she refrain from adding to it, the bird would continuously attack in that manner and leave itself open to recourse. All he needed to do was ensure that her focus was elsewhere for a time.

"*Raylin*," he started, voice pleading though the grin never left his jaw, "I'm sorry! I had to take the—"

He tapered off as the last expression he expected to

find took its place on her lips. A disbelieving—though clearly still disapproving—smile soon spread to match his. And before he could say another word, she grabbed him by the neck and united the two, kissing him with the same fiery passion with which she did everything. Jay, still lost in the moment and the exhilaration, returned it in full force, pulling her into his arms and laughing.

Wade must be losing his mind right about now.

"That's a yes, by the way," Raylin said as the crowd cooed at their display of romantic sportsmanship. "I guess if I have to accept it from anyone, it might as well be you."

She took his hand, leading them into a sweeping bow. Jay kept his eyes on her even as they did.

She really was something else.

****

When the swift ceremony was over, and the trophy had been handed to Jay and Blaze, they gave a final wave to the departing crowds. Fireworks were snapping and popping all across the island, signaling the start of their annual celebrations of the birth of Arken Isles. Jay stepped down from the stage and caught Raylin's attention.

"Hey," he said, jogging up to her. "This is yours."

He extended the trophy toward her, but her immediate reaction was disdainful of the offer. He held up a placating hand.

"Not trying to rub it in or offer any pity," he said, chuckling. "Though I did win with a little underhanded tactic, I still claim the victory one hundred percent."

Raylin put a hand on her hip and narrowed her eyes. "So what then?"

"For safekeeping," Jay started, "And for a reminder

that this time next year, I'll let you have a rematch."

She took the trophy hesitantly. "I'll toss it in the closet or something, I guess. As long as you'll come back for it." But even as she said it, she tucked the golden semblance of the four Arken Isles gingerly under one arm.

"I always come back for what's mine," he said, eyes still trained on hers.

They smiled and turned together to join the rest of their crew. Wade was standing with Kylie, of course, but Raiza had apparently rounded up the three others from the night before. And that wasn't all. A crowd of hundreds still stood by the stands, cheering them on as they approached. Raiza was leading the charge, and as one, the mass of people rushed them.

Jay was taken up on the shoulders of two beefy fellows while Raylin found herself swept up into her brother's arms and offered to another pair of giants. A gothic girl from their assembly surged out from the crowd bearing aloft two cups of frothing, electric blue drink. One found Jay's hand, and the other was passed to Raylin. Raylin extended hers toward him, laughing all-the-while, and Jay gave a 'why not' shrug. He clinked his cup to hers and downed it in one fell swig.

"That's my man!" Wade's voice roared out from the crowd. He fought his way to the front and slapped Jay's knee repetitively. "That-is-my-man!" He yelled again, punctuating each word with another slap.

Vicariously celebrated with the statement, Wade suddenly found himself hoisted up by a multitude of hands and crowd-surfed along as the entire horde began to move. Blaze, hovering in the background, tried to dodge it all, but his attempt at moderation was declined.

A bumble of girls hemmed him in, and before long, he was riding in the arms of each, passed around like a communal plaything.

Jay lost track of everything after that but the consuming high of the fete. It became a buzz to him, something only to feed and feed more. He laughed, he sang, he chanted his own name, then Blaze's, and then Raylin's. Hers tasted like summer sweetness on his lips. He found that his voice yearned to sing it more.

Then a new song came to them, inspired by some drunken bard among their company, and with it, they rocked the city.

Fiery phantoms, virtues two,
They came, they dueled, but one subdued.
A blazing wolf a phoenix fought,
Cannons fired and waters came,
But their heat an end to water brought,
And the match was on once again.
A bash, a clash, a shaking strike,
A winner stood in dead of night.
Though wolf did win, the crowd was still,
A romantic proposal unfulfilled.
But sly was the man that spoke,
For in the end, our stupor broke,
And the Manifestival was sealed!

Jay slurred more words than he got right. The rainbow of beverages never ceased to find his hands. When one was empty, it was snatched from him and replaced by another, full and frothing and radiating a need to be consumed. Jay obliged more times than he could count, and by the look of Wade, who now floated alongside an airborne Kylie, his friend was in a similar state. The pair kissed and cooed amongst the arms that carried them onward, and Jay vaguely realized it was the first time since they left Glendale that his friend actually looked happy.

But he couldn't stay in that thought long before the festivities brought him back to the moment. Fireworks continued to light the night, blues and reds and yellows burning out in the sky like dying stars. He was placed next to a swaying Raylin as they neared the edge of an overlook. The water danced in his vision, gentle waves rippling in mesmerizing fashion along to the thumping music. He felt his body move with it in one accord.

Then he had Raylin by the hips, her arms perched on his shoulders. They were flowing like reeds on the wind, stepping in perfect time with one another as if driven by one mind. The music swelled. It cast everything else away but its incessant beat. The strings, the horns, the heavy bass that thudded in time with their hearts. Two orbs of amber followed Jay wherever he went, locked onto him by tethers of trust that he would not lead them astray.

He didn't.

They danced until the world grew quiet. The music faded, but their steps did not. Jay was no longer intoxicated only by drink. He could not take his eyes away from her, could not separate her from his hands. Even as the fireworks beyond met their earsplitting crescendo, a finale that would have been a once-in-a-lifetime sight, Jay could see only one thing. *Her*.

****

Though the primary portion of the night had passed them by, Jay and Raylin sat alone in a small quad adorned with outdoor lounge furniture. An abandoned bar sat open just to their right, dilapidated by rowdy partakers and left with half-empty bottles of alcohol and mixers scattered all across its surface. The music still thrummed in the distance, taken up again after the firework finale, but it was quiet enough here that they could talk.

Jay grabbed two *hopefully* unused cups from the stand and mixed up a conglomerate of leftovers into them. Honestly, he wasn't sure that his inundated senses would care how it tasted. Topped off with ice from a nearby chest, he returned to Raylin's side to find her staring off into the night sky.

"Find what you're looking for?" Jay asked, plopping down and offering her one of the concoctions.

"*Not sure*," she said mystically, taking the drink and then a sip. Her nose wrinkled. "What is this?"

"Jay's Special," he answered, taking a sip of his own. Despite earlier assumptions, his taste buds actually *did* care. "Yeah, it's not very good, is it?" He laughed.

"Worst thing I've ever had," she agreed with a snicker.

Jay tossed the drink aside and fell onto his back and into the cool grass. He stared out into the starlit night much as Raylin did. She joined him, falling next to his side.

"So what happens now?" Raylin asked quietly.

Jay waggled his head against the ground and pulled in a deep breath. "I don't know."

"*Godsreach*, huh?"

Jay turned to her. "Yeah."

"That's a long way off, J-Jay."

Jay smiled. "Can I tell you something without you thinking me a total idiot?"

Raylin shrugged. "Depends on what it is."

Jay caught the hint of a smile on her lips. "I have a dream."

"Even though you're awake?" she teased.

He nudged her. "You know what I mean."

"What kind of dream?" she asked seriously this time.

"Don't laugh," he started. When she didn't say anything, he unveiled it all. "Wade and I aren't just touring the world. I'm trying to bind all twelve virtues. It's called Full Bindature. No one's ever done it."

She tilted her head to study him. There was no judgment in those gorgeous amber eyes, though. "Is *that* why you want to?"

"Partly," he said, but he quickly corrected, "*Mostly*."

She was silent for a long time after that. When she next spoke, the words came slow, as if she was considering them even as they fell forth. "I was curious when you revealed that you had bound *two* virtues already. Makes a little more sense now."

"I still have a long way to go," he confessed.

"And that's why you're rounding the world, then?"

"Can't find them all in one spot, can I? And Godsreach is, well…it's an opportunity I can't pass up."

"What's waiting for you there?"

"I honestly don't know," Jay whispered. "But I feel like it's something *big*." He recalled the illusive invitation given to him by Mayor DeMoro what seemed like years ago now. "Someone wants to meet me, someone with resources and reputation."

The corners of her lips twerked upward. "Two things you're gonna need for an impossible task."

"*Impossible*?" he asked, fearful that she might dive down a road of ridicule.

She shrugged. "Well, there's gotta be a reason it hasn't been done."

Jay flashed back to the conversation he had with the late Walter von Quake. "You're not the first to tell me that," he said.

"And I won't be last," she inserted. "*But*." She let the word linger. "That doesn't mean you shouldn't try."

Jay rolled onto one side to frame her in full. "You think?"

"It's your dream, Jay. Of course, you should chase it."

He smiled. "Other than Wade, I think you're the first person to ever tell me that."

She wrinkled her nose. "Then you need to pick better friends."

They lay there, staring at each other for another long, quiet moment.

"What's your dream?" Jay eventually asked.

Raylin's expression seemed to regress. "What if I don't have one?" she asked soberly.

Jay saw through it. "I would say that you're lying. Everyone has a dream. Some just happen to be impossible."

Her smile came back in fractions. "Some dreams more than others," she said, Jay wondering to which she was referring.

"I wanna hear it," he pressed.

She drew a deep breath and forced it out her nose. "To have a family," she said softly.

Jay parted his lips to speak, but she went on before he could interrupt.

"And to give them everything that I never had."

She looked away from him then, eyes scanning the

midnight skies for a shooting star upon which she could wish it true. Jay knew there was pain in that gaze, a longing for a mother she had never known, for a father who had abandoned them. Despite her fiery front and all the assumptions Jay had formed about this girl, her desires were simple ones, not at all the grandiose goals he had expected. And yet something about the way she said it gave the quest a mythical texture, like a fairytale told to children at night, but the morning light would burn away the fog and reveal it all to have been unreal.

He suddenly ached at his deceptive ploy from the tournament. The watery look in her eyes when he had dropped to a knee. The eager tremor to her hands as he held them in his.

Could she have.

"Raylin," he started, voice sorrowful, "I'm really sorry for misleading you—"

Her head snapped back to him, brows quirked. "Mislea...*oh*." She laughed aloud. "Oh, Jay, *no*. That's not what I'm saying." She giggled again and added, "I would've said *no* even if you *had* proposed."

Jay recoiled slightly. "*Okay, ouch.* Not your type then?"

"Oh, you're my type," she said with a wink. "But *I'm* not the type to go swooning for someone I just met."

"I'd be worried if you were," he said quietly.

She reached over to take his hand. "I may be reckless at times. Speed might win the tournament, but slow and steady wins the heart."

Jay entwined his fingers through hers and watched her with wanting eyes. He could feel his heart enter his throat before the words did. "Can I...can I kiss you again?" he whispered.

Raylin laughed lightly. "Do you have to ask?"

Jay flushed. "I'm not very practiced," he said with a weak grin.

"I'd be worried if you were," she mimed, leaning in closer. "But I don't mind practicing with you."

****

The morning crept slowly in. The sun crested the small gap between two buildings, sheltering Jay from the streets burning at the fore of his eyelids. He stirred but refused to open them.

He lay there for a moment longer, anger welling up at the loss of the night, but a sharp *whap* of something soft took him on the bridge of the nose. He flinched and drew up to find Blaze mounted on his chest, beady red eyes staring down at him. Jay let the panic fade and dropped his pounding head back to the grass.

Seeing that his party-animal cohort had no intentions of getting up, the virtue leaped off of Jay's chest and moseyed away. Jay waved him happily onward.

With painstaking effort, he wiped at his sun-scorched eyes wearily. His skull throbbed like he had been repeatedly kicked by a band of nightmare gremlins. With a quick and wincing survey of the quad where he had apparently ended his romantic escapade, Jay found no one else nearby but Blaze.

Raylin had gone.

He partly wondered if it was all a dream induced by alcohol, bright lights, and adrenaline. But if he paused for long enough and pressed back the ache, he could still taste her on his lips. It was a sensation he hoped would last forever.

He stood with creaking effort and balanced himself

on a nearby wicker chaise. Blaze returned to him in higher spirits than Jay could justify. He had gum and sticky bits of some unknown substance matted in his windswept hair. His left front paw looked like someone had taken a razor to it and shaved it down to a stubble. His tail had been brushed back, groomed, and lined with ponytail bands and little beads of jewelry. Apparently, Jay was not the only one who had a wild night.

Together, they meandered back out of the quad and into the deserted streets of the Isle of Providence. The skyscraping buildings all around them showed no signs of life, not a soul stirring in sight. They walked for half an hour, kicking at empty cups and strands of ribbon littering the streets, and still, no one wandered the walkways to meet them. Jay was beginning to wonder if he was still dreaming when he finally caught voices on the river wind just ahead.

They rounded a corner to find none other than Wade surrounded by a posse of six rabble-rousers that looked vaguely familiar from Jay's hazy memories. Wade spotted him and released a groan of relief.

"I've been looking everywhere for you!" he reprimanded as if Jay had been hiding all morning.

"Obviously not everywhere," Jay mumbled.

Wade broke away from the group that Jay now recognized held Kylie and five of her female friends that had, at one point during the night, carried Wade away with excited chatter and giggles. One of Wade's feet was void of both sock and shoe for the second time during their trip, and his crinkly hair was colored with what appeared to be spray-on dye. What were once dark curls now stood segmented in three varying shades of green. Another line of the verdant paint zigzagged down his exposed chest, contrasting against his brown skin behind a ripped shirt.

He stepped close enough to Jay that his femininely perfumed scent was unmistakable. "*Night of my life*," he whispered, jiggling his eyebrows.

"Yeah?" Jay asked with a smirk.

"You might have beaten me to the punch," he went on, "But I bet you didn't kiss *six* girls in one night." Again, his brows rose in challenge.

Jay laughed under a breath. "You got me there, man."

Wade's grin exploded across his face. He slapped Jay on the back and turned to the waiting women. "Ladies, it looks like my friend, and I need to um...*freshen up*. We'll see you this afternoon?"

The request was met with excited agreement, especially by Kylie, who hadn't taken hungry eyes off Wade since Jay approached. Jay watched Blaze inspecting a pair of them with an air of wariness, and he wondered if they might be the culprits behind his makeover.

"Meet us at Raylin and Raiza's," Kylie said, eyes twitching to Jay for the first time.

He made a mental note of the growing grin on her lips. She, and likely all the others, knew about his evening spent with the female twin.

"Definitely," Wade answered and led them away toward the ferry. "Okay, he started when they were far enough from the group, "*Details*. And don't spare a thing."

Jay sighed, but he gave it up. Wade wouldn't let him off with a simple explanation of his absence. He dove back through as much as he could remember while Wade listened intently and generated more questions than he had answers for. Jay wondered, not for the first time if Wade's lady-killing attitude was like an insatiable black hole.

"Dude, she's got you by the ring finger!"

"It's not like we're getting married," Jay scoffed. "We just had a good time, and the topic came up. There and gone."

"But it's her *dream*," Wade said with mystic emphasis. "How cold-hearted are you?"

Jay smiled and swerved to shove him with a shoulder. "What about you? Kylie looks like she's ready to propose herself."

"Yeah, we gotta get outta here."

"*What*?" Jay asked with a laugh.

"She's in too deep, bro. I can tell it. Something about the way she looks at me, you know?"

"*Wade Wilkes*," Jay chastised, "Talk about crushing someone? You get a woman all riled up, and then you just bail on her?"

Wade backed up into a defensive stance. "*You're* the one who roped me into this trip," he answered, "I can't help it if the women fall for me. I'm like an innocent magnet."

"*Roped you in*," Jay repeated drolly. "I recall telling you that I was going it solo."

"And you would've bit the dust before you reached the Cliffs if not for me. Learn to be grateful."

****

They stayed in the city for two more days, whiling away the hours with the Hargraves and their many friends. They laughed and enjoyed the comradery, told stories of things passed and things to come, and Jay was able to spend a little longer with a woman he would come to miss dearly.

On the morning of their departure, Jay woke with a hollow pit in his stomach. He tossed and turned on the mattress, roiled and wrapped himself in blankets only to unwind again and get up to greet the parting day. On the way down the stairs into Pierre's sitting room, he met the man himself, already awake, dressed, and ready for conversation.

"*Sit*," he said as Jay entered, a sluggish Blaze at his heels.

Jay did as requested and fell into the sofa cushion nearest the host. Pierre reached across the coffee table and let a wad of sleek black fabric fall to its surface. It landed with a light clink.

"What is that?" Jay asked.

"An upgrade," Pierre answered in his usual, grumpy tone.

Jay leaned over and plucked the fabric warily from its puddle. When it fell erect by gravity's insistence, Jay saw a new binder's sleeve with five metallic plates stitched across its surface. He looked up in surprise.

"I believe Walter would want you to have that," Pierre said simply.

"Mr. Kabolt, I—"

"Will accept it with thanks," he finished for the flustered recipient.

Jay took a moment to gather his thoughts. "But I thought you didn't want me to continue pursuing this?"

"Did my warnings make a difference?" he countered.

"No," Jay answered cautiously.

"Then the least I can do is prepare you for what's to

come." He took a sip from his teacup and studied Jay carefully. "Transfer your binding stones to it. Do you know how to remove them?"

Jay nodded, picking at the clasp that held the stones inside the sleeve he now wore.

"Beware that you do not part from those stones for long, Jameson. Maintain contact with them as often as you can."

"Why?" Jay asked carefully.

He knew, of course, that in order to summon the magical abilities of the virtues that he bound, he would need to be wearing that sleeve, but the way that Pierre said it hinted at other truths.

"Because Alden would often take his sleeve off when he slept. I cannot say whether the prolonged separation from the stones affected him in any way, but it is better to do the opposite of what he did all those years ago if you wish to turn out differently."

Jay nodded soberly. He swapped the sleeves in swift fashion, fearful now. He had never really considered being apart from his sleeve for long. Honestly, he had only ever seen the stones as something used to initially bind the virtues and maintain his connection to them. He wondered now what might happen if he somehow lost them. Would Blaze fade away again? Would he be trapped to stay near his stone? There was so much that Jay still didn't understand.

"Take this, too," Pierre said, pulling him back from his reverie. He rolled a new and blank binder's stone across the tabletop.

Jay caught it between his fingers and examined its opaque color.

"Your fourth stone will be much different. I cannot

help you there. They are designed in larger fashion and require much more intricate cuts to house the energies gained. Much like your soul, Jameson."

"I won't, you know?" Jay said quietly.

"Won't what?" Pierre replied over the rim of his cup.

"Turn out like Alden. If I see that it's changing me, I'll stop."

Pierre sighed, the breath blowing against his tea to create a cloud of steam. "*You will never stop*, son."

Jay looked up. "*I will*," he defended. "I have Wade with me."

"And for that, Wade is in more danger than you could ever know."

"Just, *stop*," Jay said. "Stop trying to derail me."

Pierre laughed like a child who had just heard a new joke. "Is that what this looks like to you?" he asked, pointing toward the gifts. "I *know* that your path is set, Jameson, just as Walter knew. You will do this and damn the ones that stand in your way. There is beauty in the commitment, I'll hand that to you, but where wisdom fails you, regret lies in wait. I am only speaking the truth as I have seen it."

"Exactly," Jay argued, "As *you* have seen it."

"It is all that I know." Pierre exhaled. "Perhaps you will find me an old fool in the end. But what I *know*, I must share plainly."

"Where can I find a fourth stone?" Jay eventually asked when the room grew still again.

"Access is restricted," Pierre answered. "They are monitored and registered to users in Tier Three. When you make it to Godsreach, you should be able to purchase one but beware the cost. They are quite expensive."

"I'll figure it out," Jay said solemnly. He peered down at Blaze. "What happens if I lose the stones?" he finally asked, fingering the two empty slots on his new sleeve.

Pierre shrugged his hunched and bony shoulders. "If only you contained a single virtue, then it would not be so bad. I suspect that you would feel the loss, like a missing limb or a shaved head. Something that should be there but simply isn't, though its absence would likely be a nuisance at most. But if you lost two or three...perhaps that is where the mind begins to fragment. It will be like a *vast part* of you has been taken. Emptiness in its place. For every virtue you bind, every stone you add to that sleeve, a greater portion of *you* is swapped out for it. That is why, I believe, when Alden bound six individual virtues, he had swapped more than his mind could handle. And when he spent nights alone without those replacements, his subconscious could not reconcile the missing majority. Therefore, he became someone he *was not*."

Just then, Wade entered the room with a loud and low yawn that rattled Jay's eardrums.

"What's everybody doing?" he asked, wiping at his crusted eyes.

"Getting ready to leave," Jay answered, gaze still locked on Pierre.

Pierre nodded a single time and stood. "I wish you boys the best. If you're ever back this way, stop in and see an old man, would you?"

With that, he trudged off toward the door opposite Wade and vanished into a conjoining room. Wade cocked his head, watching curiously as he went.

"*Strange guy*," he said, coming to sit next to Jay. "Woah, where'd you get that?" he asked, spotting the new sleeve. He held his up to compare and was clearly put off that it wasn't as fancy.

"Pierre gave it to me, along with some more of his grave advice."

"Eh, don't worry about them, man," Wade said, stopping him before he could sulk. "I got your six. Nothing gonna happen to us that I don't see coming."

Jay grinned. "Eagle-eyes."

"I dig that," Wade said, bobbing his head. "*Eagle-eye Wade*. I could be a comic hero."

Jay stood and ruffled Blaze's hair, waking him back from the brink of sleep. "Let's go. I'd rather not waste the sun."

"Eager as always," Wade lamented, but then, he stood too, and together they gathered their meager belongings, suited up, and put Pierre's residence to their backs.

****

As they walked the eclectic streets of the Isle of Promise one last time, Jay could feel that pit in his stomach swell. His mind never wavered from the image of a girl that might well haunt him for the rest of his life. They had said their goodbyes the evening before and not without a few tears shed by two solemn, amber eyes. So when he saw her standing at the gates with Raiza, Kylie, and a few others, he was both surprised and heartened.

"This our farewell party?" he asked as they drew near.

Raylin held out her hands to welcome him into a hug. "You could call it that."

Raiza clapped him on the shoulder, and there was a

gleam in his eyes that seemed somehow sad and relieved at the same time. "Be careful out there, hero. It's a dangerous world."

"I got Blaze," Jay said, looking back to find the dog encased with pats and attention from the two girls that had allegedly refreshed his look.

"*And me,*" Wade offered in a hurt tone.

Kylie snuck up and wrapped him in an embrace that Jay noted he didn't fully return.

"I'm gonna miss you," she said, and Jay took that as a cue to look away before it got awkward.

His attention came back to Raylin. "And what about you? Going to miss me?"

Her eyes fogged over like misty, moonlit lakes. "Of course," she said quietly.

He squeezed her into his chest and pulled away in time to see Wade peel apart from Kylie as well. They shared a few more words and eventually set their feet toward the opposite end of the bridge. Jay looked back as his hand touched the edge of the gate threshold. Raiza had his sister wrapped under one arm. She met his gaze.

"I always come back for what's mine, remember?"

Raylin offered a sad smile. "Yeah."

"Well," Jay sighed, "Just don't forget."

The guard clicked the gate shut behind them as they parted, and the trio traced their way back out across a massive bridge that would return them to the road.

Jay shuffled along, eyes cast down to his feet. One after another, they carried him away from Arken Isles and Raylin Hargrave. Blaze pattered alongside him, watching him with a deep, red contemplation, but Wade suddenly stopped when their boots scuffed dirt instead of stone. Jay looked back at him.

"You can stay, you know," he said softly.

Jay looked away again, fearful of letting him see the watery conflict in his eyes.

"I've never seen you like this, man. *Stay.*"

"I can't do that, Wade."

Wade blew out a long breath. "Yeah...I know."

Wordless, they stepped off again.

Epilogue

Three days brought them within sight of the Tier-Wall. It stood huge and imposing in the distance, a solid line of cloud-gray concrete and rusted steel that stretched from eternal east to west.

The road had grown muddy and slick ahead of them. A series of rain showers had sprinkled their trek, offering cool but wet weather. Now, their boots and Blaze's fur were caked with sloppy muck which only added to the ample weight each leg carried forth.

As they neared the endless barricade, Jay began to see the outlines of large black turrets resting atop the wall in succession, just as the guard in Effervescence had warned. Seeing them now seemed such an overkill statement to any group of interlopers that might attempt to illegally cross. They stood stark against the dull sky and the barren façade, a threat to those who did not belong. But Jay maintained a steady and undeterred pace. He had passage; they would not deny him.

He wasn't really sure what he expected to find when they made it to the wall, but in his mind, he had painted a scene that was wholly opposite to what awaited. He thought there would be immaculate gates of gold, perhaps as tall as the wall itself and opened by some mystic art of virtue magic known only to a few. He thought there might be a squadron of armed guards at the head of the road, ready to fight off anyone, be they man or beast, that neared. He even thought that there might be a small settlement of people stationed nearby, a home for said guards and operators and whoever else may be required to maintain it. But when he led their ragtag party of three within yards of the ward, it was as barren as a desert waste.

There wasn't a soul to be seen anywhere nearby. And though the peak of the wall stood at over eighty feet, Jay could see no movement there save for the automated cannons that swiveled about in constant vigilance. Even *they* appeared not to notice his presence, though, as they simply glided past him in their eternal survey of the land.

And the gates were, frankly, something to be ashamed of. They were nothing more than thigh-thick columns of steel welded together to create a square door of ten feet in both directions. In contrast to the gargantuan backdrop, the doorway was like a speck that did not belong, a blemish unintended by the designers.

Jay slid to a slimy stop and turned to Wade. "*This* is the Tier-Wall?"

Wade nodded with mirrored disappointment. "Count me *underwhelmed.*"

Blaze, covered head-to-toe in filth and somehow pleased by it, offered his own dissatisfaction with a low and fearsome growl.

"I feel ya, buddy," Wade echoed the sentiment.

But even as he said it, Jay realized that something else might have drawn the virtue's ire. The squat, steel door seemed to shiver on its ancient hinges. Before Jay could ask Wade to verify his sanity, he saw the portal swing wide and birth a single figure onto the road between them. It came at them in full sprint, and Blaze's growl grew in decibels.

"*What the—*" Wade started.

And then the man—as his coming voice foretold—shouted ahead in eager tones. Jay couldn't quite make out what he was saying.

"Blaze," he said firmly, cutting the dog's aggression off.

"…nis? Is that you?"

"I'm sorry!" Jay called back, stepping forward to meet the man. "I didn't catch that!"

"Are you Jameson Innis?" he asked again, this time through heavy puffs of breath.

Jay cocked his head. "Uh…yeah, that's me."

"Oh, *thank the stars*," the man praised.

He stopped just before the stunned trio and doubled over to catch his breath. "I've…been waiting for you…for days," he heaved.

"For us?" Wade asked skeptically. "*Who are you?*"

Jay took a moment to study the strange greeter. He wore sophisticated attire, a small velvet cap to crown his dark brown hair, and a suit that had recently accrued a few shades of dirt brown in addition to its tan and white plaid. He was thin and pale and seemed in *no way* a traveling man.

"I am," he started, pulling on another breath, "In the employ of Mr. V. He requested that I meet you here and offer my services." He stood back to his full height and smiled. "Hubert Thylinger at your disposal."

Jay exchanged a glance with Wade. "And what *services* would those be?"

"Why, I operate a wind carriage, of course."

Another wide-eyed glance between the pair revealed their surprise.

Hubert found it his turn to look confused. "You *were*

expecting me, were you not?"

"Not in the slightest," Jay answered plainly. "We had expected to walk the entire way to Godsreach."

Hubert's eyes widened in kind now. "Dear me, you were going to *walk*?" He seemed to size them up again. Apparently, they, too, were not what he expected to find at this gate.

"So let me get this straight," Wade started, "You're here to offer us a carriage ride to the capitol? Courtesy of Mr. V?"

Hubert nodded slowly. "Yes. But, you *are* Mr. Innis, are you not?"

"Yeah," Jay said, pulling out the writ signed by the Mayor and his mysterious patron.

Hubert read over the parchment with resignation. Handing it back, he said, "Then you are my charge. Mr. V is eagerly awaiting your arrival. Perhaps he simply wanted to offer you a speedier journey."

Wade looked to Jay. "Well, *I'm* not about to turn this away," he said with a wide grin.

Jay agreed wholeheartedly. "Never been in a wind carriage before."

"There is a first time for everything," Hubert answered. He waved them to follow. "The carriage is just on the other side of the gate. Show the men inside your writ, and you should be fit to fly."

"I'm Wade by the way," Wade offered, stepping giddily next to the carriage pilot. "So tell me, how much do you normally charge to ride on one of these things?"

Hubert gave an amused chuckle, apparently realizing the type of passengers he was sent to entertain. "Well, Mr. Wade, it would depend on the number of passengers and the distance traveled, as well as some other limiting factors, but to carry a couple such as you from here to Godsreach, I would say around twenty gallea."

Wade nearly choked. "*Gallea*?"

"That's right," Hubert said sincerely.

"Isn't a gallea like a thousand pips, though?"

Hubert smiled. "It is indeed, Mr. Wade. It takes a substantial amount of skill to maintain a wind carriage. That skill doesn't come cheap. Most wind-binders who have mastered the art charge inordinate amounts for their services, which, in turn, forces operators such as me to forward that charge to my clients. They are scarce commodities; therefore, they are highly sought."

Wade studied his fingers, and Jay could feel the faint traces of forged wind lapping over from him. He may have just found his calling.

"Hubert," Jay summoned their guide's attention to another line of inquiry, "Why is it so empty around here? Shouldn't there be people stationed at the wall?"

"For what?" Hubert asked in kind. "The Tier-Wall is a highly dense, nigh-impenetrable barrier. And anyone or anything attempting to breach it by force would earn the wrath of the weaponry placed here to deter just such things."

Jay furrowed his brows. "Yeah, I guess you're right. I just thought we would see…*more*."

"Well, don't fret. You will see greater things soon enough. Ah, here, let's just give this a tap."

Hubert stopped before the rusted panel from which he had earlier escaped. He pecked a similarly rusted handle against its surface like a knocker. With slow and squealing motions, the door creaked open to allow them entry into Tier Two.

Jay stepped across the threshold with a feeling of excitement despite the missing fanfare. It was a marked moment in his life, and he intended to make the best of it. True to his word, Hubert pointed out a pair of men that awaited them in a booth just inside the wall. The tunnel that led from one opening to the next was more than twenty yards in length. Jay had not realized just *how* dense the wall might be, even as Hubert alluded to it.

"Show them the writ, and they will mark you," Hubert instructed.

Jay and Wade approached the booth together. Jay extended the parchment and the man inside reviewed it much as Hubert had.

"Hand," he grunted, returning the page to Jay.

Shrugging, Jay thrust his hand across the countertop. The man grabbed it roughly and raked a strange, oblong device across his skin. A flash of heat surged across it, causing Jay to wince. He tried to pull away, but the guard held fast. Setting the device down, he grabbed a small, engraved metal square and thumbed it against the back of Jay's hand. He pressed it in, brought the oblong device over it once more, and Jay nearly shouted in pain.

When the man finally relented, he pulled away and cradled the hand with its newly melded augment.

"What was that!" he cried.

"Customary," Hubert said, approaching to calm him. "See the number '2' there?" He pointed to the metal square now sunk into his inflamed and swollen skin. "It's a permanent token of passage between the Tier-Wall of Tiers One and Two."

Wade backed away from the guard. "*No way*. Not doing that to me."

"No need," Hubert explained soothingly. "The writ

of passage only pertained to Jameson. You are allowed through on his merit this once."

"A little warning would have been nice," Jay brooded, rubbing at his sore hand.

"Better to just get it over with," the second man in the booth mumbled.

"Right, well, let's move on, shall we?" Hubert encouraged.

They shuffled away, but Blaze barked at the pair of sentinels before joining, causing them to jump from the confined echo of it. Jay only grinned at their salty looks.

They pressed through the second gate and back into the sunlight together. Hubert escorted them to the fore of a large canopy erected nearby. With hurried motions and a little edgy conversation with four other men and women that Jay thought to be the wind-binders who would drive the carriage, Hubert rounded up his makeshift camp. Jay and Wade only stood by and watched as they scrambled, eager for them to wrap it up and get into the air.

Jay had to admit that he felt the dreary depression lifting from his shoulders for the first time since they walked away from Arken Isles. The past three days had been dull and discouraging, with little excitement left for what would come on their trip. In his defense, though, he had fully expected to be hoofing it across half the continent on another six-week journey. But now, there was a thrill in his veins. He was going to ride a *wind carriage*.

Wade's earlier astonishment had been merited. Twenty gallea—or *twenty thousand* pips—was an extravagant amount of money. The average household income in a place like Glendale was approximately five thousand pips per year. To be able to afford such a ride across the world as they were about to enjoy would be the better part of ten years' worth of savings after living a bare-minimum lifestyle.

Hubert, freshly cleaned and changed from his muddied attire, signaled them forward toward the large sled of wood and steel. It looked like something that Jay would use if he planned on skating down the side of a snowcapped mountain without a means to steer, brake, or generally anything for that matter. It had a foldable awning that was currently tucked and clasped away to allow the sunshine to bathe the wooden benches. There was light cushioning riveted to each beam with high backrests. There were also six stations around the perimeter where a person could sit in a small, open cockpit and face directly away from the others. And to cap it all off, there was a large drape of thick fabric fastened to stout ropes that were secured at over a dozen points to the sled.

Wade was first to rush ahead in eager stride, but Hubert stopped him.

"Eh, let's get you some fresh clothing, shall we?" He was looking at all three of them as he said it. "And I assume that you plan on keeping your virtue summoned, Mr. Innis?"

Jay nodded curtly.

"Very well. I would suggest that you bundle him in this for the ride." He handed over a wide and soft roll of cloth.

Jay took it and looked down at his sidekick. "You heard the man."

Blaze huffed but let Jay wrap him up in the blanket and hand him over. Hubert took him at arm's length and practically dropped him inside the carriage like a lump of baggage. Blaze would have bit the man if not for being tangled in the wad too tightly to see.

One of the women then approached Jay and Wade, prowled around them with perusing eyes, and walked away. Before they could really contemplate what that meant, she was back with a set of clothing for each that looked both ostentatious and comfortable.

"These should be close," she said, handing them over in tandem.

"You just keep extra clothes lying around for your clients?" Wade asked, stunned.

Hubert laughed aloud as though Wade had told a particularly funny joke. "Mr. Wade, we would not be in business if we didn't." As if that answered every question that Wade could possibly ask on the subject, Hubert waved them into two closed portholes of the nearby tent to change.

When Jay was in his new and improved suit, he stepped out and handed his gear over to Hubert. The lady from before studied him with that acute gaze once again and seemed satisfied with what she saw.

"You clean up well," she said simply before climbing into one of the cockpits.

"Um, thanks," Jay replied.

Wade joined, spiffed and clean, and Hubert ushered them both into the carriage.

"A few rules before we set off," Hubert started, sidling past Blaze to take a seat on the bench. "When the coach is in the air, please remain seated at all times. Please keep all your belongings on the floor and do not reach outside of the carriage. In the case of an emergency, listen carefully to my instructions and remain calm. If you have any questions, please ask them now. We will all need our full focus for liftoff. Once we are in the air, I will rejoin you, and we can continue any conversation."

Jay waited patiently for Hubert to finish, then he asked, "How long should this trip take?"

"No more than eighteen hours. We should be to Godsreach before morning."

"*Eighteen*?" Wade whined.

"It is nearly one thousand miles to Godsreach, Mr. Wade. If you know of a way to travel more than sixty miles per hour, please share it so that we might go into business together."

Wade narrowed his eyes at the sarcasm, but he quickly relented. Jay thought the time sounded a measure better than six weeks, anyway.

"Once the carriage is in motion, the rear benches can recline beneath the umbrella to provide you a suitable place to sleep. We will make this trip as comfortable as possible; I assure you."

"Yeah, well," Wade sighed. "You got any food?"

Hubert produced a basket that seemed equipped for a large-party picnic from beneath one of the benches. Wade peeled the top back, face lighting up.

"Now, *this* is what I'm talking about!" He plucked out a wheel of cheese that was bigger than his head. "Jay, look at this!"

"Hard to miss," Jay said, snorting.

"And wine? And bread?" Wade went on. "We're gonna feast!"

"Help yourselves," Hubert answered, standing. "I must see to the preparations. We'll be off shortly. If you need anything else in the meantime, just let one of us know."

Jay fell back against his seat as Hubert stepped out of the sleigh. He watched Wade gorge himself on the many different delicacies from the basket. Blaze curiously wriggled out of his confines to see what had his neighbor so excited. But all Jay could think about was the sky and the mystery that beckoned him toward Godsreach.

Who was this Mr. V really? What did he want with Jay? And most importantly, could he help them get one step closer to their goal?

Full Bindature.

There were so many questions that surrounded the source of this wild and fanciful journey they had been on, but, as if it had been tucked away until now, Jay had not really taken the time to consider them. But Godsreach was only hours away now, and he found that concept both exciting and a measure worrisome.

Jay's reverie suddenly faded, though, as the five-person team took their places around the aircraft and rattled off a stretch of code language that obviously meant *ready*. Wade shoved his basket of dwindling goodies back onto the floor and paid more attention to the scene as well. When the last person had spoken, Hubert fell into his seat at the front of the rig and finalized the checks.

"All is ready. All pilots at maximum thrust."

With the verbal command, Jay felt the sled shudder beneath him. He looked to the nearest wind-binder and watched as she channeled her mint-green magic toward the earth in a cone of translucent energy. The air whipped up around them, and the craft began to teeter off of the ground. Wade gripped the seat with both hands, eyes wide.

The wind continued to churn around them, most of its force pressing into the ground at forty-five-degree angles from the cab. Slowly, the carriage rose farther and farther into the sky, the strain of each of the casters evident. Even Hubert, who Jay had not realized was a wind-binder himself, was taut with the effort.

Higher still, they climbed, and eventually, the large bay of fabric fluttered upward and caught a gust strong enough to unfold it into a bulky balloon that hovered high over their heads. It snatched them hard as it inflated, pulling them toward the clouds faster by the second. Jay peered over the side, close as he dared, to see the ground shrinking away. He looked to Blaze, then, who seemed to care little for the increasing distance from safety.

"We're good," he soothed, though Blaze wasn't paying him much mind.

He turned back in time to see low-lying rainclouds racing ever closer to their heads. Just when he thought they would pass that atmospheric barrier to breathing, they slowed. With visible relief, the casters eased their collective focus, and the carriage planed out on a sheet of air with only slight wobbles to tell of their continued work. Then the two back magi turned their forceful gusts to the rear of the craft and surged another pulse of pressure outward. The carriage and its overhead balloon lurched forward, carrying them off toward the southern horizon.

One by one the crew members pulled focus away from the collective and called forth their wind virtues into existence like Blaze. Each of them formless as midnight mist, they emerged onto the plane and picked up the work of their binders, maintaining the altitude of the carriage and keeping it level. In swift seconds, the entire crew was relaxing, their summoned virtues doing all the work for them.

Jay was exultant. He pulled in a deep and chilling breath, releasing it back into the endless blue sky around him. More and more clouds raced by, keeping just enough of the sun off their skin to enjoy their presence. The oversized, hazy bladders held fast to their contents, fending off the dread of rain ruining this experience.

He was flying.

Together, he and Wade watched the land pass by beneath them for a time while Hubert busied himself with the many means of upkeep and direction. The greens of wooded glens seemed to fill most of the faraway canvas, snakes of river blue crisscrossing between them. Jay thought he could even see the Arken Isles in the distance of what was certainly the Ark Waterway—large as that major line of cerulean was. He looked away before his heart could sag back into the slump that was sure to follow.

But the rest of the world spread wide beneath their airborne feet. On a foggy day such as it was, Jay couldn't see back as far as the Cliffs, but he thought he could tell the region of decay blacken from the deep greens that signaled the slope into Effervescence. And ahead was a new land of rocky mesas and sallow shrubbery and long stretches of bald and barren grounds. It was like the Tier-Wall had been a dividing border not only between social and economic districts but geographic as well.

Jay searched for a time across the near-empty landscape for any telling signs of civilization, but nothing stood out aside from occasional packs of grazing animals and clear-cut groves. He had studied the map of the land many times since receiving his new portable and digital version, and though he knew that societal developments were especially sparse in Tier Two, he still could not believe that so much land was going to waste.

People only ever seemed to huddle in large cities and walled estates; he had never heard of anyone other than the enigmatic crazies outside Eff choosing to live beyond such safeties. He couldn't fault the general population for their circumspection, but something about the view bothered him in a way that he couldn't explain. Where were the free spirits? The men and women like him with dreams bigger than a city wall could contain? Surely, he was not alone.

Still, the blank slate was a soul-stirring scene. He floated amongst these wispy lumps that had so often looked down on him even as he now looked down on the world below. How many people could say that they had witnessed this? How many had touched the sky and soared with the birds? From Tier One, that number was critically low, he was sure. Among the wealthy, though? This could be commonplace, *expected* even.

Could he gain a patron like Crazy Zane's? Someone to fund his travels and fuel his dreams? Perhaps that was the opportunity Mr. V wanted to present, a patronage offering to the bizarre kid from Glendale. He would adopt Jay as a pet project, some strange topic that he could bring up at extravagant dinner parties.

"*Darling, you must hear about this young man I've espoused. He believes he will be the first person to bind all twelve virtue types. Isn't that just adorable?*"

Jay grimaced at the thought, but honestly, he would take all the ridicule in stride if it meant he could cruise in a wind carriage and see the world.

Eventually, Hubert rejoined them and offered light conversation as well as a detailed brief of what would come when they arrived. Wade was quieter than Jay had seen him in a long while. Whether it was for the sights or some lingering fear that they might plummet to their deaths, Jay couldn't really know. Either way, he settled back into the reclining benches and let the words wash over him.

The day eventually tarried into night, offering a more lustrous and unforgettable sunset than even the riverfront of the Arken Isles could provide. When it finally kissed the horizon goodbye for another long slumber, the clouds followed suit. One after another, they dissipated as the carriage continued its onward trek through the sky until there was nothing but that inky black ocean surrounding them. Small dots of fire were scattered like thrown embers above and below. Only the faraway specks of city lights could be seen to break the monotony.

Jay was kicked back near a snoozing Wade, Blaze likewise curled up in his lap and breathing with heavy, dreamless sighs. But he could no more sleep than he could leap from the carriage and fly himself the rest of the way to Godsreach.

There was a new pit in his stomach now, and it had nothing to do with the girl he left behind. Though she still tugged at his heartstrings from what had swiftly become long miles, he was wrapped around a completely different thought that had plagued him only once in his life and not long ago at that. Like a foreign entity had sparked a tiny fire in his mind, he could not let go of the single question: *who did it*?

Who made this world and all its intricate details?

Who painted that picture below them and above them and *of* them?

Jay was no philosopher. He knew that he had no credentials to his name to consider and weigh in on such an enormous concept. But during their brief—albeit absurd and intense—travels from Glendale to here, he had seen too much to dub it all happenstance now. There was design to this world and its workings, carefully considered functionality. From the slinking of the rivers to the sprouting fields of plants, both edible and not, to the human anatomy that allowed him to live and breathe. And even to the virtues that held a measure of power over the elements that operated in it all.

He stared down at Blaze then, studying his red and black lines of fur, the slow rise and fall of his chest even though he had no need of oxygen to sustain him. *Where had he come from?* He was essentially just energy. To all of Jay's studies and understanding, Blaze was a *substance*, not a creature. And yet, he had a personality more potent than most people Jay knew. Had he always existed, just taken on different forms over the eons? Or did he, too, have a beginning just like Jay? A birth into this wild world.

Jay pinched the bridge of his nose. *Why did this even matter to him?* But even as he tried to press it away, a new shoot sprouted and carried him with it.

How could we not know? He felt at a loss. *Why is it even a question?*

If it *was* all created, would it not be like Wade said on the ferry between the Isles? The creator would surely want his creations to consider the feat a big deal. Jay couldn't quite believe that the culprit would fashion reality and walk away, leaving it to its own devices. But there was no record of anything substantial, no books that Jay had ever seen written on the subject, no tales told by people of authority to allude to some omnipotent creator. But then again, could that information exist and simply be *withheld*?

So many questions had come to Jay over this stint across the Tiers. Leaving Glendale was like opening a portal to a new world. He had been faced with circumstances that countered everything he had built his life around. The Academy had either been woefully underequipped to prepare him for this lifestyle, or it had purposefully avoided teaching him things that he was now coming to know. And the claims of the strange Sylvester of Eff seemed to surround it all.

Vices.

Suddenly, Jay felt the carriage jostle through a patch of turbulence. Wind not created by the tireless virtues cut across the bow and through his suit coat. He shivered once before pulling Blaze's sullied blanket up over them both. The virtue stirred only slightly before bedding back to warmth. When Jay attempted to return to his own focus, though, he found that the gust of wind had carried its importance away. It would come back to him, he knew. But for now, he felt the gentle pull of sleep finally reach his eyelids.

Answers would come.

Eventually, they would come.

End Book One

A word about the author...

A native of the deep south-Montgomery, Alabama to be specific-I am a fan of fiction, a connoisseur of creativity, and a jack-of-all-trades...master of none. But I write, I read, and I continue to hone my crafts. Hopefully, you will enjoy the fruits of my efforts. www.stevencmccullough.com

www.ingramcontent.com/pod-product-compliance
Lightning Source LLC
Chambersburg PA
CBHW072305020726
47501CB00002B/406